FORTUNE'S PRICE
A GOLD RUSH ODYSSEY

A NOVEL

FRANK NISSEN

Black Rose Writing | Texas

This is a work of fiction. Names, characters, businesses, places, events, and incidents are either the products of the author's imagination or used in a fictitious manner. Any resemblance to actual persons, living or dead, or actual events is purely coincidental.

ISBN: 978-1-68513-598-0
PUBLISHED BY BLACK ROSE WRITING
www.blackrosewriting.com

Printed in the United States of America
Suggested Retail Price (SRP) $26.95

Fortune's Price is printed in Baskerville

PRAISE FOR FRANK NISSEN'S
FORTUNE'S CALL:
A GOLD RUSH ODYSSEY

"*Fortune's Call* is superbly written. Great contrast in characters, and the historical detail is incredible. I read and thought, He couldn't have written this unless he time traveled back to the historic days of the gold rush forty-niners and brought home a tale worthy of being called an odyssey. Great authenticity. Once you start reading, I dare you to put it down!"
–James Robert Daniels, author of *The Comanche Kid* and *Jane Fury*

"'A homegrown Twain for California's Gold Country', *Fortune's Call* reminds me of stories I loved as a child: a young hero … impossible odds and an evil scoundrel… Telling the story from, 14 yr old, Pegg's perspective, Nissen lets you feel what it was like to travel thousands of miles across the country, the sights and smells of wagon trains fording rivers and climbing mountains, the deprivation and pain, and the unexpected joys. Crammed with action and peppered with convincing detail, the pace never lets the reader down…"
–Bill Baynes, author of *The Occupation of Joe*

"This book would be great for adults who appreciate historical action adventure, and for young readers. It should be in public and school libraries… I love how the author weaves historical details into the fictional story without turning it into a boring history lesson. I felt transported back to gold rush days…"
–Nicolle Goldman, author of *That Pilgrimage Book*

I've had many teachers—whether they knew it or not.
Whether one lesson or many, I am grateful to them all.

FORTUNE'S PRICE

FROM THE PEN OF JOHN S. HITTELL (1825-1901)

AMERICAN AUTHOR, JOURNALIST, HISTORIAN

The business of California is conducted boldly. Men make money rapidly, spend it freely and hastily. Changes in occupation are frequent and in wealth rapid.

Hazardous speculation is the body of our commercial system.

Most of our business men are young, and they are still under the influence of the feverish times of '49.

Hereditary wealth is unknown. Our rich men all came to California poor, and they are prominent advertisements of the victories that may be achieved by enterprise and bold speculation. . .It is no uncommon thing to see men who have been wealthy on three or four occasions and then poor again. . .

When men fail, they do not despair. . .they hope to be rich again.

CHAPTER 1

Sun Shu and I sat on opposite sides of the campfire outside our tents. I added more sticks to give us better light. The modest blaze was a nightly ritual, around which we sat to review the day's doings in the year-old gold camp of Grizzly Bar. But we usually never kept it going this long. Fuel was scarce, so used sparingly. But this night was no ordinary night.

Sun Shu sat erect on an empty spice crate, poised as a crane in a river, her hands cupped and resting in her lap. She kept watch toward the boisterous street. Despite her graceful, oriental composure, I knew she, too, dreaded what we were waiting for. An angry mob might appear at any moment.

Fred Hoyt, my irksome partner, had escaped into the darkness hours before, claiming a mob was right on his heels, bent on revenge. He insisted I, being his partner, was in equal danger. Hoyt had stooped to his lowest to convince me to go with him. But his cruel insults toward Sun Shu provoked me to rebuff him. Though clearly startled at my rebellion, he wasted no more time and lurched off into the dark, swinging his crutch as if he would stab the ground. I wondered how he could ever hope to outrun anyone with a broken leg hampering his progress.

Still, Sun Shu and I couldn't ignore his predictions of disaster. Hence our vigil.

Bugle, our faithful family beagle, left his place by my boot and trotted over to the flimsy rope fence that marked the limits of Yang Ho and Sun Shu's would-be store. What I was pleased to call a store was currently no more than a patch of dirt at the east end of town. This bustling gold camp had burned to the ground only weeks before, and was now in a frenzy of rebuilding. It was the only spot on the town's single street not yet graced with a new structure. Bugle came back from inspecting the entire perimeter, tongue lolling. I leaned down to give him a scratch.

"Well. What do you think, boy? Can we send them packing?"

Not for the first time I wondered what Fred Hoyt had done to incite strangers to the deadly pitch he claimed. I checked the Colt once more, petrified at the thought of having to use it to defend ourselves. The chambers were full. Only a dozen rounds remained in the shot bag on my shoulder. But if it come to that, there would be no time to reload.

How many would be in pursuit? Could I talk them out of their lust for vengeance? I didn't have Hoyt's silver tongue. How could I hope to mollify their frustration with my partner's chicanery?

I had been scared plenty of times on the way west. Losing my dad to fever had been the worst. Crossing the desert as backpackers after we'd lost our oxen was another. But none of them involved shooting people. At such moments my youth and inexperience were brought into sharp relief. I had celebrated my fourteenth birthday in Saint Louis, but nonetheless, I was green to the rougher ways of the world.

I glanced again at Sun Shu. Firelight glimmered off her soft silk trousers and coat. Celestials, as the Americans called the Chinese people among us, dressed very differently. I had never seen a woman wear trousers before. Sun Shu was only a few years older than me, but already married and wise above her years. The soul of modesty, she should not have to suffer the ire of these men.

Maybe I should leave this place and draw the danger away. But my promise to Sun Shu's husband rooted me to the spot. Yang Ho had gone to San Francisco after the fire to hire men and buy supplies to rebuild their store. He had asked me to look out for Sun Shu until his return.

As the hours dragged on, the street grew quiet. Late revelers stumbled out of the saloons and gambling halls. Those too sauced to make their own way found willing helpers, or collapsed alone. Still, no mob descended on us.

Though her posture did not soften, Sun Shu could not keep her eyes open.

"Get some sleep." My voice cracked. "We may be keeping watch for nothing more than another of Fred Hoyt's wild tales."

She dipped her head, fretful. "I am sorry, Mr. Pegg. I am not helping you." She looked out to the street. "The longer we wait, the more I am inclined to agree with you." She shifted to face me more directly. "But if it turns out Mr. Hoyt is *not* lying you must promise me you will escape at the first sign of trouble."

"I can't keep my promise to Yang Ho if I run away."

She frowned. "He only asked you to look out for me—to help with the store. I don't think he meant for you to put your life in danger."

"If they don't find me here, they might take out their frustration on you." My tone sounded harsher than I intended.

Sun Shu's delicate features showed no offense. "If you go, I will go to Chen Yi's." She knitted her brows and looked out to the street again.

In the short time I had known her, I had learned that her knitted brow meant she wanted no more argument.

I gestured to her tent. "Go on. I'm sure you'll hear the ruckus if anyone shows up."

She rose to go, a slip of a girl in clothing that seemed too big for her. "Thank you, Honorable Pegg. I am sorry."

I worked up a half-hearted scowl. "Shush. What do you have to be sorry about? I should be apologizing to you." I levered myself up to stand. "I do apologize to you."

She stepped lightly and smiled. "Fiddlesticks."

My eyes popped wide. I broke into a smile myself. "Where'd you learn that one?"

She did not stop or turn. "From you Americans." And she ducked into her tent.

I sat back down, still smiling. Sun Shu was normally demure to a fault. In the several weeks since her husband Yang Ho's departure, she and I had shared each other's company many hours of the day. Mornings, I helped her set out merchandise that Gao Chung brought from a makeshift market west of town. Then I headed off to work the Frenchmen's claim while they were in town making better money as carpenters and bricklayers. Afternoons, Sun Shu came out to the Frenchmen's claim, to help me prospect. Through it all she was ever biddable and circumspect. It was a delight to see even a little cheekiness from her. It reminded me of my sister, Amy, back home in Vermont.

I looked down to give Bugle a scratch, but he was asleep. I settled back and resumed my vigil.

Hoyt had taken off before—only to reappear, seeking to take up his old spot in the partnership. While my dad was alive, Hoyt wheedled and groveled; with me he invoked my need for his superior experience of the world.

Was his departure for good this time? If that mob caught him, would they even bother to bring him back to town for a trial? I fretted how I would word a letter to Mr. Pruitt saying that I had "lost" his stepson. I dreaded revealing the particulars.

Mr. Hoyt had been the source of many irritations, but I had honored my father's deathbed counsel to stick with him. Indeed, more—to trust him, despite my fledgling doubts. If Hoyt was truly gone, who would be my adult? No matter how many responsibilities I had back on the farm, I was still shy of my majority in the eyes of the law.

I slept where I sat. It's a wonder I didn't fall off the box. Nor was my slumber disturbed by a bloodthirsty gang. When I blinked awake, the first pale light already tinted the eastern sky. I got to my feet and paced around the store to loosen up, threading my way among the roughly hewn benches that would display the day's goods Gao Chung brought. Once Yang Ho returned from San Francisco with men and lumber, they would have a real store again.

I drew a dipper of water from the barrel outside Sun Shu's tent and poured it into my hat for Bugle. I ladled another for myself.

When she came out of her tent, Sun Shu found me looking up the slope where Mr. Hoyt had made his escape.

Sun Shu bent to greet Bugle, then straightened to look up the street. "No one came," she said.

I looked with her. A few of the earliest risers were about their business. The sun, cresting the eastern ridge, made new-sawn lumber almost gleam. The whiff of griddle cakes and coffee drifted on the morning air.

"Mr. Hoyt has a lively imagination. . . and a partiality for dramatic stories. And I, at one time, had craved them." I shook my head at the thought. "But it was still a good idea to keep watch."

Sun Shu turned her gaze to the hill behind the town. "He will be having a hard time of it with his crutch."

I marveled that she could find even a shred of compassion for a man who had treated her so wretchedly. After weeks of rudeness and slights, last night had been the most grievous. He had actually called her a doxy.

She turned away. "I will make tea. Gao Chung will be here soon."

.   .   .

We were just reviving our fire when we heard a shout in Sun Shu's language, Cantonese. She looked up in alarm. The shouter was none other than Gao Chung. He maneuvered a wheelbarrow down the street toward us as if the hounds of hell were nipping at his heels. His short, wiry figure was all but hidden behind the heap of our daily allotment of goods for sale. This might be the first of several loads. His usual demeanor, one of imperturbable calm, was gone. He was in a state, calling out, careening between the few people already in the street, scarcely controlling the wheelbarrow.

Bugle set to barking, straining at his lead.

I leaned down to him. "Hush, boy. You'll wake half the territory. It's only Gao Chung."

Gao Chung wore a similar loose-fitting outfit as Sun Shu, but his was cut from humbler cloth, rimed with the dust of the road and stained with the sweat of his exertions.

Sun Shu set down the teapot on one of the crates and rushed to meet him.

Gao Chung's long braid, called his queue, swung wide, as if to balance him as he swerved the wheelbarrow into the store space. He was winded. It appeared he'd run all the way from the improvised market where Chen Yi, Sun Shu's adoptive father, bought our goods. Sun Shu and Gao Chung exchanged a few hurried words before Sun Shu led him over to the water barrel and gave him a dipperful to drink. He gulped it down and they launched into an urgent exchange, punctuated more than once by worried glances in my direction.

Bugle strained at his lead to join them, but I held him back. I, too, fought the urge to ask the cause of the agitation. Clearly, I was somehow part of it. But I knew Sun Shu would translate for me in good time. I didn't have long to wait.

She approached with a stark look of alarm on her pale features. She began to speak even before she reached me, making no preamble. "You must go. Without delay." She looked anxiously toward the center of town, as we had for most of last night. "Gao Chung says Mr. Hoyt was not lying. Men are after him. And if they can't get him, they are coming after you. They think you know where he is."

My whole body froze with dread. It wasn't Hoyt's fevered imagining after all. I looked from Sun Shu to Gao Chung. "Who?

Why?" Bugle caught my alarm and moved between us, barking, wanting information.

Sun Shu went on. "Gao Chung heard it on his way back from the market. A group of miners were trying to draw more men to their cause. The anger was mounting by the minute. He said the fellow doing most of the shouting brandished a rope."

I turned to Gao Chung. "How many?"

Before Sun Shu could ask, he barked "Shiwu!"

"Fifteen, at least," she translated, but Gao Chung kept talking. She translated, "More were gathering. Very angry."

My mind raced. I had dismissed Hoyt's story as an exaggeration. Hoyt was out there, stumbling through the night, with a hurt leg, running for his life. I had turned him out, sent him off with righteous disdain.

Sun Shu reached into the wheelbarrow and brought out two bean cakes, intended for our breakfast. She thrust them into my hands, then dragged me toward our tents. "You must go at once. Gao Chung said he heard your name as well as Mr. Hoyt's."

"What about your breakfast?" I handed back the cakes.

She pushed them back. "There is no food out there."

She's almost right. It will be hard to forage or hunt on the run. "Did Gao Chung say why they didn't come last night?"

She looked cross. "He didn't. It doesn't matter. They are coming now. You must hurry."

Sun Shu stopped outside my tent, and I stumbled into her. I righted myself, flustered. "But Gao Chung pointed at you, too. Are you in danger?"

Her voice hardened. "Don't worry about me. I will go to Uncle Chen's. These ruffians are schoolboys compared to Zhou Chow's army."

I recalled the story she'd told of the marauding army that had destroyed her childhood home and killed her father, as well as the beloved old Jesuit who had taught her French.

Sun Shu urged me into my tent at the same time she plucked the blanket from my shoulders.

Aside from what I had on, I had only one extra shirt—one from Grizzly Bar Sun Shu had mended—and three pairs of socks. I had outgrown or worn out everything else. I stuffed the shirt and socks in the hunting satchel and hung my two pouches—one with the compass, one for fire-making—around my neck.

I emerged from my tent to see Gao Chung and Sun Shu scooping the wheelbarrow empty. The merchandise lay haphazard, forsaken. She spoke urgently. "Do not worry. Yang Ho will be back in a day or two. He will understand."

A sickening recognition intruded. I was thrust back in the same place as last night. I was breaking my vow to protect Sun Shu. Only now I wasn't being coerced by my manipulative partner. It was my own decision, despite Sun Shu's reassurances. I handed her the Colt and the satchel. "Here. At least—"

Sun Shu refused them, pushing out her hands. "No, no. You will need it more than I."

"But I can't just leave you." I searched her face. Her eyebrows arched, fear in her eyes, she darted glances at the street behind her.

"You must. You must. Please go." She reached for my sleeve but then drew back.

I shoved the Colt in my belt, but my feet refused to move.

"Leave Bugle with me," she urged. "He will warn me. He can be with me at the store."

No! How can I leave Bugle? He'd walked all the way to California with me. He'd shared the endless miles, the scorching deserts, the treacherous mountains.

But Bugle chose that moment to bark, wanting me to explain things to him. Instantly, I knew I had to leave him. One outburst like that on the run would give us away. Bugle was my inseparable companion, but now I had to abandon him. Anguish tore at me.

I knelt and took Bugle's face in my hands. "You be good for Sun Shu. You hear? I'll come back for you."

He whined, shifting from one front paw to the other.

Sun Shu's voice was anxious. "Don't worry, Mr. Pegg. Uncle Chen and I will take good care of him. Please. You must hurry."

I straightened up and took one last good look at her. "I'll be back." Immediately I felt like a fool. *If I run, how will I know when it's safe to come back?*

"I will pray for you, honorable Pegg."

As I trotted toward the back of the store, behind the tents, I realized I could not alert the Frenchmen who had also trusted me. I called back, "Tell Ormond I had to go. Please?"

Sun Shu's voice rasped with despair. "I will do that, honorable Pegg."

A pale light crept farther into the sky. I didn't have much time before I would have to go to ground and try to elude them. All I needed was a place to hide.

I had just stepped over the rope fence when Sun Shu darted up and thrust the rolled-up sleeping blankets into my hands. "One for you, one for Mr. Hoyt—if you find him."

"You are too good. I should be calling you 'honorable.'"

"Hush." She pushed me on my way. Her stern expression softened. "Godspeed."

I shut my ears to Bugle's barking. It was all I could do not to turn back. I knew his distress. *Won't somebody tell me what's going on?* Leaving him tore at me more than fear of the pursuing men. But it was the only way. I swore to myself I would come back for him.

A small, scorched shed stood a short distance beyond the new buildings. I crouched behind it just in time to see Sun Shu climb into the wheelbarrow—Bugle was already aboard—before Gao Chung threw a canvas over them both.

I rolled the two blankets tighter and tucked them under my arm. Taking one last look at the street, I dashed up the slope, away from trouble.

I had two things to do. Stay clear of the pursuing mob, and find Fred Hoyt. The ground cover was a loose mulch of dried oak leaves and pine needles, bits of deadfall. While I was looking for Hoyt's tracks, I wondered if I was leaving any of my own. I glanced behind. A skilled tracker, a hostile, as the scout Gideon MacIver called the Indians, might see the least disturbance in that confusion. Back home in Vermont, my friend Will and I had practiced tracking plenty of times while playing "Injuns." But that was just a game. It was never a matter of staying alive. Did the mob chasing Hoyt and I have a good tracker?

When he stepped over the rope fence and hobbled into the night, Mr. Hoyt was headed north. He had at least a six-hour head start, but he was hindered by the black night and his crutch. Did he keep to the northward heading, or did he veer off, picking his path for ease rather than direction?

And if he did diverge, would he choose east or west? I could waste precious time trying to second-guess him.

Scrambling through the predawn forest, I realized I couldn't leave Mr. Hoyt's fate to his means alone. My partner might not be the most admirable specimen—a braggart and a gambler, high-handed, and unpredictable, but he didn't deserve to meet his maker at the end of a rope.

Mr. Pruitt came to mind. This jovial good friend and neighbor had helped fund our expedition to the gold fields. Dad had taken on Fred Hoyt, Mr. Pruitt's stepson, as a partner at the request of his elder friend. We had started out full of high hopes. Unfortunately, Mr. Hoyt soon proved my mother's misgivings about him. He was a poor hand on the trail, no matter the chore. The only good turn he managed was to find the Chalmers group. Abraham Chalmers, in quiet command, was seconded by the guide, Gideon MacIver. Led by these two competent men, our small party traveled in the goodly company of some fifty wagons.

When Dad took sick, Mr. Hoyt changed his spots. He nursed Dad devotedly until the bitter end. Now Dad lay under a heap of stones on some nameless hill out on the prairie, and I was obliged to trust my fate to Fred Hoyt. To my growing dismay, Hoyt soon reverted to his old, imperious habits. Whatever my vexations, I could never admit to Mr. Pruitt I had abandoned his stepson to a maddened rabble.

Topping the canyon's rim above Grizzly Bar, I looked out on endless ranks of humpbacked hills, carpeted in tall yellow grasses and scattered with groves of oak and scrub. Hoyt might be anywhere out there. The sun would soon breach the eastern horizon. The growing light would make it easier to catch up with my partner. But more light would equally aid our pursuers. If I was going to help Fred Hoyt, I had to play the fugitive, as well. More importantly, I had to find him before the mob did.

CHAPTER 2

Gaining the upland on the northern lip of the canyon, I listened for the approach of the pursuing mob. Crouching low behind a manzanita bush, I looked back the way I had come. Chill morning air played across my back. No pursuers, yet. Would they be on foot? If they were on horseback, they would be here soon enough.

Having no strategy of my own, I assumed Hoyt would head for the richest strike we'd heard about: the North Fork of the American River. Setting my course north, I used every scrap of shadow to hide my progress. I had little idea what lay ahead. More hills, without a doubt, and steep defiles. Tangled forest? Jumbles of boulders? Hoyt's struggles must be desperate, indeed.

What hope did I have of seeing any sign of his passage? With the loose-leaf mulch, boot prints were not likely. Perhaps a poke hole where he put his weight on his crutch?

To better the chances of seeing any sign of my partner, I set a zigzag course. I convinced myself if Hoyt veered off at all, he would strike west, to San Francisco, as he said, and lose himself in the crowd.

While my mind was distracted with worry, my eyes were on point. Up ahead, just off to the right, a small hole punched into old, dried leaves. It could just be a mouse hole, or some other small critter's burrow. I approached and knelt for a closer look. It was a depression, not a tunnel; it didn't even go in the length of my finger. But it seemed the right angle for a crutch. I rocked back on my heels, looking ahead, hoping to see more of them.

Blue jays squawked in the trees to the south, back in the direction of Grizzly Bar. Jays usually made such a racket when they were upset at intruders.

A laugh—high pitched, almost like a whinny. At a distance, from the same direction as the jays. A solitary prospector? The vengeful mob in pursuit? I poked curled brown leaves into the depression and raked my fingers over the immediate area to blend it all together. They would close the distance fast. I did not want to leave any sign for them to follow.

I was in a patch of open ground. A grove of oak and manzanita stood some twenty yards ahead. Scooping up my blankets, crouching low, I scuttled to the stand and pressed down on my belly behind a forked oak. Luckily, it had a lot of sucker growth sprouting from its base. I pulled off my hat, pushed leaves into my hair to obscure my silhouette, and watched to the south.

Their voices reached me before they did. I couldn't make out what they were saying, but I could tell by their contentious tone they were squabbling. Four men came up over the rise into the meadow. They were some sixty to seventy yards to the southeast, heading north, as I had been. The tallest man, solidly built, carried a pistol thrust through his belt. He kept his eyes on the ground, looking side to side.

Two men of middling stature, a portly one with a bushy beard, the other with long blonde locks and a clean chin, appeared to sport only knives. The fourth man, small and wiry, lugged an old musket from a strap over his shoulder. This man also carried a coil of rope in his right hand. With nary a shovel or pan between them, it was a good bet these four shambling men weren't miners out looking for a lead. They were most certainly hunting Mr. Hoyt and me.

But they made a poor show as an implacable mob screaming for blood. What's more, the lightness of their armament announced they considered us easy pickings.

I had a sudden worry for Sun Shu. Even merely belligerent men sometimes became dangerous if they judged their prey vulnerable. I could only hope she'd been able to avoid them, and that Chen Yi and Gao Chung had been able to protect her.

I put aside worries I couldn't do anything about to concentrate on worries at hand. The men had come abreast and were drawing away into the trees. I had to make certain, beyond a doubt, these were the men sent to apprehend us. Cautiously, I raised my head enough to gauge a following distance. They were not seasoned woods runners, by any stretch. They were bound to stop and rest. When they did, I was sure I could get close enough to suss out their purpose.

They were only bits of color and sliding shadows among the trees when I crept out of hiding to follow. The trickiest part for me was crossing open ground. The grass was high but sparse, clumps of thistle few and far between.

Not long after they entered a grove of oaks, the smallest man whined for a halt. The two middling men were quick to agree. The grove provided a collection of rocks on which they could take their ease.

I found my own rock in the meadow just south of their position. My stone was large enough to hide me, and leaning strongly, it allowed me to spy through the thistles that crowded at its base.

The tall man, to all appearances their leader, continued a few paces farther into the grove, then returned to his companions, grumbling. "We'll never catch him, sittin' on our duff."

The portly one had his back to me, but he had already revealed himself to have a high, reedy voice. It was full of contempt. "He's on a crutch. How far can he get?"

The others offered no opinion on their fugitive's progress. The small man tamped impatiently at the ground with the butt of his musket.

The portly man could not abide the quiet. "Did anyone think to bring water?"

Nobody answered.

The blond man hid his worry behind a belligerent question. "How do we know this guy isn't armed to the teeth?"

The portly one huffed, "I seen him plenty of times at the tables. He was never wearin' iron." He turned to each of his companions. "Any o' you?"

The blond man was unconvinced. "What if he puts up a fight?"

Their leader drew a short clay pipe from his shirt pocket. "Shoulda thought of that b'fore you gambled away your weapon."

"It's four against one," jeered the smallest man, brandishing his rope.

"The kid could be out here, too," countered the worrier. "He's got a gun."

The musket man scoffed at him. "How much trouble can they be? Hoyt's on a crutch, and the kid'll turn tail the first sign of rough play."

The leader pressed tobacco into his pipe. "Maybe. Maybe not. We got to find him first."

What if they can lead me to Mr. Hoyt? Whatever obligation I felt toward Mr. Pruitt, I wondered if I'd be able to shoot somebody to save Mr. Hoyt's hide.

The tall man lit his pipe. Sweet tobacco smoke drifted my way.

The smallest man leaned on his musket and resumed his complaint. "I tell ya, this is a wild goose chase." He spat out a gob of brown tobacco juice. "Hoyt's headed for San Francisco, if he's headed anywhere. Riddick and his bunch will nab him and get the money."

I pricked up my ears. *Money? There's a reward for Mr. Hoyt's capture?*

The tall man unclamped his pipe and assumed the tone of a weary schoolteacher. "Sweeney set it out fair and square. Longest stick goes west. Second longest goes east, shortest stick goes north." He pointed the stem of his pipe at the musket man. "You picked the shortest stick." He went to reinsert his pipe. "If there's blame to be laid, it's on you."

One more piece of the puzzle fit neatly. Sweeney was the fancy man I'd seen scolding Mr. Hoyt not long after we'd arrived in Grizzly Bar. He must be quite the operator to have marshaled three groups of men to hunt down Mr. Hoyt—and offer a reward, to boot.

The portly fellow adjusted his bowler hat. "Why'n't Sweeney send anybody south?"

No one spoke up. The tall man finally replied, "Ain't nothin' between the American River and the San Joaquin but weeds and rattlesnakes. Slim pickin's for a man like Hoyt."

Their leader knocked his pipe out against a tree trunk. "All I know is, Hoyt suckered twice that reward out of me, and Sweeney's hundred dollars will go some way to making it up." He ground out the tobacco with his boot. "My claim sure ain't producin' it."

The blond man nodded. "Gonna buy me a new Colt with my hundred."

To which the portly man smirked, "And the rest'll go to John Barleycorn and sweet little Marie."

I blinked. It looked like Sweeney was paying each man in the successful posse a hundred-dollar bounty. If this bunch caught Hoyt, Sweeney would have to lay out four hundred dollars. How grievous was Hoyt's transgression to inspire such a reward?

The tall man put away his pipe and got to his feet. "Well, we can't horn in on Riddick's patch. Let's get a move on and hope Hoyt's headed north."

"If only for the sake of my hundred dollars," chortled the little man.

They set off. The tall man growled, "Keep yer traps shut, or we'll never see that reward money. Your jabberin' will only let him know we're comin'."

I stayed down behind the boulder. *Just like the jays let me know you were coming.*

A few paces farther on, the leader had another chastisement. "And spread out. We won't find anythin' bunched up like this."

I wondered if Hoyt knew enough to heed the birds' calls as a warning.

I had a decision to make. Did I shadow these men? Or should I try to get ahead of them and hope to find Hoyt before they did? Or should I take a gamble and head west to avoid this bunch altogether? No. Riddick was leading another party west of here. I might easily stumble into them. North was the only way.

A squirrel dropped an acorn on my back to urge me on my way. Looking up to locate my tormentor, I saw no critter anywhere near. I had a keen eye. Even Will said so, and I called him "Eagle Eye." Vexed, I made to follow "my" mob. A second acorn hit the back of my head. That was not from a squirrel in the trees. I whipped around and searched the manzanita and buckeye. I could see nothing but tangle and scrawny, leaning tree trunks. I glimpsed movement, but it was gone by the time I turned to it.

Yet another acorn struck me on the arm. This had to be Hoyt. Who else would be out here playing hide and seek?

He bobbed up briefly and lobbed his next missile. I saw it coming and caught it.

I watched the same spot and waited for him to show himself. He had good aim, I had to give him that.

Was my partner a complete fool? How could he be sure I wouldn't make some outburst that would give us away? I stayed put and kept mum. He waved his hat. I couldn't miss that. At least he had sense enough not to call out.

I stood up, hoping to end the game.

The hat disappeared and Mr. Hoyt rose laboriously into view, not much more than twenty feet from me. I must have passed within eight feet of him.

Another skill I had to credit him. He was good at hiding. He glanced after the departed men as he hobbled toward me.

The same thing that had happened after the Grizzly Bar fire was happening here. Hoyt chose his time to reappear. As before, I found myself torn between relief at his safety, and vexation at his playing puppet master. When he got close, he put on his crooked grin and spoke smugly. "Now do you believe me?"

I crouched back behind the boulder and gestured for him to do the same. I spoke in little more than a whisper. "How long were you going to wait to show yourself?"

He leaned down and hissed through gritted teeth. "I could've left you here, you know. I could've left you to deal with those scoundrels on your own."

That jolted me. I was fourteen. I was no match for hardened men.

As quickly, he regained his jovial air. "Did they chase you out of town?"

"No. Gao Chung brought us warning." I whispered, hoping to encourage him to do likewise. "He heard Sweeney whipping up the posse."

Hoyt glanced north. "I'm impressed you finally saw the wisdom in tearing yourself away from the wench."

I ground my teeth but made no reply.

Then, with a pained look, he pronounced, "It grieves me, lad, that a Chinaman's words compelled you to action, while you found mine lacking."

I was flummoxed. Where was the stuttering terror he displayed last night? Hoyt seemed to be heedless of the danger; heedless of the fact that he could never hope to outrun those men if they got sight of him. I blurted the only thing that made any sense. "I came to warn you."

That caught him by surprise. He blinked and shifted his crutch. "Despite what you might think, I don't sling words around carelessly. And it's safe to say I've seen a little more of the world—and its perils—than you."

I rose again to my feet, watching north for danger to reappear.

Hoyt raised his chin, seeking my obedience. "Perhaps in future my opinions, not to say my judgment, will find more credence in your eyes."

I bent to pick up the blanket roll. He was doing a good job of testing my resolve. Something deep inside forbade me to leave him to his fate. And the same impulse that urged me to seek him out, despite the danger, now convinced me to do what I had to do to help him reach a safe place. After that. . .

He wasn't done. "I do not take lightly that your father asked me to stand by you. I don't think it unreasonable to ask the same allegiance of you."

If my father was a knife, you could not use it better. Finally, I looked at him. "For the sake of the partnership."

He let a moment lapse, studying me. "Good lad."

With the pecking order reestablished, my partner stumped himself around to retrace his steps, heading westward.

"Where are you going?"

Mr. Hoyt didn't stop. "To San Francisco. Where else?"

A shot rang out. We froze. A moment later, another shot. Not far distant, to the north. What, or who, had our posse encountered? I edged back toward the boulder. We waited. No more shots followed. Likely not some showdown. Perhaps they shot a rabbit for supper, or were just working off their frustration.

He obviously has no thought for the danger he's in.

My immediate concern was that he'd had such difficulty descending the western slopes of the Sierra Nevada mountains with a broken leg. Did he know a wide valley and *another* mountain range lay between him and San Francisco? "Do you think it w—" *don't question his wisdom* "—would be practical to attempt it on your crutch?"

Mr. Hoyt took another step and halted. He looked down at his splinted leg.

I came up beside him. "And didn't they say Riddick and his party are checking that way? He might be smarter than this bunch."

The blue jays split the silence that had settled over the grove. We both looked toward the racket. We had barely time to get back behind the boulder before Sweeney's bounty hunters reappeared. Heading south, they trudged doggedly, with the purpose of covering ground, no longer hunting.

The small musket man groused, "If Sweeney wants Hoyt so bad, let him get out here in the weeds and look for the scalawag himself."

Their leader was silent, moving steadily out into the bright meadow. He held the limp, swaying, headless bodies of two large rattlesnakes, one in each hand. He had the side arm.

Two shots, two snakes. A good shot.

The portly one jeered. "See if he thinks Hoyt's worth wadin' through a field full of rattlers for."

To which the small man brayed, "I'd rather keep my limbs, thankee."

The last we could make out came from the blond worrier. "Riddick's probably got Hoyt by now, anyway."

We waited a good while after the jays settled down, to make sure the aggrieved posse did not change their minds again. During that time, I lectured myself to remember to let Mr. Hoyt "man the helm," to use Mr. Pruitt's phrase.

At last Mr. Hoyt struggled to his feet and looked down at me. "Did you happen to come away with any water?"

"No, Sir. There was no time."

He watched where the men had disappeared among the trees, southward.

For all his bravado, is he actually worried about them? Once again, I gathered up the blanket roll and set my face west. But to my surprise, Mr. Hoyt stepped off to the north. I scurried to join him.

Without prompting, he explained. "Our best course is to head in the opposite direction from those vermin."

Emboldened, I chirped, "Maybe we can look for the North Fork." I almost added, *It's bound to be closer than San Francisco*, but shut up.

CHAPTER 3

To keep him happy, I trailed Hoyt a pace or two. But I was surprised I had to make an effort to keep up. Could it be my fatigue? Or because we were on a flat? He was certainly moving more briskly than I would have expected.

His fall had happened as we approached the gold fields, in mid-September, during a heavy snowstorm. The scout MacIver said heavy snows were known to come that early in the mountains. Now it was early November. In all, Hoyt's leg had been healing six weeks, maybe a bit more.

Dad broke his arm once when I was seven. That break had taken three months to heal. Would it be the same for a leg? Maybe Hoyt is a good healer? Did this mean he could start helping with the prospecting when we got to the North Fork? Even so, he stumbled many times. I wondered whether he had slept at all the previous night.

I began to wish for water, too. I did the pebble-sucking trick Mr. MacIver had taught me in the desert to stave off thirst. I was glad this time I didn't have to worry about water or food for Bugle. He was safe with Sun Shu and Chen Yi.

When the sun was well down in the west, Mr. Hoyt slumped on a handy rock. "I'm done. I can go no farther." I was glad for the rest, myself. We had pushed hard all day. Hoyt spoke, expecting disappointment. "Since you don't have any water, I assume you likewise have no food."

I produced the two bean cakes. "No, Sir. I *do* have food." I unwrapped the cloth and offered him one of the cakes.

He did not take it, but leaned back a little and stared skeptically at the pale, plump ball. "You're suggesting I eat raw bread dough?"

I laughed. "No, Sir. It only looks that way. It's been steamed. There's a filling inside. Chen Yi calls them bean cakes." I moved it closer to him. "It's not griddlecakes and syrup by a long shot, but they're right filling."

He leaned a little farther back, regarding it askance. "Thank you just the same, but I am not inclined to subject my stomach to such foreign fare."

Still, I held out the cake. "But aren't you hungry?"

I rewrapped the one cake, stowed it away and made quick work of half of the other one. Mr. Hoyt watched me as if I would turn blue in the next moment, but then swiveled his head to make a study of the western horizon.

While there was still light, I found a clump of trees nearby that had a shallow bowl at its center. The depression proved to be thickly bedded with the mulch of many seasons' leaves. It didn't seem wise to have a fire, but at least we would be out of the wind. I handed Mr. Hoyt one of the blankets, without mentioning who it came from, and helped him settle himself to the ground. I tucked the blanket around him. He managed a weary smile. "Much obliged, Pegg, boy. Much obliged."

I only nodded.

His eyelids succumbed to sleep even as he kept up his prattle. "Now don't you worry. We'll make a new start, and, before you know it, we'll be rich as kings."

I could not cheer such blandishments.

Mr. Hoyt set to snoring before I had wrapped myself in my own blanket.

My mind was wracked with worry, but I, too, dropped off quickly and slept through to dawn.

In the morning, we trudged on, without breakfast or water. I wanted to save what remained of the bean cakes as long as possible. I marveled that Mr. Hoyt made no further complaint about food.

We came upon a spring, barely more than a trickle, but with patience we drank our fill from cupped hands.

The country didn't harbor a soul. We had only the jays for company, and they merely scolded our passage. A flick of movement among the trees, a rustle in the grass hinted at other creatures. We flushed coveys of quail, and a couple jackrabbits, but often they disappeared as I pulled the Colt from my belt. Just as well, since I couldn't shake the fear that a gunshot might give us away.

If we weren't going up, we were going down. We were grateful for whatever level ground we came to, what the prospectors called "flats," where we made good progress among the scattered oaks. I kept the sun at our backs, heading north. The North Fork of the American River couldn't be that far away.

A cold rain passed through, making the old leaves and dry grass slippery. I skidded plenty of times, but managed to keep my feet under me. Mr. Hoyt was not so lucky.

.   .   .

By the afternoon of the second day, my partner's cursing and grumbling grew ragged with despair. We rested more often. During one such break, I caught a whiff of smoke coming over the crest of the ridge ahead. Everything was too damp for it to be a forest fire. *An Indian camp?* I had seen no Indians since we arrived in California, though I had learned a few survived, working for some of the miners.

Dread spurred me to think our pursuers had not only returned but had gotten ahead of us. A burst of song soon dispelled my fear. There couldn't be much malice in a lusty rendition of "Oh! Susannah," though the singer's earnest bellowing did not contain much of the melody.

Soon Mr. Hoyt and I emerged at the south edge of a sizeable meadow, and the singer came into view. This scarecrow of a man tended a fire while singing at the top of his lungs. He was attired in typical miners' garb, except for one particular. His hat had a very tall crown and an extremely wide, round, decorated brim. Such generous headgear clearly provided plentiful shade for his face and neck. I had seen a few like it in Saint Louis and Independence. Uncle Rafe said they were worn mostly by Mexicans.

The singing scarecrow's outfit consisted of only a well-used tent, as patched as the owner's duds, and a heap of collected firewood within easy reach of the fire. His prospecting equipment appeared to be no more than his pan, pick, and shovel—a placer miner. His claim featured a small, almost dry, streambed. The set-up gave the impression his chief activity had been making piles of dirt.

The prospector spied us coming down the slope. He straightened his long frame to watch us approach. Without his caterwauling, you could hear the slide of grass against our boots. A huge jackrabbit jumped up out of the thistles ahead of us and bounded straight for the singing prospector, who, spotting the movement, yanked a sidearm from his waistband. The rabbit, seeing its error, disappeared in a sharp right turn.

The scarecrow man restored his weapon and called out, "Well shuck my peas and hatch my chickens! Pilgrims in from the wilderness! Orphans of the storm!" His voice rasped like a rusty gate hinge.

As we drew closer, I realized the scarecrow man was well over six feet tall. He swept off his great hat in a courtly bow, then straightened back up, grinning a nearly toothless grin. He stuck out his hand. "Name's Elijah Cooder. Late of Kane-tuck."

I knew that meant Kentucky. My friend Linnaeus, the teacher who had traveled west with us, had been skilled at mimicking the speech of many regions. He had, with his many stories of olden times, continued my education. Linnaeus wasn't obliged to, but he stayed close all the way to California. Now he was making his way in San Francisco playing Dad's fiddle.

Mr. Cooder interrupted my thoughts. "But you can call me 'Ee-lie…" He pronounced carefully. "Proud to meet you. Proud, indeed." He pumped our hands in turn. "Welcome to Poison Acres."

I glanced at the stream. "Is the water bad?"

Eli Cooder crinkled his eyes and chuckled. "No. Water's fine. Just got a passel o' the demon weed, poison oak, hereabouts."

I wanted to ask him what poison oak was, but I was more interested in his food. I had consumed only the two bean cakes in the better part of two days. Mr. Hoyt had eaten nothing since leaving Grizzly Bar.

A pot of beans hung over the fire. A sack of flour and a side of bacon lay on a square of canvas in the grass to the side.

Eli cast a skeptical glance at Mr. Hoyt's crutch. "Good thing you ain't got a bear chasing you, Mister. You'd be hard put to get up any speed in that rig." His face bunched into a dozen leathery creases when he grinned. I could make out no more than half a dozen teeth in Mr. Cooder's head.

"I was just fixing supper," he went on. "Can I offer you gents a place at my table? If you can find one." He grinned again. "A table, that is!" He threw back his head and cackled. His Adam's apple danced a wild jig. When he recovered himself, he said, "No… seriously. That's a gen-u-ine invite. It ain't much, the three B's. Beans, bacon, and biscuits." Eli winked at me and pointed at the Colt in my belt. "Seein' as how you didn't pick off that rabbit for the pot—"

I forgot my manners and interrupted him. "You were right in the line of fire. You mighta thought I was aiming at you." But the man's jolly spirit was irresistible. I made bold. "Why didn't *you* pick 'im off?"

Eli's grin widened. "Why. . .you two was the same. Well? Whadaya say? You game?"

I didn't wait for Mr. Hoyt. I said, "Thank you, Sir. We'd be happy to. And be much obliged."

Eli did a little dance. "Excellen—tay! Sit yourselves down and I'll have us in vittles in two shakes of a lamb's tail."

"Can I help?" I asked.

He squinted over his shoulder at me. "How you at frying bacon, Boy?"

"Pretty good, Sir. If I do say so." I tried to stay serious.

Eli leaped up and spun around. "Sir! You hear that? Sir!" He did another little dance. "Why, I ain't been called 'Sir' since I was knee high to a corn jug. I'm gonna keep you on steady, Boy!" He pointed a long, flour-coated finger at a frying pan and the sack of bacon. "Slice off some for you and your dad, there." He spun back around, "Sir! Indeed!" and continued preparing his biscuit dough.

I cast a quick glance at Mr. Hoyt. He gave me a look that warned me against correcting our host for referring to him as my dad.

He addressed himself to Mr. Cooder. "How long you been out here, Eli?"

Eli placed lumps of dough in his biscuit pan. "Came out to Oregon Territory in 'forty-three with the missus and the bairns, bent on raisin' apples, like ever'body else."

He put out his biscuits to face the fire and stirred the beans. "Came to Californie in June of 'forty-eight. Fetched up on Weber's Creek. There were maybe 200 prospectors on the whole blamed creek, not counting Weber's Indians. I took out 8,000 dollars my first four days, just scratchin' around with my pocketknife."

Mr. Hoyt broke in with a laugh "That would certainly whet a man's appetite."

I looked over at my partner, glad his spirits had improved.

Mr. Cooder responded with a grin of his own. "You betcha. And I wasn't the only one. Five fellas up on the Yuba River washed out 75,000 dollars in three months. Another fella took out 700 dollars in four hours! Stories like that were a dime a dozen…still are!"

I tended to the bacon, trying to grasp those kinds of riches.

Eli brought out two more plates and forks for his guests. "I got Irish linen and candles, but you boys don't mind roughin' it, do ya?" He winked at us and threw back his head and cackled up a storm. His Adam's apple was hard-pressed to keep up. He sat on a stump to watch the beans and biscuits. "Where all you folks from?" He snuck another look at us.

"We're from Vermont," I said.

"Well, that's right fine, but what I meant was, where'd you all come from in the past week or so? You come at me from the south, so I figured you were maybe coming from Coloma or Hang Town."

Mr. Hoyt spoke up, quick as spit. "We're new to the country. Been to both those places. Weber's Creek, Mormon's Island, too."

"Them's all overrun." Eli scratched up under his hat. "But there's plenty other places."

"That's what we found out," Mr. Hoyt concurred.

"Can't be easy, trussed up like y'are," Eli said casually, eyeing the crutch.

I heard Mr. Hoyt closing up. "The boy's handy. We'll make out."

Eli adjusted the tin pan with the biscuits, his back to us. "You fellas're travelin' awful light for prospectors. You get robbed?"

I blurted, "No, Sir." *How to tell our story quickly?*

Mr. Hoyt scowled me into silence.

Eli spun around, his Colt in his hand, waving it around, trying to cover both Mr. Hoyt and me. "Don't go for the gun, Sonny."

CHAPTER 4

I thrust my hands in the air. "Sir! We don't have any evil intentions towards you. None at all!"

"You show up, no outfit. A man takes note. Maybe you two're livin' off other people's sweat." Eli drew his sagebrush eyebrows together in a scowl and swiveled his Colt between Mr. Hoyt and me. "Maybe it ain't a bear chasing you, but a posse!"

I reached higher. "We didn't do anything." *That he has to know about.* "We just want to get to the American River! That's all."

"Jolly me along, just bidin' yer time, waitin' to get the drop on ol' Eli…"

"Mr. Cooder, Sir," I said, "Does it look like either of us could get the jump on you, let alone overpower you?"

He blinked a couple of times, and the gun drooped slightly in his hand. His bluster vanished. "Well…now that you call it out: a cripple and a whelp who ain't dry behind the ears yet. . . ain't exactly. . ." He put away his gun and went back to checking the biscuits as if nothing unpleasant had occurred.

I checked for Mr. Hoyt's reaction. He rolled his eyes. I tended the bacon, but kept an eye on Eli Cooder. He was out here all alone. Maybe he had been robbed before by seemingly innocent, friendly visitors.

"Can't be too careful, you know," Eli announced breezily. "There's as many two-legged varmints as there is four…" He cleared his throat and stirred the beans.

"Yes," agreed Mr. Hoyt in a solemn voice. "Treachery is everywhere these days."

"Ain't it the truth," replied Eli. "I am aggrieved that I took against you. I ask your pardon."

"No, Mr. Cooder," replied Mr. Hoyt. "It is we who are in your debt for your generosity."

This was an aspect of my partner I hadn't seen in a long while. I threw him a quick glance. He gave me a curt nod.

I jumped in. "Yessir, that's true!"

Eli grinned and shook his shaggy head. "Sir! If that don't beat all."

We were all quiet for a minute. Eli tasted the beans. "Now, you want to talk about bandits…" he waved his spoon at us. "We got our own special breed— but they might be the only smart ones among us. That's the Sam Brannans in this whole circus. Fellas like him ain't muckin' around in the river. No! They're selling us the gear, so we can muck around in the river! And they're making a BIG, FAT profit off us, too, when Aunt Martha ain't lookin'!"

"Disgraceful…unforgivable," replied Mr. Hoyt.

"Brannan's got four stores, last I heard. And they say he already owns half o' San Francisco!" Eli tested the beans. "No grubbin' in the gravel for Sammy Brannan. Noooo-o, siree!"

"I prefer to make my money honestly—in the diggings," Mr. Hoyt allowed with a righteous air.

"Well, then, you boys'd best hustle." Eli started dishing out beans and signaled for me to bring on the bacon. "I guarantee you, before this is over, there'll be ten—a hundred—times as many of us as there is now, all looking for the same color!"

I made a vow to myself we would waste no time once we got to the North Fork.

While we were eating, I asked Eli, "How far are we from the North Fork?"

"Depends on which way you go," he replied.

"Isn't it north of here?" I pointed.

Eli waved his spoon. "Straight north'll likely bring you to the Middle Fork, not the North Fork. If you set yourself more west than north, you'll come on the North Fork, and sooner." Eli popped the last of a biscuit into this mouth. "Can't miss it. Big ol' notch in the land, it is."

"We hear it's rich diggings," I said.

"That's the word. Probably is. Heard tell of a fella took out a five-pound specimen above Horseshoe Bar. That's on the North Fork. One nugget— five pounds!" Eli shook his head in amazement. "Heard he lost it the same night in a game of monte. Another fella— he took out 16,000 dollars in one day! Spent it all on oysters and turtle soup! No, that was another fella…"

"Is a 'nugget' and a 'specimen' the same thing?" I asked in his pause.

"You *are* a greenhorn ain't ya?"

I wasn't exactly, but I felt like one right then. "I guess so."

Eli Cooder set his plate on the ground. "They are, but you'll find almost ever'body you talk to in this circus has got a differ'nt name for shovel, britches, or bread."

We sat up half the night, listening to Eli's stories of Sullivan, the Irishman, who went home with 26,000 dollars, of a man named Reading way up north, on the Trinity River, who, with a crew of men, took out an unbelievable 80,000 dollars in one month! I soaked up these dazzling stories, anxious for the day when I would have my own triumphant story to tell.

. . .

Eli woke me with the smell of coffee brewing. The sun had already cleared the horizon. Mr. Hoyt snored on.

Eli said in a low voice. "I'll show you poison oak." He couldn't believe I hadn't yet run afoul it. "Somebody's smilin' down on you. That's sure."

I shrugged. "Just lucky, I guess."

After learning about the demon weed, we walked back along the stream. Pointing to some ferns bowing over the water, Eli said, "I 'spect you know 'bout fiddleheads and watercress. Just like back home."

"Yessir. I do." I had seen them on my ramblings around the South Fork. Mother put them on the table often.

"They keep the scurvy away. Too bad more people don't know that, or believe it." He half turned. "Heard about miner's lettuce?" He showed me a patch of ground cover made of a plant with odd, round leaves. "You see a lot more of it in the spring. Tasty eatin', this." He picked some.

When we got back to camp, Mr. Hoyt had roused himself. Eli made us breakfast. My partner declined the greens our host offered him, so he then heaped the extra portion on my plate.

Eli didn't want us to go. "'Preciate the company, Gents. Surely do."

We all shook hands. I said, "So did we, Sir."

Eli chuckled quietly. His Adam's apple jigged. "Keep that up, Sonny. You'll be governor quick enough."

Mr. Hoyt and I crossed the stream and headed into the trees.

Eli called after us, "You boys want some more abuse, come back by, hear?"

I turned and walked backward a few steps. "What if you're not here?"

"My loss, then!"

"Ours, too! Good luck, Sir."

. . .

Mr. Hoyt and I didn't see another living soul for the next three days. It was difficult finding places to sleep. The nights were cold. Thanks to Sun Shu we had blankets, but they weren't enough. I took to building big fires to keep us warm, and to fend off critters who might consider us dinner. Though I missed Bugle terribly, I was glad he was with Sun Shu and Chen Yi.

Water was scarce, most often no more than a trickle. But it was even more difficult finding something to eat. Mr. Hoyt flat out refused to eat weeds, as he called the watercress and fiddleheads I collected. I found a handful of dried-up berries and he ate them. In the morning of the second day, Mr. Hoyt declared, "I'm not going to make it if I don't get some real food in my belly, Pegg, boy. And I surely have no desire to leave my bones bleaching on these wretched hills."

I remembered my night lost on the prairie with the other kids. Every last bullet had been precious. "I haven't got that many rounds. I think we should save—"

Mr. Hoyt jerked his crutch high and stabbed it into the ground. "Confound it, Boy! Will you condemn me to a slow death with a few sprigs of grass?"

I started. "No, Sir."

He swayed, hanging on his stick. I thought he might keel over. He grumbled to himself, "Good, red meat's the only thing will serve a man's needs."

So, we sacrificed progress while I lay in wait near a rabbit hole. After an hour or more, I picked off dinner for my starving partner. Mr. Hoyt soon had his "real food" roasting over a fire. I'll say this for him, he had the discipline to make that rabbit last into the next day, even after sharing a scrap or two with me.

Soon after we began on the fourth morning, we came to a gap in the trees that revealed our arrival at the southern rim of a sizable canyon. It looked pretty much as Eli had described the canyon of the North Fork: a deep, wide notch in the land, running roughly east-west where we encountered it. We couldn't yet see the American River itself. The other side, the north side, was a fair distance away.

The land dropped away in ridges and folds toward the river. As we descended, it was possible to see, on the opposite slope, that the lower elevations had been shorn of most all of their timber. Every last stick had fed a fire or gone into building a shelter.

What growth remained on the upper reaches consisted mostly of several kinds of oak tree and the odd pine, with buckeye and manzanita among them. We were moving through much the same on our side. Grateful for Eli's instruction, I avoided the poison oak.

Many places were steep, and we slipped repeatedly on the dried mulch. It was especially hard for my partner, finding a place to brace his crutch. His spills were grievous to witness because they happened so suddenly I couldn't come to his assistance in time. That he didn't snarl and blaspheme worried me.

Food crowded out all other thoughts. If there was no store handy, then I'd buy some from a miner. I had to be very frugal with the few nuggets I retained. Mr. Hoyt must've forgotten about them, or he would have insisted on keeping them, that being his self-appointed responsibility in our partnership. I was pretty sure he didn't have any money on him, gold or otherwise.

As we worked our way lower down the canyon slope, we began to catch glimpses of the river, still far below us. We also began to hear the sounds of chopping and voices, and soon encountered the stumps of cut-down trees. Then came shouts, and the crash of a tree falling.

As we passed the wood-cutters, they waved and called out what I assumed were greetings. Mr. Hoyt spoke at last in a peevish grumble. "More foreigners."

I waved back and smiled at them, but kept going. Another thing to look for: somebody who spoke English.

CHAPTER 5

Finally, we approached the river itself. Mr. Hoyt and I had fetched up on the south shore. Prospectors swarmed the banks. The rattle of gravel, the 'chunk' of picks and shovels, the shouts of men, as well as the churning of the river, made for a boisterous din. I realized how quiet the last several days had been.

There was no doubt this was a "strike." Could it be Rattlesnake Bar, itself? As with Simpson's Creek, the area had been dug up so much it was hard to tell what it used to look like. Both banks, as far as you could see upstream and down, were a confusion of heaps and holes. The claims looked small, which meant rich diggings. Rickety timber flumes snaked along the shores, moving water to places where it was needed.

We came to a tree that had been unaccountably spared, which cast a scrap of shadow.

I turned to Mr. Hoyt. "Why don't you wait here in the shade?" I pointed. "I'll go find out if this is the North Fork. Get us some food. Maybe one of those miners has some to spare."

"Much obliged, Pegg, boy," he grinned wearily. "Hopefully you'll come up with something besides grass and weeds."

The first person I came to was a Negro man. I had seen a few in Saint Louis, but Negro people were a rarity where I grew up. Here was the first one I'd ever had a chance to talk to. He appeared to be making a repair to his flume. I stood back, waiting for him to finish hammering a board in place.

I remembered how my dad would approach strangers. "Good afternoon, Sir."

He turned and looked at me, blinking. Then he broke into a big grin. "And a good afternoon to *you*, Sir." His voice was rich and deep.

"May I ask if this is the North Fork of the American River?"

His grin got bigger. He cast quick glances both ways on the stream. A younger man—a white man carrying lumber—joined us. The black man asked him in a joshing tone, "Hey, Dick. This the North Fork of the American River?"

The man named Dick was a tall, lanky youth, only a few years older than me, with dark hair, dark clothes, and bright blue eyes. He looked at me, and then up and down the river. Last, he inspected the gravel underfoot. An easy, unguarded smile spread across his sunburnt face. "It was this morning. I dare say it likely still is."

Both men laughed. I turned beet red, but since I couldn't feel much more the fool than I already did, I asked, "Is this Rattlesnake Bar?"

The Negro man beamed with delight. "Right again, young fella."

I got right to it. "I was wondering, Sir, if I might buy some provisions from you. If you have any to spare. Some bacon, or flour... coffee." He was staring at me so fixedly that I lost my nerve. *Best back up and start right.* "My name is Bartholomew Pegg."

"Well, ain't you a sight for sore eyes, Bartholomew Pegg!" He held out his hand. "Jacob Harper. Welcome to the gold rush."

We shook hands. Then Jacob Harper gestured to the younger man. "This here's Richard Barter. He goes by Dick."

I shook Richard Barter's hand. "You can call me 'Pegg.'" I pointed back the way I had come. "That's my partner, Mr. Fred Hoyt."

The two miners looked in his direction. Mr. Hoyt lifted his crutch in salutation.

Several other miners close by stopped their work. Word spread—there was a kid in their midst. More miners came over. A crowd soon formed, and people called out.

"Where you from, Sonny?"

"I got a kid brother about your age!"

"How old are you, boy?"

"Hellfire! I got a son about his age!"

A man old enough to be my grandpa called out, "I gotta older brother 'bout his age! Haw, Haw!"

His friend scolded him. "Jasper! Shut yer trap. You got the brains of a gnat."

A sudden recollection came to me from our time in Grizzly Bar. At the eating hall, the American House, I had been an object of curiosity. Except here, thankfully, I was not being stood up on a table.

Jacob Harper held his hands up in the air. "Hold on! Hold on!" he called in a powerful voice. "The young gent wants to buy his supper!"

Only those closest to us paid him any mind. But people noticed and the quiet spread. "What say you?" Jacob called out to the crowd.

Voices erupted in a lively babel. "He ain't buying as long as I have anything to say about it!"

"We got fresh bacon! Com'on over, Sonny!"

"That's nothing! We got venison stew!"

At a gap in the noise, Richard Barter said, "Maybe he'd be willing to sing for his supper."

The hubbub started up again. Miners called out "Carrier Dove," "How Can I leave Thee," "Old Virginia Shore," and a multitude of other songs, many of which I had never heard of.

At the American House, after I had been hoisted up on the table, somebody had asked me to sing. But that was after I had eaten my supper. Then and now, I dreaded the thought of performing alone.

But I was very hungry after a difficult journey. I asked Mr. Harper, "What do you want me to sing?"

Jacob said, "Do you know 'Amazing Grace'?"

I yelped, "Yessir, I know that one. It's my mom's favorite."

"That's my sister's favorite," said Richard.

I started to sing "Amazing Grace." Everybody hushed up, looking at me. It felt awfully naked without the other parts coming in, but I kept going. I feared my voice would break in an awkward place. It was doing that a lot, lately. I closed my eyes and imagined singing with my family. On Sunday evenings we'd sing it with four-part harmonies. It was the most wonderful feeling you could imagine: singing together. There were many things to pine for out here—that was one of the sweetest.

When I started the second verse, other voices joined in. I opened my eyes to see Jacob Harper, Richard Barter, and a bunch of others singing. Their harmonies blended in like flowing honey, high and low. By the end of the third verse, the air filled with the blending of dozens of voices singing, "…And grace will lead me home."

People from other places didn't know the lyrics, but being surrounded by the beautiful, soaring harmonies, they smiled. The singers stayed with me for the fourth verse, and even more came in for the fifth. When we got to, "…A life of joy and peace," the river canyon fairly boomed with all the voices. I was sure nobody heard my voice anymore, but I didn't care. I sang full out—for my father, for my mother. I sang with my spirit lifting and lifting.

The power rising up with the sixth and seventh verses shook the heavens. A shiver ran through me. We finished, "…Than when we'd first begun," with more than a few faces wet with tears. We drew the last notes out, slow and sweet, like nobody wanted it to end.

A moment of quiet held before a great cheer burst from the throng. Jacob Harper clapped me on the shoulder, grinning at me. I laughed silly, like a girl. Something thumped against my chest, just like it had happened at Grizzly Bar. I looked down to see a little leather sack hit the ground at my feet. As I bent to pick it up, a second one landed on my back. A third one knocked my hat off. Jacob and Richard helped me pick them up. When I couldn't hold any more, I started stuffing them into my pockets. Richard found a discarded biscuit tin, and we put the rest of the sacks in it.

When the cheering died down and the miners began to drift back to their work, I emptied my pockets into the tin. We tallied a dozen sacks of different sizes. Some had nuggets, some had dust. There certainly had to be enough to buy equipment and keep Mr. Hoyt in a hotel where he could get a good rest… for a few nights, anyway.

Richard hefted the biscuit tin. "You have a hundred dollars here, maybe more." And he handed it to me.

Inside my head, my friend Will snickered, *Maybe you oughta sing your way through this gold rush*. That was not a bad idea, except my voice was changing—an embarrassment I had no wish to display voluntarily.

I turned to Jacob Harper. "I'd still like to buy some bacon and beans from you—if you have any to spare?"

"Only after you have sampled the goods as my guest," Jacob said.

Mr. Hoyt hobbled up. "That Pegg! He's a regular magician, ain't he?" He favored Richard Barter with his quirky smile while completely ignoring Jacob Harper. "Pulls gold right out of thin air!"

"Mr. Harper, Mr. Barter," I said. "This is Fred Hoyt, my partner. Mr. Hoyt—"

Mr. Hoyt thrust out his hand to Richard. "I gotta thank you for helping us out."

I threw a quick glance to Mr. Harper. He had gone real quiet, watching Mr. Hoyt. I felt bad for him. *Why would Mr. Hoyt ignore him?* I thought back to how Hoyt had treated Chen Yi and Sun Shu back in Grizzly Bar. *Maybe it shouldn't be a surprise.*

Richard shook Hoyt's hand, still smiling. "Well, Mr. Hoyt, you're very welcome, but I think it rather more appropriate that you thank Jacob, here, since it's his generosity—"

Mr. Hoyt broke in. "This isn't your claim, then?"

"No, it is not," replied Richard in a cautious, measured tone. "This is Jacob's claim. I work for him."

"Ahhh…." said Mr. Hoyt, as if seriously considering. "Ah. You'll have to pardon me. I just assumed…" He paused, grinning apologetically. "I'm used to the normal situation being the other way around."

Still Mr. Hoyt addressed himself to Richard Barter as if Jacob Harper wasn't there. *What is he playing at?*

"Well, Mr. Hoyt," grinned Richard, "This is California." His voice had a certain edge. "Not Mississippi, not Alabama. I'm sure you've heard your Congress voted it a free state." Getting no reaction from Mr. Hoyt, he went on. "It was official in September. The southern boys aren't too happy about it, but it's done."

"We've been on the move," huffed Mr. Hoyt, looking down his nose. Hunched against his crutch, he wasn't as intimidating as he expected.

"Be that as it may," Richard replied mildly, "at least here, Jacob has the same opportunities as you or me."

In all this time, Mr. Hoyt had not once looked at Jacob Harper. He made a sour smile for Richard Barter's benefit, and took the biscuit tin from me.

Mr. Hoyt got some of his manners back, but kept his gaze fixed on young Barter. "We appreciate your help in gathering up Pegg's earnings." He shifted on his crutch and tucked the tin under his free arm. "Is there a town around here with an express office or a bank?"

"Auburn's up at the top of the canyon," Richard replied. "But you won't make it before dark. Best wait 'til morning,"

Mr. Hoyt brought out his grin. "Much obliged, Son. Much obliged."

Richard added, "I'll be taking some letters into town in the morning. I'll show you the way."

Mr. Hoyt grinned even wider. "That's most generous of you, young man, most generous."

Richard excused himself and went off to his family's camp.

Jacob Harper said, "The offer of supper still holds, if you're interested." He looked at me, not Mr. Hoyt.

I was scrambling to think of how I could make up for Mr. Hoyt's rudeness, but hunger got the better of me. "Thank you, Sir. We'd appreciate that very much."

Jacob started off for his cabin. I hustled after him. My partner stayed put. Jacob stopped and called back. "You're welcome, Mr. Hoyt, if you're so inclined."

Mr. Hoyt unstuck himself and followed.

Our host's cabin wasn't much bigger than our root cellar back home, nor nearly as well made. Jacob ducked inside to get his supper fixings. My partner and I waited outside. I looked around for kindling to lay a fire. Mr. Hoyt settled himself on a stump, hugging the biscuit tin to his belly.

I pointed to the tin and smiled. "That ought to give us a good start, a fresh start." I hoped it wouldn't disappear like the gold I supplied him with at Grizzly Bar.

Mr. Hoyt had an odd, sleepy look. "More than enough," he said.

Served around his modest campfire, Mr. Harper's beans and bacon tasted no different than others I'd tasted in the last seven months. But after four days of almost nothing to eat, my partner and I wolfed down his humble repast as if it were a king's feast. Mr. Hoyt allowed himself only the tersest of responses to Jacob's efforts to engage him, and could not manage so much as a thank you.

After supper, Jacob laid a few more sticks on the fire. While bats swooped overhead, he and I swapped stories about ourselves and where we were from. Mr. Hoyt kept his place by the fire, inspecting the contents of the biscuit tin.

When we hit a quiet spot, I asked Jacob, "Why is this place called Rattlesnake Bar? I've heard of other places with Bar in the name." Mr. Hoyt had cautioned me against mentioning Grizzly Bar. "Why are these places called, this Bar, or that Bar?"

He smiled. "'Bar' is short for sand bar. They're islands in the river where the water scoops up sand from one bend and dumps it farther downstream at another bend. You'll find them on all the big rivers. There's dozens of places up and down the gold country with names like Mississippi Bar, Neptune's Bar, Wildcat Bar." Jacob swept his hand over the scene. "You'll only see them in the quieter parts of the river; never where the water's too fast." His smile grew bigger, revealing he retained a full set of chompers. "But to answer your question, probably the first fella to show up here ran into a rattlesnake— or a bunch of 'em. Just like Mormons were probably the first folks to prospect Mormon Island. That's usually how it works."

While the front of me was toasty warm, the chill night air settled on my back like a blanket. I reminded myself not to complain. Novembers were usually some colder in Vermont. I looked at Mr. Hoyt. His chin had sunk to his chest, and he was sawing some very large, noisy logs.

I spoke cautiously, in a whisper. "I'm sorry about my partner. He ain't been the same since he broke his leg. He's right friendly most of the time." I left out the quick-tempered part.

"Don't trouble yourself," replied Jacob, equally cautious. "Some people see a darkie, all they can see is a slave." Jacob gave a smile that had no humor in it. "But the truth is, I was born a free man." He regarded Mr. Hoyt for a long moment. "However, regardless of what I say, your partner would probably like nothing better than to haul me back to the states and collect a fat bounty he imagines is on my head."

"I hope not. But I'm sorry, just the same."

"Well, I appreciate that, Pegg. I do." He was quiet for a minute. "If you don't mind my asking, I couldn't help but notice you didn't show up with much gear. Did you leave your outfit back up the hill?"

I didn't want to raise the same suspicions in Jacob that we had raised in Eli Cooder. "We don't have an outfit. We're just starting out." I didn't want to admit we were starting over, much less explain the whole shameful business of being chased out of Grizzly Bar. "We're looking to stake a claim."

Jacob leaned forward to add a stick to the ebbing flames. He arched his eyebrows in sympathy. "That'll be hard to do around here."

I tried not to feel discouraged. "We heard the North Fork is rich diggings."

He let out a low chuckle, shaking his head slowly. "So has everybody else, as you can see."

"I can work for somebody. I worked for Ormond Bonnet and…" I realized Jacob wouldn't know the Frenchman back in Grizzly Bar. "I can work a cradle 'til a claim comes free, or we find a spot."

Jacob smiled and held up his hand to stop my babbling. "I'd be glad to hire you, son, but I've already hired Dick and his kin." He rubbed his chin for a minute and then said, "R. C. Simpson's been talking about hiring help. But I don't think he has yet. I'll take you to meet him in the morning."

"I'd be much obliged, Sir. Much obliged. Thank you."

"Such fine manners, not to mention beautiful singing, deserve no less."

Sudden homesick almost fell me. I imagined my mom smiling at such compliments—her glad, dark eyes telling me not to let them go to my head, they had nothing to do with getting your chores done. Her hair was dark, too, lustrous dark. Mine was dark like hers. I was almost as tall as her when I left home. I'd be taller now. How I missed her hugs. I shook loose of such maudlin recollections. We'd get our gold and head home.

I sent up a silent prayer that the letter Yang Ho had mailed for me when he got San Francisco would reach her. But I owed her another letter. Richard Barter said he was taking letters to mail in the morning. I asked Jacob if he had writing materials. Luckily, he did. "I'll pay you back," I said.

I planned to write just a note. I didn't want to worry her with all my worrying, so I concentrated on asking about things I knew they would be doing on the farm. Was she making a strudel with apples and raisins, a favorite winter dish with our family? Was Amy milking Patience and Penelope, our cows? Normally, it would be another year before she had that chore. Did Adam have the forge going, fixing tools and making new ones? He might even be married by the time I got home. I said I was looking after myself, as well as looking for gold. I talked about my claim being on a very promising part of the river. Knowing how she cared about my reading, I wrote I was reading the newspapers regularly. I didn't say anything about missing Dad—I knew that would upset her—or about Mr. Hoyt—which would upset *me*. Besides, it would likely get back to Mr. Pruitt. The note ended up being a two-page letter.

I had an urge to keep writing, but Jacob didn't have very much paper. So, I contented myself with staring into his fire and thinking about what I would write to my friend Hally, from the trip out, when I got some paper of my own.

Did her family settle close to Lilly's family, the Chalmers? How different my lot would be had I accepted the Chalmers' offer to go with them to Oregon. I would be welcomed, without a doubt. I wouldn't have to worry so much. I recalled little Lilly, who was about three, riding on my shoulders or on Boreas, our ox. Mrs. Chalmers always treated me with the respect due an adult. I might even have more time to spend with Hally. How we had passed endless miles: trading stories about what she or I had seen along the way, or what we'd learned from Mr. MacIver, with plenty of laughter thrown in for good measure. That led to thoughts of all our friends in what we called the Buffalo Chip Gang, and our night lost on the prairie.

Somehow, remembering of any sort led to thinking about a lonely gravesite where my father lay, on a windswept hill somewhere west of South Pass. Then I would have to shake myself and find something that didn't cut me so deep.

That usually ended up being thoughts of Linnaeus Peabody, the schoolteacher who traveled west with us, playing music with my dad, teaching me countless wonderful things about the world. Did he make it to San Francisco, playing his beautiful music? And where, oh, where was Gideon MacIver? The guide for the Chalmers company had taught me the difference between the Cheyenne and Arapaho.

CHAPTER 6

In the morning, Jacob Harper shook me awake and handed me a couple pieces of cold bacon and a biscuit. "We'd best make tracks. R. C. will already be hard at it."

Mr. Hoyt was still asleep. The young Barter sat on a stump, waiting for him to wake. He held several letters in his hand. I asked him if he would mail my letter, too. "Of course," he replied cheerily, adding my missive to his sheaf. Jacob urged us on our way to meet my prospective employer.

"Good luck to you," Richard waved.

"Thanks." I scurried after Jacob.

Even with the smoke from cook fires, the air smelled fresh and cool. Jacob and I threaded our way through other claims. Some people were up and about, rubbing sleep out of their eyes, coaxing fires back to life. Others slumbered on. Jacob asked what I had done in the way of prospecting. I told him about finding the cradle, and then working for the Frenchmen, and how Ormond had given me lessons with the gold pan.

As Jacob predicted, we came upon Mr. R. C. Simpson already at work. He was bent over a long tom, which worked something like a cradle, but was much longer, and didn't rock. The best part was it had a constant supply of water, channeled from the river, so you could wash more dirt at one time.

"Good morning to you, R. C.," Jacob called out as we approached.

Mr. Simpson straightened up to face his visitors. He was a lean, wiry man, as tall as Jacob, with giant, bristling whiskers and a floppy gray hat. Despite the chilly morning, he was dressed only in his long, red underwear and a pair of battered boots. Such a getup would draw curious glances back home, but apparently not here.

"Same to you, Jake," R. C. called back, with a careless wave of his hand. "Same to you. Be better when I get some color in hand." He gave a quick glance back to the long tom and pushed his hat up on his forehead. "If you see Dame Fortune, send her my way, will ya? She's been a little scarce, lately."

"I'll sure do that, R. C.," replied Jacob, stepping over to the long tom. "This why you been talkin' about takin' on help?"

R. C. didn't answer. He was staring at me. "What you got here, Jacob? A boy-child, looks like."

"This is Bartholomew Pegg," said Jacob. "Goes by 'Pegg'. Late of Vermont. Can rock a cradle or tip a pan with the best of 'em."

R. C. ran knobby fingers through his salt and pepper whiskers. "You swear by it?"

Jacob ignored the challenge. "If you're still looking for help."

I blurted, "I work hard, and I don't complain." I instantly regretted my bad manners, but I was desperate.

Both men seemed unperturbed. R. C. went from scratching his whiskers to scratching his backside. "That so?" he said. "Look a little wet behind the ears, Sonny."

I jumped in again. "I worked for Ormond Bonnet—on Simpson's Creek, over on the South Fork—"

R. C. cut me off. "Whereabouts in Vermont?"

I almost said "What?" but I knew I had to be quicker than that. "Richford. Up top—near the border," I said.

"Know a man named Pruitt?" asked R. C. "James Pruitt?"

I started, but I hoped it didn't show. "Yessir. He made it possible for us to come here."

R. C. hitched up his elbows. "Us?"

"My dad, Mr. Hoyt, and myself. We have a partnership."

R. C. eyed me warily. "Why ain't you workin' with them?"

Jacob spoke up. "He lost his dad on the way out, and Hoyt broke his leg."

I tried to keep a straight face, even though it felt like a kick in the stomach. *No tears. No playing for sympathy.*

"Sorry to hear that." R. C. shot a glance at Jacob. "Cholera?"

"Thank you, Sir," I said. "No. Fever, I think."

R. C. drew his eyebrows together. "Ever been to Irasburg?"

I grinned. "We have people there. My mother's sister and her family."

R. C. went back to inspecting his long tom, swirling the water with his fingers. "And who might they be?"

I leaned toward him to make sure he heard. "Joanna Calder and Enos, her husband, and my cousins—"

"Good man, Enos Calder." R. C. levered himself upright. "I got a place on the river, a little farther out of town than him."

This man was practically a neighbor. Irasburg was only a whisker over twenty miles to the southeast of Richford. I tried not to show my surprise. The coincidence was uncanny, but I chose to see it as a good sign.

R. C. broke into my thought. "This Hoyt kin of yours?"

"No, sir, he's not. Mr. Hoyt is Mr. Pruitt's stepson."

R. C. raked at his whiskers again, like he was sorting out who was who. "So—you know how hard this work is?"

I put on a scowl, hoping to look sober and diligent. "Yessir, I do."

R. C. picked up a battered gold pan and held it out to me. "Let's see what you can do, Bartholomew Pegg."

I took the pan and picked up a shovel lying close by. I fretted if I would be able to show him some color. Then I reminded myself that I only had to show R. C. my skill, not my luck.

By the look of it, he had already worked over most of his claim. I scooped up a shovelful of dirt, dumped it in the pan, and took the pan over to the river. Jacob and R. C. stood over me. I knelt and started washing the dirt, tossing out the bigger pebbles as they showed themselves. I took off my hat to let them see better. It was quick work to get rid of most of the larger gravels, dirt, and coarse sand. I sent a silent, "Thank you," to Caleb Johnson and Ormond Bonnet for teaching me to pan.

When I got down to the fine silt and black sand, I proceeded with more caution. As I tilted the pan higher, I had to go even more carefully. It was easy to wash too much away. Gingerly, I still picked out the odd piece of small gravel.

Jacob said, "What'd I tell you, R. C.?"

The grizzled prospector only grunted.

Pretty soon, out of that whole shovelful of dirt, no more than a few spoonfuls of black sand remained. R. C. and Jacob bent to peer into the pan. Now I had to go very carefully. I took another dip of water and moved the dark sand out along the crease in the pan.

A tiny speck of yellow glinted right in the middle of my spread of sand. Being even more careful, I washed out a little more of the black sand without losing any of the gold. More flakes and granules appeared. No matter how tiny, they glimmered richly against the black sand. They amounted to less than a pinch. But that was one pan. If you kept at it all day, and had that kind of luck all day, you might have maybe a thimbleful of gold for your efforts. I looked up at Jacob and Mr. Simpson.

Jacob grinned. "I take it back. Come work for me."

"Oh, no you don't." R. C. thrust his hand out as if to keep Jacob at bay. "You brought him over. I got first dibs." He looked down at me. "You're hired. When can you start?"

"Right now." I stood up and handed him the pan.

Jacob gave me a wink. Still smiling, he said, "So be it." And he turned to go. "I'll tell Mr. Hoyt you're here when he gets back from town."

"Thank you, Sir. I'd appreciate that."

Since the long tom had a constant supply of water from a ditch R. C. had dug, I helped him keep the device supplied with dirt. We spread each shovelful out so the water could do its work quickly and thoroughly. Once in a while, R. C. would leave off shoveling to pick out river pebbles and debris, and sift through the tailings caught behind the riffles.

When the sun was behind the hills to the west, coloring the cloud bellies orange, R. C. cleaned out the riffles for the last time of the day. He washed those last tailings out in the pan, and then paid me my wages from the day's take.

"Come back tomorrow, long as you can get here before the sun does."

I suppressed a grin. "Yessir." I'd been doing that almost since I could walk.

I hurried back to Jacob's camp, eager to show Mr. Hoyt we were part of the Gold Rush again! I found Jacob, outside as before, tucking into his supper. "Well, there you are, Pegg," he smiled. "Did R. C. work your tail off?"

I sensed it wasn't a serious question. "I guess I did okay. He wants me to come back tomorrow."

"Oooooo-eee!" Jacob threw his broad shoulders back, his dark face beaming. "He's got no time for a man who doesn't work as hard as he does. I think you did okay, indeed."

I cast a quick glance around the area. "Is Mr. Hoyt around?"

"Don't rightly know. Young Barter came back from town by himself. Told me to send you right over so he could fill you in."

"Where's he camped?"

Jacob pointed downstream with his spoon. "With his kin. A hundred yards. Maybe a bit more."

"Thank you, Sir!" I called over my shoulder as I bolted for the Barter camp.

"You want me to save you these beans?" he called out, holding up his cook pot.

"Yes, please!" I shouted back.

As I moved downstream, I walked through the claims, dodging tools, sidestepping pits and piles both, ducking under flumes. I met with someone new every ten feet. Because Rattlesnake Bar was deemed rich diggings, each prospector's claim consisted of a ten-by-ten-foot plot of riverbank and continued into the river to halfway across. Those who'd put up living quarters, whether cabin, tent, or tangle of brush, set them at the back of the claims.

Plenty of fires lit my way. Many miners were still at their supper—others had settled in for a pipe or some stories with friends.

Different languages came to my ear, but everybody seemed to know what a smile and a wave meant. I turned down more than a few invitations while keeping an eye out for the Barter camp. Fiddle music began upstream, behind me, and I had a powerful urge to seek it out, but I was on a more urgent errand.

At last, I spied Richard Barter, taller than most, holding forth while half a dozen others sat around their fire. Among these were two men of equally impressive stature and dramatic features.

Richard sprang to his feet as if he would leap into flight. "Pegg! There you are. Welcome." He thrust out his hand.

We shook. The others looked on expectantly. Richard spread his arms to take in the group. "Gentlemen. Allow me to introduce the latest inductee into this fevered multitude." He lifted a hand to indicate the entire canyon. "Bartholomew Pegg. Otherwise known as Pegg. From Vermont."

I received a volley of nods and greetings, bobbing my head in return. Richard went on to introduce his companions, ending with, "Her Majesty's loyal sons, everyone." The two larger fellows proved to be, indeed, his kin: his brother, Andrew, and a cousin. Everyone called Richard, Dick. I thought they were British, but it turned out they were from Canada.

I could hardly wait to get past the pleasantries before I blurted, "Where's Mr. Hoyt?"

"I expect he's on his way to Coloma, or will be in the morning," Dick said, grinning like he had some private joke up his sleeve.

"What?" I yelped. "What do you mean?"

"Thought that might get your attention." He motioned me to a stump a ways off. "Sit down. Let me tell you about it."

I sat down. The others returned to their stories.

"Tea?" Dick offered me a tin cup and poured from a blackened tin pot.

"Thanks." But I was too impatient to drink. Mr. Hoyt was up to his old tricks, hying off to chase a new whim without so much as a by-your-leave.

"An impressive chap, your Mister Hoyt," Dick Barter began. "We weren't in town more than half an hour before he's hobnobbing with none other than Sam Brannan, who *just happened* to be in town. How they sniffed each other out, I'll never guess. To hear Hoyt tell it, you'd think they were long-lost chums. Brannan, himself, must have sensed a kindred spirit, because he offered Mr. Hoyt a position at his store in Coloma."

Dick paused to take a sip of his tea.

I gaped at him in disbelief. Just like in St. Louis, my partner had bolted, chasing after some scheme that promised easy riches, with no regard for his obligations. But this time I didn't have my dad to take refuge in.

Dick had more to tell. "Hoyt made me swear on my mother's grave that I would impart this news to you, and give you his solemn promise that he still considers your partnership in full force. Indeed, he pronounced hooking up with Brannan the best way that he can contribute to it."

I stared at Dick Barter, speechless. *What possible use can this Mr. Brannan make of a man with a broken leg?* "Did he say when he would come back?" My stomach hollowed out. *What if, this time, things actually work out for Mr. Hoyt? Would he come back at all?*

Dick swirled the tea in his cup. "He said he would come back when he was established, when his leg was fully healed, and mining activity picked up again."

He didn't even ask! But then I scoffed at myself. *When did Mr. Hoyt ask permission to do anything? Couldn't he have asked me to go along?* He was my last connection to home. Who else would understand when I talked about my family or Richford? This was a new feeling, and it turned my knees to water.

I realized Dad was right. I needed an adult to depend on in this wild, lawless place, maybe not breathing down my neck, but around if the need arose. There was great comfort in that. Many times since Dad had died I felt his absence keenly. Now I really was—no bones about it—on my own! Without even Bugle to confide in.

My friend Will scolded me in my mind. *Enough of this weeping and wailing. Get your oars back in the water.*

Who was going to carry on with the responsibility for sending money back East? Him or me? Who was going to make the decisions?

I turned to Dick. "Did he deposit the gold I got for singing 'Amazing Grace'?"

"Yes, he did," Dick replied. "I was with him. We did that straight away."

A glimmer of relief broke through. At least we had an account. I could buy food.

Presumably, Mr. Hoyt would live off what Brannan paid him. Questions came crowding back, but I voiced only one. "Did he take out a bank draft?"

Dick brightened. "As a matter of fact, he did. Yes."

But I had to make certain. "Did you happen to see who he sent it to?"

"I tried not to be nosey, but I did hear 'Pegg' and 'Vermont.'"

I sighed inwardly with relief. At least Mr. Hoyt had done that part right. I could only hope that he'd been sending drafts all along, since I had been supplying him with gold.

CHAPTER 7

With Mr. Hoyt off chasing another whim, my immediate concern was making myself useful to Mr. Simpson. That way, I would be ready to jump on any claim that came free. I tried not to fret about how long that would take. The canyon gained new arrivals every day.

Jacob Harper very generously shared his camp and his victuals until I could find my own accommodations. On my third day at Rattlesnake Bar, while sharing his supper, I said to Jacob, "Looks like rain any day now."

Jacob glanced at the sky. "We may get some before Christmas."

The days grew steadily shorter, and much of the time the sky was overcast with clouds that threatened rain. People stirring their beans looked up and wondered when the skies would open.

Jacob went on. "But the true rainy season, if we have one, will be early in the new year. January, February, March." He handed me another biscuit. "Once the rains come, the river will rise and we won't be able to work until the spring." He shuddered as if shaking off the rain. "Besides, it'll just be too cold and wet."

"Why can't we just keep working?" I squared my shoulders. "I worked in the cold and wet all the time back home on the farm."

Jacob smiled. "Well, maybe you're tougher than most. There's lawyers here, piano teachers, and bookkeepers. . .tailors. People who've never even held a shovel, let alone mucked out a barn. They'll scuttle into town at the first sign of bad weather—if they can afford it."

"What about you?" I said, not realizing I might be insulting him.

Jacob shook his head, smiling. "I'm no braver than the rest. When the rains come in earnest, I'll go help my brother. He has a ranch west of Auburn, near Spanish Corral. Raises melons and potatoes and strawberries, any fool thing people crave." Jacob chuckled in a contented way. "Makes better money than I do."

I thought about my dad's long-nurtured dream of a big dairy farm. He'd died trying to realize that dream. I couldn't fail my family. "Well, I want to get back home. I'm going to work as long as I can."

"As long as the river will let you," Jacob added.

On the fifth day working for R. C. Simpson, he said, "I got another claim farther upstream, on the south bank. It needs looking after, so people don't get any ideas. You think you can handle that?"

I was excited by the chance. "Yessir. I think I can."

R. C. tied two biscuits and a few strips of bacon in a handkerchief. "Here's your dinner." Then he handed me a shovel, a pick, and an old, battered wooden bowl. "This here's called a batea," he said, showing me the bowl at different angles. "I used this early on, 'til I could buy a metal pan." He brushed his fingers around the inside of the bowl. "It'll serve." He gave me the batea. Last, he produced an empty tobacco tin. "If you fill this up, come and get me."

I went bug-eyed. "Yessir!" That would be a bonanza. I shoved the tin in my back pocket.

Picking our way upstream past the other claims, people called out a greeting or a good-natured insult to R. C. Sometimes he answered, sometimes he just waved. When Rattlesnake Bar slipped under water, we splashed across to the southern bank. Finally, we reached a spot that wasn't as dug up as the claims on either side of it.

"This here's it." R. C. opened his palm to the ground at our feet. "To the west," he pointed behind us, downstream, "is Emerson Abbot Marshall, who is no doubt sleeping off last night's drunk. No relation to James Marshall, the fellow who started this whole whirligig." Then he pointed upstream, to the east. "On the other side of you is Wilford Mahoney."

A small man with a dark, curly beard looked up from his pan and scowled. "'Bout time you showed up, Simpson. We thought you'd seen the elephant and tucked tail and run."

R. C. frowned and grunted. "Don't bet on it, Mahoney." He pointed to me. "This here's Bart Pegg. He's my official, bona fide representative. Gonna work the claim for a few days 'til I can get back up here."

I stuck out my hand and tried to make my voice as low as possible, but it broke, despite my best efforts. "You can call me Pegg, Sir. Good to meet you." Mr. Mahoney gave a startled look, like he was unaccustomed to such gestures.

He set his pan aside and rose to his feet, offering his hand. "Sure."

R. C. scowled at Mr. Mahoney. "He's good at minding his own business. See if you can do the same."

"Ha! Better'n I can say for you." Mahoney tossed his head and went back to his work.

R. C. pointed out the stakes marking the limits of his claim. According to the local agreement, as well as the land, R. C.'s claim went halfway out into the river. There were stumps and tangles of brush, as well as a lot of sand and gravel. A collection of larger stones made their way from the shore out into the water.

"Have at it," he said. "Come by tonight and tell me how it went." He turned and headed back downstream to his claim with the long tom.

I tied my dinner handkerchief high up on a manzanita branch. I imagined Bugle and Sun Shu sitting under the tree back in Grizzly Bar while I worked the Frenchmen's claim. She spoiled him with more petting and scratching than one dog had any right to expect. My shameless mutt would sprawl in her lap like a drunkard, lost to his pleasure. I missed all the good talks Sun Shu and I had walking back to town at the end of the day.

How were they getting along? I hoped Sweeney, or his men, were leaving Sun Shu alone. I was anxious to go back and check on them and reclaim my dog. I scolded myself to stop wallowing in worry; I had a tobacco tin to fill.

I got the feel of the wooden batea after a few shovelfuls of dirt. Being more like a bowl, it had no well-defined crease between the bottom and side. I had to be even more careful when I got down to the black sand. It could all spill out so easily. To my intense delight, I caught a few grains of color.

A blue jay called. I looked up in time to see him land on the manzanita branch that held my handkerchief. I lobbed a couple of pebbles his way. "Git!" The jay flew off, protesting.

Mr. Mahoney commented from behind me. "You'll use up every pebble on this river keepin' them jays away. Best hide your food under a rock or something.'"

I turned to him. "Thanks. That's a good idea."

Mr. Mahoney froze in mid-stoop, like I'd tricked him. "You're welcome."

I hid my dinner under a rock. The biscuits would suffer, but I could abide that.

Wondering if the idea I'd used back in Grizzly Bar would hold true here, I wrestled aside one of the larger rocks in the shallows at the edge of the water. That stirred up a lot of silt. I waited until the river carried the silt away before digging out more sand and gravels from the cavity where the rock had been. I got some color, enough to make me try the same idea with another boulder.

As soon as I had some dust and flakes, I tipped them ever so carefully into the tobacco tin. Those few flakes glinted way down at the dark bottom of that tin. It would take some doing to fill it up, let alone before the day was out.

When the sun was at its zenith, I had a teaspoon of color in my tin. It was nothing like the bounty I'd found at Grizzly Bar, but it felt good to be working in the gold rush again.

Upon inspection, I discovered my dinner was completely covered in ants. It was every bit as careful an operation picking off all the ants as it was washing black sand out of a pan. I held up a biscuit in triumph to Mr. Mahoney, who was likewise settled to his dinner. He nodded and saluted in return with a piece of bacon. He took his ease in the shade of a grand old oak tree at the farther corner of his claim.

While I munched on my dinner, I looked around R. C.'s claim. What I had taken earlier for a pile of brush and trash turned out, upon closer inspection, to be the remains of a dwelling sitting at the back of his claim. Three log walls and a low-pitched shed roof declared it a cabin, though a very small one. The back wall seemed to be the hillside itself.

In the afternoon, a few drops spit down from the cloudy sky, but nothing more. I kept working the larger rocks. With the heavy cloud cover it got darker even earlier than usual. I stayed until I thought I would lose my way back in the dark. I had washed another dozen pans of dirt in the afternoon and got a thumbnail's worth of color for my trouble, which went into the tin.

I was looking for a place to conceal the tools when Mr. Mahoney spoke up. "You comin' back tomorrow?"

"Yessir. I hope so."

He gestured carelessly toward R. C.'s claim. "You can leave your tools out. That way people will know you're working the claim. They'll leave it be."

I gave him a nod. "Thanks. I appreciate that." My dad often said that to people he had dealings with. I laid the shovel and pick in the shape of an "X" on the sand at the center of the claim. I rested the bowl where the two handles crossed, but it kept sliding off.

I heard Mr. Mahoney say, "Don't worry, Son. They'll get the idea."

I turned to see him smiling.

"Okay." I rested the bowl up against one of the handles. "Thank you, again, Sir. Have a good night. See you tomorrow."

He grunted, "Uh, yeah… You, too." He tipped his finger to his hat.

I did the same and set off, shoving the tobacco tin deeper into my back pocket.

As I made my way back downstream, I thought about R. C. Simpson and Mr. Mahoney. Mr. Mahoney didn't seem all that bad a sort. Maybe not the most outgoing, but then, R. C. could be pretty crusty himself. Maybe there was some bad blood between them. I had no reason to be sour toward Mr. Mahoney on what I'd witnessed of him so far. I just hoped I wouldn't get in the middle.

It was near dark by the time I got back to R. C.'s first claim and handed him the tobacco tin. He hefted it gingerly.

"Four—maybe five—ounces?" he said. "Well done, young 'un."

"There's more, I'm sure." I wanted to sound like I knew what I was talking about. "I just worked with the larger stones by the river today."

"Jacob's invited us to supper," R. C. said as he measured out my wages.

I still had that little square of paper that held the wages from my first day working with the Frenchmen back in Grizzly Bar. I fished it out of the pouch around my neck and put what I had just earned in there. Then we went over to Jacob's camp.

R. C. and Jacob swapped cordial insults, the way good friends do, the way Will and I did back home. Over supper, they shared news of somebody's good luck downstream.

That'll be me someday.

During a pause in their banter, R. C. asked me, "Did you notice the oak on Mahoney's claim?"

"Yessir, I did. One of the bigger ones I've seen out here." The trunk was six feet across, maybe five.

"A good landmark. You can use it to find my claim."

I was glad to be in the conversation. "Why do you suppose nobody's cut it down?"

R. C. looked thoughtful for a minute. Jacob put another biscuit on his plate.

"Thank you kindly." He nodded to Jacob, then he answered my question. "If it was me, I'd say respect for an old'un. But more likely because smaller stuff was easier to cut."

Jacob put another biscuit on my plate. I nodded my thanks as R. C. had.

Jacob added, "Somebody's taken a few of the lower branches, though."

I glanced over at R. C. He seemed lost in a moment of melancholy. Maybe I could draw him away from it. "R. C.? Was Simpson's Creek named after you?"

He took a bite of bacon. "Not likely, since I never set foot on the South Fork, that I recollect."

I speculated to myself how many Simpsons could be among all the miners in the Gold Rush. Then R. C. offered, "Could've been my cousin, Meriwether Simpson. We came out together, but parted company at Fort Hall over who's cooking was worse. He's out here somewhere, ornery cuss!" R. C. gave us an impish grin. "If he ain't kilt himself with his own cookin'. Could be him it's named after."

After much genial banter, R. C. took himself off to his claim and I helped Jacob with cleaning up. The heavens opened in earnest that night, heavy drops pelting down, sheets of rain drifting. Jacob urged me to share his small shelter, which I was only too happy to do.

The rain continued into the next morning, making a fire a fool's errand. Jacob produced a cold breakfast of last night's sliced bacon and biscuits. Washing dirt was pointless, as well. I went up to R. C.'s other claim anyway, to be ready to work in case the rain let up. I was also curious how Mr. Mahoney fared.

As I trudged on my way, I became aware of a continuous scene of very different activity on both banks. No miner washed dirt or rocked a cradle; they carried their tools and gear away from their diggings, hauling them up to higher ground behind their claims. No joking, no joshing. Food, blankets, everything movable was hauled away.

Just when I was about to ask Mr. Mahoney what the odd activity signified, R. C. appeared, soaked to the skin. His old, floppy hat sagged over his ears, spouting water out past his shoulders. He scooped up some of my tools and the batea and took them up into the trees high above the claim.

I grabbed up the rest and followed him. "What's going on?" I shouted over the pelting rain and wind.

"Come help me take down the long tom, move my kit," he shouted back. He was already trotting off the way he'd come.

I ran after him downstream. We got back to R. C.'s claim amidst a great commotion. Miners were shouting and running everywhere. Jacob added braces to his flume. Richard and his brother hauled all their tools to higher ground.

R. C. handed me a hammer. I asked again, "What's going on?"

"Gullywasher comin'!" R. C. shouted. "Sure as the day is long!"

We dismantled his long tom into two ten-foot sections, carried them up the hill, and lashed them to the uphill side of a tree. Then we went for his other tools. It was none too soon, for just as we came up the hill with our last load, we heard a distant roaring. I spotted a pick we had left behind. "I'll get that pick!" I started back down the slope.

R. C. put out his hand to stop me. "Tools can be replaced. More angry water than you want to think about's comin' our way any minute now."

Above the drumming rain, the roar grew louder. All along the south slope a line of sodden miners stood with their kit and kept watch upriver.

"Here she comes!" R. C. yelled.

Some scrambled instinctively to even higher ground.

The already muddy flow began to swell, grow more rambunctious, pushing beyond its normal boundaries. Suddenly, a churning, thrashing wall of water, four to five feet higher than the earlier flow, pushed into view. It reared and plunged like a stampede of wild horses.

The flood rolled right over Rattlesnake Bar. It filled the whole river bottom. The debris of who-knew-how-many miles' worth of miners' gear tossed and heaved, turning a mute waltz with uprooted trees and broken limbs. Some of the prospectors had waited too long. They were barely able to save themselves.

Much of the flotsam was what couldn't be easily moved—bits of cabin, lumber, barrels of provisions, canvas from tents, anything that would float. Jacob Harper's flume shattered into matchsticks. The wreckage twirled away into the surging chaos.

The higher water did not subside. A sloppy, heaving, many-headed monster swallowing everything in its path followed. The level of the rushing flood rose to perhaps ten feet below where we stood. It was a sight to cause the stoutest heart to quake.

Expensive sawn lumber, precious flumes and cabins, food and clothing were being swept away. *How many of these men, have the means to rebuild—to start over?*

I looked upstream to see what might be coming. Somehow, in the roiling, surging confusion, I saw a bowl bobbing along. I was sure it was R. C.'s wooden batea, the one I had been using. I thought we had stowed it safely. Apparently not. I had no time to wonder because right next to the bowl up popped Mr. Mahoney. I had only a glimpse of him before he went under. I pointed. "Mr. Mahoney!" How had the snarling waves caught him unawares?

"Darn fool!" growled R. C. "Too stubborn to get out of the way in time."

Mr. Mahoney came up again, sputtering and gasping. The way he was thrashing around, I was sure he didn't know how to swim. I threw off my hat, yanked the Colt out of my belt, pulled off my shoes and dove in. I heard R. C. yell before the roar of the water closed over me.

Boulders grinding along the bottom rumbled like angry river trolls. One part of my mind said, *This is stupid!* But my mind wasn't in charge at that moment.

I had to get some air. The world weaved and thrust and fell. I had only an instant to look around. I caught a glimpse of Mr. Mahoney, still upstream, but not by much.

If I swam straight out, knowing the river would carry me downstream as I swam, I might intercept him. The surge pushed me under. *Up!* I fought to get my arms working. The water twisted me around, picked me up, pushed me down.

I narrowly missed getting clobbered by a stout timber. I grabbed it, but the river wrenched it away.

I couldn't see Mr. Mahoney. A hogshead's worth of water caught me full in the face, leaving me gasping and sputtering. Another surge slammed me in the back. *Under! Up! Air!*

I tried to work my way to the middle of the river, but in such a lurching, liquid confusion I couldn't tell where I was.

There he is! We're almost abreast! Only eight feet more—! Slammed under again! Fight my way up. Twisting, I saw R. C. Simpson running along the south shore.

Twist more, look for Mr. Mahoney. Beyond me, downstream. He went under again.

A wave tumbled me under. *Mr. Mahoney is past your help now. Time to look after yourself.*

I was underwater as much as above. Suddenly I was very much afraid. I struck out for shore; it didn't matter which. My efforts were scarcely better than flailing. *Remember to kick*, came my father's voice from so many years ago.

I glimpsed the shore through the sheets of rain, a little closer. I swam crossways to the current, the only sure way to reach shore.

A barrel loomed up, ready to smack me. I gulped air and dug at the water to get below it. The staves scraped across my back. When

I came up, a piece of somebody's firewood splashed into the water next to me. A length of rope was tied to it.

I grabbed the wood, hugging it to my chest, praying the rope meant something. It drew taut. A mound of water broke over my head, but I hung on to the piece of wood. Through driving rain and plastered hair, I saw a figure up past his knees in the churning current, hauling on the rope. He was almost as much a fool as me.

The man didn't stop gathering in the line until he hauled me out. I lay in a heap, coughing and gasping. Even then I didn't let go of that chunk of wood. On the other end of the rope stood R. C. Simpson.

He was all akimbo. His whiskers bristled with raindrops falling or ready to fall. His saturated long johns sagged against his tall, bony frame like a loose hide. He was hopping mad. "Of all the crazy, fool-hardy, dingle-headed—What were—I never…" He sputtered to a stop. He threw aside his end of the rope, now that I was safely beached.

I got to my hands and knees. "Thank you." I coughed up more water, wiping hair out of my eyes. "Thank you. Much, much obliged."

R. C. bent down, as if I couldn't hear him. "What'd you go and do such a crazy, fool thing for? You could've drowned!"

"I can swim." I finally released the life-saving chunk of wood.

Leaning yet closer, R. C. flapped an accusing finger at the raging water. "Neptune hisself couldn't swim in that!"

"I didn't know that before I jumped in."

"That Mahoney varmint wasn't worth it," R. C. blustered, relenting a little.

"I didn't know that either." I sat back on my heels. "Did you see him? Farther down, after he passed me?"

R. C. stood glaring down at me, hitching his elbows in agitation. "I did not," he grumbled, straightening. "I had other priorities, if it's all the same to you."

"Well, I thank you again, Sir." My body sagged as the tension left me. "I surely do."

"The river's got enough rocks in it, as it is. You don't need to go addin' the ones in your head."

Richard Barter came up, grinning like a co-conspirator, bearing my hat, gun, knife and shoes. He handed me my gear, tipping his head toward R. C. "You see this old coot out in it up to his knees? I thought I was going to lose both of you." He offered me a hand up. "I know who I want by my side next time I'm in trouble."

R. C. snorted, raking water out of his beard with stiff knobby fingers.

The wind that drove the rain increased the chill of our wet clothes. Everybody was equally soaked. Water dripped from noses, hats and fingertips. We were stranded on the south bank with a score or more of other miners until the river went down enough to cross, assuming the flood hadn't erased our crossing spot.

I recovered my spirits enough to wonder which fate would befall Mr. Mahoney. He was either ashore or drowned. *Or, he could still be afloat.* Will always said it was my curse to look on the bright side.

R. C. looked around and pointed up the slope. "There's some fellas vacatin' that tree. Let's get out of the wet." We scuttled to crowd against the trunk before anybody else got the same idea. Several other miners took shelter, such as it was, on the other side.

We stood in silence for a few moments. Then Richard offered, "Somebody's bound to fish him out before he gets to the Golden Gate."

R. C. snorted again. "He's probably already presentin' his sorry self to St. Peter at the *Pearly* Gates."

I watched the churning water. I could easily be the one presenting myself to St. Peter.

R. C. wasn't finished. "Still, we gotta give him his week. If he don't show up by then, his claim'll be up for grabs, same as anybody's."

I remembered the Englishman in Grizzly Bar; Mr. Galloway's instruction about miner's respecting each other's absences. "Will people respect that if they know he's—not coming back?"

Richard wrinkled his eyebrows. "You mean like if they find his body washed up downstream?"

R. C. gave us a withering glare. "Am I keeping company with nitwits? Use yer noggin. As soon as everybody knows he's dead, his claim'll be buried in people fightin' over it before you can blink."

"An apt turn of phrase, I must say," observed Richard.

R. C. turned his shaggy scowl on the younger man.

I stood up.

R. C. groused, "Where you goin'?"

"I gotta see."

He swung his hand out to remind me of the river. "He can't have survived that. What's there to find out?"

"I just want to be sure."

CHAPTER 8

I started downstream. Will snickered in the corner of my mind. *It ain't exactly grave-robbing, but it's close.*

The rain let up and then stopped while I was looking. The cloud cover moved off, but the sun offered no warmth. About a mile downriver I found Mr. Mahoney. By some miracle he had made it to the south shore. He was sitting a few feet from the water's edge, surrounded by a gaggle of curious prospectors.

I walked up to him with a big smile. "Mr. Mahoney. You made it. Hallelujah."

He didn't reply. He didn't look up from staring at the cobbles. Maybe he didn't quite believe he was still alive. He was completely soaked through, hair plastered slick to his head. Only his curly, dark beard defied his generally bedraggled state.

I squatted beside him. "The good Lord smiled on you this day, that's for sure."

Mr. Mahoney continued to stare between his knees. "Can't thank Him for much else."

Perhaps this surliness was why R. C. took a hard line with Mr. Mahoney. Some of the onlookers began to drift away, presuming somebody that ornery wasn't going to keel over anytime soon, and thus did not merit further concern. I tried a little good cheer. "Well, at least you're here for another try."

Mr. Mahoney raised his head to look at me. "That was a blame fool thing to try."

It was my turn to look at the cobbles. "Well, I wasn't much help to you, after all."

"But you tried." He waited for me to look at him. "Not many would. People say I've got a short fuse. Maybe so. But I'm not one to ignore a kindness."

I didn't have anything to say to that.

Mr. Mahoney's voice took on a rasp of desperation. "Looka here. I'm done. I've had three different claims on three different rivers, and I've got nothin' to show for it." He turned his angry glare at the tumbling river. "What little color this cussed place gave up—" he kicked at a stone— "just about kept me in vittles, and no more."

He turned to me again. No peevishness remained, only despair. "Getting washed out was the last straw," he said. "I'm through." He struggled to his feet and wobbled uncertainly. "You want my claim, it's yours."

I grasped Mr. Mahoney's elbow to steady him. "You sure?" Did he truly mean it? This was no trifling matter in a place as rich as Rattlesnake Bar. Maybe he was just dazed from his ordeal.

Mahoney swayed, getting his balance. "It's yours. Maybe you'll have better luck." He said it like he was pronouncing a hex.

I stood up. "Don't we have to tell somebody? Sign a paper?"

He turned away, looking for his next step on the uneven stones. "I'll give notice at the express office. The quicker I'm shut of this place, the happier I'll be."

I stayed with him, my hand hovering close, just in case. "How are you going to cross the river to get into town?"

He drew ahead, gaining determination. "You don't have to worry about that," he called over his shoulder. "Just go in and tell 'em who you are."

I watched him stumble upstream. A few other miners watched him pass. I hoped it would be as simple as he said. Just to be sure, I called after him. "That's Bartholomew Pegg. Not just 'Pegg.'"

He said no more, picking his way among the rounded cobbles.

"Thanks…" I didn't move. If I wasn't mistaken, I had just been handed a claim on the North Fork of the American River, one of the richest strikes in the Mother Lode! I reviewed our exchange as carefully as if it were nuggets of gold. 'You want my claim, it's yours.' That's what he'd said. I wanted to run after him, to make doubly sure. But I didn't want to give him a chance to change his mind.

"Hey, Boy! Can we get a hand here?"

I turned in the direction of the hail. Half a dozen miners were wrestling a drowned cow to shore. *Where in heaven's name did that come from?* No matter. It was here now. The meat would make a welcome change from beans and bacon.

Only one other man besides myself knew anything about butchering. Being the more experienced, he took the lead, starting with the cut down the belly. I was happy to help and learn. I marveled at how light and sure the man wielded his knife. The work was quickly done with several of the miners helping hoist the carcass around as we progressed.

No one wanted to bother with tanning the hide, so I cut two sections out of it to wrap the two tenderloins I'd chosen as my share. With hasty farewells, I rushed back to find that Jacob had joined R. C. and Richard Barter. They were standing in the sun, drying out. I handed one parcel to Jacob and the other to R. C., explaining about the unexpected bovine bounty that had washed up close by where I'd discovered Mr. Mahoney.

R. C. studied his bloody present. "If the other fellow was the lead, how'd you come away with the two best cuts of the whole shebang?"

"He was happy with the tongue." I couldn't suppress a smile. "And nobody else recognized what they were."

Richard chimed in. "Probably because it wasn't on a plate with a side of potatoes."

Jacob said, "Thank you kindly, Pegg. This is surely welcome." He gestured with the parcel. "What about *you*?"

I grinned. "Oh. Well, if you're willing, I'll share some of yours."

Jacob grinned back. "Gladly."

Then I told them what had passed between Mr. Mahoney and myself. Their eyes grew wide at my first pronouncement. Their excitement turned to concern when I got to the part about Mahoney's hasty departure.

R. C. grumbled, "Ornery to the last."

Jacob said, "We'd best get over there and stake your claim."

.   .   .

When we arrived at Mr. Mahoney's claim, we found someone waiting for us.

I sensed we were going to have trouble as soon as I saw him. He perched jauntily on a keg in the middle of Mahoney's claim. The man reminded me of a blue jay, except he was dressed entirely in green: coat, britches, waistcoat, hat—the works. This wasn't one of the mellow hues my mother got from dyeing cloth with wildflowers growing around home: Queen Anne's lace, or lily of the valley, and the like. No, this was a brash, store-bought green you could never wear to church. The hat was low and round, with a tight brim—a type I'd never seen before.

As we got closer, it was evident the fellow hadn't suffered the drenching the rest of us had; more to the point, he had not been prospecting recently, or had yet to start. The only thing that belied his having dropped out of the sky was the mud on his boots and splatters of the same on his trousers. His bold costume hung on a very slight frame; you could even say he was skinny. His hands were draped over an odd-shaped walking stick. The stick, most of it anyway, seemed to be sheathed in a tightly gathered bundle of cloth. Something nicked my memory. Maybe the device was the "umbrella" that Mr. Hoyt had suggested buying for the trip west.

This Mr. Green was a young man; not as young as me, but not many years older than Richard. The impression of youth was made stronger by his being clean-shaven. His blond hair was short-cropped. He regarded our approach with an amiable smile.

Jacob said in a low voice, "A city slicker, without a doubt."

R. C., winded, lagged someway behind us. Richard, Jacob and I stopped just inside Mahoney's claim. The fellow came to his feet and doffed his hat. He wasn't much taller than me. His umbrella stayed stuck where it was. "Good day, gentlemen," he said in a honeyed politician's voice.

Foreboding choked off my manners completely. "Who're you?"

Bowing at the waist even as he replaced his hat, he announced, "Louis Absalom Shrivington, the fourth." By the time he finished, he was standing upright again. "Your servant." His tone suggested we should be *his* servants.

Something about this man got my dander up. "What're you doing here?"

"Well, it's obvious, I should think?" He looked about to make sure. "I'm staking my claim. I believe that's the correct term."

R. C. came up in time to hear this speech. He stuck out his chin. "It ain't yours to claim."

Mr. Shrivington got a surprised look. "Oh…but Mr. Mahoney said it was."

I rocked back on my heels. *How did this man have a chance to talk to Mr. Mahoney before I did? Maybe after, while I was butchering? How many other people did Mr. Mahoney, in his despair, promise his claim to?*

R. C. spoke up for me. "Mr. Mahoney gave his claim over to Pegg, here."

Mr. Shrivington brushed invisible dust off his coat. "I'm afraid I have a different view of the matter."

Richard jumped into the fray. "Where'd you come from, Mate?"

The dandy was unfazed by the challenge. "That should be obvious, too. From speaking with Mr. Mahoney, naturally. Time and tide wait for no man. Don't you agree?"

R. C. hitched his elbows in agitation. "There's only one way to sort this out."

"I'm afraid you've missed him," observed the green man. "As you can see, he gathered up his kit and is gone."

Jacob gave the dandy a stern, assessing look. "How—" But he broke off and turned to me. "Did Mahoney say where he was going? Into town?"

I tore my gaze away from the green man. "That's what he said, to the express office. But how could he cross, with the river like it is? Maybe he's headed for Coloma."

Shrivington spoke right on my heels. "I don't see that there is need for any further discussion. Mr. Mahoney was quite clear—"

Richard broke in. "He can't have gotten far. Jacob, you look downstream. R. C., can you look upstream? I'll strike inland. We'll give it an hour and rendezvous back here, with or without Mr. Mahoney."

R. C. and I exchanged a look, a mutual silent question. *Do you have a better Idea?* We both nodded at Richard.

Jacob was already pacing downstream.

I spoke up. "But if he headed downriver from his claim, wouldn't we likely have run into him on our way here?"

Jacob, still within earshot, stopped and turned.

Richard furrowed his brow. "Righto." He looked to the tall negro. "Jacob, you take south and east. I'll take south and west. "

This was my fight, too. "What can I do?"

Richard smiled grimly. "Stay here and keep an eye on your claim."

My compatriots set off on their searches. I stood staring stolidly at my rival, who gazed off as if I didn't exist. But then I felt witless, and went over to sit among the roots of the grand old oak, as I had seen Mr. Mahoney do. I kept my eye on Louis Absolom Shrivington, the fourth, who sat almost with his back to me, one leg crossed over the other. He gave the impression of having complete mastery of the situation.

Mr. Mahoney's claim was my first real foothold into the gold rush under my own steam. It was no bonanza, or he wouldn't have walked away from it. But I was counting on stories of "played out" claims giving up new, unexpected, wealth.

I brooded over the same questions, like rolling acorns around in my hand. Where was this fellow from? How did he get here? Where had he run into Mahoney? When had he talked to him? He was claiming exactly the same thing I was claiming. Where had Mahoney got to?

I was jarred from my musings when Shrivington rose to his feet. He turned just enough to speak over his shoulder. "If you'll excuse me. I'll be back." He tapped the handle of the umbrella lightly with two fingers. "Try not to do anything unwise." He sauntered on upstream, as if he didn't a care in the world.

I sat tight, with only two wrapped tenderloins for company.

An hour later, Richard and Jacob came back at Mahoney's claim without their quarry. The green-clad Shrivington had not reappeared.

Richard cast a quick glance at the umbrella. "Where's the green man?"

I shrugged. "Upstream somewhere. He didn't say where he was going." I was glad Shrivington was absent. Our deliberations could be voiced more candidly. Richard and Jacob fell to speculating on how Mahoney could have eluded them. If he kept to the river, we had to hope R. C. had the wind to catch up to him.

Another half hour passed before R. C. came shambling into view from upstream.

Richard gave him a grin. "Looks like you've had no better luck than we did." He jumped up and offered the older man the keg he had been sitting on.

R. C. lowered himself to rest. "Thank you kindly, Mr. Barter." He shook out his lanky frame and adjusted his hat. He, too, glanced at the umbrella. "Where'd the peapod get to?"

"He just took off." I pointed upstream. "Didn't say what he was up to. You didn't run into him?"

R. C. shook his head. "No. But I reckon I had the better luck, if you take the longer view."

I was too impatient for coming at it sideways. "But you don't have Mr. Mahoney, either."

"That is so, young'un. That is so. But I did speak to him. Mahoney, that is." He adjusted his hat again. "I took the greatest care to keep a civil tongue in my head and presented the situation to him."

"You spoke to him?" I was about jumping out of my skin. "Did he go to the express office like he said?"

R. C. sighed and resumed. "Since I encountered him on the south bank, I presumed he had not yet visited the express office. Any fool could see the river was still in a plenty mean mood. After every other stratagem failed, I invoked his sainted mother, even though I have no precise idea of her present location. The long and the short of it is, Mahoney had no interest in lingering to complete his part in the transaction."

If Mr. Mahoney wasn't going to help clarify the matter, it would be my word against Shrivington's. "Did you *ask* him *who* he left his claim to?"

R. C. hunched his shoulders and squirmed, contrite. "I was already sold on it bein' you. I never thought to ask him straight out." He raked his fingers through his beard. "I was fixed on persuadin' Mahoney to do his part." He looked up at Jacob and

Richard. Then he looked at me. "Don't make me feel worse. I'm sorry, Young'un. You can't expect much from an old sandhog."

Instantly, I felt my own remorse. "No, sir. I don't mean to do that." I looked quickly to Richard and Jacob, then back to R. C. "Please. I appreciate everything you're doing. I do."

The only thing I could think to do was put out my hand. R. C. and I shook. These were good people. I vowed to keep a better watch on what escaped my mouth.

Jacob slid his thumbs through his suspenders, making a show of looking over the other miners stranded on the south shore. "Can't think of a better specimen of sandhog I'd squat by a river with."

Richard and I concurred with murmurs. R. C. touched his hat. His voice got some of its vinegar back. "Obliged, gentlemen. obliged. There's a tad more, if'n you'd care to hear it."

Richard grinned wide. "The oracle of Delphi was never more eagerly awaited."

R. C. took a firm grip of his knees. "Mahoney proclaimed Missouri his next stop, and nothin' better get in his way. To make his point, he was gracious enough to show me his Dragoon, denoting it was fully loaded, should I feel compelled to press my case." R. C. went quiet and ran his fingers through his wiry whiskers, letting us absorb his story.

Jacob gave him a wry smile. "Well, I'm glad to see you didn't press your case."

I looked from one to the other. "But with Mahoney gone, who will pass judgment on which story is true? Mine or the green man's?"

"Miners' court. It's all we've got," R. C. said.

Richard shook his head slowly, gazing at his boots.

I knew that miners' courts were informal affairs, and the verdicts could be fickle. It all depended on the mood of the mob.

The judge and jury were plucked from that same mob. With no police force, sheriffs, or judges, the miners meted out their own rough justice. Shootings were rare, and came to trial only if somebody objected to the deed. Stealing, on the other hand, was a different matter.

"What if nobody comes?" I asked.

"It's about claim-jumpin'," R. C. replied sternly. "That's somethin' everybody cares about. They'll come."

CHAPTER 9

What the miners hadn't saved from the raging waters boots, clothes, cooking gear, food—the flash flood swept away. Those on the south shore waited for the river to subside, and shared what food the miners salvaged in their camps. Thankfully, no more rain fell, but the November days were chilly. Those of us who were restless spent our energy gathering firewood for the storytellers who stayed close around the fires.

On the morning of the third day, the river subsided enough to cross to the north shore. I went with R. C. and Jacob to replenish what of their outfits they had lost. We were in the company of scores of other miners streaming in from the surrounding canyons. The multitude converged on the budding town of Auburn, the very place where my partner, Fred Hoyt, had found his escape with Sam Brannan.

The town sat in a hollow, surrounded by higher ground, or "flats." We came at it from the south. From the ridge above, Auburn looked much like Grizzly Bar, except smaller: a motley clutch of log buildings, tents, or make-shift shelters, all clapped together in the haste to get on with business.

Sounds I had so recently left in Grizzly Bar came faintly to us on the breeze—saw and hammer. Auburn was still growing. The normal bustle of commerce was made yet more tumultuous by the trader wagons up from Sacramento, resupplying the miners like R. C. and Jacob.

R. C. flexed his elbows in agitation. "Well, we'd best hustle on down there if we expect anything to be left."

We rejoined the miners trudging down the slope, following one of the streams, stepping around prospectors at their diggings.

The stream led us into Auburn's single street. Indeed, the stream continued up the middle of the street toward the north end of town. What became apparent, once we were in the midst of the clamor, was a battle between miners and merchants. In Grizzly Bar, the street was filled with people and wagons going soberly about their business. Here in Auburn, the street convulsed with a horde of miners tearing up the ground, prospecting the stream flowing up the middle of the self-same street. People wishing to buy a sack of beans or a new hat were obliged to fight their way past miners digging up the merchant's doorstep.

I pitied the shopkeepers trying to make an honest living, but I also knew the excitement of scrambling after a promising lead. I was surprised when R. C. said Auburn had been in existence for most of two years.

I protested, "Grizzly Bar is only a year or so old, and it's lots bigger."

"Most of that time," R. C. went on, ignoring my interjection, "Auburn wasn't more'n a couple of tents. People came and went. Not enough water, much of the year."

Jacob added, "That's why it used to be called "Wood's Dry Diggings."

As I had been when entering Grizzly Bar, I was all but overwhelmed by the signage that encrusted every available surface, offering everything from baths to billiards, fresh oysters to cigars.

I spied a dry goods store under the name of Gwynn's. I darted up to the man standing at the door, placidly observing the parade. He sported a long bib apron; I took him to be the merchant. I had no more opened my mouth when the man said, "Whatever you're wantin', Sonny, I'm fresh out. Sold my last pair o' britches not five minute ago."

I gave him a wordless salute and raced back to my friends.

R. C., Jacob, and I worked our way up the street with the other prospectors, toward the north end of town, where the Conestogas had clustered. The crowd got thicker and the commotion grew livelier as we drew close to the big wagons. Beyond the wagons, the creek we had followed emptied into another stream flowing west. As far as the eye could see its banks swarmed with miners trying their luck.

There were pack trains as well, loaded with all manner of goods. Both wagons and mules were caked to their knees in dried mud. It must have been a hard crawl up from the valley. Word had traveled fast of our misfortune. There was money to be made, and it would take more than a little mud to discourage these hardy traders.

I recalled the rebuilding of Grizzly Bar after a fire leveled it. The frenzy to buy was such that miners besieged the freight wagons as soon as they rolled into sight, and the traders had merely to step to the backs of their wagons to do business. It was the same here in Auburn.

We visited three of the wagons and two pack trains before R. C. and Jacob had purchased everything they needed—clothes and cooking gear and food. They hired a mule and Jacob offered to pack both their outfits back to the river while Richard, R. C. and I set about drumming up interest for a miner's court.

I soon learned a trial was the next best thing to a fight in the entertainment line, if you didn't count hangings. R. C. observed dryly, "And they're about as spontaneous."

Richard leaned in. "Good way to empty out the saloons, unless the trial is being held in the saloon."

But more importantly, Mr. Shrivington, the mysterious man in green, had to be located and notified. The process could take a few days. I still wanted to find Mr. Mahoney. He very nearly drowned. How far could he get before he needed to rest? On the other hand, the man had made it very clear to R. C. he did not want to be found.

The following Saturday, three days hence, was chosen as the day. Everyone agreed the judge should be a prospector by the name of Ira Bovee, who had served as a judge on previous occasions, and was highly regarded for his sagacity. He had been a deacon back in Virginia.

I stayed in town, harboring a fading hope of finding Mr. Mahoney. R. C. grubstaked me a bed and meals in a cheap hotel. Despite persistent questioning of all and sundry in the following days, we could discover no firm trace of Mr. Mahoney. Some said they'd seen him on the road to Sacramento. Others swore they saw him leaving Spanish Flat, the next gold camp north. If that was true, he had the Bear, the Feather, or the Klamath rivers to lose himself in, not to mention the various forks of those rivers. But he'd told RC he was heading back to Missouri.

By Friday morning, I was fit to be tied. Without Mahoney, it was my word against Shrivington's. It was anybody's guess who the miners would believe. The thought of losing Mahoney's claim sickened me.

At breakfast, Richard reported he had found the green man and learned that Shrivington had already been informed of the imminent trial. Richard finished with a wry smile. "Shrivington said he wouldn't miss it for the world."

I could hear the smug confidence of victory in the words. My own confidence wavered.

R. C. snorted in derision. "Snivelin', sidewindin' scalawag."

I could sit still no longer. I put down my fork, my griddle cakes unfinished. "I'm going out to look at the claims today."

"What about your pancakes?" R. C. asked.

"Sorry. I'm just not hungry." I pushed back my chair.

Richard came to my aid. "Not much else to do, I suppose. The defendant is champing at the bit, the key witness has vanished, the judge is being sobered up. The jury will be scraped together from what's available at the moment." He gave us a self-satisfied smirk.

R. C. frowned at him.

Richard wasn't daunted. "Did I forget something?"

"Next you'll be suggestin' sacrificin' a goat, or somethin'." R. C. turned to me. "Be sure and be back by mornin'. You don't show, they'll give it to green britches straight out."

I touched his shoulder. "I'll be there." I hesitated. I didn't want to leave my two friends glaring at each other.

R. C. caught my elbow and gave me a stern look. "While you're at it, keep an eye out for salvage. Anything that looks like wreckage likely is. Gather it up. Anybody else out there will be doin' the same. You never know what'll come in handy: rope, canvas, tools, bottles and such for your dust."

.   .   .

I looked over R. C.'s first claim, which had a new coating of mud, then salvaged some stakes and remarked his holding. After, I checked the long tom pieces and tools we had stacked behind the tree up the slope. As Mahoney had said, people seemed to be respecting the signs of ownership.

R. C.'s other claim and Mahoney's claim, side by side farther upriver, were likewise covered with new mud. I reset the stakes here, too. I gave a hard look at the insolent umbrella that stood guard in the center of Mahoney's claim. I had an impulse to leave something of my own to indicate that claim was in dispute. Then it occurred to me less scrupulous types might feel free to jump the claim if I did.

I got in an hour or so of scavenging before the light began to fade and I had to head back. I kept close to the river, looking for single items that were scattered. I saw only two other miners on the same errand, far apart.

Auburn was sunk deep in a bowl of evening shadow by the time I arrived. Even yellow squares of window light below and points of cold starlight above couldn't hold back the night. I found R. C. at the same pancake place that I had left him at breakfast. He was in company not with Richard Barter, but with Jacob Harper. Jacob and I shook hands. He pulled out a chair for me.

Jacob clapped me on the shoulder. "R. C. told me you were feeling a might nervous about today. If you don't mind, I'll tag along tomorrow, for what it's worth."

I gave him a smile and a nod. "I'd be glad of that."

"Any room left for me?"

We all turned to see Richard striding up in a very dramatic suit of clothes. All black.

R. C. smirked. "We wouldn't want to deny you the opportune-i-tee o' showing off your fine, new duds, now, would we?"

Richard shook hands with all of us and sat down. "Kind of you to notice, Radcliffe."

I turned to R. C.

"It's what the R stands for," my weathered mentor groused. "I gave him an express injunction against usin' it, but he don't listen."

We all had a good laugh while the waiter set down plates stacked with golden brown griddle cakes. I was thankful for the good company.

Saturday dawned clear and bright. Out of anxiety, as well as habit, I was up at first light. We same four wolfed down a quick breakfast and set off for the trial.

The wide, ransacked swath of dirt that served as Auburn's town square stood in for the courtroom. The official judicial furniture, set precariously among the diggings, consisted of a wide, stout plank laid across two barrels, and a chair. Several wagons had been commandeered to provide additional, raised galleries, forming a half circle at the back. Prospecting in the streets had ceased, as those attending the trial would be standing in the claims. R. C.,

Jacob, Richard, and I took a place favoring the plank, as I was part of the proceedings.

R. C. pointed to a large, beefy fellow standing next to the plank bench. He had a sullen set to his jaw. "That's Ned Archer. He's going to be bailiff. Wanted on several counts for assault and battery back in New York City, they say." Bailiff Archer had tiny ears, a bull neck, and equally massive arms crossed over his broad chest.

Will whispered at the back of my mind. *Bailiff Archer doesn't appear to be the sharpest tool in the shed.*

To the bailiff's right, two rough rows of barrels, boxes and chairs were no doubt provisions for the jury. I tallied seating for twelve. Soon those seats began to fill as more of the gallery appeared.

The crowd packed in around the judge's bench, filling the square and the wagons. Some had a better view by perching on piles of dirt. The bailiff pushed everyone back to establish a respectful eight or ten feet between the crowd and the justice. My adversary, still in his lurid green suit, appeared, and Bailiff Archer placed Shrivington and me at the front, facing the bench. R. C., Jacob, and Richard took up positions right behind me.

A moment later, a wispy skeleton of an old prospector tottered forward and took his place at the bench. Dressed in his threadbare Sunday best, he sported a fulsome beard, snowy white except for the long tobacco stain descending from his lower lip.

The bailiff bellowed, "All rise!"

This request went unheeded since most everybody was already standing. A boisterous jabber filled the square. Before the bailiff could repeat himself, the judge raised his pistol and fired into the air. The racket fell to a murmur. Bailiff Archer puffed up his chest and bellowed, "This court is open for business. The honorable Ira Jackson Bovee, preceding."

The honorable judge shoved his gun back into his trousers.

The crowd broke into whistles and cheers.

"Order!" bawled the bailiff. The man's voice could turn back the tide, but it struggled in vain to prevail against the din of rowdy miners.

Judge Bovee extracted a quid of chewing tobacco and placed the soggy lump on the plank. "Ned? Where's my gavel?"

The bailiff handed him a bottle of beer and stepped back in deference.

His Honor polished off the bottle in one long pull and thumped the empty sharply on the bench. Several times. "This court is in session!" screeched Judge Bovee, his high, reedy voice like a rusty saw. "Y'all shut yer traps." He ran his eye over the crowd, stopping at the twelve men seated to his right. "This our jury?" he addressed Bailiff Archer, pointing.

The bailiff nodded. The group of twelve miners were in no way different from the general audience, except that they sat quietly and attentively.

Judge Bovee leaned in their direction. "You gents have some idea o' what's required of you?"

They nodded somberly, as one.

The judge then proclaimed, "The two defendants step forward and state yourselves."

Shrivington took a step forward and stuck out his chin. "Louis Absalom Shrivington, the fourth."

The crowd chortled in delight. "Hey, Louis, buy us another round," piped a miner. Another hollered, "Yeah, Louie. Time for another drink. I'm dry." Still another, thinking of his hogs back home, shrilled, "Louie, Louie, Looo-uu-i-i-i-eee." That got a burst of laughter from those who had also kept hogs.

R. C. fumed. "The scalawag's been tryin' to buy the court."

Judge Bovee couldn't resist adding his two bits. "Lord, A'mighty! With a moniker like that, how can you even get up and walk around?"

The crowd roared at the judge's wit, which caused the bailiff to cry, "Order! Order!"

Soon, all eyes turned to me. I didn't have nearly as impressive a handle. Still, I dreaded what this crowd would do with it.

I took a deep breath and spoke boldly. "Bartholomew Pegg… from Vermont." My voice squeaked in the middle of "Vermont."

Judge Bovee didn't give them the chance. "What's the offense?"

"Claim jumpin'," shouted R. C., upstaging the bailiff.

A sharp grumble erupted from the throng. That was a crime as bad as horse stealing.

Judge Bovee brandished his gun again. "Hold it down! Hold it down, ya bunch o' tally whackers! Which is the commit-tor, and which is the commit-tee, of this foul deed?"

A miner near the judge leaned closer to him. "It's a dispute, Ira. Both these gents're claimin' the same thing: a spot near Rattlesnake Bar was give over to 'em directly by Wilford Mahoney, who has lit out for parts unknown."

Sudden dread gripped me. What if the jury decided in the green man's favor? Did that make me the claim jumper? *Why did I agree so readily to a miners' court? It could just as easily wind up with me at the end of a rope.*

The judge fixed Shrivington and me with his flinty gaze. "Each man will present his case. The youngster first. The slicker next."

So I told my story, starting with going to work for Mr. Simpson and meeting Mr. Mahoney, and ending with my talk with Mr. Mahoney on the riverbank during the flash flood. When I finished, R. C. grabbed my elbow. "You left out tryin' to save him." He jumped up, waving his hand. "Yer Honor. There's more to the story."

"Order!" shouted Bailiff Archer.

The judge snapped his head around like a hawk spotting prey. "Simpson?" He leaned forward over the bench, as if to get a better look. "Izzat you?" Satisfied with his identification, Judge Bovee settled back. "The proceedin's wouldn't be full bore without your two cents."

R. C. snatched off his hat as a sign of respect. "Beggin' the indulgence of the court, yer Honor, I'm a witness to the whole story, which should be heard."

"And clearly in the camp of my adversary," sniffed Shrivington.

Judge Bovee pointed his beer bottle, bottom first, at the slicker. "It ain't yer turn yet, Shivershanks. Shut yer trap. Be quick about it, R. C. People're gettin' thirsty. That could lean some on the verdict."

R. C. told about me jumping in the river when it was "runnin' like hell itself broke loose" to go after Mahoney, ending his tirade with, "Yer honor, he put his own life in peril trying to save the poor Mahoney." He left out the part about how he, R. C., saved me by going in the river himself.

"And it was I who pulled Mahoney out after you abandoned him!" shouted Shrivington.

"Order!" bawled the bailiff.

"No you didn't," shouted a miner standing up in one of the wagons. "He crawled out himself. I was there. I didn't see *you* anywhere around."

I grasped that shred of evidence. Were there other possibilities? Could Mahoney have spoken to Shrivington before I got there?

Another man called out, "I seen the kid talkin' to Mahoney."

Judge Ira banged his bottle on the plank bench half a dozen times, his shouting swallowed in the general commotion.

R. C. reared back in disgust, stabbing his finger at Louis. "You lyin'—"

Once again, the judge resorted to his gun and shot at the sky. Quiet swiftly returned. Laying his pistol ceremoniously on the plank, he pitched forward on his elbows. "Whether Mahoney got pulled out, or hauled hisself out, has got nothin' to do with who he promised his claim to."

Those who were listening laughed. Somebody called out, "You tell 'em, Bovee."

Judge Bovee took aim at the crowd with his gavel, sweeping it from side to side. "Quiet!" he roared. "Hold it down or I'll discommunicate the bunch o' ya!" He jabbed the bottle in Louis' direction. "You, there. Mincemeat. It's your turn. What say you?"

Louis Absalom Shrivington stepped forward, slipping his hand inside his coat like Bonaparte, his head held high. Such posturing earned him more than a few snickers. He waited for as much quiet as he was ever going to get, and then spoke with a pronounced humility. "I had so recently arrived in this vicinity by way of Coloma and Yankee Jim's, where I enjoyed modest success. The proceeds from those activities enabled me to avail myself of the latest expression of the haberdashers' art." He passed his free hand down his fine green suit.

Amid more hoots and catcalls, Richard muttered, "Did you have to choose green, mate?"

"Can't you just say 'duds,' like a normal person?" called a member of the gallery.

The judge pounded the plank once again.

"Pipe down!" bawled Ned Archer, forgetting the proper protocol.

Louis went on. "Like so many of you, I followed the siren call of the North Fork, only to arrive at the very moment the calamitous flood descended upon us. At that juncture, I found myself by the river's edge in time to have words with one Wilford Mahoney, which resulted in his transferring title to his claim to me." He paused only a heartbeat.

"Naturally, I thought it only prudent to take immediate possession, so to avoid just such an unfortunate misunderstanding as we have here." He lowered his head modestly and stepped back.

Will sniggered in my mind, *You'd think he was courtin' his honey at her balcony.*

Someone in the audience had the same impression. That man warbled, "Aw, shucks. Sure, I'll marry you."

The gallery erupted in merriment. Bailiff Archer shouted "Order! Order in the court! Order!" to no avail.

Judge Bovee beat the bench unmercifully with his bottle, his face red. Under such incessant pounding, the judge's tobacco quid danced off the bench and plopped in the dirt.

The beleaguered bottle could endure no more. It shattered. A dozen shards flew, throwing off winks of sunlight. People ducked. The judge had only a moment to stare at what remained of his gavel before he was handed a new one.

The audience gradually regained its composure. But Will's voice in my head would leave me no peace. *Shivershins copied your story down to the punctuation.*

The judge ran his stony gaze over the crowd, now waiting on his next word. "Barbarians." He stopped at his jury. "Well, Boys. There you have it. These two yahoos're both sayin' Mahoney passed his claim to them… him…" he shook his head in frustration. "…the plaintiffs… each…" he hunched his shoulders and grimaced as if to reorder his wits and thumped his new gavel on the bench. "You boys deliberate on it and come up with a verdict. And don't be all day about it."

Richard expressed my thought. "I wouldn't want to be on that jury."

The twelve put their heads together right where they sat. A jug was passed. I couldn't help but worry about how much that jug might influence my fate.

The gallery crowd, remembering their own thirst, adjourned to the surrounding saloons. I spent most of the recess fretting. Since I had been taught not to pester the Almighty with trivial matters, I just hoped the jury would find in my favor.

The defendant, Mr. Shrivington, occupied himself with paring his fingernails.

Most of an hour passed, after which the gallery, reduced some in number, reconvened.

A miner brought Judge Bovee a fresh bottle of beer, which he polished off in short order. He stared at the jury, as if willing them to finish their work. At last, the tallest of the twelve stood and nodded mutely to the judge.

"Gentlemen," exclaimed the wizened magistrate, taking a fresh grasp of his beer bottle gavel.

This roused the dozing bailiff, who obediently bawled, "Order in the court!" to nobody in particular. The judge glared at Ned, his bailiff, who retreated.

Judge Bovee addressed the tall man. "Mr. Hawthorne. Has the jury come by a verdict, so we can all get back to our business?"

Mr. Hawthorne cut an impressive figure. He squared his shoulders and raised his chin. "We have not, your Honor. 'Pon my word, Ira, we are at an impasse."

Ira made a fist and shook it in frustration. "Goldang it, Pete. Your job ain't to get stuck at impasses. Your job is to get over 'em." He struck the bench with his fist.

The foreman of the jury looked chastened. "It's neck and neck, 'far as we can see, your Honor. Without Mahoney—"

The judge swept his hand to shut the man up. "That's good corn liquor gone to waste if you boys can't settle on a verdict."

Hawthorne braved the judge's ire. "We looked at it six ways from Sunday, but these two fellas have 'xactly the same story, not countin' the amendments by Simpson, there."

The judge turned his stormy brow in our direction, muttering, "King Solomon had it easy." Then he swiveled to the jury. "I got a good mind to hang the bunch o' ya." Returning to us, he muttered on. "No court of mine is gonna end in a pussyfootin', prevaricatin' hung jury." He cast his gaze around, vexed. "Here's what we're gonna do. We're gonna have us a race."

He ignored the confusion his announcement provoked. "From here to Mahoney's claim. Whichever of you two rapscallions gets there first, gets the claim." He slammed his bottle on the bench to ratify his ruling.

Bailiff Archer stepped forward. "Court is now—"

Judge Ira Bovee thumped the hapless bailiff on his arm. "Shut yer trap, Ned. We ain't done yet." The judge hobbled out from behind his bench and came over to the two of us. He squinted at us for a moment as if we were livestock. He bent with some effort and, in the space between the toes of his boots and ours, drew a line in the mud with the neck of the bottle. "From here."

Someone called out, "You got 'em pointin' the wrong way, Bovee." The judge looked around and had us move to stand on his side of the line, facing south toward the river canyon.

Louis asked, "What are to be the rules?"

Judge Bovee blinked at the green-suited man like he had just popped out of thin air. "Rules?" he cried. "What rules? It's a race." He tilted at Louis, thrusting out his whiskered chin. "No trippin', kickin', or eye-gougin'! How's zat?"

During the exchange I sized up my opponent. He was half a head taller than me, which gave him a few more inches in the leg. Properly employed, those few inches could, by the end of the race, add up to a sizable lead. But only if he was a runner. Long legs weren't the whole answer. Hunched on a bookkeeper's stool day in and day out doesn't make you a racer. But he was lean and sinewy; he could easily be fleet of foot. Whatever his capabilities, I had to win this race.

I gave my friends a worried look.

Richard said, "Don't worry, Mate, we'll be your seconds."

R. C. scowled at Richard. "Maybe you can. I ain't run a hunert yards since I was his age, much less four miles."

Richard looked contrite. "Actually, I had Jacob in mind."

We all looked to Jacob.

"I'd be honored," the big man grinned.

I handed R. C. my Colt, my knife, and the pouch around my neck.

R. C. eyed Louis and spoke in a low voice, echoing my concern. "We got no idea if that varmint is fleet as a deer or if he'll fag out after fifty yards." Then he held his finger against my shirt. "Pace yourself, save some wind for the end." He stuffed my Colt through his belt. "You'll need every break you can find." He leaned a little closer. "Since you're so partial to the swimmin' line, you might keep the river in mind." He straightened. "It's goin' in the right direction."

The judge interrupted our huddle. "Ready?" He turned to a gaggle of miners idling close by, none of them too steady on their pins. "Hawthorne, Belshaw, Connoly. You pace 'em. Make sure there ain't no hanky panky goin' on."

I recognized Belshaw and Connoly from the jury. Belshaw was a short man with a slight build. Connoly was as big and imposing as Jacob Harper. Hawthorne replied, "Sure thing, Ira."

"No Hinkle pinks," burbled Belshaw and sagged in a heap, laughing. Connoly reached down and helped him stand again.

Judge Bovee held the bottle gingerly by the neck, out in front of him. "Ready?"

After a heartbeat, he let it drop.

We were off!

I sprinted up the street. Behind me the sturdy bailiff yelled, "The court is now adjourned," amid shouts of encouragement for us.

CHAPTER 10

Racing headlong, we reached the top of the rise at Rich Flat. The big miners, Hawthorne and Connoly, were already huffing and puffing. Shrivington had doffed his coat and waistcoat, but he was catching up fast. We would be neck and neck soon. To my surprise, he proved to be a good runner.

Richard, being taller than either of us, used his long legs to advantage. Jacob, as tall as Richard, but heavier, kept right with him. Belshaw, a small, wiry man, though thoroughly soused, managed to keep up.

We turned westward onto the wagon road and charged on. A few riders on horseback overtook us, calling, "We'll see you there!"

Louis said he just came from Coloma. How well does he know the country along the North Fork and around Auburn? He knew enough to find Mahoney's claim, but maybe he was directed to it.

Louis, Richard, Jacob, Belshaw, and I formed a small knot pounding down the road. Hawthorne and Connoly—Connoly was a giant—steadily fell behind.

After another half mile or so, I glanced at Richard and tossed my head to the left. He nodded. I picked a clear spot with not too steep a drop and veered to my left off the wagon road. Richard and Jacob stayed right with me.

Louis skittered to a halt. Belshaw plowed into him. "Hey!" shouted my opponent. "What're you doing?"

"Tryin' to win this race!" I yelled.

"That's not the way."

I didn't answer. I concentrated on picking out the next twenty feet. I didn't go perpendicular to the road. I angled south and west, picturing a line running diagonally from the road to the river.

Behind me, voices shouted, getting fainter as I plunged and leapt down the slope. They argued what to do. Hawthorne and Connoly caught up and joined the debate.

I might not hit Rattlesnake Bar exactly, but once I reached the river I could look for a place to cross over to the south shore for the last leg of the race.

When next I glanced back up at the road, Shrivington had set off again, still on the road, pounding hard, a little ahead of me. Belshaw now lagged behind him. The other two miners had dropped yet farther back.

Louis and Belshaw still argued, but raggedly, and I couldn't make it out. Soon, their voices were lost altogether for the crunching leaves and snapping twigs underfoot. Richard was right on my heels, and Jacob trailed him closely.

Smaller watercourses crossed my path, cutting their way down to the river. The first one I came to that I couldn't jump fortunately had a bridge. A tree, one of the Digger pines, had fallen across it. The first half was a straight trunk, but the upper portion splayed in a great jumble of limbs. That slowed me down some.

Gaining the other side, I waited to see that Richard and Jacob got safely across. Clambering, Jacob shouted, "Go!"

I heard a shrill oath higher up on the slope. I glanced back. My adversary had finally left the road. He had lost his hat. He picked his way cautiously, a hundred yards back. Belshaw came after, making most of his progress by rolling and tumbling.

That glance cost me. I tripped and went down, sprawling. Scrambled up, flailing, and plunged on.

It rattled me that Louis was on the same tack. He showed remarkable grit, and was gaining.

I felt my dad looking down on me—my mom and Amy hoping and praying. It didn't matter whether Mahoney had promised his claim to two people or ten. His claim was key to making this whole mad enterprise worthwhile. I had to win this race.

A faint, sibilant thunder came to me. The river. The canyon welcomed me like a wide trough. Richard stumbled and fell. "Keep going," he panted, rubbing his knee. "I'll catch up." Jacob, steps behind, helped him to his feet.

R. C.'s suggestion had found fertile ground in my mind. The river, cold as it might be, wasn't an obstacle, it was a means.

The lower I got, the easier it got. So many of the trees had been cut, the manzanita and buckeye harvested for cooking fires. A stitch stabbed in my side. Nothing to do but wince and look forward for your next twenty feet. Stumps to dodge. Slipping on dry leaves. My throat burning dry, my lungs about to burst. *Is he gaining on me? He can't be. He's a city slicker; he needs orderly sidewalks, neat pavements.*

I didn't go right down to the river. I stayed up on the slope, maybe a hundred yards, until I could recognize features of the land that told me I was close to Rattlesnake Bar.

Suddenly I spotted a familiar outcrop on the south bank. A disordered tumble of gray stone jutted into the channel about a mile above the bar. The eddy downstream from the stones had made a pool. It was time to use the river.

I clambered my way down to the wide, cobbled stretch on the north shore. Out of my clothes in a flash. Long johns, everything. I had to be slippery as an eel.

Louis had no doubt reached the more open ground by now. He would be making better time.

Into the shock of cold water, I swam like a madman; the current added to my progress. Just above the warble of the water close about me, I heard a howl far back upstream. "No fair!"

That had to be Louis. He must have found my clothes, and was loathe to follow my example—or couldn't. Louis would have to look for a place to cross.

I stroked for the south bank, keeping an eye out for the old oak tree that marked Mahoney's claim. The river ran strong, but with nowhere near the force of the week before.

I pulled harder; the old tree would be coming into view soon. It had to!

Louis's shouted again. "Treacherous scoundrel! Blasphemous rogue! No fair!"

There! The stout old monarch with its heavy, winding limbs, set back from the shore.

A crowd of prospectors surrounded Mahoney's claim, awaiting the outcome. A few perched up in the branches of the oak. All watched the bright green Louis pounding along on the north shore, still shouting.

Then the miners spotted me and sent up a shout. Four more strokes and I felt the bottom.

I took a heartbeat to see Louis casting about for a way to cross. His fist whipped the air; his shouts heaped terrible abuse on my character. He must have more wind in him than we gave him credit for.

That brief pause carried me farther than I planned. I clambered out and ran back upstream to Mahoney's claim. The frigid air froze the water on my skin. My legs were knotted with cold, my lungs were on fire. This was the finish of four miles of running "flat out."

The miners set up a jubilant racket, and parted at my approach. I staggered up to the umbrella, dripping and shivering like the last leaf of autumn.

Somebody threw a blanket over my shoulders. I was treated to claps on the back, praise, and cheers.

"Din't know you was part fish!"

"The Mississippi's just waitin' for ya!"

"Hell! Go for the Atlantic!"

Through the gaps in the crowd I spied Louis picking his way across, a dozen claims downstream, even so, in up to his knees. I looked upstream for Richard, hoping his fall was not serious. There they were, Richard and Jacob, some way up, loping steadily along the north bank. Richard had my clothing tucked under his arm.

Will our referees be appearing soon?

Amongst the well-wishers stood Osher Phelps, who held the claim on the upstream side of Mr. Mahoney's. We had exchanged greetings, but not a lot more. He was a mild-mannered, good-hearted wainwright from Missouri. Osher wore a big smile.

"Could we build a fire?" I chattered, pulling the blanket tighter and pointing to the ground at my feet.

He gave a sharp nod. "For the champeen swimmer? You bet."

In minutes a goodly fire burned warm and welcome. I huddled as close as I could without catching fire to the blanket, and waited for the referees.

Louis limped through the throng, breathing hard, and confronted me. His fancy shirt and green trousers had suffered for the snags and twigs that had caught at them. Clinging leaves attested to one or more spills along the way. His trouser leg at the left knee was badly torn and smeared with blood. "There was nothing about swimming. I call it a foul." Louis glared at me. "You have not won fairly."

"There was nothing about *not* swimming," I countered. "Judge Bovee said to win. He didn't put any limits on how."

Somebody in the back called, "That's right. I heard 'im myself." A few others rumbled agreement. Another offered, "'cept for bitin' and gougin'."

Richard and Jacob entered the circle. Richard handed me my clothes and looked around, finally settling on Louis Absalom Shrivington. "From your expression, Mate, I must conclude that Pegg, here, won the day."

"And I must protest," sneered the loser. "He won only by the most under-handed means imaginable."

Richard laughed. "Ah, do not assign limitations to my imagination, good sir." He looked around to see if his wit was appreciated, and raised his voice a little. "Was Pegg here first?"

A chorus rolled out in reply, clear and loud, if ragged. "Yes!"

I was busy climbing into my clothes. I knew I had won the race. Mahoney's claim was mine. I felt as if I could float up to the sky.

Louis curled his lip. "We will settle the matter when the officials arrive."

Our referees appeared in due course, although winded and disheveled. Louis lost no time in making his case. "The scoundrel cheated," he fumed. "He should have stayed on the road."

A quick wit piped up. "If he'd stayed on the road he be in Sacramento by now."

Hawthorne furrowed his brow, Belshaw, and Connoly looked befuddled.

Louis ranted on. "Worse! When he saw he was losing, he leapt in the river and swam across. A desperate, cowardly ploy."

I looked hard at the fragile figure in green. *Why do you want this claim so badly?* Was he as desperate as I was?

Hawthorne was not hornswoggled. "Was he first?"

Louis neared apoplexy. "I insist you disqualify him and declare ME the winner!"

Miners called out. "The boy was first."

Hawthorne's brows gathered into a thunderous scowl. "I'm askin' you, shiver sticks. Who was first? Him or you?"

Louis lifted on his toes, trembling with outrrage, making fists. "He only won by—"

Connoly came to life and grasped the back of Shrivington's neck in his massive hand. "The only rule was to win, skunk piss." He commenced to squeeze. Shrivington grimaced.

Connoly tipped his head in my direction. "And ever'body but you says the youngster came first. That's all that counts."

I was not above a little show of triumph. I pulled Louis Absalom Shrivington's umbrella out of the ground and handed it to him.

Connoly leaned close to him and asked cordially, "Are we ever going to see you around here again?"

Louis managed to shake his head despite his confinement.

The big miner continued, softer yet. "And do you know what will happen to you if you do show yourself?" Without waiting for an answer, Connoly jerked Louis into the air in a very effective mimicry of what a rope would do.

Dangling a few feet off the ground, Louis nodded the affirmative.

Connoly opened his hand and Shrivington the fourth dropped to the ground in a heap. He came to himself in short order, scrambled to his feet and scuttled away, hounded by a volley of rough laughter.

The show was over; the race was won. Jacob and Richard stood by while well-wishers lingered, slapping me on the back, offering encouragement. But most headed back to their camps or to town. Now I was just another sandhog. I looked around at the plot that was now mine, full and true. Was there a bonanza lurking here? Deep in the gravels? Would Fortune smile on me? Or should I be heedful of Mahoney's frustration?

I found a stick and planted it where Louis's umbrella had been. Now was the time to sacrifice my hat, at least until I could get a more substantial sign of possession. I allowed myself a satisfied sigh. Finally, I had a real chance to keep the promises made to so many people back home. A letter to Mother and Amy with the good news was certainly in order, and to Mr. Pruitt, too.

CHAPTER 11

The overcast broke up enough to allow the westering sun to light the town as Richard, Jacob, and I came down off the last ridge. Now that I had a real claim in this gold rush, Auburn felt a little more like *my* town. The ever-present smoke from cook fires and forges drifted up and hung in the still air. It being Saturday, the street was already full of miners making merry.

R. C. must have been keeping a watch for us; he met us as we came into town, right outside the Empire Hotel, which lay near its southern limit. His whiskers couldn't entirely hide his smile. His eyes crinkled with mirth. He held out his hand to me. "Congratulations, Young 'un." We shook. "River come in handy, did it?"

I gave him a big grin. "It was good advice."

Jacob said, "It appears the news got here before us."

R. C. scoffed at his friend. "I thought the second coming was gonna get here 'fore you did."

Jacob shot back, "Did you miss us that bad?" He put his arm around R. C.'s shoulder.

R. C. frowned and tugged at his hat. "'bout as much as I miss the pox."

Richard and I stifled laughter as we stepped into the Empire to celebrate my good fortune with supper.

The Empire Hotel, being a large log cabin, was one of the only substantial buildings in Auburn. Upon entering, its great room accommodated most of its offerings; a bar, gambling tables, and a dining area. The room also boasted the largest fireplace I had ever seen. It provided welcome warmth, and fitful light. Several miners took their ease around the blazing hearth.

Many more were at the bar and gambling tables, filling the room with a genial noise. The air was a pungent fog of tobacco smoke, damp wool, and a lack of bathing. Lamps were few and scattered, favoring the gaming tables, producing the feeling of being snug in some critter's burrow.

Jacob and R. C. hustled toward the last available table in the dining area. We had no more seated ourselves than a tall, heavy-set man in a long apron approached. This imposing gentleman was the selfsame bailiff from the morning's court session, Ned Archer. His judicial bellowing was now reduced to the timbre of a large cat, purring. "What'll it be, gents?"

R. C. looked up at him. "What's on the ticket tonight, Ned?"

Ned wasn't looking at anybody in particular. "Roast beef."

Richard wrinkled his brow. "Anything else?"

"Boiled beef."

I thought back to all the wonderful dishes I had shared with Sun Shu at Chen Yi's restaurant in Grizzly Bar. Those dishes contained flavors that were wholly new to me, but that I quickly came to relish. A half dozen questions about my Celestial friends and Bugle, my dog, suddenly crowded into my mind.

R. C. looked at each of us in turn. "Anybody for boiled beef?" He had no takers. "Roast beef all around, then, Ned." He looked up into the ruddy face. "Any horseradish in the house?"

"A dollar."

R. C. thrust out his chin. His wiry whiskers jutted even farther. "Bring it on. This here's a celebration, ain't it?"

Ned went away to do our bidding.

I only half-listened to the haggling for supper. I had already moved from triumph to worry, despite my new claim. I knew I didn't have enough gold to stay in town all winter, even with what Mr. Hoyt had deposited for my singing "Amazing Grace." I supposed I could spend the winter singing, but that seemed like a very uncertain business. R. C., Richard, and Jacob fell into a lively discussion of state's rights. When they came to a pause, I spoke up. "Excuse me. May I ask a question?"

They all looked at me.

R. C. said, "You fixin' to be a lawyer, young 'un, with all these fancy manners?"

Jacob offered, "It only sounds that way because there's so few manners on display in these parts." Jacob nodded for me to go ahead.

"R. C., would you mind if I hole up for the winter in that cabin behind your other claim? The one I'm working." I was flattering him by calling it a cabin.

R. C. shifted in his seat. "It was like that when I took over the claim," he frowned. "Ain't fit for nothin' but spiders 'n' snakes. You'd be better off running with the coyotes."

Richard gave me a worried look. "What's to say it won't wash away in the next flood?"

R. C. shook his head. "The one we just had missed it, didn't it? It's high up enough, it should be out of harm's way."

I jumped in. "Yessir. That way I could work the claim on the good days."

"And work your own claim?" R. C. lifted a shaggy eyebrow.

"Yessir. One day, yours, one day, Mr. Mah—mine."

Jacob jumped in. "Now there's an idea that ought to appeal to you, R. C."

R. C. pushed back his hat and scowled at Jacob. "Would you *kindly* give me the opportunity to consider the proposition without a lot of extra foo fah?"

Jacob settled back in his chair, grinning. "Cogitate on, there, Midas. Cogitate on."

Ned came out with two platters balanced on each arm, a stack of five griddle cakes on each one. He set them before us without comment. The diameter of the griddle cakes was generous enough to hold three fried eggs arranged in a triangle on top of each stack. A great, irregular lump of butter, likely scooped fresh from the churn, melted at the center of each egg arrangement.

R. C. stared down at his stack of golden-brown cakes. "This is the strangest lookin' roast beef I ever saw."

Richard and Jacob were equally transfixed.

"That table over there got the last of the roast beef," Ned said, with some reluctance.

Richard was trying very hard not to laugh. Jacob was digging in. I thought that a good idea. The last time I had eggs was thanks to Mrs. Chalmers on the wagon train out.

"You still want the horseradish?" Ned said.

R. C. gave him a wave of his fork. "Maybe when you get in some more roast beef."

Ned went away.

R. C. fell on his griddle cakes. After a few bites, he turned to me. "You're welcome to the cabin, such as it is, but are you sure you can put up with the lonesome?"

"I think so, Sir. I'll have to come into town now and then to bring you your gold, anyway."

I heard Jacob stifle a laugh.

"You ought to be a lawyer," R. C. grunted. He accepted the jug of molasses I offered him. "It's yours. Go to it. But if you get et by rattlers, don't come whinin'. Ya hear?"

Everybody knew rattlers don't eat people. Their bite might kill you, but that was different. I tucked into the warm, doughy griddle cakes, smiling. "Thanks, R. C."

This was my chance to play *Robinson Crusoe*. My dad had read that book to me when I was little. And I had read it for myself not a year before we set out for California. Now I could see if I was up to the challenge.

Before I could play Robinson Crusoe, I needed some supplies. In the three days it took to prepare for the trial, the stores in town had restocked and the big trading wagons were gone. On my way to Gwynn's, I spotted only a solitary pack train at the north end of town.

Gwynn had only a patchwork canvas emporium supported by poles that had yet to be debarked. However humble his shelter, it housed an inventory of essentials to every miner. Much of his merchandise was displayed in the very crates and barrels it arrived in. Others were heaped or stacked on tables. Frying pans and gold pans, shovels and socks, and sou'westers for wet weather. Picks, pickles, and pants. Holding a picture of my mother in my mind, stern-browed, arms crossed, I moved through the store. I restricted myself to a gold pan, two blankets, a frying pan, and an axe. For food, I added a sack each of flour, rice, and beans, five pounds respectively.

I deposited my purchases on a fancy table, deep red in color, ornately carved, that had once been highly polished. It was likely a castoff from some wagon train. A ledger and pencil sat in the upper right corner and a scales that almost every merchant had for weighing gold sat in the upper left.

"Starting a new claim?" Mr. Gwynn asked.

"Yessir."

"We have a very good selection of picks and shovels. Did you see them?"

I smiled smugly. "I already have those, thanks."

"Very well." He looked at my pile again, and rested his hand on the sack of beans. "How are you planning on eating this food, once you've cooked it?" I looked up sheepishly, but he only smiled, pointing behind me. "Over by the cook pots and dutch ovens."

I had thought to use my gold pan for a plate but still needed a fork. In the end, I brought a tin plate and cup, and a fork back to the counter. "Thanks."

"Salt?" said Mr. Gwynn.

I could do without tea or coffee. And sugar. But not salt. I added a small tin of salt. I thought back to how much of all these tools and provisions I had seen thrown out along the trail to California. My purchases took just about all the gold I had to my name.

. . .

Jacob and Richard helped me carry my kit out to R. C.'s claim. Richard peered into the ragged, overgrown hole that marked the entrance to the cabin. He came back, brushing cobwebs off of his black hat. "That'll take a little work."

Jacob said, "You forgot something." He handed me a sack of slugs and caps for the Colt. "For the occasional dinner—or unwelcome guest. I'll trust you can see to the powder as you need it."

"Thanks. I'll pay you back. I promise."

He clapped me on the shoulder. "Sing me a song sometime."

After they helped me collect enough wood for a night's fire, I walked them back down to the river. I stood watching them until they started climbing the slope on the other side, back toward Auburn.

I made a fire and fried some bacon.

With the light fading, the start on the cabin could wait 'til morning. I tied my food high in the great oak on Mahoney's claim. I'd come to think of it as the Grandfather Oak. Then I sat by the fire planning my daily regimen. I'd spend the mornings making the cabin livable, and do other chores to take care of myself, like hunting for firewood. The afternoons I'd work the claims. As I told R. C., my plan was to work his claim one day, and Mahoney's claim the next.

The yap of a coyote jerked me awake. I put a few more pieces of busted lumber on the fire and rolled up in my blankets to sleep next to it. I missed Bugle especially at times like this. He was a boon companion after Dad died. I'd confided in him more than ever, proposing ideas, clearing my own mind just by trying to explain things to him. It had only been eight or nine weeks, but even so. . .I hoped it wouldn't be too long before I got him back from Chen Yi and Sun Shu.

.   .   .

The first thing I did to improve the cabin was to beat on it with the butt end of the axe, what we called the "poll." I walked around the three sides that stuck out from the hill, giving it good thumps and shaking the looser-looking parts. If the whole thing collapsed under one blow, at least I'd know where to start. It also gave any critters who had made it a home the chance to leave gracefully. I threw in a little whooping and yelling to help things along. Nothing of any size came out, and—to my relief—no snakes.

I ducked inside, stepping cautiously. It was dark. Right away I got a face full of dusty spider webs. Wiping them off, I stood still until my eyes adjusted to the gloom. A musky dirt smell filled the interior, but it had a dry quality, not moist, like the turned earth back home. The room was bigger than I thought it would be. The space had been increased by digging into the side of the hill, forming the fourth wall. It gave the place a cave-like feeling, strengthening my Robinson Crusoe fantasy. Gossamer filaments hung everywhere like shreds of ghosts, giving way to the least stir of air.

I cleaned out all the cobwebs using a cedar branch from my salvage, then swept the floor—not as good as my mom, but then, I never had much practice at home; she was always doing it.

Anything movable, or that might pass for furniture, I carried outside. Then I paced off the inside. It was about four paces by six, with the long side parallel to the river, about the size of Adam's and my bedroom back home. It would be easier to make it bigger, though, for the back wall—which was just dirt and rocks—had slumped in and spilled over part of the floor. The floor was dirt, too, but hard-packed, so somebody had used it for a while. The shed ceiling sagged a foot above my head at the back wall, and rose another foot higher at the front. I'd have to see if I could raise it a bit. The few sticks of furniture needed work.

For less than a minute, I thought about which wall would accommodate a fireplace, but I had neither the patience nor the knowledge to do it safely, and I could easily destroy the structure, so I abandoned the idea.

The first order of business was a door. You couldn't really call it a house until it had a door. I found lumber and nails down by the river, but I didn't have hinges. Maybe in my hunting I'd find a pair of boots and make hinges from the leather. In the meantime, propping the door in the opening and bracing it with a keg would have to serve.

The next chore was shoveling out the dirt that had fallen from the back wall. Soon I'd line the back wall with stones. That put me in mind of the chore I'd grumbled at back home. I leaned on my shovel. How safe and tidy and predictable life in Vermont had been. Chores waited patiently for you to get to them, and provided a reward for doing them, like milk or eggs or firewood. Always a warm, snug house to come into, a tireless mother lading the table with good things to eat. A father who would listen and offer good advice. And, somehow, always time for fishing or exploring with my steadfast friend, Will. *What's he doing right now?* I couldn't help but wonder.

The second day, while I was washing out some of the backwall dirt, I heard a shout. It was quite a ways off, downstream. Were people coming back to their claims? I set aside my pan and went looking for people and usable wreckage.

I gathered up everything I could carry for a mile downstream on my side. If I saw something worthwhile on the north shore, I waded across and brought it back. I saw no one and heard no other voices that day.

Along with the wood, I gathered up clothing, pieces of canvas of different sizes, four buckets, lengths of rope, and a shoe. Now I could make my door hinges. By the light of my supper fire, I sorted the lumber and wood and folded the canvas and the clothes.

On the third day, I searched upstream and came upon several barrels and kegs of various sizes, a couple of blankets, and a number of bottles and tins. But the real treasure of the day's scavenging was a toolbox. It was out in the water, wedged in some rocks. At first, I took it to be just more lumber, but when I waded out to it and realized it was a tool box, my heart leapt for joy. Then it sank just as fast. Flipping it over, the toolbox was empty—except for a chisel wedged in the seam between the side and the bottom. My joy rebounded. Who knew how far it had been carried—and tumbled—by the flood?

I peered down into the water where the box had lain. A hammer lay on the rocky bottom. I said a silent, fervent prayer of thanks. That hammer couldn't have been more valuable if it had been made of solid gold. The handle was badly split, but it would be nothing to carve another handle with Uncle Rafe's Bowie knife.

For three or four days, I ranged farther and farther, both upstream and down, bringing back everything I could carry, even if I didn't have an idea for its use right away. I used a piece of canvas as a sling. In all that roving, I encountered no other miners. I was pleased with what I gathered. *I might make a decent Robinson Crusoe yet.*

I scooped some glowing embers from my supper fire into my gold pan and brought them into the cabin. That provided a little light to find places for everything. I put the door in place and rolled up in my blankets, thankful for the extra ones, occupying my thoughts with how to put some of my loot to use. Extra clothes for winter, canvas on the walls to help keep out the cold… I was soon asleep.

I woke with a start. I had heard a cough—I was sure of it—outside the cabin. Hours must have passed; the embers had died out. I couldn't see anything.

Another cough.

I waited for somebody to knock on the door. Then I heard him on the roof. The timbers and roofing material creaked, shifting under his weight. The thin planks let in brief slivers of moonlight. The way the boards sagged told me there were two men up there, one following in the other's path, or was it a bear? Bits of grit and chaff sifted down on me. I followed the sounds as they walked slowly around the roof.

Should I call out? I groped for the Colt and gathered it to me. Then the roof gave one last wheeze and all went quiet. I was sure whoever was out there would knock on the door now. *Why didn't he speak up?* I tried to make myself get up and open the door. I waited… and waited some more. Silence became like a great dread, pressing on me.

I didn't get much sleep that night. I kept expecting my visitor to come back, bash down the door, and demand his tools or his clothing back.

CHAPTER 12

In the morning, I found the tracks of my visitor in the dirt around the cabin. Cat tracks! Our tabby back in Vermont left a paw print little more than an inch across. This cat's print was at least four inches across. And wide, not narrow, like a dog's. Unless there was another animal Mr. MacIver hadn't told us about, these were the tracks of what back home we called a catamount—a big one. When I told R. C. about it later, he said out here they were called mountain lions, or cougars.

The whole story was there in the tracks. The cat had inspected everything, climbing on the roof, as well. I went back inside, got the Colt, checked the cylinder, and stuck it in my belt. Then I took a good look around, up and downstream. I lost his tracks in leaf litter on the rise behind the camp, and I didn't go any farther. There wasn't much in the way of trees or bushes for the cat to hide in, but I was in no hurry to hunt the beast down with only a handgun. *If there were mountain lions, could there be bears?*

Such thoughts led to somber reflections. Yes, I had a house, but it wasn't by any stretch a fortress. It might well collapse with a good shove. With the miners gone to town, I couldn't count on anyone coming to my aid if my visitor returned. The realization sank in that I was truly on my own. I didn't even have Bugle.

For the first time since my dad died, desolate loneliness sapped my resolve. How fared my family back in Vermont? The news of my dad's death must have been a terrible, terrible blow. If I met some untimely end, how would they ever know? I cast a thought to Chen Yi, Sun Shu, and Gao Chung back in Grizzly Bar. I realized how much I had come to take comfort in their friendship.

The day was clear and bright, but the coldest I had yet experienced in the gold country. *Back home, this would be considered a nippy autumn day.* How much colder would it get here? Would the river freeze over? I put on two of the salvaged shirts over my own shirt. I challenged myself that I would resort to my coat only when it got colder.

If I was going to have these kinds of visitors, I had better see to the sturdiness of my dwelling place. The first thing I did was make hinges for the door to hang properly. I managed to cut two out of the one shoe. I retrieved nails from my salvaged lumber.

I opened my new door wide to let in as much light as possible. The roof was only one thin layer of planking. Before my worry had been keeping out the rain, now I had to worry about keeping out animals, too.

Looking up, I saw right away why the roof sagged so readily under the weight of the cat. Other than the walls, it had only one support. One tree trunk, not much more than a sapling, spanning the length of the ceiling, something like a ridge pole.

What I needed was a post to prop up that ridge pole. The best place for the post would be smack in the middle of the room. Not ideal, but simple and easily done.

Any young tree of a proper dimension had long since gone to some prospector's fire. I cobbled together my post from salvaged lumber. I planned it to be square, but, with the oddities of my lumber, I settled for a rectangular shape. Lastly, I carved out two saddles in the top for the ridge pole to rest in. In what daylight remained, I washed some dirt, and while so employed thought about ways to weatherproof the roof.

The next morning, I stepped gingerly from solid ground onto the roof and was glad to see that my center box post firmed up the roof well. But, if I was going to keep out the weather, I needed more roof than one layer of planks. I covered the original roof with pieces of my salvaged canvas. Over that I added a layer of patchwork lumber, crossways to the original roof planking, and sacrificed a few precious nails to fix some of this third layer to original, to discourage shifting.

I had just enough canvas for one final layer. I anchored the whole shebang with stones from the river, and all around the edges to keep the wind from playing mischief with the canvas.

I stood back and surveyed my handiwork. A reasonable fortress. I silently thanked the miners for building so many flumes— all that lumber came in very handy. Now I could divide my time equally between gold mining, salvaging, and fixing up the cabin.

The back wall of the cabin remained only dirt. I imagined waking up one morning, after a rain, buried in mud. Unless I shored it up some way. I had devoted most of my lumber to building the post and to strengthening the roof, so I reverted to means of which I had considerable experience: a rock wall. And the river shore right outside my door sported a limitless supply of rocks.

. . .

In the days that followed, it rained frequently. If it was only drizzling, I kept at my prospecting. Firstly, I washed the pile of dirt that had fallen into the room from the back wall. It yielded perhaps a teaspoon's worth of dust and flakes. Then I moved on.

R. C.'s claim produced a small but steady amount. Mr. Mahoney's claim—my claim—was a disappointment. I worked what were called the tailings: the piles of dirt and gravel left over from his previous efforts. I'd heard stories of the Celestials—the Chinese people—finding gold in tailings other people had washed out two or three times and had given up on. I got a little, but it was slow work.

My most important job, after prospecting, was collecting firewood. The easiest and best kind was deadfall—branches on the ground and snags, trees that were dead but still standing. But miners before me had picked clean the lower slopes of the canyon, and then gone after the living trees, leaving only stumps behind. I had to go farther and farther up the hills to find anything. After I brought back the first armload, I thought, *at this rate, I won't have time to do anything else.* Shortly after that, I began using the sling I had made for scavenging flood debris to carry a great deal more wood each trip.

R. C. came out once in a while "To make sure the coyotes ain't got ya." He'd look around and ask how it was going. I could tell he was just being sociable, and I'd show him where I was working. Sometimes he would bring a newspaper. Other times, we'd just sit and talk about Vermont. One time, Richard came along. There was a lot of joshing that day.

When the sun was sinking toward the western horizon, R. C. would say, "I'd best let you get back to the pursuit of your riches." He'd lever himself up, study the sky and predict rain, and set off.

Whenever it rained, I chafed. Every day lost to rain was another day's delay in earning enough to go home. I kept myself busy inside. I fixed the table and stool, added a couple of shelves to the walls, and made a bed from lumber and rope. It made the cabin feel crowded, so I dismantled the stone wall and started digging out more space for a bedroom.

It was the usual reddish dirt, salted with old, round river stones. In one shovelful I spotted an oddly shaped pebble about the size of a walnut. Unlike the other stones, it was uneven and pitted, and felt heavy for its size. *Could this be?* I tried not to get my hopes up even as I rubbed some of the dirt off with my thumb. Then I ran down to the river to wash off the rest. The nugget gleamed in the cold winter light. Gold!

I dumped the shovelful of dirt in my pan and took it down to the river. Four nuggets, that same size or larger, and many more smaller ones—and flakes, too, lay hidden in the dirt. Despite the drizzle drifting down on my shoulders, I went very carefully so as not to lose a single grain of the precious metal.

The next two days I spent digging and washing the dirt from the back wall. I had achieved what I needed for my bed, but kept on, wanting to make sure I got every speck of ore. I felt crumbs of dirt sift down the back of my neck, and, looking up, realized that this could all cave in on me. I stopped digging to scavenge more lumber to build a ceiling for my new room.

It took another day to wash the remainder of the dirt from my excavation. In the end, I filled five bottles of assorted sizes with gold dust and flakes. The bottles also held any nuggets bean-sized or smaller. I made a separate bag for the bigger nuggets. I hefted the bag. It had to weigh at least fifteen pounds!

This was surely more gold, even, than I'd found with the Frenchmen on Simpson's creek. My first impulse was to run and show my dad. *Look! Can you believe it? This is enough to build at least a barn and a house. Did you ever think—?*

Then I sobered up. Firstly, my dad lay under a pile of rocks out on the prairie. Secondly, this was R. C.'s gold. It wasn't mine. This was found on his claim. My claim was next door, and we had yet to see what would come of that.

I put the bottles of gold dust on my top shelf. Even half of one of these bottles would keep Mother and Amy in lamp oil, and no doubt much else, through the winter. Lord, how I missed them.

But in our family wallowing in self-pity was not tolerated, and would earn you a good dose of mockery. Pushing away my melancholy, I reconstructed a new back wall and sides with river stones and moved my bed into the greater space.

The following morning, under a gray, overcast sky, I came back from gathering firewood singing "Roll on, Silver Moon" at the top of my voice, just like Eli Cooder would. When I got closer to the cabin, I was surprised to hear two voices join in my song. One was Jacob Harper's. I could tell that quick enough. I had to listen a little harder to the other voice, but then I recognized Richard Barter's faint British accent.

I came around to the front of the cabin already smiling. They had seated themselves on two of the smaller kegs from my scavenging trips.

"Hello, Master of the Chorus!" beamed Jacob, rising with his big hand out.

"I give you joy, Pegg-o, on this fine day," Richard said, rising also. He was dressed in what most people would consider their Sunday best: a black broadcloth coat, pinstripe woolen trousers, boiled shirt, and black silk vest.

"Thank you. Hello to you, too!" I set my load of firewood on the ground.

"Do we merit thanks?" Richard asked, feigning bewilderment.

I was stymied for a minute. "Well, for coming to visit…" I stepped forward to shake their hands. "Have you been waiting long?"

Richard said, "Long enough for the coffee pot to grow cold."

Flummoxed, I gestured at the cook fire. "But I don't have coffee."

Richard gave a sly smirk. "Seeing no coffee pot, we surmised as much."

"I've been hunting firewood. I'm sorry to have kept you waiting."

Jacob chuckled. "Don't fret, Pegg-son. We've come to do more than visit." I gave him a questioning look, and he went on. "Have you lost track of the days? 'Tis the Yuletide Season! Indeed! It's Christmas Day!"

I gaped at him. Christmas? I had, indeed, lost track of the days, the weeks, so bent on survival. Memories swirled through my mind, worry, too, about the occupants of a small farmhouse in Vermont this Christmas.

Richard jumped in. "And we've come to rescue you from your solitude!" He rubbed his hands together in glee. "We have been sent to bring you back to town for a celebration. R. C. insists you stop working and join us for 'some seasonal vittles and good cheer,' as he says. If we step lively, we may yet enjoy a few of the leftovers."

Step lively, indeed. It was almost noon, and a two to three-hour hike into town. I spilled the wood out of the sling and took it into the cabin, calling to them to follow. The three of us filled the cabin. They both ducked their heads to avoid hitting the ceiling. I spread the sling on the table and got the bottles of R. C.'s gold down from my shelf. I could sense my two visitors growing still as I filled the sling with the bottles and then the bag of nuggets. Jacob lifted the bag and tested its weight.

"It's a foolish question," he said quietly, "but is this gold, too?"

"Yes, it is." I didn't try to keep a smile off my face.

"From the river?" Richard asked, equally hushed.

I shook my head. "Closer to home."

Richard's eyes widened. He looked around the room.

Jacob laid the bag of large nuggets back on the sling. "Now, Dick. Let's not be too nosy. You know how word travels."

Richard glanced over his shoulder, then back. "Has it played out?"

"I think so." I put on my salvaged coat and hoisted the bulging sling onto my shoulder. "I'm sorry I don't have presents for you both, but at least I have one for R. C."

"Oooooo-eee," exclaimed Jacob.

"I don't think he could hope for a better one," said Richard, and we set out for Auburn.

We climbed out of the canyon until we came to the wagon road. A cold wind pushed us along. When we got to town, we passed by the Empire Hotel for another establishment. The room featured long tables and benches, and the walls were festooned with pine boughs and great swoops and bows of red ribbon. The warm air was rich in pine resin, pipe smoke, and roasted meat.

Richard, Jacob, and I exchanged glances of dismay. It was only too evident that the Christmas feast had, indeed, been consumed. The room was all but empty; only scattered knots of miners lounged in casual talk, sucking contentedly on clay pipes. Workers in long, spattered aprons cleared the last articles from the tables.

R. C. and I saw each other in the same moment, but he spoke out first, cheerfully. "What's kept you, Young 'un? You missed the feast!"

He was seated at one of the long tables, surrounded by other miners. It put me in mind of a thicket of wild, untrimmed whiskers topped by a crazy assortment of hats. R. C. touched the sleeve of a worker headed back to the kitchen with a load of plates. "Garçon."

The man paused and looked down at R. C.

"Do you think you could rustle up three more plates of Christmas vittles for these varmints?" He gestured to Jacob, Richard, and me.

"See what I can do," replied the man, and he lumbered on his way.

Most of the men sitting with R. C. made their excuses and left us. We three "varmints" settled onto benches with those few who remained. While he was busy making introductions, I settled the sling under the bench by my feet.

He turned to me. "Good to see you in one piece, Young'un. Wouldn't want you to be gettin' cabin fever. Mahoney's claim worth anything more 'n a hoot an' a holler?"

"Too soon to tell. It's going pretty well, though." I swapped a quick glance with Richard and Jacob and moved my sling a little farther under the bench with my foot.

"Ahh," chuckled R. C. "You're learnin' to hold your cards close to your chest. A lesson too few learn."

"Yessir," I replied. Everybody seemed in a good mood. I wondered if I could manage a jest. "Pete Hawthorne passed by your claim the other day. You remember him? He was the foreman of the jury at our miner's court."

R. C. only nodded, raking his beard.

I charged on. "He asked if you'd seen the elephant. I told him I was holding down the fort while you were busy running for governor." It was nonsense: I hadn't seen a soul for a week, at least.

R. C.'s eyes popped wide, Jacob let out a whoop, and Richard broke into a big grin. The other miners' enjoyment was less assured. A few laughed; most made do with smiling. Luckily, the server came back with three plates of food just then. Slabs of turkey and mutton, a big mound of bread stuffing, boiled potatoes and onions, all covered in gravy. It wasn't piping hot, but it sure tasted good. He came back a few moments later with three slices of mincemeat pie. "On the house. Merry Christmas," he said in a tired voice.

"Thank you," the three of us said in unison.

R. C. left us in peace to tuck into our meal, but he was clearly itching to ask questions. The remainder of his companions bade farewell and drifted away to other tables, or out the door entirely. When it was just the four of us, R. C. leaned forward on his elbows, lowering his voice. "Well? Has Dame Fortune been any nicer to you than she has been to these other poor saps?"

"For all love," said Richard. "Do we have to talk business on Christmas? I'd rather talk about our loved ones back home, waiting for us…"

R. C. reared back. "So why aren't you handing out presents, there, Sainty Nicholas?" He waved his arm to take in the room and the food before us. "This ain't Christmasy 'nough for you?"

"Ah, ha! There you are!" Richard smirked. "I'm not the one to be handing out presents." He leered at R. C. "But I know somebody who is!" He turned his gaze on me.

Jacob, who had been content to concentrate on his dinner, murmured, "Up. Cat's out of the bag."

R. C. looked from one to the other of us with suspicion. "What's goin' on here? What—?"

I hauled up the canvas sling and settled it on the table. The glass bottles shifted and clinked. "Merry Christmas, Mr. Simpson."

R. C. jerked back and stared at his present with some consternation. Richard and I held our breath. Jacob said, "You gonna make us wait 'til Easter before you open it?"

"If'n it was from you," growled R. C., "I know it'd be a pile of dead skunks."

"Be thankful for small favors, then," Jacob replied with a rumbling chuckle.

R. C. opened the canvas cautiously, his eyes growing wider by the minute. Halfway, he threw a quick, questioning glance at me. I just smiled at him. Then he threw another glance around the room, which was now even more deserted. The few folks left were across the room and minding their own business. Even so, he hunched over the sack as if to shield it.

With the canvas unwrapped, he picked up one of the bottles, which used to hold Dr. Peeb's All Purpose Tonic, and turned it slowly. It was full to the neck with gold. The tiny flakes glittered in the murky light.

"Looks like Dame Fortune hasn't been so scarce after all, eh, R. C.?" Jacob said quietly. "She just ain't been sitting in your lap."

Richard added his anthem. "Looks like Rattlesnake Bar is living up to its reputation."

R. C. arranged the bottles in a row, lying side by side. Then he settled his hand gently on the lumpy cloth bag stuffed with the bigger nuggets. He raised his eyebrows at me in question. I nodded. He set the bag up, untied the draw strings, and peered inside. His eyes got even wider. He reached in to pluck out one of the nuggets but snapped his head up to look around the room.

Drawing the nugget out, he gave it no more than a glance before he closed his gnarled fist around it. He lowered the bag to the table. "The whole bag like this?" He moved his fist forward.

I kept a sober face with difficulty. "Yessir. Mostly. Some are bigger."

R. C. put the nugget back and closed the bag and cinched the strings tight. "You hadn't ought to be showing off your takings like this, Young 'un," R. C. muttered gruffly. "You'll attract unwelcome attention." He looked around again. Then he folded the canvas back over the whole treasure.

"It's not mine, Sir," I said. "It's yours. It's from your claim, not Mr. Mahoney's..."

R. C. went back to looking at the bundle. "On my claim, Peggson?"

"Yessir. In the cabin," I said. "The back wall was just dirt. I was digging it out to make the room bigger."

R. C. mumbled, "I never would have thought to look there. . ."

I leaned forward and whispered, "If we dig on the same level of the hill right outside the cabin, there might be more. Could be an old riverbed."

R. C. reached under the canvas, brought out one of the bigger bottles and slid it to me. "That's yours, then," he said.

Both Jacob and Richard were still. My heart was thumping. I stared at the bottle. "Are you sure, Sir?"

"You'll need it for lawyer school. Go on."

He took out another bottle and slipped it into his coat pocket. Then he wrapped the jars and canvas bag all up into a bundle again. "I'd be much obliged if you'd take this over to the express office and put it to my account."

I stared at him. "You'd trust me?"

He fixed me with a stern gaze, his shaggy brows drawn down, and pushed the bundle across the table to me. "In your shoes, many another man would have dug this up without breathing a word. And I'd've been none the wiser."

Jacob nodded.

I was still dazed. "Will it be open? It's Christmas."

"They're always open," scoffed R. C. "Whether they want to be or not. Miners won't let 'em rest."

"Yessir," I said quietly. "I'd be happy to." This was like being entrusted with building a barn all by myself.

R. C. rose from his seat. "I am much obliged to you, Sir." He turned and called out to the room, "Drinks're on me over at the Temple!"

Will whispered in my head, *He called you "Sir." Did you catch that? After all his bellyachin'.*

R. C. bellowed toward the kitchen. "Kitchen, too! Dishes'll wait!"

The workers barreled out of the kitchen, throwing aside their aprons. The room emptied in a flash. Richard and I found ourselves alone at the table. I slipped the bottle of gold R. C. had given me into my pocket. It seemed to me he wasn't following his own advice about keeping mum about one's luck, but I figured he knew what he was doing.

"I'm not much for that kind of celebrating," Richard said with a sheepish look. "I'll tag along to the express office, if I may,"

"Be glad of the company," I said, rising.

CHAPTER 13

I hadn't done this part of the gold rush yet—depositing the gold you found, which made it official. Then it was on record as yours. Some miners sent it on to San Francisco, a few sent a portion back home, like we did. Mr. Hoyt had always done the depositing for our partnership. I had to admit, I was a little puffed up about this new responsibility.

We got to the express office to find a "Closed" sign hanging on the front door. I was worried about safeguarding all that gold through the night. "Let's find a place to hide this 'til morning."

"Nonsense," Richard said. "The sign may say closed, but their work is never done." He rapped on the door. We waited. "There'll be packages to wrap for the morning stage." He knocked on the door again.

Finally, we heard movement, and the clerk unlocked the door and pulled it open with a jerk. To my surprise, there stood a lady. She was a little taller than my mom, and trim, like her. But this lady was dressed in butternut brown, with her hair pulled tight against her head. She looked tired, and she did not look pleased to see us.

Richard turned on the charm. "We're awfully sorry to interrupt your work, dear lady." He made a little bow. "But we have a late deposit that we must entrust to your care."

She stepped back and waited for us to enter. Richard led the way into the dimly lit room. She closed the door behind us. By the look of it, we had, indeed, interrupted her wrapping packages. "Do you have an account with us?" she asked, taking her place behind the counter, directly under a sprig of sage hanging from the ceiling.

I spoke up. "Yes, Ma'am. But I am also making a deposit for someone else, as well."

"Let's see to them first, then." She opened a large ledger. "The name?"

"Simpson. R. C. Simpson."

She flipped through some pages of her ledger, ran her pencil tip down one page, and stopped. "Simpson, R. C. Yes." But she was already writing something in the book. Then she looked up expectantly.

We stared at each other. The clerk creased her brow in irritation. Richard nudged my arm that held the bundle, and twitched his chin in the direction of the counter. Flushing with embarrassment, I hoisted the bundle onto the counter. I felt like a greenhorn. I *was* a greenhorn!

"Have pity, Ma'am," Richard said. "We're new at this. Not accustomed to all the particulars, as it were. We greatly appreciate your indulgence…"

"Sugary talk will earn you no favors, young man." She flipped the canvas open briskly and emptied the first bottle into the metal dish on one side of the scales. While picking through her counterweights, the clerk held out the empty bottle to me. I was just a breath too long in realizing my part, and she withdrew the bottle and dropped it behind her. She put counterweights in the dish on the other side until the needle in the middle stood straight up. She peered closely at the weights in the right-hand dish and made a note in the ledger. She emptied the brass dish into a sack, poured the next bottle into the dish, and repeated the steps— except for the offering-me-the-bottle step. Just as briskly, she processed the remaining bottles and noted the ounces.

I knew better than to ask questions.

Surely the bag of large nuggets would impress her. It was heavier than she expected. She had to take a second grip. Still, she made no remark.

With a great clattering and clanking of metal against metal, she tumbled the nuggets into the brass dish, and the bag followed the bottles into the collection box. Then she put the nuggets in the dish with what seemed no more care than if they were common river pebbles. All of the largest counterweights were in the right-hand dish, and we waited for the needle to settle, watched her add up the weights and make her notation in the ledger.

"You have other business?" said the clerk, while finishing her entry.

I fumbled in my pocket to pull out my bottle of dust.

Richard spoke up. "If I may ask, Ma'am, what was the total weight?"

She looked up sharply at Richard. "Are you Mr. Simpson?" She must have known he wasn't, because she didn't wait for his answer.

Richard opened his mouth for a retort, but as quickly realized his chance was gone.

The clerk had turned back to me. "What else?"

I held up my bottle of dust. "Yes, Ma'am. I'd like to deposit this under the name of Hoyt."

She flipped back though a number of pages in her ledger, running her pencil up and down the page several times. Her brow drew down in consternation again and her mouth pressed into a thin, straight line. "I have no Hoyt."

"Hoyt," I said. "H-O-Y-T--"

"Thank you," she said with a tight jaw, and looked again.

"Fred Hoyt," I said in a small voice.

"I have a 'Hall.' I have a 'Harper,' a 'Hill,' a 'Howley,' a 'Hixon'... 'Haydon'..." Down the page she went, keeping her place with her hovering pencil. "'Hicks'... 'Hobbs'... 'Hoy'."

I jumped on the last name. "That's it! Hoyt."

She sighed, still looking down at the page. "No. That's Hoy. Not Hoyt."

I fought down my disappointment. "Might there be a second page—of H's."

The clerk looked downright cross for the blink of an eye, but then composed herself and turned the page. After studying it for the briefest moment, her brows stitched into a frown, but it was gone as quickly. She looked up. "I'm sorry. We have no 'Hoyt'."

I rocked back as if I'd been kicked by a mule. My jaw dropped. *What does she mean, "no Hoyt?" There has to be! Where did he put the money from my singing "Amazing Grace."* Richard and I stared at each other in disbelief.

I turned to the lady and blurted out, "Are you sure?" She was not at all pleased at my questioning her thoroughness.

Richard exclaimed, "I was with the man. I brought him here! To this very office!"

I was desperate. "Could it be in a different ledger?"

Richard flapped his arms. "Hold on, hold on! It was a man! The clerk on duty that day was a man!"

"That would be Mr. Hamblin," offered the clerk reluctantly.

"Could we talk to him?"

"Young man. Do you have the least grasp of how many people come into this office every day—day in and day out? Regardless of who served him, your Mr. Hoyt is not in the book. That is the only way we have of knowing whether he has an account here. Since his name is not in the book, we must conclude he has no account here."

She closed the ledger, resting one hand over the other, flat on the cover.

"Will there be anything else?" she asked primly.

CHAPTER 14

I stared in stunned disbelief at the stern express office clerk. *This can't be right!* How could Mr. Hoyt not be in the book? *There has to be a mistake! An explanation!*

Richard saw him make the deposit. *Maybe he made the account in my name.* "Do you have a Pegg listed? Bartholomew Pegg? With two g's?"

She opened the ledger, found the "P" page, and looked from the top to the bottom of the page, tracking with her pencil, without calling out any names. "No. I'm afraid not."

I had to risk her wrath. "Is there another page of 'P's, perhaps?"

I was too worried to think about what trouble I might be causing her. She turned the page and ran her pencil down it, again without singling out names. Then she looked up at me with a slow blink. "I have no 'Pegg'."

She closed the ledger carefully. She was a small woman, and it was a hefty book.

"How about Pruitt? Did you see a Pruitt? James Pruitt?"

She did not reopen her ledger. "I'm sorry. But I have a lot of work yet to do, and the hour is late. Perhaps when you solve your mystery you can come back."

I put my bottle back in my pocket. I had a dozen questions. *Did Mr. Hoyt send it all to Mr. Pruitt? Did he send any of it to my family, like he said he had been doing? Maybe he took it to another place later. No, Richard said they had deposited it here.*

When she saw I wasn't moving, she said, "Was there something else?"

"No, Ma'am," Richard and I answered.

She wrote out a receipt, stamped it and handed it to me. It read R. C. Simpson. "Thank you for your business, Gentlemen."

I stared at the slip of paper, wishing I had one for our account.

She assumed I knew what I was looking at. "I'm sorry it's not the regulation form. I've been assured the printed forms will be arriving from the San Francisco office—soon."

"Thank you, Ma'am," In a daze, I put the receipt in my shirt pocket.

Richard broke into a smile. "Then it only remains to wish you a very Merry Christmas, Ma'am." And he touched his finger to his hat.

"And to you, young man. Now, if you please…" she gestured toward the door.

It closed behind us with a firm thump, and we heard a key scrabble in the lock.

Richard and I walked away from the express office with no particular destination. Merrymakers caroused up and down the street, stumbling in and out of the saloons. A few lay prostrate in the mud, overcome by their celebrating.

I was in a lather of confusion, humiliation, and resentment. I brought out my bottle of gold dust. "I forgot to deposit this."

Richard hunched his shoulders and chafed his hands. "You don't have an account. Or rather, your partnership doesn't have an account."

What had Mr. Hoyt done with the gold I got from singing? Had he taken it with him when he went with Mr. Brannan, to make himself more commendable to the man? *Maybe he sent a bank draft to Mr. Sweeney in Grizzly Bar to pay off his debt.* I hoped that would mean I could go back and get Bugle.

Maybe he took it so he could keep sending money back to my family.

No matter what he had done with it, he left nothing to help see me through the winter. I had no idea how far the bottle in my pocket would stretch. If I didn't find any more gold, what would I live on?

Your wits, my lad, chided Will. *Let's not forget those.*

Richard was still trying to figure it out. "I brought him there! We've got to go back when the other clerk is there."

I turned up my collar. "Did you see him deposit the gold with the man?"

"I wasn't exactly hanging off his shoulder," Richard replied defensively. "But, yes! I saw the clerk weigh the gold. I saw him make the entry in the book."

"So what happened to the entry?" I kicked a lump of dirt. "This is just like Grizzly Bar! He ups and disappears without a word! The gold disappears! What kind of partnership is this?" Instantly, I knew my mother would not be pleased at such an outburst, much less in public.

Richard leaned back, blinking at me as if I'd grown an extra pair of ears. "I wish I could give you an answer to the first of your questions, and I have my opinion about the second."

We found an empty bench and sat. We stuffed our hands in our pockets and hunched forward against the cold. Singing and music swelled and ebbed by turns on the chill air, not a few of them Christmas carols. Empty bottles littered the street.

I told Richard about the time in St. Louis when Mr. Hoyt had left the partnership to go build steamboats, and had returned with his tail between his legs, claiming to have been robbed.

Richard looked out at the street. "So, he's a riverboat man, then. Or was."

"I think he's anything he wants to be—whatever the moment requires." That led me to the story Vernon Tucker had told about his time on the Mississippi showboats with Mr. Hoyt, and the unfortunate Miss Mirabelle.

"So what became of the lady?"

"Mr. Tucker didn't know and Mr. Hoyt wasn't saying."

"Mmmmm. That *is* unfortunate," Richard mused.

A moment of quiet passed. A man marched by, head held high, waving his arms wildly as if conducting a band.

Richard cupped his hands and blew on them. "This is nothing like Quebec, but it's still plenty cold."

I patted the pocket that held my bottle. "Why don't we use some of this to get rooms for the night?"

Richard held up his hand, "Save it. One chilly night won't do us in. You've got the whole winter to think about."

I rubbed my arms vigorously. "Maybe the express office lady knows a place that will give us credit."

"Right," Richard said. "Do you want to bother that lady again?"

I smirked at that prospect. "Freezing to death would be no worse."

We shared a rueful laugh, sending little clouds into the air, only to be interrupted by a woman's voice.

"Excuse me."

The express office lady stood ramrod straight at the end of our bench. She held a lantern and clutched a shawl tightly around her shoulders.

Richard and I jumped to our feet. "Ma'am?" he said, sweeping off his hat.

I yanked my hat off, too.

"I must apologize," she said. "It was on the next page," Her brow was wrinkled up, attempting to say she was sorry.

"Ma'am?" I asked.

"Hoyt's name. It was the last entry on the next page." She squeezed her eyes shut and shook her head. "I shall have to speak to him about it. It's highly irregular." She took a deep breath, as if she was taking on all the guilt. "It is my mistake. I should have been more thorough. I am terribly sorry. I know these misunderstandings can cause a great deal of trouble."

I said, "That's all right."

At the very same time Richard smiled and said, "Don't give it another thought."

We all shared a nervous laugh.

"I am afraid there's more." She knitted up her brow again and took a new hold on her shawl.

Richard moved forward a little. "Should we go back to the office to discuss this? It's awfully cold out here."

Heedless of his concern, she went on. "His name was crossed out and the amount of his account was crossed out, as well. That's most certainly not our designated procedure. Mr. Hamblin had written 'Closed' to the right of his entries." The lady frowned as if she were somehow at fault. "That is proper procedure. In any event, it appears that your Mr. Hoyt made his deposit, changed his mind, withdrew it and closed the account. It was irresponsible, not to mention foolish, of Mr. Hamblin to attempt to make it look like the entry had never been made."

"Can you tell me the amount?" I asked her.

"I'm afraid I am not permitted to give out that information, except to the account holder." She was still trying to apologize.

Richard spoke up. "But the account's closed. The gold is gone. Shouldn't that absolve you of any such stricture?"

The clerk got some of her starch back. "And I would offer your thought back to you, young man. The gold is gone. Knowing the amount would only be a torment."

"Yes, Ma'am. I see." I sensed I would need this lady's good will in my time here. Richard, in his candor, was not helping my cause. In any event, the rules weren't of her making. "Thanks just the same."

"Even if I were willing to break the rules, I couldn't help you. I'm afraid Mr. Hamblin did rather too good a job of crossing out the entries. I could barely make out 'Hoyt.'"

"I hope that's been of help to you. I do apologize for the earlier confusion."

"Yes, Ma'am," Richard and I chorused, shivering.

"Then I will say good night. If I may be of further assistance—" She caught herself. "Good night—and Merry Christmas," she said and hurried away. The shadows swallowed her up.

Still looking after her, Richard said, "Was that the same lady?"

Mr. Hoyt was gone, and the gold with him. This was my first Christmas away from home. Even though I had friends in R. C., Jacob, and Richard, I felt very much an orphan isolated in a strange land.

Fortunately, our bellies were full of the Christmas dinner R. C. had "saved" for us. We got up to be moving again. We tried tucking ourselves unnoticed into corners of noisy saloons, but were shown the door when we declined to buy drinks.

Walking up and down the street, we shared Christmas stories. I told him about my mom cooking for a couple of days. We always had a house full of people, and her chestnut stuffing was the envy of the neighborhood. Mom made special red-colored tallow candles, something her mother had done, and her grandmother before that. A new custom came along, when Amy and I were little, of bringing a small evergreen tree into the house and decorating it. My dad strung popcorn and made ornaments.

Richard talked about how his dad would go out and collect holly and decorate the parlor with the dark, shiny leaves and bright red berries. They'd buy sticks of cinnamon to put in their cider. Both our families, it turned out, had yule logs. They had Christmas pudding with hard sauce; we had mince pie. . .

"We sang 'Deck the Halls'," I said. "And 'The First Noel.' What did you sing?"

"The same! And 'Joseph and the Angel' and 'God Rest ye Merry Gentlemen.'" He blew into his cupped hands. "You know, we're tormenting ourselves with these memories, and it's not making us any warmer."

Richard looked around the empty street. "I certainly don't fancy hiking back to the river in the middle of the night, despite the coffee and blankets waiting for me. You think it will get down to freezing?"

"It feels like it has already." I imagined them finding us stiff and frosty behind a building in the morning.

"Ever sleep in a haystack?" Richard asked.

I kicked myself. Why hadn't I thought of that? "Yes. In fact, I have!" I remembered Grizzly Bar. But Chen Yi had saved me from it by sending Gao Chung to invite me back to their restaurant. "For a little while, anyway."

Richard said, "I've never had the pleasure myself, but I've heard it'll serve in a pinch."

"Let's go have a look at the livery." We set off.

Richard hustled along. "I presume the idea is to use fresh hay."

I grinned at him. "Unless you want to be fragrant in the morning."

We had a good laugh. Then I filled him in on the benefits of sleeping in a pile of hay. "The pile itself makes some heat, even without piss and manure. It's very scratchy, and there's always one or two straws set to poke you good. You're breathing straw dust, but it smells good. And it's tolerable warm once you've heated it up."

"Sounds lovely," replied Richard.

I couldn't tell if he was being sarcastic or not. "And at least you're out of the wind."

The livery stable, indeed, had a large pile of fresh fodder for the animals behind the building. A great patched canvas covered most of it, except for a few feet from the ground.

I sucked in one of my favorite smells, cut hay. "Which side do you want?"

"Is the hay different on your side?" Richard smirked.

I dug in and curled up, assuming Richard could tend to himself. Once more, I wished I had Bugle with me. Not only could we help keep each other warm, he would listen patiently to my musings about what Mr. Hoyt might be up to. With the perk of his ears or the tilt of his head, Bugle could always get me to reconsider whatever I was wrestling with from a different angle. My sister, Amy, used to laugh at me when I would credit Bugle with helping me figure something out. I would even forgive Mr. Hoyt for using my singing money to pay his debt if it meant I could go back to Grizzly Bar to get our pet beagle back.

I told myself to stop thinking about home. But remembering Christmases with Richard had set me down that road. Last Christmas, before Dad and I left for California, had been extra special. Maybe because we all knew Dad and I were going away, maybe it was Amy and I seeing things being expressed between Mother and Dad we hadn't appreciated before. But whatever it was, it made the memory of it ache hard. A haystack on the edge of a town at the edge of the world was poor doings for Christmas, compared to a warm house full of love and good cheer.

.   .   .

Come morning, Richard talked himself into a job at the livery stable. Jacob had gone off to his brother's, so Richard needed work. I sought out R. C. and gave him the receipt for his deposit. Then I did something that took most of the grit that I possessed. I went back to see the express office lady. I dreaded that grim manner and stern expression I'd endured the night before. Of course, she had apologized, but I had a strong sense it wasn't something she did often.

I had two pieces of business to conduct with the lady. Firstly, I had to put my bottle of gold safely in her hands. Since there was no Hoyt account, that meant there was no partnership account. I couldn't worry about what Mr. Hoyt was or wasn't doing. It was up to me to open one. And hopefully fill it to bursting soon.

But how to keep it safe from my partner's grasping fingers? For he was just as good at reappearing as he was at disappearing. I could just imagine him walking in and dipping into the partnership account to bankroll some new scheme, or to buy a new hat. I'd had enough of that in Grizzly Bar.

Second, I wanted to ask her if I could get my bottles and the cloth bag back. Smaller containers like that were hard to come by, and I wanted to spend less time scavenging and more time prospecting.

There was plenty of light, but the sun had yet to break over the rim of the hill overlooking Auburn. My breath came out in little clouds as I hurried along, my hands stuffed in my pockets. The morning stagecoach stood in front of the express office. The coach was a beautiful new Concord, gleaming deep, red body paint, bold, buttercup yellow wheels, and goldleaf detailing. A few people hovered close by, more than likely passengers waiting to board. The horses' harness jingled whenever they stamped their feet or shook their heads. The big leather flap that covered the rear luggage platform, what we called the boot, had been pulled aside. The driver was nowhere in sight.

The express office lady was coming down the steps with her arms full of packages. She slid her load onto the floor of the boot, pushing parcels already there farther into the space. It was clear they would need to be arranged more securely for the rough journey. As she turned to go back inside, one of the packages teetered for a moment and fell. Quick as lightning, she snatched it just before it struck the ground and set it in the boot and hurried away. The package fell again as she disappeared into the office. I picked it up and slid it farther onto the boot. Should I take a chance and rearrange the packages? If I did it wrong, she would be angrier than ever. I didn't want to give her any reason to refuse my request.

Just then the clerk reappeared carrying more packages, while dragging a huge sack of mail. It thumped down the steps like a reluctant child. She seemed to not even notice me. She slid the packages onto the boot, pushing the others as she had before, and dropped the rope that cinched the heavy mail sack. Then she went back for more!

"So, she's finally hired some help!"

I spun around, my hand still resting on the boot. The stage driver—the whip, as he was sometimes called, was striding toward me. A big, sun-browned man, he wore a dusty, dilapidated, wide-brimmed hat; a great, shapeless, faded bandana about his throat, and a long, loose, travel-stained coat. Huge, drooping mustaches, the color of ripened wheat, all but hid his mouth until he grinned.

"Well, hop to it, Sonny. Time's a-wasting!"

"Yessir!" I hefted the mailbag into the boot. Then I climbed up and rearranged the packages around the other luggage so it was all as tight as one of my Vermont stone fences back home.

The express lady came out with the last couple of packages and stared at the boot.

"Looks like you hired yourself a keeper, Lila," beamed the whip. "The boy packed up that boot like he's been doin' it all his life."

"I didn't hire him."

"Well, you ought to!" The whip's generous smile lifted his moustaches.

"Where's the mail bag?" she fretted, craning her neck to find it.

"It's right there, Ma'am," I pointed, and jumped down off the boot.

"Safe and sound, Lila," reassured the whip as he pulled down the big leather flaps that covered the packages and luggage. "Packed almost as good as you do." He gave her a wink. Then he turned to call out, "All aboard, folks! Next stop, Spanish Corral." He snugged down the straps that secured the big flaps. The waiting passengers clambered into the coach.

The whip gave Lila, the express lady, a squeeze and a kiss on the cheek. "Until the 'morrow, Sweet Pea."

Lila blushed, protesting with flailing arms and a frown. "Wallace Evans! I will report you to your superiors if you persist in such outlandish behavior!"

The driver let her go, but her blush lingered. "Do that, Lila Mae," he beamed, before fairly springing up into his seat. "Then we can get married—and I can sit on the porch and mind the brats!" He cracked his whip over the heads of the team, gave a shout, and the stage rumbled away.

Lila tarried in the street, watching the stage disappear up the road. At last, she turned to go back into the office.

I cleared my throat. "Excuse me, Ma'am."

"Were you addressing me?" Then she narrowed her eyes. "Aren't you the boy who came in last night to make a deposit?" She wrinkled her brow. "You were with that young man dressed in black who thought a little too much of himself."

"Yes, Ma'am, I am. I mean, that was me. But don't mind Richard. He just tries to keep everybody in a good mood."

"Is there a problem?" She wrinkled her brow up even more.

"No, Ma'am. No problem at all." I smiled. "I was hoping to open an account this morning."

"You're at the right place, then."

Fortunately for me, no other customers waited for her when we entered. She marched up to the counter and took up her place behind it, regarding me expectantly. "It really should be your father doing this, you know."

The floor seemed to lurch under me. I gulped. *I would give every last nugget in this benighted country if my father could be here.* I clamped down on the tears that threatened. "My father died on the way out, at South Pass."

Her censure shifted to concern. "You're on your own?"

"For the present. Yes, Ma'am."

She settled back a little. "I see." She took her pencil from her ear. "Well, we'll deal with that, later. You have assets, I assume, with which to begin."

"Assets?"

"Money." She gave a little sigh. "Gold."

"Yes, Ma'am. Of course." I pulled R. C.'s bottle of gold out of my pocket. "But may I ask a question first?"

Having begun to open her ledger, she held it as far as she got. Cautious. "I will answer it if I can."

"I was wondering if there is a way to make it harder to get into an account."

She closed the ledger slowly. "Only the person whose name is listed with the account may make withdrawals from that account." She put her pencil back behind her ear. "I can see you are in a quandary. What is your concern?"

Now I have to let the cat out of the bag, as Jacob would say. "Well, Ma'am, I'm not, strictly speaking, on my own. I have a partner. He's not here right now. As a matter of fact, I don't know where he is. And he's supposed to be in charge of the money." *If Mr. Hoyt sees my name on an account, he will declare his right as the senior partner and do as he pleases.*

"I think I know what you mean."

A slender ray of sympathy? "We need to get back home as soon as possible, but we seem to be having a hard time hanging onto the gold I find, so it's going to take longer and longer. . ." I ran out of steam.

"Out of the mouths of babes," she said, more to herself. To me she said, "Let me assure you, you are not alone in that dilemma. You might consider a joint account." When she saw my look, she said, "Have two names on the account."

I was on the scent like Bugle after a raccoon. "And as long as his name isn't on the account, he won't be able to get at it."

She almost smiled. "That's the idea." Then she got serious again. "But the drawback is, the other person named has equal access to what's in the account as you do."

I stood up a little straighter. *My friend from the wagon train.* "Hally Forsyth."

The clerk held up her hand. "My land." She reached for her pencil again. "First things first. Who are *you*?"

She didn't remember from last night. It was one of a welter of names bandied about, after all. "Bartholomew Pegg. The Pegg has two g's.

"Thank you." The clerk opened her ledger but paused again. "In this situation, you have a choice of which party you would like the account registered under."

I didn't want to waste time guessing if, by situation, she meant her ledger, or my predicament. But I knew which party it had to be. "The other one. Hally. Hally Forsyth."

The clerk opened her ledger the rest of the way, found the "F" page and bent to write. She glanced up. "F-O-R-S-Y-T-H?"

"Yes, Ma'am. I'm pretty sure."

She wrote, and looked up again. "Do you know how she spells 'Hally'? With a 'y', or with 'ie'?"

Somehow over all the miles Hally and I walked together, that had never come up. "I'm going to guess. H-A-L-L-Y."

"Forsyth, Hally and Pegg, Bartholomew." She fixed me with a stern gaze. "I assume you'll remember to ask for Forsyth when you want access this account."

"Yes, Ma'am, I will. Thank you. But you can call me Pegg."

Her frown deepened for about half a second. "You're welcome, I'm sure." She moved to the scales. "Well, let's see your color."

Now I felt back on familiar ground. I fished the bottle of gold out of my pocket. Things went briskly, indeed. I marveled at how quickly she could find the right counterweights to balance the dishes. She entered the amount in her ledger and put the gold into a waiting sack.

I breathed a sigh of relief. "Thank you, Ma'am. For everything."

At just that moment another prospector came in.

The clerk closed the ledger. "I'm only doing my job. Will there be anything else?" She put the counterweights back on the table.

"Yes, Ma'am. I was just wondering if I might trouble you to retrieve the bottles and the bag I brought the gold in—last night."

She reared back a little. "You can if you've a mind to."

I realized I had spoken carelessly. Before I could try again, she went on. "I don't have time for such niceties. They're in the trash behind the building. Help yourself. Next time—if you have a next time—you'll know to take them when I hand them to you." Her tone suggested she considered me her dimmest pupil, for stern schoolmarm she was, every inch.

I found the bottles and my scrap of canvas fairly easily since they were some of the most recent additions to a sizable trash heap. But there were a number of other bottles, tins and bags that would come in handy. These items were buried and scattered, but I had been in a scavenging frame of mind almost since leaving St. Louis. If it wasn't buffalo chips, it was firewood, or a discarded pair of shoes. I found a flour sack to carry it all in.

I was busy collecting when the express lady called from the back door. "I've made a pot of tea. Would you like a cup?"

I looked up. *Maybe the dimmest pupil. But worthy of a little hospitality.* "Yes, Ma'am. I'd like that very much."

She led me to the wrapping table and pushed aside the twine and scissors and paper trimmings. Two cups and a porcelain teapot waited for us. A thin line of steam drifted up from the spout. She sat in the chair opposite me. "I could get into serious trouble for letting you help load the packages. It's strictly against the rules." She dropped her gaze to the table. "As you have seen, in spite of my threats, Wallace doesn't give a fig for the rules." She looked up. "But I just wanted to say thank you."

I almost said, *For what?* But made do with, "You're welcome." Better safe than sorry when it came to manners.

CHAPTER 15

Rounding the corner of the express office with my bottles and tins, I pulled my jacket close. Despite being the day after Christmas, it didn't feel like winter yet. The crisp morning air felt more like fall in Vermont. If you stepped outside on December twenty-sixth in Vermont, the hairs in your nose would freeze. There'd be snow to crunch through, and icicles a foot long hanging from the eaves. Here in Auburn, the only other sign of winter was a thin skin of ice on the puddles. Heading back for R. C.'s claim, I followed the stagecoach road until it was time to cut down into the canyon.

I had a lot to mull over.

Having been kicked by the mule, I could not go back to being un-kicked. And once trust was gone, everything about Mr. Hoyt came into question.

What had changed him? True, he had never been one for stick-to-itiveness or hard work, but that was a trifle compared to the foul-tempered, unpredictable, secretive wretch he had become once he got his hands on our gold. I thought back to the times he'd snatched up every scrap of gold that came my way. He assured me he was sending money back to our families, but had he? Or had he spent it all on himself, like that fancy suit of clothes?

Now he was off to Coloma, taking our gold with—unless it was gone already. And I still had the same question. What could Mr.

Hoyt, with his broken leg, do for Mr. Brannan that would earn him wages?

It boiled down to this: I didn't know what Mr. Hoyt was doing, and he didn't know what I was doing. I didn't want to admit this partnership was in trouble, because it wasn't just me and Mr. Hoyt. It included Mr. Pruitt, who'd grubstaked Dad's idea in the first place, as well as a passel of neighbors who'd jumped in later for a share. A lot of people, not just my family, were counting on us. If Mr. Hoyt *had* been sending money back east as he said, would he continue doing the same with his earnings in Coloma? Or did Hoyt expect me to do that?

Was it worth the risk to go back to Grizzly Bar to see if any of our gold was still there? That put me to wondering when I could go back to get Bugle, and see Chen Yi, Sun Shu, and Gao Chung.

I heard the muted, hissing rumble, and a few minutes later the river came into view. I struck west, keeping an eye out for the Grandfather Oak down on the south bank.

I was still a half mile distant when I spotted the old tree. Bereft of its summer leaves, it was easier to marvel at the great, twisting tangle of arms that sprang from the massive trunk. The old tree stood at the very eastern corner of my claim. It was even more distinctive for the pale stumps of the limbs it had already given up to the miners. Which reminded me, I had to reregister Mahoney's claim in my name.

My vantage point on the north side of the canyon allowed me to see the larger pattern of a low ridge of rock that stitched its way up the southern wall of the canyon. The ridge seemed to be leading off from the base of the old Grandfather Oak.

A closer look revealed it to be two uneven ridges of rock, running side by side, separated by a narrow gap. The gap varied in width. The seam, as I came to call it, might be worth looking into sometime. But I doubted I'd be the first to do so.

As I approached the cabin, my grumbling stomach reproached me that it was dinner time. I set the bottles aside, got a fire going, and fried up some bacon. After dinner, I dug outside the cabin, in a line to the east, to see if there was more to the lead that I had found *inside*. I hauled every last speck of dirt down to the river to wash.

It was only two feet from the cabin to the edge of R. C.'s claim. Happily, my claim was right next to his, so I could keep following the lead, if I should be so fortunate.

But Dame Fortune decided it should rain. I scuttled inside to tend to chores that otherwise languished. As the drops patted on the roof and the sweet damp of wet earth seeped in, I wrote letters, washed clothes, of which I now had a goodly collection, or carved stoppers for my "new" bottles. Of course, it was the best time to fix leaks.

While so employed, I thought about the new farm we would have when I returned to Vermont. The most important requirement was that its soil be free of rocks! Even if that meant moving out of Vermont. My mom would have a nice, big house, with tall trees to shade it, and we'd have a grand barn, as big as the ones Dad and I had seen in Pennsylvania, for all our cows!

    .   .   .

During other rains, I wrote letters to Hally and added them to the stack that awaited her address. I took stock of my provisions. I had plenty of flour and salt, but I would soon need bacon and beans. I was eager to start digging on the other side of the cabin, the west side. Back in Grizzly Bar, Mr. Galloway told me a pocket of gold could be five inches long and an inch deep, or a hundred yards long and ten feet deep. And it could change from one to the other in the span of a hand, if it continued at all. Your shovel could be bringing up bare dirt inches away from a strike rich enough to dazzle a king!

I became aware of the world gone quiet. When I opened the door, the rain had turned to snow. *At last, a real winter.* But it was already melting. I promised myself I would keep working until the ground froze and the river iced over.

When the snow stopped, I got back to it. It was the same slow business on the west side of the cabin. As before, I took everything down to the river to wash. I built a fire to warm my hands and feet from the frigid water. The first five pans turned up almost a teaspoon of color. Then nothing more to the edge of R. C.'s claim. My last shovelful produced a nugget about the size of a walnut. My heart beat faster. I dug deeper in that spot and came up with a dozen more nuggets. *Is this it?*

When washed, these nuggets revealed themselves to be slightly different. They weren't as lumpy. The color, though a little lighter, had the same soft shine. I kept digging until there definitely wasn't any more of it. I couldn't wait to show R. C.

The following day I started out early. I put on four layers of shirts; one of my own and three I had found in my scavenging. I wondered if, when I walked into town, someone would call out, "Hey! That's my shirt!" Stepping outside, my footstep crunched. Frost covered everything. The sky was perfectly clear, and blue as blue could be. I tried to remember if the skies were that blue in Vermont in the winter.

In Auburn, I found R. C. in Gwynn's Dry Goods store, taking his ease with several other prospectors around a toasty-warm stove. I recognized only two. Mr. Ira Bovee, the judge from the miners' court, sat to R. C.'s left, and almost opposite, across the circle sat Mr. Osher Phelps, who had the claim next to mine, upstream.

Even the storekeeper, Isaac, was listening to the talk. But he was standing, like he could step back behind the counter if a customer came in. Which he did when I appeared. I smiled and shook my head, and when he saw me heading toward the group around the stove, he came back over. The miners' wool clothing made the bunch of them smell like wet dogs, drying by the fire. The spittoon had been missed several times. R. C. had his back to the door, and the talk didn't die down until I came up and stood by his shoulder.

He turned and broke into a grin. "Well, now, lookee here. The hermit in from the desert! How be you, Young 'un?" He didn't wait for my answer. He turned to the others. "Ladies and Gents. This here's Bartholomew Pegg. Goes by Pegg. He's lucky enough to hail from Paradise. Otherwise known as Vermont."

A couple of his companions ridiculed R. C.'s boast. A rumble of greetings came from the rest. I nodded my head and said, "Pleased to meet you." I gave an extra nod to Osher Phelps and he returned it.

Judge Bovee—it was hard to think of him any other way—gestured with a sinewy hand that looked like it was made from parchment. "Pot of passable coffee on the stove, Son, if you want some." He pointed to some cups stacked at the edge of the stove.

"Thank you, Sir. That would be welcome." As I stepped toward the stove, I gave a quick glance to the store keep. He not only nodded, but handed me a cup. When I had my coffee, I went back to stand by R. C. and relish the heat of the drink.

Judge Bovee lobbed a gob of juice at the spittoon, adding a bit more to the stain on his snow-white beard. He squinted up at me. "The cold finally chase you inside, Sonny?"

"Not exactly, Sir. I'm here to see Mr. Simpson."

One of the miners raised his eyebrows high and exclaimed, "*MISTER* Simpson?"

R. C. held up his hands. "Settle down, you sidewinders." When they did, he went on, "The boy's practicin' to be a lawyer. Count yourselves lucky to be in the presence of such fine manners."

R. C. turned to me again, grinning. "What you got there, Young 'un? Another bonanza?"

I was confused. I thought miners were supposed to keep quiet about what they found. I bent a little toward R. C. "I have something to show you."

Everybody fixed on us now.

"Well, let's have a look," R. C. said in a jolly voice.

I still hesitated. Finally, he understood. "Oh!" He swept his hand around at the circle. "Don't mind these varmints! This here's the 10,000 Dollar Club. Every man here has found at least 10,000 dollars—and lost it! 'Tomorrow's a new day!' is our motto!" He held out his hand. "Nothin' to hide here."

I handed him the cloth bag. He hefted it to show its weight. Murmurs of approval went around the circle. R. C. rested the bag on his lap and untied it. There was a stir and mumbling, even a few smiles, as R. C. pulled out the first nugget. I had put the biggest one on top. It was a little bigger than a horse chestnut. Everyone went quiet in awe. R. C. studied the nugget, turning it over, looking at it from different angles.

Finally, he said, "You'll need somethin' bigger 'n this if you're lookin' for a doorstop."

I stared at him, even more confused. He was making fun, and I didn't know why.

"Can I deposit it for you?" I said, wanting to save a little of my pride.

"Miss Lila would toss you out on your ear if you took her this passel o' rocks. I guarantee you," R. C. grinned.

Now I knew for sure something was wrong.

R. C. understood the look on my face and said, "Uh, oh. . . I'm sorry, Lad. Hasn't anybody told you about fool's gold?" Chuckling and murmuring welled up as the other miners cast glances at the nugget R. C. held. He turned to the storekeeper. "Isaac, any chance you can scare up another chair so our fellow argonaut, here, can warm his bones?" He motioned to the men on his left. "You fellas. Can you squeeze up a bit?"

Scraping chairs and muttered joshing followed. I sat in the chair Isaac had moved into the space. I felt like a dunce. I tried to remember if, indeed, anybody had ever advised me about this kind of gold. I thought back to my time with the Frenchmen at Grizzly Bar. We had never encountered such specimens. Still, I had to salvage some scrap of pride. "I've heard tell of it, but I've never seen it," I said.

He held the nugget closer to me. "Well, you're looking at it."

"Why's it called fool's gold?"

He offered back the false nugget. "Because greenhorns are fooled by it all the time, just like you were, thinking it's real gold."

I wasn't ready to give up. "And it's worth less than the other kind of gold?"

R. C. gave a little snort. "It's *worthless,* period, Son. It ain't gold at all."

I stared down at the nugget. I had dug out and washed a whole bag of nothing.

R. C. said, "Aw, now, Son. No need to be down in the dumps. It's an honest mistake. Most all of us have made it." He turned to the others. "Ain't that right, Boys?"

The miners rumbled genial agreement.

"Think of it as an initiation." R. C. clapped his hand on my shoulder. "Like crossing the equator on a ship and havin' your head swabbed with tar."

A younger man, with new whiskers darkening his jaw, across the circle, got my attention. "I found pyrites—most call it fool's gold—two weeks after I got here. Thought I'd found King Solomon's mine. Took a bag of it— about what you've got there— into Sacramento City to celebrate. I got laughed out of town." He chuckled at his own folly. Others nodded, smiling, perhaps remembering their own stories.

Ira Bovee took the nugget from me. "There's different grades of gold, Son, but like R. C. says, this ain't one of 'em." He turned the nugget a little. "Look here. The color is different. See? Not quite as rich. Less golden, you might say. Sometimes it's even a touch greenish." He looked up to see if I understood. I nodded.

He pointed with a calloused finger to fine lines and streaks on the surfaces. "And these streaks, here? Looks almost like it's been scratched? You never see those on real gold."

I kicked myself for not taking note of them before.

A big miner with a red shirt and what had once been white suspenders leaned forward and stretched out his calloused hand. "Here. Lemme see that."

Redshirt eyed me sternly. "Here's another way you tell the difference." He twisted and struck the pyrite nugget against the iron stove. A sharp, high clang sound. Sparks flew and died. He held up the nugget. "*Real* gold don't do that."

A man across from Redshirt said, "So, Jeb. You want he should lug around that there stove while he's prospectin'?"

I settled a little more at ease. Something in the way they spoke told me I was now part of their circle.

Redshirt lobbed the pyrite nugget at his heckler, who shied. The miner next to him, Osher Phelps, caught it handily. He gazed thoughtfully at the nugget in his open palm while he spoke. "There be an easier way."

He held the pyrite out to me and took a sizable gold nugget from his vest. It was easy to see the difference. He bit cautiously into his nugget, as I had seen Mr. Hoyt do. Osher held out his gold so I could see the teeth marks. "You try that with your pyrite, there, and you'll break your teeth."

The heckler had the last word. "That's if you got any left to break."

R. C. took the pyrite nugget from me and put it back in the bag. "Now you've seen it," he said gently. "Now, you know. You won't be fooled again."

His circle of friends offered agreement and encouragement, and then proceeded to pay me no more mind whatsoever, which was the surest sign of acceptance. My pride crawled out from under its rock.

R. C. smiled through his wiry whiskers. "Now, drink that 'fore it gets cold. Isaac's coffee's guaranteed to dissolve granite."

I took several gulps, then showed him the bottle with the few tablespoons of dust I had got from digging outside the cabin. "At least this is some real gold for your account." I shook the bottle to make it seem like more. "If you want, I'll deposit it. Then buy some provisions and get back."

R. C. took hold of my arm gently and wrinkled up his brow. "You're making me feel bad, Young 'un. If you must work, work on your *own* claim. I'll come out and bang around a little, so people know mine's mine. You look to your own claim now, hear?"

"Yessir. Thank you, Sir."

"*Sir, sir, sir,*" he growled, smiling. "Go on with you, then, if you insist on freezin' your fanny off."

As I headed for the door, R. C. called out, "We'll hang on to this here bag o' pyrites to pay Isaac for his coffee and hospitality."

I closed the door on rowdy laughter and headed over to the express office, vowing never to be fooled again. As I made my way up the street, I consoled myself with a small nugget of knowledge I had gained: The express office lady's name was Lila.

CHAPTER 16

While at the express office, I told Lila the story of how I got Mahoney's claim, and described where it was located on the river. "Mr. Mahoney should have come in with you to verify the transfer," she said.

"He left town, Ma'am."

"I know that. He didn't come by the office to say anything about transferring his claim."

Did he have an account to close out? "Maybe he didn't know he had to…" I didn't know what the rules were; maybe Mr. Mahoney didn't either.

"I'm afraid your word is not enough," she said, almost apologetically. "There is so much bold talk—that people take back the next day."

I was getting a little scared this wouldn't go right. "What about the miner's court? What about the race Judge Bovee set up? I won that fair and square."

Lila looked stern, but there was no hardness in it. "Have you no adult who can stand for you?"

Hope was sinking fast. "No, Ma'am." *Mr. Hoyt can go hang. Dammit. Dad should be here.* But wait! "I had a couple dozen miners standing around the finish line, which was Mr. Mahoney's claim, who'll speak for me."

It was easy to see she didn't put much store in the lawfulness of the miner's court.

"It really should have been Mr. Mahoney," said Lila. Then she sighed and gazed down at her ledgers. "I suppose it can't be helped." Then she looked up at me, frowning. "This is highly irregular. If a dispute arises, I am sure you will fight it out, or shoot it out. Just be good enough to advise me of the result."

"Yes, Ma'am."

She stepped over to a big map on the office wall. Auburn was drawn in near the top right corner, and a winding line snaked through the middle of the map. I took that to be the river. She peered close at the river line and ran her finger along the south bank the same way she ran her pencil down the pages of her ledger, then stopped, her fingertip against the map. "Is this it?"

I went up for a closer look. Hundreds of tiny squares had been drawn along both banks of the river. Each square had a number written inside it. Her finger rested under a box with the number 806. "I'm afraid I couldn't be sure, Ma'am," I said. "Mr. Mahoney didn't tell me a number. He just said I could have his claim, but that looks right. . ."

Lila dug out a different ledger from her stack, opened it and briskly ran her eyes down several pages. "Yes. 806. Mahoney. Wilford Mahoney." She took her pencil from behind her ear. "So you are claiming it?"

"Yes, Ma'am."

"Forsyth, wasn't it? What was the first name?"

I realized how complicated I had made things. "No, Ma'am…I mean, that's right for the deposits ledger. But for this one—" I tapped the edge of the claims ledger, the one she hovered over. "I'd like to use Pegg."

Lila gave a sigh. "It will be on your head, young man, to keep all these convolutions sorted out. If you get lost in your own muddle, these books will be as stone walls to you."

Before she could paint the picture any darker, I jumped in. "Yes, Ma'am. I understand."

She began to write in her book.

"That's with two g's," I said, ready for her to bite my head off.

"I remember. Thank you," she said crisply.

She slid the pencil back behind her ear. "806. Bartholomew Pegg. Congratulations, Mr. Pegg."

"Thank you, Ma'am."

I deposited R. C.'s gold without a hitch and was on my way.

I bought a side of bacon, a sack of dried beans, another of dried apples, and headed back to the river. It sure would have been nice to sit out the winter around that warm stove, telling stories. But then, I could only dream of finding the 10,000 dollars' worth of gold that would earn my place in that circle.

That evening, I stood at the edge of my claim, studying it while biscuits baked by the fire. Mr. Mahoney had worked it over pretty good. I looked out at the river. More claims crowded along the north shore.

What if all I find is fool's gold? I shook off that thought right away. If there wasn't plenty of gold around, all these people from all over the world wouldn't be here. This part of the American River was supposed to be a rich strike, so I would work my claim until it played out.

I had twelve and a half ounces of dust in the Auburn express office to keep me going. And, since I couldn't count on Mr. Hoyt to contribute anything to the pot, I would scour these hills until we could go home with everything we'd hoped for.

As soon as I stepped outside the cabin the next morning, I could see my breath in white puffs. My nostrils burned. Frost covered everything. It was cold! I went back inside and put on more shirts. I chided myself for being a sissy. California winter was nothing compared to Vermont. Even so, I regretted the heavy coat I'd left back in the desert, when Mr. Hoyt and I became back packers.

Of all the holes Mr. Mahoney had dug, the deepest was about four feet. A couple inches of water sat in the bottom of it, which did not bode well for going deeper. Of course, if I hit a pocket, I'd keep digging until it played out. I told myself I would take the part of my claim on dry land down to four feet before trying the river itself.

Often, whether digging or washing dirt, or cooking dinner, I glanced up the north slope of the canyon, hoping to see R. C. shambling down to work his claim. I even put off going out for firewood, in case I missed his visit. My wish was granted on another bright, crisp morning when I heard a shout from across the river. "Ho! The camp! Is Vermont the best place to be from? The only place?"

I stood up and faced the river and shouted back, smiling. "Yes! The only place!"

R. C. stomped right through Jock Sturgis' claim and into the water. He wore a long duster like Wallace Evans, the Stagecoach driver, wore, and had a load on his back.

I went down to the shore and watched him pick his way across the river.

How be you Young'un?" he grinned, as he stepped onto dry ground. "Coyotes ain't got you yet, looks like." He held out his hand and we shook.

"The rattlers neither," I said. "You got an early start." I helped him shrug off his pack. "I have a few biscuits still warm. And I can fry up some bacon quick enough…"

"Why, thankee kindly, Young'un. I surely won't refuse."

While the bacon fried and R. C. munched on a biscuit, I asked him for news.

"What's it been, a week and some since I seen you last?" He raked crumbs from his beard. "Well, let's see. Auburn ain't burned down, yet, even with every closet in town taken up with fools sitting out the cold." He chuckled, shaking his head.

The memory of Grizzly Bar burning struck me: a lurid nightmare of roaring, towering flames, exploding buildings, panicked shouting, choking smoke.

R. C. brought me back. "You know Jacob's gone to winter with his brother over near the Spanish Corral?"

"Yessir. I do."

He squinted into the distance and scratched at his beard. "Heard tell the other day they're starting to call it 'Ophir' now, there's so much gold over there." He popped the last of the biscuit into his mouth.

I recalled one of Linnaeus's stories. Ophir, renowned for its wealth, was a land mentioned in the Good Book, Genesis ten. The whole city was made from "stones of gold."

R. C. accepted another biscuit. "Our young Barter has taken up work as a carpenter. He's got a winning way about him, but he's a restless cuss. Only thing he's certain about is that Rattlesnake Bar will make him his fortune." R. C. snorted. "If he can ever get a claim."

I handed R. C. a plate of sizzling bacon and the other biscuit.

"Thankee kindly, Young'un. You are a prince among men." He set the plate on the ground and reached into his pack. After a bit of rummaging, he brought out a dark bottle. As soon as he opened it, I smelled molasses. He picked up his plate and proceeded to cover the biscuit and most of the bacon with the thick, brown syrup. He recapped the bottle and handed it to me.

I had grown up with a mother who prided herself on letting each flavor of her cooking hold its own. She would roll her eyes in dismay at the custom of smothering everything in the sugary brown ooze, a usage I had first witnessed at the American House in Grizzly Bar.

R. C. said, "A timely addition to your pantry, I'll warrant."

I held up my hands. "That's okay, Mr. Simpson. You'll need it for your own pantry. Thank you just the same, though."

"Ha!" R. C. cackled. He reached into his pack again. "I knew you'd say something like that." He pulled out a second bottle of molasses. "I have provided for my own pantry, thank you very much, so I'll hear no more about it."

"Yessir." I grinned and took the bottle from him. "Thank you, sir. I'll enjoy every drop."

"Think nothing of it, lawyer-man." And with that he took up the biscuit. No small amount of sticky molasses dripped into his beard.

·   ·   ·

After we had eaten, and I had asked him about Lila, the express office lady, whom R. C. declared as ornery as ever, we walked over to look at my claim. He cast an appraising eye at the hole I was digging. "Looks like you're aimin' to dig your way clear on through."

I stood next to him. "I want to be sure there's nothing left here before I start messing in the river."

He squatted to scoop up a handful of dirt and gravel, pushing at it with the ball of his thumb. "You gettin' any color for your labors?"

"Some… not much." I had to keep my hopes up. "There might be more in the river."

R. C. stood up and brushed grit from his hands, looking over my claim for another couple of minutes. A pronouncement was coming, I could tell. Without looking my way, he spoke quietly. "There comes a point when you got to move on. You ought to give that some thought. There's plenty of rivers, plenty of canyons. Despite appearances, they ain't all overrun, yet."

He meant it kindly. He wasn't pushing me; for that I was grateful. It made me realize how much I valued his friendship. "Thank you, sir. I understand. But not just yet." I scuffed at the gravel with the heel of my boot. The thought of going anywhere else smacked too much of starting over again.

From what people said, the Gold Country stretched for hundreds of miles to the north and to the south. Besides, I'd already told my mom to use Auburn as a mailing address. And if I went running off to some other river, some other canyon, how would Mr. Hoyt find me, come spring? *If,* indeed, he came back. With a wry, private smile, I had to admit that skepticism was my own; I didn't need any prompting from Will anymore.

R. C. stayed five days and worked both his claims: the one next to mine, and the one downstream, where I had first worked for him. We had the river pretty much to ourselves. When other miners did show up, if they were within hollering distance, there was always time for a palaver.

R. C. spent some of his time at my claim, washing the dirt that I dug up. When I protested, he told me to hush. Crouched over the pan, he squinted up at me. "I'm just helping you realize quicker that this claim is played out." I began to think he might be right.

He brought his own pan over, so we'd both be hunkered down, washing dirt at the same time. He was a master with the pan. He could get down to black sand in no time at all. I watched him to learn more. He brought his provisions over, too, and we cooked and ate and talked, often late into the night. I told him about Gideon MacIver and Linnaeus Peabody, but a lot of the time we talked about Vermont.

His family had moved north from Bethel, Vermont, to Irasburg when he was just a tyke. "Lost my folks when I was about your age," he said, regarding me. "Worked themselves into early graves tryin' to make a go of it." His six older brothers and sisters raised him, mostly.

He threw another stick on the fire, chuckling to himself. "My pap always said he was just lookin' for the place that growed the most rocks."

Thinking of our rock-strewn farm, I laughed so hard I almost fell over.

He asked me about my family, my mom, my sister Amy, my older brother Adam. I talked a lot about my dad, how hard he worked, how patient he was, teaching me everything he knew. How Mr. Pruitt would seek his counsel. How he could play not only his own violin but Linnaeus' banjo, too. I told about his dying. My heart swelled to bursting, but it felt good, somehow, to recollect him, and I thought maybe the healing was underway. Our gabbing used up a lot of firewood, but I didn't mind. I was glad for his company.

"Sorry to hear about your pap," R. C. said simply, but I could hear the care in his voice. I was grateful for that, too.

R. C. bellyached more about the cold each day, so I figured he would be heading back to town soon. On the afternoon of the fifth day, it rained. That decided him. We ate cold dinner in my cabin. R. C. sat on the stool, his plate perched on his knees. I sat on the bed, facing him.

"I'll be back out again," he said, swigging the last of his coffee. "To make sure the rattlers ain't carried you off." He handed me what was left of his bottle of molasses.

I knew better than to refuse it. I put his bottle on the shelf next to his gift. "Thanks. That'll come in handy. And thanks for all your help." I gave him a letter I had written to my family, in which I had included a note to Will, and asked him to mail it. Then we walked down to the river crossing and stopped at the water's edge. The low clouds brought the dark earlier. The rain had stopped, but a fine mist drifted down.

R. C. hoisted his pack on his back. "Think what I said about beatin' a dead horse with that claim of your'n, will you, lawyer-man?" This time he looked at me, almost smiling.

"Yessir. I will." I smiled back. "Don't forget to trim your whiskers so Dame Fortune will sit on your lap."

"Ha!" R. C. scoffed, waving his hand in the air dismissively as he splashed across the river.

On the other side, he stopped and turned, calling out, "Where's the best place to be from?"

I thought I'd have some fun, so I lifted my chin and called out, "Mississippi!"

"Ha!" he shouted in scorn, but with a smile, and waved his hand in farewell. I waved back and he turned to trudge up the rising ground.

I watched after him until he was lost to view. The quiet yawned wide but for the garbling river. Across the canyon the blue jays protested R. C.'s passage. I was already recalling our conversation and planning how I could respond this evening at supper. Except he wouldn't be here this evening. I turned away and walked back to the cabin, missing my crusty friend.

CHAPTER 17

With R. C.'s help, I had worked my claim down to the four feet I had planned, except at the water's edge, which I left undisturbed so I wouldn't create a swimming hole. The pit was shallower at the back side of the claim by the Grandfather Oak. Perhaps six inches of water sat in the lowest parts of the excavation.

Over the next day or two, while I washed the dirt we had dug out, I mulled over R. C.'s advice. I supposed I should heed his words, given the experience he had, but I couldn't give up here just yet. Two parts of my claim had not felt the bite of my shovel: the area around the roots of the old oak, and the portion that continued on the riverbed, out to the center of the river.

I had an instinctive reverence for that old tree. How many storms and floods had it withstood while growing into a monarch? Poking around the roots a little would do it no harm. Stepping cautiously from root to root, I imagined great, knobby fingers grasping the ground, holding the tree fast. There might be some gold trapped between them. I scraped around, hoping for the best.

Just like Mr. MacIver had warned us out on the trail, the mountain lion dropped on me as silent as a snowflake. Except this was a ninety-pound snowflake!

The cat bowled me over. We rolled down the sloping roots into the water. The cat lost his grip and fell away. I scrambled to my knees, turning, and reached for the Colt in my belt. Gone! *It must have worked loose in that first tumble.*

All teeth and claws, the cat leapt at me. Just enough time to throw my arm across my face. Teeth closed on my arm, claws stabbed my shoulders. Searing pain. His momentum bowled us over again. His jaw tightened its grip.

I went from surprise to fear to survival in a flash—drew my knees up into a ball. The cat relented for a second, searching for a way to open me up. I clamped into an even tighter ball, and got both arms over my neck. He bit my wrists where they crossed. New pain.

He was on my back now, front paws ripping, digging into my shoulders, back paws tearing my legs, teeth trying to rip my hands off my neck for the kill. I pushed off with my feet to roll us backward and get his head under water. The cat let go to save himself, but in a flash he was back on top of me.

He clawed at me everywhere, looking for purchase, but I was still in a ball. Instinctively, I denied him my belly and throat. My scalp burned like fire.

Blood ran into my eyes. I glimpsed a chance and opened up enough to jam my arm into his mouth again, this time way back, like the bit for a horse, hoping he couldn't snap it in two. At that instant I had the cat's head backed against a root. I pushed until his tongue bunched up behind my arm. He tried to squirm away, but I pinned him with my knee against his belly. That gave him new places to claw.

I got on top of the cat. With my free hand, I reached for the Bowie knife, praying the heavy blade was still in its sheath. Yes! I yanked it out and drove it into the cat's belly to the hilt. Hot blood gushed out over my hand. The cat didn't even seem to notice; he was trying to shred me bodily.

I stabbed again and again—frantic, wild stabs, angled higher up under the rib cage.

Suddenly the cat went limp, like an empty sack.

I pulled my arm free of the jaws and rolled away. I lay in the water, catching my breath. I still gripped the knife, the dead cat next to me as if we slumbered together.

I pushed myself up to my hands and knees. The pain of my cuts swarmed over me. I let loose something between a cry and a howl, reassuring myself I was alive.

It felt like a lifetime, but the fight had probably lasted little more than a minute. I washed off the blade and shoved the knife into its leather sheath, all the while thanking my Uncle Rafe for giving it to me. The water around me was the color of my mother's strawberry jam.

I had to find the gun. Couldn't leave it to rust. Still on my knees, I felt around in the water... nothing. Groping under the carcass. . .*There!* I stuffed the Colt in my belt and pushed myself to stand. Dizzy and winded, I sat right back down again in the red, muddy water. I took a few moments to let my heart stop pounding. *Up, one knee at a time.* Finally, got my feet under me again.

My trousers and the two shirts I wore hung in ribbons. My arm was mangled, and blood still ran into my eyes. My head was blood-clotted hair and cuts. Taking one last look at the cat's lifeless body, to reassure myself that I had won, I crawled out of the pit.

My body was as badly sliced up as my clothes. I staggered back to the cabin and used a blanket to wipe away the blood, but I kept bleeding. If I couldn't stop it, I'd bleed out. I'd end up dying alone in this cabin, and the dream of a new farm would die with me. What would become of my mother and sister? They might never learn of my fate.

At least they'd know what happened to Dad from Mr. Hoyt's letter. Would Hoyt take the gold I'd found home to my family? A creeping dread told me I couldn't entrust such a task to Hoyt. While I could draw breath, I would not abandon my family.

A sudden, desperate thirst seized me. The water barrel was empty. I stumbled down to the river and scooped up water in my hand. The water turned pink even as I slurped it up. I needed help.

I was in no shape to sew up my own cuts, even if I had the articles necessary. The blanket was now soaked to a dull red. I threw it aside and sacrificed one of my shirts to makes some quick bandaging with limited success.

Only one place to get help. . .can I even make it back across the river? I wrapped myself in another blanket and headed for town.

The climb out of the canyon usually took an hour or so; now it became an ordeal. I stumbled over the smallest twig, weaved and lurched into trees that weren't in my path a breath before… went to my knees more than once. But I'd remember how my father held on for so long fighting the fever that eventually took him and forced myself back to my feet.

Finally, I gained the wagon road. I pulled the blanket up over my head and held it close under my chin. Headed east toward town. . . Almost no traffic. One or two prospectors, heading west, gave me curious looks, but kept going. No time to stop and explain… *Probably quite a sight, anyway. Can't blame them for their caution.*

A wagon approached from behind, rumbling heavily, and passed, loaded with firewood. The wagon pulled ahead, but then stopped.

Another step. Just one more. I approached the wagon on the off side, the driver's side.

When I came to the front wheel, a voice floated down, familiar… "Say, aren't you Lila's help?"

Wallace Evans, the stagecoach driver, bent over, peering down at me. "You look a little roughed up, lad. Can I give you a lift?" Wallace asked.

"Thank you, Sir…" I plodded around in front of the team. They snorted and shied at the smell of blood. On the shotgun side, I reached to haul myself up. Then he was beside me, helping me onto the seat. I tugged the bloody blanket close around… shivering.

Wallace got back in his seat, slapped the reins, called to the horses. The wagon jerked into motion; he reached out and steadied me.

Once under way, he turned to look me over. "Son, you look like you took on half the Sioux nation single-handed."

"No… mountain lion."

Mr. Evans gave a low whistle. "Since you're here, I'll assume you got the better of him." He flapped the reins and urged the horses on.

"Yessir… did. Thanks to. . .Uncle Rafe." Patted my Bowie knife under the blanket.

Wallace gave me a wry grin. "I'm sure Lila Mae will thank your Uncle Rafe, too."

We went on. The jolting of the wagon was nothing compared to the burning of my cuts. *Get your mind on something else.* "You… got… firewood business… on the side?"

"Not so's you'd say." He smiled. "I'm clearing some land west of here for when I give up stagecoachin'."

"Not… going back… home?"

Mr. Evans scoffed. "'Back home' was an attic room in Cincinnati."

"Lila will miss you," I said.

He looked at me, puzzled. "I hope it don't come to that, but thanks for the thought."

We drove quiet for a while, his arm still holding me on. My vision grew fuzzy; my ears seemed plugged with cotton. I slumped into his side. The world shrank to the thump of the wagon, jangling harness, hooves beating an urgent tattoo.

.   .   .

Wallace Evans gave me a nudge. I blinked and lifted my head. We were approaching town. He gave me a stern look. "I'm takin' you over to Doc Lewis's. Get you sewed up."

"Obliged…" My voice was barely a whisper.

Wallace didn't hear, or maybe I didn't actually say it. He pulled up in front of the Shamrock Saloon and ran to the stairs on the outside of the building. I gripped the seat with one hand, and my blanket with the other. Passersby who bothered to look up stared curiously. Everything seemed so far away, cloudy, muffled—even though it was a bright afternoon.

Is this how death closes in? There was blood all over the seat, my hands. *Is this it? Don't get to say goodbye to anybody?*

The big coach driver reappeared on my side of the wagon, a worried look on his face. He glanced up and down the street. "Doc Lewis's over in Spanish Corral, cleanin' up after a brawl." Wallace looked around again as if hoping a solution might appear, then he squinted up at me. "Ain't another sawbones in thirty miles, but you need tendin' to."

He started walking around to the driver's side. "I heard tell of a fellow up the street patches people up sometimes, those willin' to trust him. That's all we've got—that I know of. If you've got no objections, we'd better look him up before you bleed out." He climbed back up and urged the team to turn the groaning wagon. I could barely hang on… Wallace reached out, kept me aboard.

I assumed we had come to Auburn; the buildings looked familiar, but they were leaning, twisting, as if to deny our acquaintance. My eyelids kept dragging down, wanting rest. The wagon stopped again. I opened my eyes to find we had come into China town. We had pulled up in front of a store that announced itself as Sam Lee's Laundry.

Wallace hopped down and ran inside. I closed my eyes again to save my strength. A few minutes later, he came out, bringing Chen Yi with him.

Chen Yi?

I blinked a couple of times to clear my head. Chen Yi was in Grizzly Bar… had a restaurant before the fire… he let go a burst of Chinese. I had never heard the older gentleman shout before. It sure sounded like Chen Yi: more trickery of an addled mind…They were rebuilding after the fire. Sun Shu had Bugle, was waiting for Yang Ho to get back from San Francisco with supplies to rebuild their store in Grizzly Bar, not Auburn!

Wallace climbed up and handed me down to Gao Chung, who had magically appeared at Chen Yi's side. We hustled inside the store, Chen Yi shouting Chinese instructions as he went.

We went through several rooms, each smaller than the one before, until Gao Chung settled me in a real bed in the last room and disappeared as simply as he had appeared. All I wanted to do was sleep. I heard Wallace ask if he could be of any help, and Chen Yi say in a calmer voice, "Maybe. Wait, please."

I heard Chen Yi talking to someone in his own language in another room. I looked over at the stagecoach driver: a big, flamboyant man trying to make himself inconspicuous in a small room. I sent a silent thanks to him.

Next thing, Sun Shu leaned over me, frowning. *More magical appearances.* I tried to speak to her. "What. . .?"

"Hush," she scolded gently.

I was surely confused. But I couldn't remember the last time I'd been so glad to see somebody.

From inside her sleeve Sun Shu pulled her wicked-looking knife and started slicing my clothes off me. The drying blood had stuck some of the shreds to me, but she didn't let that stop her. She ripped away the stiff ribbons without a hint of mercy. The first one made me screech, but after that I gritted my teeth.

Sun Shu glanced over her shoulder, shouting something at the top of her voice. Gao Chung burst into the room. She fired some instructions at him, and he disappeared as quickly. A minute later, he came back with a steaming bowl of hot water, and a minute after that, he returned with an armload of clean cloths.

Sun Shu looked me over. There wasn't much of me that wasn't carved up good, but my head and my bottom were the worst: they had stuck out the most. She spent a lot of time inspecting the top of my head.

Wallace, hovering in the corner, spoke in a low voice. "Anything I can do, Miss?"

At first, Sun Shu ignored him. She touched my shoulder and leaned closer to me. "Can you turn over?" While I struggled to turn over, she answered Wallace, "Outside. The tub at the far end of the yard, the smallest tub. Can you stir it? Then put out the fires under all the tubs. I would appreciate it." Without waiting for his response, she returned to her work.

"Yes, Ma'am." Wallace Evans's voice was full of concern.

"Thank you," Sun Shu replied, slicing away at my clothing.

Sun Shu had to wash out all the cuts and gouges, and it burned like crazy. Gao Chung kept bringing in fresh bowls of hot water, and more clean cloths. He carried out armloads of the bloodied ones. I couldn't see much with my cheek half-buried in the pillow, but it sure looked like a lot of my blood was leaving on those towels. Added to what I was sure I'd already lost, they needed to sew me up quick or I'd drain dry.

Chen Yi came in with a wooden chest and opened it. Chen Yi and Sun Shu spoke quietly to each other. I couldn't understand their words, but I could sure hear the tense urgency in their speech. Chen Yi fished out a couple of bottles and set to mixing up a vile-smelling concoction. Somewhere in all the commotion, Bugle dashed into the room, over to the bed, and put his paws up on the bed frame, whining and wagging his tail. Almost as quickly, a pair of hands scooped him away.

"Bugle!" I wanted it to be a shout, but could only manage a mutter. Sun Shu gently pressed my shoulder when I tried to rise. If my Celestial friends were here, it stood to reason that Bugle would be with them—I had left him with Sun Shu, but it certified that I was not dreaming.

Bugle was smart enough to stay out of the way, but I saw him looking at me. I blinked at him, it was all I could manage, and he whined.

Wallace Evans came back from his chore and brought R. C. Simpson with him. "Sweet Jesus!" I heard R. C. gasp.

Sun Shu shot back, "No blasphemy, please."

The little room steamed up with tension.

But R. C. wasn't muzzled. "Did you do battle with Lucifer himself, Young'un?" His voice was scolding but that didn't hide his concern.

Wallace offered, "Fires're out, Ma'am. I see things are well in hand. Mr. Simpson here, has offered his assistance. I'll be gettin' back to my wagon if you don't require anything more of me."

"Thank you," replied Sun Shu distractedly, without turning away from her inspection.

Wallace stepped closer but didn't disrupt the doctoring. "Miss Lila Mae is going to want to know why you aren't comin' 'round. She'll have my hide if she learns I knew and didn't tell her." He chuckled like he looked forward to that confrontation. "If it's all right, I'll apprise her of your situation."

I managed a small nod. I guess it was enough.

The coach driver and the crusty miner held a muttered exchange. Then I heard boots scrape the floorboards and the door open and close.

As soon as Sun Shu finished washing my wounds, Chen Yi followed up with his rank concoction. It took three or four batches of the stuff to apply to all my cuts. He slathered an extra helping on my chewed-up arm, and then they wrapped it in clean cloths. They both got to work, sewing up the deeper cuts with needles and thread. The pain of that finally convinced me I was in a bad way.

R. C. held a lantern close to their work.

Sun Shu and Chen Yi spent a good while patching up my scalp. There was no way to be gentle. It proved too much for me. I dropped into a black pit of nothing.

When I came to myself again, they had finished. My whole body felt like it was on fire. Sun Shu laid a couple of blankets over me and put her hand on my forehead. "There will be some fever. We must watch closely for infection."

Gao Chung brought in food. I had to lie on my stomach. Sun Shu pulled up a chair and fed me soup with a spoon. I heard R. C. say, "Might I trouble you for a fork?"

Floorboards creaked, doors opened and closed and opened. "Thankee kindly," said R. C. with genuine gratitude.

After we ate, Sun Shu propped me up while Chen Yi helped me drink a cup of tea. "I add potion help you sleep," he said.

Whatever he had added to the tea worked. I was pleasantly groggy in no time at all. The sharpest of the pain dulled. Through my haze, I heard Sun Shu urging everyone out of the room, and saw her come over to sit in the chair close to the bed.

"Sorry. . ." I mumbled, ". . .trouble. . . you. . ."

Sun Shu leaned forward and touched two fingers to my lips.

I managed, ". . .Beautiful. . .pirate. . ." Then, I slept.

CHAPTER 18

I felt as helpless as a newborn babe, drifting in and out of sleep, which Sun Shu pronounced as what the healing body needed most. I was happy to sleep while the pain of being sliced up in so many places slowly ebbed. I couldn't say how much time passed while I was under the spell of Chen Yi's wonderful tea. Each time I woke up, I looked to the window. It would be morning, night, twilight, midday, all mixed up, willy nilly.

Bugle was always at the foot of the bed. When he saw I was awake, he'd lift his head, grin, and thump his tail on the bed covers. Often, Sun Shu would be sitting in the chair, sometimes with a bowl of soup, or leaning over me, inspecting my wounds. When she changed my bandages, she had Gao Chung standing by to lift me and turn me. I hated being so helpless.

I woke one time feeling like I was burning up. *This must be the fever.* The feeling was worse than any heat I had endured while crossing in the desert. My head felt crammed to bursting with hot stones.

This time I was alone. Someone had moved the chair closer to the bed and left a cup of water on the seat. I reached for it and knocked the cup over. Sun Shu came in and picked it up. *How did she know? Did she hear?* She came back with a full cup and helped me drink, then stayed until I slept.

The next time I came around, I was still roasting alive. Sun Shu was applying more salve and new bandages. She looked worried. Chen Yi stood at her shoulder, looking more serious than I had ever seen him. R. C. Simpson peered over Chen Yi's shoulder. I slipped under again, worried about their worrying.

I never knew who would be sitting in the chair. Chen Yi, R. C., Sun Shu, Richard.

.   .   .

When I woke again, the window was dark. The lamplight showed raindrops sliding their crooked way down the glass. Sun Shu knelt at the side of the bed. At first, I thought she was inspecting my bandages, but her eyes were closed and her graceful fingers steepled together in front of her. I must have moved; she opened her eyes and saw me looking at her and scrambled up into the chair. But I was already drifting off again.

I spent most of my time lying on my belly since the majority of my cuts were on my back and head. One of the few times Sun Shu let me lie on my back, I had a look around. I was in a small bed in a sparsely furnished room made with peeled logs. It featured a window and a door to the other rooms, the door through which Sun Shu came and went. A small packing crate served as a bedside stand. The chair sat close to the bed.

There came a blessed day when the hot stones were gone from my head. I still hurt, but not nearly as much. The chair was presently empty. I speculated on who would come through the door next. The winner was Sun Shu. She held a tray with a cup and a folded cloth.

"Good morning, Sunshine," I croaked. My dad said that to my mom all the time. Sun Shu looked up in surprise and smiled. Setting the tray on the chair, she laid her hand on my forehead and closed her eyes. When she opened them, she smiled. "The fever has broken. Heaven be praised."

"Heaven and you," I added.

She smiled more and then frowned. "You have the strength to be sacrilegious. For once, that is a good sign."

"Well, I'm sure the good Lord appreciated your help. I know I did."

Sun Shu was not mollified. She ran her hands over the sheets, all business. "These sheets are soaked. The fever must have broken during the early hours."

She made me sit in the chair, wrapped in a blanket, while she changed the bed. I was feeling my oats and got up to help tuck in one of the sheets.

Sun Shu gave me a fierce look, then pointed stiff-armed to the chair. Boss nurse. I scuttled meekly back to my seat.

Chen Yi brought in a bean cake on a plate and handed it to me. "To celebrate. You back in land of the living."

My mouth watered, and I knew that meant I was getting better. In between mouthfuls, I asked him, "How come you are in Auburn?"

Chen Yi made a scoffing sound. "Grizzly Bar burn down again. Time change luck with feet."

"When did that happen?"

Chen Yi shook his head, smiling apologetically. "Sun Shu say. Chen Yi English not enough for it." A bell chimed and I heard a door open followed by some steps. "Customers." Chen Yi nodded at the bean cake as he made for the door. "Eat now. Get better."

When he was gone, I looked to Sun Shu. "Will you tell me the rest of what happened?"

"I must change those bandages," she insisted.

While I savored the bean cake, she changed the bandages. Nobody had ever taken such liberties with my person before, except my mother, and that was when I was a tyke. The wounds I could see were still angry red, but were closed up. My arm wasn't pretty to look at, but at least it was still there.

Questions backed up in my head like a log jam in a river: *Was the fire as bad as the one I was in with them? The whole town went that time. Did she and her husband, Yang Ho, get their store rebuilt before the next fire? Did Chen Yi build a bigger restaurant? What became of the Frenchmen, Ormond and his friends?*

"It happened so fast. It was the third fire in the space of a year. You remember the terrible confusion. This time. . .without you or Yang Ho to help, I couldn't save much."

I forgot my manners completely. "Yang Ho wasn't there?" *Wasn't he back from San Francisco, yet?* Sun Shu and I had waited weeks for Yang Ho to return with supplies and men to help rebuild the restaurant and their store. "What about the helpers he was going to bring back?"

I sank back and drew the covers around me. "I'm sorry. I spoke out of turn."

Sun Shu leaned forward and fussed with the bandages. "I know you must have many questions. I have many myself." She settled back, her hands coming to rest on her lap. "Without your company, I felt Yang Ho's absence much more keenly. As the weeks went by, I did not show my worry, but Uncle Chen knows me too well. He wrote a letter to a relative who had a trading house in San Francisco." She brought her hands together. "So, then I had two things to pray for, Yang Ho's return, and the letter."

Sun Shu looked up and smiled, as if she was grateful for something. "When no word came back from his relative, Uncle Chen sent Gao Chung to look for him. I took Gao Chung's place cooking while he went to San Francisco. I prayed every night that Gao Chung would find him. But the Chinese community there was in a terrible uproar. A tong war had been going on for months. Many had died or were missing. Gao Chung barely escaped with his life."

"And he didn't find Yang Ho."

"No." She barely whispered. "Gao Chung came back saying no one knew of Yang Ho. Also, he discovered that the relative we had first written to had gone back to China. It felt as though our ancestors had turned away from us. Then the fire came."

She seemed to slump a little. After a pause, she went on. "In truth, there wasn't very much to save. I sold what little remained, and we moved here. Uncle Chen lost everything, too, except for some gold he had hidden under his bed. He thought it would be good to try a new place."

I thought about Gao Chung carrying me into the laundry regardless of my bleeding all over him. "And Gao Chung, too."

"Gao Chung, too." She tried hiding her smile again. "We are limpets to Chen Yi's rock."

"That's good. I mean, that he's here, not that he's a limpet."

Sun Shu rocked back in the chair. "So, now you know why we are here."

"Well," I said, "I'm sure glad you are."

"We will see. Uncle Chen is already gaining respect in the Celestial community."

I burst forth with the one question that crowded out all others. "So, in all this time you've had no word from Yang Ho?"

I thought of my mother. Of her waiting for months with no word from her husband. Of her hoping and praying. . . not knowing. . .

Sun Shu was quiet for a moment, then she raised her head. "Even after we got here, Uncle Chen arranged for notices about Yang Ho to be placed in all the San Francisco newspapers. He wrote another letter, this time to the leader of his tong. That man wrote back, saying that he could find no one of that name in San Francisco."

Sun Shu straightened, summoning her resolve. "But he will come back. I know it. I pray for it..."

.   .   .

The fever passed and the danger of infection with it. The fourth day after the fever had broken, I made the most desperate face I could.

"I'm almost as good as new. Please. I can do easy things: Get to the outhouse and back, fold clothes, keep Gao Chung's irons filled with coals…"

Sun Shu was unmoved. She handed me a bowl of soup with plump wontons in it. "If you go jumping around, many of your cuts will open again. The healing is not strong enough yet."

.   .   .

The view outside my window told me it was a sunny afternoon when Lila surprised me with a visit. "I thought you could use something to read during your recovery." She hesitated. "I assumed since you have dropped off letters at my office, you know how to read."

"Yes, Ma'am. And thank you for coming to visit." I pointed to the chair by the bed, imagining what my mom would say. "Please, Ma'am. Have a seat."

Her eyes darted around the tiny room, which was bare to the bone. The only grace note was supplied by a small, framed daguerreotype image of Sun Shu and her husband, Yang Ho, on the bedside stand.

Lila probably had a nicer room, maybe even with curtains and such. I couldn't tell what judgement Lila reached, but Sun Shu's room, not to mention the care that came with it, was a Heaven-sent palace to me. Lila obviously wanted to ask how I'd come to stay with Celestials, but refrained. Instead, she said, "I can't stay," and offered me the slim volume. "It's poetry. Alfred, Lord Tennyson. Have you heard of him?"

I accepted her gift, feeling very smug. My mother had read some of the man's poems to our family on Sunday evenings. "Yes, Ma'am. I have."

"This is his best, so far. It has a much-improved version of 'Lady of Shalott.'"

I was on the point of asking Lila about the Lady of Shalott, when there came a soft tapping at the door. "Come in?"

Chen Yi opened the door just enough to peer in. "Busy boy. More visitor."

I could make out R. C.'s whiskers and floppy hat in the dim light of the work room. He stood behind Chen Yi, impatiently trying to see into the room. Lila turned toward the door, then back to me. "I'll say good day."

Chen Yi opened the door farther and R. C. sidled by him into the sick room while Lila slipped out past them.

"No long stay," Chen Yi decreed to R. C. in his sternest voice. "Pegg-son still wobbly, like Xinsheng."

R. C. gave him a mock salute. "Whatever that means. Aye, aye, Sir."

Chen Yi closed the door.

I was glad, for the women's sake, that my cantankerous friend dressed in more than his usual long johns when he came to town. He crooked his eyebrows at me in a mocking way. "Glad to see you're back to bein' in one piece, Young'un."

I smiled at him. "And you, R. C. What have you got there behind your back?" It looked like a rolled-up blanket. I leaned to get a better look.

R. C. wrinkled his brow, reprovingly. "Now, is that how your momma taught you?" He was half smiling, like he had something up his sleeve. "The presumption." R. C. huffed. "I declare." He stepped forward. He made me close my eyes while he made his presentation.

I felt something soft and limp, but with some weight, land in my lap. I looked down at an animal skin lying in my lap. In the next blink, I was sure it was a cougar skin. *It's my cougar's skin.* In all the times I'd thought over the encounter, the cat had gotten bigger and bigger in my mind. What lay in my lap seemed too small.

I gave R. C. a big grin. He gave me a short nod, and I went back to running my hand back and forth across the thick fur.

Bugle sniffed at it, adding a low grumble.

I spread out the tail. *Had I bested this beast?* The pelt was in perfect condition, the hide on the underside soft and pliable. It had been expertly tanned.

R. C. pointed at the edges of the pelt. "Sorry it's a little ragged along the edges, there. You carved up his belly pretty good, gettin' the upper hand."

Bugle barked at the pelt, quivering with excitement. I held it up by a front leg and a hind leg, showing off the tawny pelage. "See what I'm talking about, Boy?" I said to him. "He would have made mincemeat out of you."

Bugle barked like he was ready to take him on.

"He came close to makin' the same outta *you*, lawyer-man," R. C. chortled.

A surge of dread coursed through me, but I kept my head down, lest R. C. see my fear. "Thank you, sir. This is a lot of work. You did a beautiful job. Thank you." I went back to admiring the pelt.

"You're welcome," R. C. said, pleased. Then his voice turned serious. "You're lucky, you know."

I knew to pay special attention to that tone of voice. "I know."

"Maybe you do. But this here's a young'un…" R. C. nodded at the pelt "…just like yourself. If it'd been his Mam or his Pap waitin' for you up in that tree, you'd likely not be sittin' here, feeling lucky." He dug into his pocket and tossed a gold coin onto the pelt.

I eyed the large coin, bemused. "What's that for?"

"Sold the teeth to an Injun." He stretched out his long skinny legs, crossing them at the ankle.

At that juncture, Gao Chung appeared with tea and moon cakes. I showed R. C. how to work the lid on the tea cup. It took no effort at all for him to like the moon cakes. Chen Yi came in with napkins. Only I knew why he was beaming with satisfaction. Even with only one guest, Chen Yi wanted to make sure everyone was well-taken care of. He made sure all our cups were full before he left.

Once my visit with R. C. was over, I started reading the book Lila had been so kind as to bring me, but found myself too tired. Pretty soon, Sun Shu brought in a cup of Chen Yi's special tea. I took a whiff. "It smells different."

"It will help build your strength," she said firmly. "Drink."

I studied Sun Shu over the rim of the cup while I sipped the tea. Back in Grizzly Bar she had been the embodiment of deference and humility. Here her gaze was steady, and she spoke with the assuredness of a straw boss.

"Are you Sun Shu's tough twin sister?" I said, after a sip.

Sun Shu looked very confused. Her face worked to find an expression. The stern nurse gave way to the Sun Shu of former days. "I am sorry. I do not understand. I do not have a twin sister…"

I kicked myself for confusing her. "No, no. It was a joke. I'm sorry. I didn't mean anything."

"What is the joke?" she said in the trusting voice I knew.

Now I really felt like a dunce. "You have been taking very good care of me. I know that. And I thank you for it. But you have been like a stern schoolteacher, or a mother. I've never seen you boss people around. It's almost like you are a different person. So that's why I said you were a twin sister."

She smiled and raised her fingers to cover her lips. "Now I understand. Thank you."

That was the Sun Shu I remembered.

"Is that why you say 'tough'? Because I have been bossy?" She looked down. "This is a new meaning for me."

"Yes. I haven't seen you be that way before."

She smiled behind her hand again. "That is because we are not married, Honorable Pegg."

I heard hope in her words, but despair in her voice. Her husband was supposed to be gone a week—most of three months had now elapsed.

I wished I could fix it for her. Mr. Hoyt had disappeared on me, too. He was supposed to be watching out for me. We were supposed to be partners, but he just took off. "I think I know how you feel."

Her eyes were shiny. She blinked a couple of times and wiped her fingers across her eyes. "You are thinking of Mr. Hoyt?"

"Yes, Ma'am."

"I remember the night of your escape from Grizzly Bar." looked out the window again before turning back to me. "May I speak, Honorable Pegg?"

This was the Sun Shu I was used to, modest as the day is long. "Yes, Ma'am. Please," I said.

"The *Gum Shan*—that's our way of saying 'the Gold Mountain', meaning here, California—the Gum Shan shows many men to themselves. . .shows them things about themselves perhaps they did not even know."

I must have looked puzzled because she began again. "I am sorry. Yang Ho says I must learn, in America, to come to the point. Forgive me. I will try again."

I nodded. I just liked to hear her talk.

"Gold changes people. Some people throw it away as soon as they come into possession of it. That is especially true here, now, when people convince themselves that they will find as much gold tomorrow as they found today."

"But isn't hope a good thing to have?" *My dad had a saying, "Have faith in tomorrow, but work hard today."*

Sun Shu thought before she spoke again. "Yes. It is. But it is hard to build a future if you are starting over every day."

That's what I'd felt like ever since Dad died and left Mr. Hoyt in charge of the partnership. "You mean like having to start over after every fire?"

She shook her head with pursed lips, making fists in her lap. "Pegg, I must tell you something very directly." She was almost whispering. "And I am not happy to do it. You may hate me, and I will bear it. But I must say this. The ancestors insist."

CHAPTER 19

Sun Shu sat primly in the chair, looking at her hands in her lap. "I have not seen this myself, but someone I trust has, so I tell it to you." She looked up and took a breath. "Mr. Hoyt threw away your gold."

I stared at her. "What?" Fear hollowed out my stomach. "How do you know?"

"In Grizzly Bar. After cooking, Gao Chung worked also in the saloons and gambling houses, in the small hours of the morning. He emptied spittoons, swept floors, repaired furniture. . . anything they wanted him to do. Gao Chung saw Mr. Hoyt many times in those places. Mr. Hoyt stayed on when few others were still awake. He was always playing cards or buying people drinks."

I swallowed hard. "And he lost." It should have been a question, but my bones told me differently.

Sun Shu laid a length of dusty, battered cloth on the covers. "Gao Chung insisted I give this to you so you would believe his story." It was the arm of the long johns she had fashioned to carry my gold, still knotted at the cuff end, the shoulder end ragged where she had made the cut." Do you remember this from your time with Monsieur Bonnet and his friends?"

I nodded. Prospecting Simpson's Creek with the Frenchmen seemed a lifetime ago, but it was only a few months back. I ran my hand over the remnant. Despair and anger consumed me in equal measure at my partner's perfidy.

"Gao Chung brought it to me. He saw Mr. Hoyt lose most of the nuggets from it, then throw the bag on the floor."

So the gold I found with the Frenchmen, though not lost in the fire, was lost just the same. It wasn't a great leap of imagination to surmise that the bags of gold dust I had received at American House in Grizzly Bar, or singing "Amazing Grace" here, on Rattlesnake Bar, had met similar fates. Had Hoyt sent *any* of it home?

"I am sorry to tell you this, Pegg," Sun Shu said quietly. "But Gao Chung knows the fever of gambling. He has suffered it himself in the past. He says he saw that fever in Mr. Hoyt."

I sat on the bed, staring at nothing, my mind whirling.

"Rest now," Sun Shu said, almost pleading. "You are getting better. You must not let worry imperil that." She rose from the chair and left the room.

I didn't rest. I couldn't. If Mr. Hoyt had not been sending money to help them through the winter, how would my family manage?

While there was no longer a reason to go back to Grizzly Bar, there was the imminent return of my supposed partner to worry about. I had to start planning for that. I sure didn't want to just keep giving him gold as if everything was all right.

Would it do any good to write Mr. Pruitt? What could he do from Vermont?

No. First, I had prove Mr. Hoyt was still squandering the partnership's gold. There was no reason to doubt Sun Shu or Gao Chung, but this was a very serious matter.

I wrote a letter home reassuring my mom that I was eating well and getting plenty of rest. Making no mention of my concern about Mr. Hoyt, much less my run-in with the mountain lion. But I did ask if she had received money from Hoyt. I told her I hoped to be sending more soon myself. When Richard visited, he agreed to mail it.

Once or twice, Richard and R. C. arrived together. Despite Sun Shu's insistence on a quiet visit, the room soon rattled with laughter. When Bugle added his bark to the general hilarity, Sun Shu reappeared, scowling, and my visitors recalled errands that needed their immediate attention.

The morning after one such lively visit, Sun Shu announced I could get out of bed and get dressed. She brought in clothes for me. Her face was flushed, her arms red from the hot water and harsh soaps of the laundry tubs. She had a bandana tied across her forehead, looking like a pirate again. I remembered seeing her marching along the bank of Simpson's Creek. That time she had a wide red sash around her waist, with my old Navy Colt thrust through it. Her loose tunic and trousers flapping to her stride had lent her a jaunty air.

"There is soup and noodles on the table." She paused at the door. "Visit the laundry room when you are finished, if you'd like. Uncle Chen will be happy to see you up. Then back to bed."

I felt like she had given me the keys to the kingdom. "Yes, Ma'am." I smiled and gave her a salute.

Getting dressed winded me. Bugle waited by the door, looking back eagerly, as if he knew it was time to go out. I sat down on the edge of the bed to catch my breath. He came and sat by my feet. As I bent to give him a scratch, I realized how much strength I had to regain before I could go back to my claim.

In the center of the next room, a bowl and a set of chopsticks sat on a small table. This room wasn't much bigger than the one I had been occupying and was almost as bare. Two simple beds were placed snug against opposite walls. A few barrels and boxes served as furniture, grouped around the table. Small open crates serving as shelves held folded clothes and a few personal possessions. The only distinctive feature of this room was a small shrine, affixed to one wall, draped in red cloth. It was not much bigger than a birdhouse, dedicated to the ancestors. I now understood the setup. I was lodged in Sun Shu's room, and the room I had stepped into was their living quarters, as well as Chen Yi's and Gao Chung's bedroom.

The bowl held steaming broth and fat noodles, "winter noodles," Chen Yi said when I had first tasted them. Floating on top was a slice of pork, slices of hard-boiled egg, and a sprinkling of chopped onion. I didn't leave a drop, not a scrap.

I opened the door to the next room—what Sun Shu had called the laundry room. The musty smell of damp wool and the toasty warmth of ironed clothes filled the moist air. This room was the largest so far, and the warmest. It was a welter of clothes, hanging, piled, folded on tables. I had never seen so many clothes in one place.

I stood a moment, trying to make sense of it. Gao Chung was hunched over a big, padded table, ironing a shirt with the same fierce concentration he had applied to his cooking in Grizzly Bar. A second padded table also seemed to be for ironing, while a third, smaller table in the corner seemed by its implements devoted to sewing and mending.

Another door, along the south wall to my left, let out to the side yard where Sun Shu worked. Straight ahead, across the room, an open doorway admitted lots of light into the room I was in. That could only mean the room beyond was the front of the store. Resounding voices, Chen Yi's and another man's, cinched it for me. Then, after the sound of a small bell and a door opening and closing, Chen Yi hustled into the laundry room.

"Ah, so, Pegg-son! You come back world!" he said.

I smiled. "Yessir."

At the second ironing table, he checked the little metal box that held coals to heat the iron. Testing the iron, he took up a sprinkling bottle and shook it over a shirt.

Chen Yi ironed with sure, fluid movements, like he had been born to it. Sun Shu had told me about his life back in China: a wealthy merchant with a large family, and probably a large, well-staffed house, who took delight in entertaining his friends with grand feasts. Now here he was, in a rowdy little claptrap gold camp, ironing shirts. Did he pine for his life back in China?

"Sun Shu say you visit." He pointed to the side door. "Fresh air do good." He pointed to a jacket hanging by that door. "She say, you must jacket."

Bugle already stood at the door. I dutifully put on the jacket and went out into the workyard. It seemed like a 'coon's age since I'd been outside for anything but visiting the outhouse. Bugle ran over to Sun Shu for a pat, and then scampered off, exploring. I waved to Sun Shu but stood close to the door, not wishing to disturb her work. She gave me a quick wave back.

Sun Shu's workyard made use of the whole space between their building and the next. The yard opened onto the street at its east end and then dropped off at the west end. In this space, seven tubs sat in two rows of three, with the last tub by itself near the drop-off. At the bottom of the drop-off I spied a small stream. Surprisingly, nobody seemed to be working it.

Each tub rested atop a circle of stones, which had an opening to add fuel. They all had fires going under the tubs. Half the tubs were for washing, judging by the suds and the scum, half for rinsing. Sun Shu moved briskly among the tubs. Tucked against the wall of their building sat six large barrels of water. *They must refill them at least two times a day, maybe more.* Sure enough, two wooden buckets and a yoke sat obediently by the big barrels.

It felt good to have the sun full on my face. The clatter and shout of the town going about its business drifted around the corner. Much as I reveled in the sun, it was without warmth, and soon the chill found its way past my jacket. I shivered and hugged my arms around me.

Sun Shu, the hawkeyed nurse, saw it, and pointed straight-armed to the laundry building with a scowl. I called to Bugle and obediently scuttled inside.

I was under the covers, warm and grateful for it, when she looked into the sick room a while later. "You are making good progress. Please don't jeopardize it."

"Yes, Ma'am—I mean, no, Ma'am."

.   .   .

The following morning, I was sitting up in bed, planning our new farm with Bugle, when Chen Yi came in from the ironing room with a visitor. I blinked in surprise. It was Lila back for another visit.

"Lady insist see you her own," Chen Yi said in a formal voice. "I stay?"

Lila was standing very stiffly, her elbows pressed to her sides.

"No. No," I said. "Thank you, Chen Yi. That's not necessary. It's fine."

"I have Gao Chung bring tea," he said.

"Oh. Please!" said Lila. "Don't go to any trouble. I'll only be staying a moment."

"Thank you, anyway, Chen Yi," I said.

Chen Yi left us.

Lila watched him out of the corner of her eye. When the door closed, she looked at me with great concern. "It's none of my business. But I didn't get a chance to ask last time: How in Heaven's name have you come to be here?"

I thought, *Where else could I be?* "They're friends from Grizzly Bar. Chen Yi had a restaurant there. Sun Shu is his daughter, or maybe stepdaughter. They've been very good to me. I'd probably be dead by now if not for them taking care of me. And Wallace, too. He helped me get here."

"Yes. He told me. It was horrible. It's a miracle you are alive." She gave a sad smile, looking me over as carefully as decorum allowed. Her concern grew apace.

I suddenly appreciated the side of that coin: Sun Shu and Chen Yi, and even Gao Chung, despite the apparent grievousness of my wounds, had tended to me with sober efficiency, as if my full and complete recovery was never in doubt. Scars, and even disfigurement, were to be seen as badges of survival.

I tilted my head at my visitor. "Gonna have a job combin' my hair into something decent."

Lila let out a bleat of dismay. She started to speak, stopped, tried again. "You are too young to bear such terrible wounds."

"Richard says it'll make a great story for the grandkids." I added a grin, hoping to lighten the mood.

Lila pressed her lips to a thin line. "First, you must live long enough to have children."

"Yes, Ma'am. Richard doesn't mean any harm. He just tries to keep on the sunny side."

"You might think about saying a prayer of thanks for your deliverance."

"Oh, I have, Ma'am. Believe me, I have." It struck me she was still standing where Chen Yi had left her. "Please, Ma'am. Come have a seat." I pointed to the chair by the bed.

Lila perched on the edge of the chair. "But they're Chinese." Her eyes darted around the room.

"Who?" I looked at her, not entirely innocently.

She gave a half-hearted wave to include the immediate vicinity.

"Oh. Chen Yi and all." *What else to say to the obvious?* I determined to turn the conversation in a more cordial direction. "Have you ever tasted Chinese food? Pork with black bean sauce? Egg foo young? They have these things called noodles…"

Lila broke in. "My sister is married to a Wop." She stopped, pressing her lips into a thin lime. "I mean, an Italian. I know what noodles are."

"Aren't they good?"

"The Italians call them pasta." She gave a short nod. "But yes, they are." She looked down, fidgeting with what she held in her hands. "A letter arrived for you last night. I thought you might want it without delay."

This was 'highly irregular,' to use Lila's own words. Express agents weren't expected to deliver letters. Miners were supposed to come to the office to collect their mail.

She handed me the letter.

I accepted her unexpected gift. "Thank you, Ma'am. That's very thoughtful of you." The surface of the envelope was badly abraded, but I could just make out the distinctive strokes of my mother's hand. "Excuse me, Ma'am. This is my first letter from home. I've been waiting for this for a long time."

Lila lifted her chin proudly. "Well, I'll leave you to it." She rose to go.

"Oh. Don't go. I'll read this and then we can visit." That outburst caught me by surprise. Without rhyme or reason, I found this lady's manner deeply comforting. There was an honesty about her that drew me like a magnet. Even when she was being stern, I could tell its well-spring was worthy.

She hesitated. "I don't want to intrude." But then sat back down, stern-faced as ever.

I smiled at her and turned my attention to the battered envelope. It read, "Bartholomew Pegg, General Delivery, Auburn, California." I opened it as it if were a fragile treasure.

My dearest, darling Barti,

Your first letter from California arrived today, and I must respond without delay. You cannot imagine the joy with which we received it. Your last was from Fort Laramie these months past, and having heard nothing since, we have been frantic with worry. We miss you so very, very much.

What happened to Hoyt's letter to her about Dad's passing?

Mr. Pruitt has visited with kind-hearted constancy. He always asks if we have had any word. I finally confessed to him that we have received nothing since Fort Laramie. He revealed, with some despondency, that he has received nothing whatsoever from his stepson, Fred Hoyt, from the outset. He said that his only correspondence was from your father, the last of which also came from Fort Laramie.

HOYT HAD DONE NOTHING! He had not written to my mother about my father's death after all! He hadn't sent money home! Her skepticism about him had been right all along.

Now we know the unbelievable, unbearable truth of why we have heard nothing more. This house has had no greater grief than word of your father's passing. The heart has been torn from the bosom of this family. I regret that I was not there to care for him, or you, once the angels had called him home. Your dear sister Amy has been my savior, showing a strength that had never been called forth before. Someday you must tell me the full story of this sorrowful episode.

Your letter from Auburn gave the impression that we already knew of this terrible news. I can assure you we knew nothing of it until we teased it from your words. My life's companion has been taken from me. I must now subsist on shining memories as a lone traveler tries to stay warm by a dwindling fire. I pray that you will never have to suffer such devastation.

This hit like a hammer blow. I wanted to scream. I wanted to punch the wall. I wanted to hunt down Mr. Hoyt and beat him senseless. I read on, dreading...

It is difficult to imagine how hard it has been for you since you lost him. I picture you tramping the endless desert miles, scaling the frozen summits, and my heart breaks. I can only hope that Mr. Hoyt has proven steadfast and kept loneliness from your tender heart.

We carry on, as we must. Adam has worked steadily to keep the farm going. But I know he itches for the day he can marry and have a place of his own.

It has been a hard winter for everyone. There has been much snow. We lost several chickens to a fox. Your friend Will bagged the varmint some nights later, for which we are very grateful. He has made the pelt into a very jaunty hat. It reminded me of the first time I met your Uncle Rafe, when your father was courting me.

We had gone through most of our candles when Mr. Pruitt began bringing over the occasional tin of lamp oil, which we use very sparingly, indeed. I have made a vow myself that we shall, by whatever means, repay his kindness.

It is hard to believe that you are well into your fourteenth year. I pray that we may be together for your next birthday. Uncle Rafe wrote to us, reciting the many pleasures you and your father shared during your brief sojourn in St Louis.

I do hope with all my heart that this letter finds you in good health and good spirits. You must be strong and come home to us. I do not care if your pockets are stuffed with gold or are threadbare. What is vital is that you return to your family that loves you.

Know that you are in my every prayer, day and night.

Mr. Pruitt's generosity compels me to burden you with a request. If you see the right moment, dear Barti, you might suggest to Mr. Hoyt that a note home to his stepfather would be most gratefully received.

Lastly, I have a letter for you from an H. Forsyth, in the Oregon territory. I will forward it as soon as I know you are receiving these mails.

Until then,

I remain, affectionately,

Your mother.

CHAPTER 20

I stared at the letter, my every fiber seething.

"Oh, dear," said Lila, leaning forward a little. "Is it unhappy news?"

It was no doubt writ plain on my face. I was torn between rage at Mr. Hoyt and anguish for my mother living for months in ignorance and false hope!

"I'm sorry. I am intruding. I should be going." But she hesitated a moment.

"No, Ma'am. Don't go," I blurted. I didn't know why I wanted her to stay. There was nothing she could do. I was jumping out of my skin with the need to pummel the stupid, arrogant, no-good lout I was supposed to call my partner.

A soft tap came at the door.

"Come in," I said.

Sun Shu opened the door just enough to look in. Lila turned in her seat and nodded to the younger woman.

Sun Shu nodded to Lila in return, then looked in concern to me. "I heard you had a visitor. Would you like tea?" She probably overheard my outburst to Lila.

I said, "Chen Yi already offered," and Lila said, "Thank you. But I was just leaving," one on top of the other, making Sun Shu blink in surprise. Time for some manners.

"Sun Shu, this is Lila Mae Rose. She's the express agent here in Auburn. Miss Rose, this is Sun Shu. She's the daughter of Chen Yi, who owns the laundry." I lifted the pages of my mother's letter off the bedcovers and said to Sun Shu, "Miss Rose brought me a letter—from home."

"You must be very happy," Sun Shu said pleasantly. "The mails are so unpredictable." Her dark eyes were full of questions. She paused just a moment before she turned back to Lila. "It is very nice to meet you, Ma'am, but you must excuse me."

When Sun Shu was gone, Lila turned to me, about to speak, her eyes wide.

I guessed what she was about to say and jumped in first. "She speaks English."

Lila blinked and then frowned. "Yes." She glanced back at the door. "I would never have guessed." She settled back in the chair.

I don't know what had gotten into me. Putting words in people's mouth was something Will would do.

"You are a trial, young man," Lila said. "Truly. A trial."

I dipped my chin. "I'm sorry, Ma'am."

"You are no such thing."

"They really are wonderful people, Ma'am. They work their tails off—sorry. They work very hard. Sun Shu works harder than anybody I've ever seen—except for you."

Lila frowned to herself. "With very few exceptions, everyone here is working their tails off."

I gaped at her in surprise. Her lips weren't smiling but her eyes were.

My thoughts went back to the letter. I was sure my mother had revealed only a fraction of the terrible grief she felt. By the same measure, what she said about their privations of the winter only hinted at the hardships they must be enduring. These terrible revelations made me more desperate than ever to find more gold and send it home as soon as possible.

"I am sorry that your letter distresses you," Lila said.

I folded the pages and put them back in the envelope, but I didn't want her to go. "May I ask you a question?"

I could see her bracing herself. "You're reaching your limit. She saw me sag back and relented. "Yes, but just one. I will do my best to answer it."

"Where are you from?"

A smile of relief flitted across her face. "Pennsylvania. And you?"

"Vermont," I said. "We came through Pennsylvania. It's beautiful country. Good farm country. Did you come overland?"

"That's two." When I didn't catch on, she added, "Yes, I did."

Then I smiled. I felt I might hazard a couple more questions.

We swapped stories about the trail. She had been with a group that had chosen to cross over the Sierra Nevada using Lassen's cutoff. They had lost all their wagons and teams and walked for most of the last four hundred miles. Before they were finished, some of their people were boiling belts and shoe leather. In none of her stories did Lila speak of her husband.

Curiosity demanded satisfaction. "Has your husband had good luck prospecting?"

She brought herself erect as if preparing once more to rise. "Perhaps that is one question too many."

I hung my head. "I'm sorry. Forgive me. Everybody says I'm too nosy for my own good."

"I have no husband," said Lila, with a defensive note in her voice. She brushed at her skirt. "I never have. I am the perfect spinster." She held her head high, but she looked down at her lap.

I knew nothing about spinsters, except, perhaps, that they were rare, and, with side-long looks, pitied. How to get this conversation up out of the ditch and back onto the road? "Well," I said, "maybe we should save a few stories for next time." That sounded like the right thing to say.

"Get well first," Lila said, rising determinedly from the chair, smoothing her dark hair.

Bugle raised his head, curious, from his post at the foot of the bed.

"Thank you for bringing my letter," I smiled up at her, hoping it would make her feel better. "Don't forget to say goodbye to Sun Shu. She'd like that."

Lila looked around uncertainly.

"She's out that side door in the workroom. Did you see it?"

"Yes. That's very thoughtful of you," Lila said. "I hope your next letter will have better news." She moved toward the door.

"Could I ask a favor of you?"

"I must be going. You need your rest."

"Could you take some gold out of my account and buy some paper and a pen and ink for me?"

She drew herself up. "Under no circumstances am I allowed to do that. I will bring you some writing materials, and you can pay me back out of your account when you come in and make a withdrawal."

"Yes, Ma'am. I understand. Thank you."

"You are very welcome." She looked at me sternly but I could tell she wasn't angry. "Put your questions away for a while. Rest." And she stepped through the door.

I didn't rest. I couldn't.

I reread my mother's letter and got all riled up again. I lay back on the bed and thought about all the things that had to be sorted out.

.   .   .

If I wasn't rereading my mother's letter, I was stewing over it, fuming at my limitations. I had to put it away. I tried to read the Tennyson, but could only manage a verse or two before I found myself worrying about my mother and Amy. I felt I was getting better, so I pestered Sun Shu into letting me do more small chores and step outside more often. I had to be careful with my chewed-up arm. I started a regimen of lifting a piece of firewood with it—adding a few more repetitions each day—to get it back in working order.

A few days after Lila's visit, I discovered where their firewood was coming from. I came out into the workyard to see what I could do and spotted a man unloading firewood from a wagon at the end where the yard met the street. *Why haven't I seen him before?*

Sun Shu nodded in the man's direction. "That's Mr. Summers. He delivers wood once each day. A face cord each time. Even so, it's barely enough."

Mr. Summers was a rough, stern-looking man with powerful arms and shoulders—what you'd expect for someone who spent his days chopping down trees or splitting firewood. The two-mule team pulling his wagon looked plumb worn out. Mr. Summers tossed wood to the ground in a scattered, messy pile, like he couldn't wait to be on his way.

After Mr. Summers drove away, I studied the careless heap of wood. It didn't look right. More to the point, it didn't look like *enough.* I'd split and stacked enough firewood in my short life to have a sense of how much wood it took. A face cord, stacked, should measure four feet high by one length wide by eight long, clean and square. My dad insisted on neat cords. "Shows a man's pride in his work," he'd say. But he said that about most of what we did around the farm.

I had to find out. Sun Shu protested, but I told her I would stop if I got tired. First, I made two towers, four feet high, four feet on a side, log-cabin style, four feet apart. Then I stacked the rest of the wood in between them.

When I finished, Mr. Summers' delivery was, indeed, short. A saddle dipped in the middle where the missing wood should be. Sun Shu had paid for a full cord of wood, but she hadn't received a full cord. I explained to her how the top was supposed to be level, four feet high, all the way across, and pointed out the lack.

She frowned at the stack. "He said he would deliver a cord each time. Is this not a cord?" She ran her fingers lightly along the uneven top of the cord. "We have never before stacked it this way."

"Probably because you use it up so fast."

Sun Shu said, "I must discuss this with Uncle Chen." She had a serious look on her face. "Thank you, Honorable Pegg. We are indebted to you for this revelation. Uncle Chen will breathe fire." She brushed sweat from my brow with her sleeve and looked sternly into my face. "You have worked too hard. If you turn for worse, Uncle Chen will be very angry with me. You must return to bed."

I made my way toward the door with a little more wobbling than I wanted to. My body wasn't up to even that small chore. I glanced back and found Sun Shu watching.

Gratefully, I crawled back under the covers. Warm and dry and clean. Bugle hopped on the bed and curled up right away. I let my head sink into the pillow. *I am so lucky.*

My folks always said, "Mind your own business," but they also said, "Speak up for what's right, no matter how hard it is." They just never explained what to do when both those things came up in the same situation. My friend Will, on the other hand, would call out mischief as soon as he saw it. He was fearless that way. But he could also run like the wind.

How I missed my best friend and envied his agility of mind. But, talking to Mr. Summers about the shortage of wood would be good practice for me before taking on Mr. Hoyt.

I called Bugle close and gave him a good scratching. "Why can't people do what they say they're going to do? Huh, Boy?" Bugle grinned and wagged his tail. "Things wouldn't get so complicated then."

Before long, Sun Shu came in with Chen Yi. He pulled the chair closer to the bed and sat down. Sun Shu stood at his shoulder.

Chen Yi nodded. "You better, Pegg-son. You already work."

"Yessir, I am, thanks to you and Sun Shu."

He made an agreeing noise, but he held his face still. After a moment he said, "Old Chinese sage say, 'Most useful part of cup what not there.'"

What did missing wood have to do with empty cups? I am sure my puzzlement showed.

Sun Shu said, "I showed him what remained of the stack and explained about a cord."

Chen Yi spoke quietly. "You understand?" he said. "Missing wood tell us problem Mr. Summers' deliveries."

I made bold. "Are you going to talk to him? If you want, I can talk to him." In my mind, my entire family gasped in dismay.

Chen Yi scowled and sucked in his breath. He turned his head slightly and Sun Shu bent to listen. They spoke quietly and earnestly for a couple of minutes. Then Sun Shu straightened up. "I am sorry, Honorable Pegg. Uncle Chen says it is a very dangerous business to accuse Mr. Summers. Anger needs so little to ignite."

I couldn't keep my mouth shut. "It's not right!"

Sun Shu leaned forward to speak; Chen Yi lifted his finger. She paused and retreated, silent.

He lowered his finger slowly. His voice was grave. I had never heard that in him before. But it was not unfriendly. "Pegg-son. Early days gold rush, enough room everyone. Plenty gold everyone. Lucky chance everywhere. Now, many, many people come *Gum Shan*. Maybe not so much for everyone. Maybe not so much luck. Feeling about people from Middle Kingdom, people from other places, change."

"The Middle Kingdom?"

"What you call China," said Sun Shu, "we call the Middle Kingdom."

"I'm from Vermont," I blurted. "*Everybody here* is from somewhere else!"

"Ah so, but you American," Chen Yi said. "Hard feelings make life tricky people from other places. Everybody love clean shirt, but blame laundry start big fire."

I was steamed. "What about candles, and tipped-over lanterns, and untended cookfires?"

Chen Yi sighed weary patience. "Yes. But people need place put hard feelings. We must step carefully, not make people angry."

That gave me a lot to chew on. Chen Yi sat with his hands on his knees, scowling to himself. Sun Shu stood still as a post, attentive to her elder.

I thought about the different people I had met, all the different languages I had heard spoken. I recalled Mr. Hoyt grumbling about "foreigners" when we came to Rattlesnake Bar.

"Summers-man price wood good price. . ." Chen Yi said. He sounded like he was trying to convince himself.

I didn't know what he was charging them, but that wasn't the point. "Of course it is. But he's not giving you what he said he would for that price."

Chen Yi frowned to himself. "I must think about this." He shifted to rise. Sun Shu stepped back.

I felt I had stirred up more than I bargained for. "I'm sorry," I said. "I didn't mean to cause you trouble." But I was already shaping a plan in my mind. I didn't stop to think it could cost me the friendship of the Celestials.

CHAPTER 21

The following day, I was so fired up with my plan it didn't occur to me Chen Yi might have his own plan. The window by the bed looked out on the workyard. I watched for Mr. Summers' return. Sun Shu stirred boiling clothes, carried loads from wash tub to rinse tub, and added wood to the fires. Periodically, she darted over to stir the single tub, which she had told me held starch. At last, Mr. Summers reappeared.

Bugle looked disappointed when I told him to stay. I put on the coat and went outside. I picked my way among the tubs, over to the wagon and watched Mr. Summers throw down wood from his wagon. Sun Shu went inside. To alert Chen Yi?

"You must have come a long way," I said, like I was just passing the time of day.

"How's that?" Mr. Summers said, tossing wood.

"To have found that much wood. Sure ain't much around here."

Mr. Summers grunted and laughed. "It gets tougher every day." He tossed a couple more pieces down and then stopped. His gaze fixed on the last few tiers of one of the bookends. All that remained of the cord I stacked yesterday. "Who stacked the wood?"

"I did." I squinted up at him. Then I bit the bullet. "Yesterday's load was a little bit shy." He threw three quick looks: yesterday's remnant, today's new pile, and me. He barked a short, harsh laugh.

"Oh." He thrust out his hand in apology. "I'll have to make it up tomorrow. I'm a little short myself, today." He picked up another piece of wood.

Not quite done. "That'd be good. I'm sure they'd appreciate it."

Mr. Summers' face hardened in a flash. "You speaking for them Celestials?" He scowled down at me, holding the piece of wood like it was a club.

It took everything I had to look him in the eye. "No, Sir. This ain't about taking sides."

"Well, if you're speaking for them," growled Mr. Summers, "you're taking sides."

I gulped. I had debated the finer points of misbehaving with my mom or my dad many a time—and usually lost—but I had never taken on a stranger. "It's just you agreed to deliver a cord of wood for an agreed-upon price." I took a breath. "And yesterday's load was short." *No sense in asking about other loads before that.*

"You're awful nosy, Boy, for something that ain't none of your concern."

"Well, that may be so, Sir," I said, "but it's everybody's concern if that's what's going on elsewhere, too." That was as close as I dared come to accusing him of cheating others. I was trying to get him to think of a miners' court. I had trusted my fate to such a mob. The judge in his dotage, the jury half liquored up, the verdict based on whim. If Summers had ever seen one of these charades played out, he should worry. Miners took a hard line when it came to cheating and stealing.

I was going places I'd never been before in my fourteen-plus years. Did I have the courage to follow through?

Sun Shu came out the side door and stopped.

Mr. Summers tossed down two more pieces of wood. "That's all I got for you." He looked to Sun Shu and held out his hand.

I turned my attention to the wood he had already thrown on the ground. "Am I going to get a full cord when I stack this up?" I asked, trying to sound like I was just pondering out loud. If Mr. Summers jumped off the wagon and beat me up, at least I'd have a witness.

I picked up a piece of the new wood to start another cord next to the old one. After I had moved the second stick of wood, I heard a growl from him, then he started tossing down more wood, more carelessly than ever. I had to jump out of the way.

He threw down another two dozen pieces. When he finished, he was breathing heavily. "Happy?" And very cross. "That's for yesterday, too."

I tried to give him a smile. "Yessir. Much obliged." I almost said, Good doing business with you, but I thought that might sound like rubbing it in, so I held my peace.

Sun Shu came forward and handed him up a small pouch of gold. Mr. Summers snatched it out of her hand. He clambered into his driver's seat, grabbed up the reins, and yelled at his mules, and the wagon jerked away.

Sun Shu and I stood quiet, like two survivors in the wreckage of a battlefield. The rattle of Summers' wagon was soon swallowed by the general din. Sun Shu asked, "What did you say to him?"

I remembered Dad and Mr. Pruitt trading "dealing" stories. "I tried to lead him to his own decision."

Sun Shu turned and gave me a long look.

Suddenly my arrogance dropped on me like a sack of flour. "Will Chen Yi be angry?"

She looked at me with concern. "Perhaps for a moment. But he values a fair deal more."

I retrieved a piece of wood. "Well, let's see if we have a cord."

Sun Shu touched my shoulder. "You have done enough today, Honorable Pegg. Gao Chung will stack the wood tonight."

I gave her a pout.

"Please. I will show him how you did it."

I flapped my arms, vexed. "But I'm doing nothing but lying around all day—"

"You have been—healing!" She sounded vexed, too.

I stabbed my finger at their building, at her workyard. "And you all are busting your fannies—m—" I blushed. "Sorry, ma'am… I—"

Sun Shu brought her hand up too late to hide her smile.

"I'll just do the towers," I said in a rush. "The ends. Then Gao Chung can do the middle. How's that?"

Sun Shu was not won over.

"Okay. How about as soon as I get tired, I'll stop? I promise."

"Your ancestors are watching, Honorable Pegg." She went back to stirring her tubs.

While I made the bookend towers for the cord, I thought about confronting Mr. Hoyt. I'd seen Mr. Hoyt angry. He was a winter blizzard compared to Mr. Summers' thunder shower.

CHAPTER 22

The day got colder as soon as the sun went down; Sun Shu scolded me back inside, except it didn't seem like scolding. I was grateful because stacking the wood had completely tuckered me out. Gao Chung finished the stacking and it came to a cord. Sun Shu worked well past dark, by the dancing light of her several fires.

Chen Yi fixed supper. He didn't have anywhere near the ingredients they had had at Chen's Garden in Grizzly Bar, but he whipped up a tasty supper, just the same.

Watching Gao Chung cook was like watching a mad, wild dance. Watching Chen Yi cook, on the other hand, was like watching a magician do card tricks—close, quick movements that you couldn't quite follow. I said to him, "You know how to do many things."

Chen Yi made his agreeing noise in his throat, still hunched over the little stove. He pointed to the table. "Chop onions, please."

When all was ready and steaming on the table, Chen Yi sent me to gather Sun Shu and Gao Chung. We all sat on salvaged barrels, eating our supper from bowls by the light of a couple of candles. We looked kind of funny; all the barrels were different sizes, making us all different heights, regardless of our true stature.

The Chinese spoke contentedly among themselves, in their language. It was the tenor of people who knew each other well, who had been through a lot together. I didn't mind, and I didn't feel left out. We huddled close around the table, slurping our noodles. Bugle curled up at my feet. I felt very much at home.

During a pause, I said, "I thought, in a couple of days, I would go back out to my claim."

Quick as lightning, Sun Shu said, "Perhaps at the end of the week. We will see then."

"But I'm feeling much, much better!"

Gao Chung said something in their language. Sun Shu spoke sharply to him. Gao Chung ducked back behind his bowl. I had never seen her cross. Stern, yes, but cross to the point of snapping at someone? Never.

"What did he say?" I asked Chen Yi.

This time Sun Shu translated. "He reminds me you are not my child."

Before I could ask her what she said in reply, Sun Shu set down her bowl with a thump and knocked over her stool as she hurried into the laundry room. A second door slam told us she went outside.

I looked at Chen Yi, mystified.

He studied his supper for a minute, and then spoke in a dismal voice, without looking up. "Yang Ho, Sun Shu marriage, no child—yet."

Gao Chung, equally subdued, said something that sounded like an apology.

By the time I finished my bowl, Sun Shu had still not returned. I topped her rice with greens and potatoes and turnips, put on my jacket and took the rest of her supper out to her.

She was shoveling ash out from under one of the rinse tubs. "Let me do that." I held out the bowl to her. "Eat."

She stood, handed me the shovel, and took the bowl and chopsticks. "Thank you." But she did not eat. "What is all that gold if you lose your life?"

"There is only one reason I am out here, and that reason is lying in the river. I have to go there."

"I am sure your family would rather have *you* return home than any amount of gold."

"I know it's dangerous. But I've been careless. I'll just have to be more watchful from now on."

Sun Shu frowned and poked at her rice.

It was hard to face down her reasoning. "I have a promise to keep. I have already failed in part of it. I can't go home empty-handed."

"At least wait until the other miners go back to the river. . .to discourage the beasts."

We stared at each other. Waiting was the last thing I wanted to do. "I can't."

I bent to scrape out more ash. Sun Shu hesitated and then worked on her supper.

.   .   .

I may not have been her child, but I continued to be her patient. Good care and good food did its work, and there came a morning when I felt fit enough to manage a walk around town. Sun Shu extracted a fistful of promises that I rest often and return directly at the first sign of fatigue. She supervised my dressing to make sure none of the few bandages I still sported would chafe. Grimacing, she settled my new hat gingerly on my plowed-up scalp as if she herself were enduring the discomfort. I set off with Bugle, feeling like Christopher Columbus on his way to the new world.

I searched for R. C. to see when he was going back to his claim. I couldn't find him in any of his usual haunts. As a last resort, I tried the express office.

Lila was having a busy morning. When I finally got to the counter there was no possibility of our usual banter. "Good to see you up and about," she said, and handed me an envelope.

I was surprised that my mother would write again so soon. But the envelope was unblemished: it could not have traveled more than six inches, let alone survived three thousand miles. The address simply said, "B. Pegg, lawyer-man." Only one person called me "lawyer-man."

I sat in a chair by Lila's wrapping table and tore open the envelope. The penmanship was measured and beautiful, but unfamiliar to me. The salutation confirmed my suspicion—R. C.

Esteemed Fellow Vermonter,

No doubt by the time you read this I will be some way up the trail. I am headed for the Feather River, as I spoke. I have engaged the services of the fine Miss Lila Mae Rose to inscribe these words, as writing was never my strong suit. When it comes to fare-thee-wells, I am the lowliest of cowards. This is what I want to say.

It has been an unexpected honor to have known you. A long time ago, I was married to a fine lady. We were soon blessed with a boy child. His mother died within days of bringing him into this world and he, not six years later, was called to his mother's side after falling off his horse. I have been a rootless wanderer that sad day to this.

I thank you for giving me the feeling of family for this little while.

The time has come for me to strike out for new ground. You are welcome to my two claims. Your best bet is to sell them to some hapless greenhorn.

Wherever your path takes you, I wish you all the best luck that the Creator has to give, that you will be reunited with your family, and that you will have a long, successful, and happy life. Our paths may cross again in this crazy, restless place. I will look forward to that day.

Until then, I remain,
Your faithful friend in the diggings,
Radcliffe C. Simpson,
Vermont

With a wrenching force, I realized I had come to have the same sentiments toward him. I wanted to talk to Lila, but she was very busy. I found a scrap of paper and wrote, "*Thank you for helping R. C. write his letter. Sincerely, B. Pegg.*" I laid my note on top of the spindle of twine, so she wouldn't miss it.

Back at the laundry I showed the letter to Sun Shu. She read it while I tended the tubs. "He is a good man," she said. "Rough as the bark of a tree on the outside, soft as one of Uncle Chen's dumplings on the inside."

When she saw I still needed cheering up, she said, "You will see him again. Look at what happened to us."

Losing R. C. wasn't anywhere near as bad as losing my dad, or Linnaeus, but his departure left an ache I would have to get over—again. I needed to start counting on nobody but myself. My mom popped into my head. *Does that mean you're not going to trust anybody?*

No. I've just got to remember anybody I meet out here is probably going to be moving on sooner or later. I've got to keep to my own path and concentrate on getting enough gold to get back home.

.   .   .

I knew I was much better when I itched to be doing. I carried in washing for Gao Chung to iron, stirred the starch, and hauled water for the big barrels until Sun Shu chased me inside to sort socks. After a few days, I even salvaged lumber and made proper stools for the dining table.

All the while, though, worry about mom and Amy never left me in peace. Whenever I tended the front counter for Chen Yi, I asked any unfamiliar faces if they had been to Coloma recently. If they had, I described Mr. Hoyt, but no one had seen him. *Is he still there, or is he even farther afield?*

I wrote my mother and sister, trying to keep my words light-hearted. I talked about the weather, about what great friends R. C. and Richard Barter were. I said nothing about a mountain lion.

"Bugle asks to be remembered to you," I wrote in one letter, hoping the humor would not be amiss. I wrote to Hally to add to the ones I had already written. With any luck, I would soon have her address. And I wrote to Mr. Pruitt, advising him of Dad's passing, even though it was likely Mother already had. But I felt the need to, just the same.

I wrote to my friend Will, who was always close by in my thoughts. We were probably better friends than we would have been brothers. I enjoyed his bracing sarcasm. I asked him lots of questions about his doings.

.   .   .

I tarried days longer than I intended, but finally my obligations could no longer be ignored. On a Saturday morning, I was up at first light, making a pack of my few belongings. A tap at the door.

"Come in?"

Sun Shu came into the room—her room. After today, it could be hers again. Usually, she came right over and sat in the chair. This time, she closed the door and stood against it, holding a slip of paper. "Uncle Chen and I have drawn up a list of things we would like to buy for you to set up your camp."

"Oh! You don't have to do that!"

"He has given me some gold and said we should go to Gwynn's before you set out."

"Thank you, Sun Shu, but that's not necessary. I couldn't—"

She tucked in her chin, looking at the floor, and took a new hold of her list. "It *is* necessary!"

I sat down on the bed and gestured for her to come sit in the chair. "Why do you want to do that? I have been living in your house for free. . .for weeks and weeks. I have been eating your food. . .I have been warm and dry all winter, thanks to you and Chen Yi." A sudden thought struck. "I am *alive* thanks to you and Chen Yi."

She was looking at the list she held in her lap.

I tried to get her to look at me. "And you've taken care of Bugle longer than you've been taking care of me! It is I who owe you!"

She looked up with a fierce expression. "Will you make me list all the things you have done for us?"

SunShu's passion was startling. She so rarely gave vent to strong emotion. I couldn't let them do this. They were struggling just as hard to make a future for themselves. "You and Chen Yi saved my life! I owe you far, far more than you could ever owe me."

"And we wish to help you continue your life with some small particle of comfort. An extra blanket, a little rice, a pot for your tea. . ." she held out the list. "It is not so much— when we have eaten so much rice together."

No matter how much composure she tried to hold in her face, I heard more distress in her voice than I ever wanted to hear. No amount of independence was worth that. "Okay. Okay," I said. I almost said, you win, but I realized this had nothing to do with winning.

She settled the list back in her lap. "Thank you, Honorable Pegg."

I went with Sun Shu to thank Chen Yi for his generosity.

He made his hissing sound. "Ah so, Pegg-son. You bring laundry—all happy."

.   .   .

The tops of the buildings caught the first light of the sun. You could feel in the air that the back of winter had broken. If it wasn't April, it was very close to it. The street was already busy. People were still wearing coats, but they weren't hunched over against the cold. They moved around us like water eddies around a stone, coming and going from Gwynn's General Store. Sun Shu got more than her share of curious glances, some more hostile than curious, but she paid them no mind. I tried to ignore them, too, but not as successfully. She did not deserve such looks.

I was loaded down with a new outfit: cooking gear, sturdy wool shirts and trousers, blankets, bacon, flour, tools, rope, ammunition. All courtesy of Chen Yi and company, all lashed to an old trapper's frame, with a tumpline across my forehead.

Bugle paced eagerly.

Sun Shu moved around, checking how the pack sat against where she knew my scars to be. "Is it binding anywhere?"

If I gave her half an excuse, she'd send me back to bed. "I carried more than this in the desert. I'll be all right." I twisted to look at her, to let her know I was joshing. "It'd be easier to carry you."

"Don't make fun." She kept fussing. "Can you come back for some of it?" She came around in front to check the extra pad she had put under the tumpline. "You're just getting well."

I smiled at her. "Thanks to you."

She cocked her head but didn't smile back. Her dark eyes held me fast. "So I would ask you not to throw all my hard work away."

My eyes popped wide. "Whoa! There's my girl." Dad would say that to Mom when she did something to surprise him.

Sun Shu looked around, then gave me a questioning look. Her eyes widened and she looked down, blushing. I'd embarrassed her for sure.

People bumped into my pack. I cleared my throat. "Well, I'd better get moving."

"Yes." She glanced at the sky. "You don't want to get caught in the rain."

I looked, too. Perfectly blue. "Not much chance of that."

"That depends on how long you stand here."

A laugh busted out of me.

She clasped her hands together. "Go."

CHAPTER 23

I walked away from town with a heavy heart. I realized how much I had come to enjoy their company, and Lila's. *Don't be stupid, they'll be no farther away than they were before.*

Up on the wagon road, I got into my stride. After so many weeks of convalescence, it felt good to be stretching out again. Bugle was just as happy, scampering ahead, sniffing, marking, trotting alongside before darting away again. I hesitated calling him back. I figured he wanted to stretch out as much as I did.

I only had to stop to rest one time, just before spotting the massive old Grandfather Oak as I made my way down the north rim of the canyon.

I had the river pretty much to myself. I looked over the claim while Bugle marked his territory. It hadn't changed much since I left it, blood-spattered, two months ago. More water had seeped into my diggings. There was about a foot of water in my four-foot-deep excavation. R. C. had stashed my tools against the cabin and laid a piece of canvas over them. It appeared he hadn't been the only visitor. Cat tracks mingled with his boot marks. I touched the butt of the Colt stuffed through my belt. It was foolish to assume there was only one mountain lion prowling the neighborhood.

I went inside the cabin to see what my absence had wrought. Bugle hopped up on the bed and settled himself in the same place he had on Sun Shu's bed. Dust and chaff, sifting down from the ceiling, covered everything. Cobwebs, like pale, silver threads, stitched together the corners under the roof. They were easily dispensed with.

I inspected the back wall. Nothing had shifted. Groundwater seeped through in a few places, but nothing to worry about. The old blankets on the bed smelled musty, so I laid a fire and dried them out. Only then did I spread all my blankets—old and new—on the bed. The rest of my new gifts from Sun Shu were soon stowed.

As darkness came on, I added a few more sticks to my fire and made a supper: bean cakes for me and three thick slices of bacon for Bugle. Sleep was long in coming, listening for visitors on the roof.

The next day, I had to see, once and for all, if there was anything worth staying for on this piece of the river, or whether it was time to move on, as R. C. had said. The only part of my claim that remained unexplored was the river bottom. I stepped up to the water's edge and peered into the ripples. The bottom looked to be mostly sand and a few rocks, and dropped away quickly. I had no idea how to go about prospecting river bottom, but then I picked out a thick, dark, wobbling line. *Could this be?* I turned to look back at the last of the seam before it dipped below ground right behind where I stood. Raising my gaze to the hillside, I spied the other parts of the seam that stitched its way down the rise. In each place where it emerged, the seam was divided along its length by a dark cleft, averaging some four fingers wide. And now here was a wide dark line, lining up with the others, on the bottom.

I took off my boots and socks, rolled up my trousers, and stepped into the shallows, picking my way across the steadier stones. If there was color that I had any hope of getting at, it would likely be trapped in that crevice. So intent was I in following the seam, I was soon in past my knees, with soaked britches. The current pushed relentlessly. If I was going to go any farther, I would need help.

I went ashore and found a stout staff. It would help me keep my balance in the current. After retrieving a blanket from my shelter, I shed my clothes, folding them neatly on a rock on top of the blanket.

I held up my finger to Bugle. "Now, don't let anybody think these are for salvage, hear?"

He stood up and wagged his tail, as if he wanted to come along. I pointed at the gravel. "It's okay, Boy. Stay. I'll be right back."

I stepped into the cold water. It would be wise to make this a short visit.

Placing the stick firmly before each step, I moved out into the river, keeping the seam close to my right. I hoped its path would stay inside my claim. When up to my waist, the rippling of the water turned the whole river bottom into a rolling, shifting kaleidoscope of colors. I lost track of the seam.

Taking a fresh grip on my staff and sucking in a deep breath, I plunged my face underwater. The seam stood out clear as day. It ran through my claim in a clean line, rising a foot or more above the sandy bottom. The dark fissure varied in width. The seam kept going into the claim of Harvey Drummond, right across from me. A ribbon of undulating light played across the seam, setting off a glint of yellow light in the dark groove.

I came up for air. I put my face under again, hoping desperately. Another golden wink in the same place. I straightened, trembling with excitement, certain that glitter was indeed GOLD. The water would be up to my chest where I had seen the glint. I wouldn't be able to stand against the current there, even with the stick. I'd have to dive for the spot.

I turned and heaved the stick back on shore. Bugle surged to his feet, ready for a game of "fetch" but he quickly discovered the stick was far too big for the game. He stood looking out at me, confused. I took a couple more steps farther out.

As soon as my feet lost hold of the bottom, the river carried me downstream, away from the seam. Dear, cynical friend Will smirked in my mind, *Ain't you never been in water bigger'n a wash tub?*

I swam for the south shore, and trotted back upstream with a mind to go at the seam again. But I didn't want to catch a chill, so I wrapped myself in the blanket, made a fire, dried off, and thought how to get the better of the current.

I put more wood on the fire and went to try out my idea. Picking my way upstream thirty or forty yards, I didn't know whose claim I ended up in. I set three rocks in a stack at the edge of the water to mark the spot. I swam out and the river carried me down toward the seam. When I figured I had reached it, I stuck my face underwater.

I was just passing over it, with no chance to grab at the wink of golden light. On my second try, I put my face under sooner, clawed my way down and grabbed where the fleeting speck of light had been.

I got a good fistful of sand and shot to the surface, gasping for air. I was already ten or fifteen feet downstream. Keeping my fist clenched tight, I swam to shore.

As soon as I got back to my camp, I dumped the fistful of dirt into my gold pan,threw a blanket over my shoulders and toasted myself by the fire. Bugle came over. I reached down and gave him a scratch. "Keep your paws crossed, Boy, that it wasn't just fairies playing tricks."

When warm, I dressed and took my pan to the water's edge to wash what I had grabbed. The black sand held a nugget and a few flakes. The nugget was half the size of my thumbnail. I bit into it gently, just to be sure.

I held the little yellow lump out toward Bugle. "Look at that, Bugle!" He got up off his haunches, wagged his tail and barked. Then I remembered and looked around. Not another soul in sight.

Are there more nuggets down there? How can I keep from being pushed downstream while trying to work? Hang onto something that's heavier than the river could move—a rock? How about a rope tied to the rock so I can move around? One hand for the rope, one hand for the work.

But I was too impatient for even that simple a plan. I had to see if there was more gold in that seam. *What else can I use to stay in place?* My balancing stick. It was stout enough. If I could jam it firmly into the gap, I could hang onto it and have one hand free to work. *It's worth a try.* Before going back in the river, I added wood to the fire for when I came out.

.   .   .

Stick in hand, I went upstream to my mark. Once in the water, the stick had a mind of its own. It wanted to float. After several tries, interspersed with warming by the fire, I got the stick jammed firmly in the crevice. The silt kicked up by this frenetic stabbing glittered with gold flakes, luring me on. Hanging onto the stick, I scooped another handful before my lungs screamed at me and I bobbed up, coughing and sputtering. Letting go of the stick, I swam to shore.

Turning in the warmth of the blaze, I glanced out at the river. The stick held. I opened my hand and quickly culled the river pebbles. The four nuggets that remained gleamed in the winter sun. One nugget was about the size of the first one, but three were bigger. Just the thing to whip up my expectations.

In the middle of the third dive, the stick worked loose. The current seized me, tumbling me end over end. With both hands occupied, I couldn't swim, and I wasn't about to let go of a fist full of nuggets. The stick bobbed and dipped on its way to the Sacramento River and beyond.

Warming myself by the fire, I reflected on the day's take. Fourteen nuggets of varying size had come from just one spot on the seam, all in the space of an afternoon. *Is this the beginning of a bonanza?* With nobody around, I did a little jig, grinning like a fool.

Bugle got up and sat down, got up and turned around. "Ah, Bugle, d'ya think this could be it?" We made circles around each other.

I gazed fondly at my haul. How much more could be trapped in that crevice? It would take a coon's age, scooping up a handful at a time to find out. I had to do much more on each trip.

The next day, after replenishing my supply of firewood, I went into the river well above the seam, and floated face-down, searching for a large rock on the bottom to serve as an anchor. While there was no shortage of rocks, none looked big enough for the job. I would have to make my own anchor.

Over supper, I came up with an idea that might be a bonafide solution.

Bugle looked up from his bacon when I gave voice to my thinking. "If one big rock is not to be had, how about adding up enough smaller rocks to equal the weight of a big rock? Bugle tilted his head as if to say, "And. . .?" And I knew I wasn't finished. "But how do you tie a rope to a pile of rocks and hope the rope won't pull the pile to pieces when you pull on it?"

I looked around my collection of salvage, which included a pair of long johns. I remembered how, back in Grizzly Bar, Sun Shu had made bags from the arms and legs of a pair of long johns. *What if the rocks are in a bag?*

I sat smug for about half a heartbeat. How do I haul a sack of stones heavier than I am into the river and drag it into position?

I tried thinking back-to-front—a trick of Will's. *Take the bag to its position first, then fill it with stones.* But it would have to be a big bag.

CHAPTER 24

By lantern light, I dug a hole under my bed and hid twelve of my new-found nuggets. I kept out two of the larger ones. Together, the two nuggets weighed close to ten ounces. At sixteen dollars an ounce, that should be enough to buy a square of canvas, a length of rope, a ball or two of sturdy twine, and an awl. But I still had no idea how I was going to turn these makings into a bag.

I hustled into town at first light and went to see Sun Shu, to ask her for her ideas, then do the sewing myself. I paid my respects to Chen Yi first. "I'd like to ask Sun Shu's advice."

Chen Yi's eyes crinkled in glee. "Chen Yi, fountain good advice. All problems."

"Do you know anything about sewing?" I asked, most earnestly.

Chen Yi threw up his hands, turning his face aside in mock horror. "Never touch needle, thread. Big lose face."

Out in the workyard, Sun Shu stirred vigorously at the boiling clothes. We exchanged greetings but she didn't stop. I went right over to the starch pot—it could always use a stir. She paused, wiping her forehead. "You work too hard." I tried a smile.

Sun Shu dragged a sodden shirt onto a washboard. "The world is full of people who do that."

"I have a favor to ask."

Her look challenged me not to waste her time. I showed her the canvas and explained what I wanted to do, right down to dropping the stones into the sack and cinching the bag shut when it was "full." I held out the twine. "Do you think this will be strong enough?"

She ran her fingers lightly over the rough canvas, she said as if talking to herself. "It must be a flower."

Why is she talking about flowers?

She took the ball of twine. "Yes. A flower. But it will work in reverse." Then she remembered I was standing there and looked up. "First it will be open, as if in bloom. You will drop in the stones, then it will be closed, as in a bud." She looked at me with solemn eyes. "Do you understand?"

Dark eyes, like the night sky full of stars— "Uh… yeah." I shook myself. "I do." But I didn't, exactly.

She studied the twine. "It will take many dives to close the sides of the bag, so we must make them simple knots."

Sun Shu was already working on details while I was still trying to imagine a giant white flower blooming at the bottom of the river. She marched to the workyard door and called to Gao Chung. When he appeared, she spoke quietly to him and he came into the yard. She shifted her gaze to me expectantly, and I hustled to follow.

She spread the canvas on the ironing room floor and cut it into the shape of a four-pointed star. At last I grasped Sun Shu's flower idea. The center of the flower formed a square about two feet on a side. She placed the flat of her hand on the square. "You will pile the stones here, like a pyramid, then close the sides together."

She cut the tips of the four petals blunt, then reinforced them. Then she cut holes in the reinforced parts. "You will close the bag by passing the rope through these holes after the bag is full."

Then, with the awl, she punched smaller holes up both sides of a triangular petal. She handed me the awl to do the other three. To these holes she added lengths of twine so I could tie the sides together as I filled the bag.

Sun Shu instructed, "Stand in the center and hold up two petals together."

Mystified, I did as I was bid. She cut lengths of twine and sewed together the first six inches of the sides, forming a shallow box. At last, she took the rope out to Gao Chung and showed him she wanted a loop on one end.

In the space of a few hours the bag was complete. "This is wonderful. Please, let me pay you," I pleaded.

"Uncle Chen would be very unhappy with us if we accepted money from you."

There was honor tied up in there, I knew, so I didn't insist. But I resolved to sneak some nuggets into their possession now and again.

.   .   .

After hasty farewells, I hightailed it back to my claim with my new bag under my arm.

My bones told me there was a lot more gold waiting for me in the seam. This was just part of the cost of getting at it.

I reckoned I could swim and carry a ten-pound stone at the same time. Collecting fifteen or twenty loaf-shaped stones wouldn't be difficult, but first I had to get the bag into position. When I took the canvas out to a spot above the seam, I took a seven-pound stone with me, to hold it in place.

When the sun dipped below the rim and the air chilled, I stopped for the day. Shivering, I hustled over to my warming fire. I was eager to collect the stones. Thanks to my fence building experience back home, I was able to quickly pick stones that would pack tightly and not shift.

.   .   .

I wolfed down a cold breakfast, after which I built up the fire to a hearty blaze and commenced loading my anchor with stones. It took four tries to get it right. I was glad there was no one around to become curious about my odd behavior. By the middle of the third day, my anchor bag contained sixteen stones and was all cinched up. Just as I had hoped it would, the current dragged at the rope, angling it downstream over the seam.

Hand over hand, I pulled myself down into the water, toward the seam. The bag didn't budge. On a second descent I scooped up a handful of nuggets. At the end of the day, I tied a bit of branch to the end of the rope, so it would float.

Warming myself by the fire, I realized I was still restricted to one handful of dirt with each dive. I cobbled together a smaller canvas bag that could hold perhaps four or five handfuls, with loops for my belt to go through.

"Keep your fingers crossed, Bugle, boy—or your paws! That Dame Fortune smiles on us." I showed him my crossed fingers, and he thumped his tail against the ground. It was definitely better, having company.

The sun rose into a blue sky for the first time in many days. Surely that was a good sign.

With my new belt bag at my side, I swam out to the rope, took a deep breath, and hauled myself down to the seam. Brushing aside silt, twigs, and pebbles revealed more gleaming yellow. I grabbed up a handful and stuffed it in the belt bag. I tried to sense if the anchor wasn't holding. The rope stretched taut. I managed two more handfuls, then shot to the surface, my lungs ready to burst. After two more dives, the belt bag was full, and I swam for shore.

Dressed, with a blanket snug around my shoulders, I sat close to the warmth of the blaze and emptied the soggy bag into my gold pan, shaking the bag to make certain it was truly empty.

After disposing of twigs and pebbles, I spread out the individual specimens across the bottom of the pan. Then I sat gazing at them.

I had just taken out more gold than the total of all my previous dives in the seam. *This might be a bonanza, after all!*

Bugle, settled at my feet, caught my excitement. I showed him the pan. "A few more pans like this and we can go home. What do you say, Boy?"

He looked up at me and licked his chops.

Giddy delight would not be denied. I counted twenty-six nuggets lying in the bottom of my pan. Several were the size of a robin's egg. One, a chicken's egg. None were smaller than a bean. Suddenly, the wild stories didn't seem so outlandish anymore. A new dairy farm for my family didn't have to be just a wistful dream. Going home in triumph was within reach! And from the color I'd seen in the seam, these twenty- six nuggets weren't the last of it!

Over the course of that afternoon, I found my limit was two or three handfuls with each dive. Each handful had at least a half dozen nuggets, sometimes more. I took out four more bags before I called it a day. I was in a lather! I might qualify for R. C.'s $10,000 club, yet!

After supper, I washed all the nuggets individually in my gold pan. My jubilation grew with examining each bulbous, pitted specimen. Having no container for such large nuggets, I folded them in a cloth and shoved them into the hole under my bed. It was time to start taking them to Lila at the express office for safekeeping.

Rolling up in my blankets, I gave myself up to reviewing the day's take, and planning a vast, wonderful barn, with milking sheds, and a big, two-story house with dormers, surrounded by towering elms—

Then the glory drained from the day. It wasn't entirely *my* gold; it was partnership gold. As long as everybody back home was counting on this partnership, I had to respect it, even if another member of the partnership—namely Mr. Hoyt—didn't.

But wait! Honoring the partnership meant turning this hard-won treasure over to a man I was certain would squander it on his own whims. He'd done it enough times in Grizzly Bar. My mother's letter proved that he had not only neglected to inform her of my father's passing—as he had promised—but had not, during all this time, sent one red cent back to them for their maintenance. And it was a good bet he hadn't sent anything back to Mr. Pruitt, either.

Perhaps it was time to make some of my own rules.

CHAPTER 25

I was up at first light, impatient to get back to the seam. Gathering up the loose nuggets was quickly done. The deeper I went, the more I had to pry the nuggets loose. I ran out of breath after only one or two nuggets. Next time ashore I added my Bowie knife to my belt and started using it to work the nuggets free. This was a sure way to ruin the point of the knife, maybe even break the blade.

How could I stop? Many of the specimens were bigger than any I had yet seen. The more nuggets I plucked from the seam, the more my excitement grew. And with each nugget, one thought grew stronger: I could not let Hoyt get his hands on this bounty.

At the end of the second day's work, a heap of gold nuggets glistened, triumphant, on my table-bench. I grinned like a fool. For supper, I treated Bugle and myself to extra pieces of bacon.

He lay against my boot, sated. I gave him a good scratching. He turned and raised his eyebrows at me. It was his *I'm all ears* look.

"We sure do have a good spot here, don't we, Boy?"

He rolled over for more.

I obliged him. "At this rate, we'll never get up to the Feather River. R. C. will have it all to himself."

One thought hammered at me. I needed a way to keep Mr. Hoyt ignorant of most of the gold I found. I would have to hide the gold before he ever found out about it. I sure didn't like the idea of lying to him, but if that's what it took, so be it.

My first impulse was to bury the gold someplace on my claim. But, I already had an account at the express office under another name. Could I open a second account for Mr. Pruitt and the neighbors under a name Mr. Hoyt wouldn't recognize? Such a stunt would probably drive Lila to distraction, but that couldn't be helped.

Then I thought I would have to shave this a little finer, to keep Mr. Hoyt thinking everything is going along just like before. That meant I would need three accounts: one that was his share in the partnership, which he could use as he wished; another for Mr. Pruitt and the other partners, and the third account would be for my family's share. This last one could be the one I already had, under Hally's name. And they should all be joint accounts.

Mr. Hoyt's account would be under his name and mine. Hopefully, that would convince him it was the partnership's account, representing all the gold I found. I just had to come up with a name under which to hide Mr. Pruitt's share.

.   .   .

In the morning, I took up the axe and my sling. "Come on, Bugle. I've got some thinking to do," I said and set off up the slope at the back of my claim.

I passed stumps of trees sprouting bushy sucker growth as they struggled back to life and I struggled to think up a name for Mr. Pruitt's hidden account. Maybe some of the people Linnaeus had told me about… *Thomas Jefferson? Benjamin Franklin?* No… Everybody knew who they were. *Julius Caesar? Gilgamesh*? No. Too fancy. The name had to fit in with names that were around every day. Like R. C. . Richard Barter. Or Lester Davies, one of the miners on the river near me. And it had to be one I could remember. Will popped into my head without even asking. That seemed too easy. His last name was Smith. *Will Smith. You can't blend in better than that.*

But we were all three from the same town. True, Mr. Hoyt had been away for most of the time Will and I were growing up. That settled it. Mr. Pruitt's and the partners' share would be hidden under the name of Will Smith.

Two of my favorite people, Will Smith and Hally Forsyth, would be easy to remember.

Then another problem crowded in: How to divide up a given batch of gold so that each account got its rightful share.

I climbed out on the flat at the top of the canyon. There were more trees surviving here: the Digger pines and majestic old oaks, their twisting arms bare and dark for the winter.

I spied some deadfall under a great oak and gave a little prayer of thanks. A large limb had fallen and shattered into many pieces some time ago. Bugle sniffed eagerly among the ruins.

"A real bonanza in firewood, eh, Boy?" Many of the pieces were a good size for a cooking fire. *And for counting.*

I laid out ten of the smaller sticks in a row. They would represent one hundred percent of whatever I was taking in to deposit. According to Dad's calculations, of whatever gold we found, twenty percent would go to the Pegg family—that was two sticks. Mr. Pruitt, who would look after the neighbor partner's shares, was entitled to seventy percent, or seven sticks. Mr. Hoyt was due ten percent—one stick.

I imagined sorting an amount of gold into ten equal piles. My imaginary piles vanished in a puff of disappointment. Piles of the same *size* would not serve. Gold was valued by its weight, not its size. Each pile of gold in my line of ten had to be equal in *weight*, not in size.

Before I could try out my idea with the nuggets I already had, I had to buy a scale to do the weighing. I added up my calculating sticks to the sling and soon filled it from the deadfall.

I returned to camp with a light step despite the load on my back. My plan involved activities that went against the grain of everything that was esteemed in our family. But knuckling under to Mr. Hoyt's demands spelled disaster for everybody.

CHAPTER 26

When I walked into Chen Yi's laundry with my small bundle, he greeted me as if I'd been away for months. He gave Bugle a welcoming scratch. "Business not so good without Bugle dog jolly customers."

Chen Yi pushed a heap of laundry down the counter toward two other piles.

I grinned, eyeing the piles. "Looks like if Bugle were here, business could get worse. Besides, I need him to keep the varmints at bay." I hoisted my bundle up on the counter. The thump betrayed that the bundle contained something more than shirts.

Chen Yi turned his gaze on my bundle. "Fortune smile you, Pegg-son?"

"Yessir."

"Not let others see her smile?"

"I tried not to."

"Shirts belong here. Gold belong express office."

"Yessir. But I'd like to measure it first. Weigh it, I mean."

"Why not weigh express office?" Chen Yi asked.

I gave him a sheepish look. "It's kind of a long story."

"I patient—until next customer."

So I explained my plan to deposit shares into separate accounts. He understood, nodding soberly. "Measure must wait laundry close. No interruption."

"Thank you, Sir. I appreciate that."

Chen Yi waved his hand in the general direction of the yard. "Go give Sun Shu happy day." He dragged the bag with my gold off the counter.

I called out as I stepped through the side door. "Don't you ever stop working?"

Sun Shu, stirring one of the wash tubs, jerked upright. "Pegg!" Her smile lit up her whole face. She forgot to cover it, as modesty required. She kept stirring as I approached. "My ancestors are not pleased with me." She said it with a serious face, then, slowly, she let a smile creep in. "They keep sending more laundry to do." She moved to another tub with her stick.

I ambled along. "From what I saw inside, they aren't going to let up anytime soon."

She wound a sodden bundle around her stick and carried it, steaming in the crisp air, to a rinse tub nearby.

"Any word from Yang Ho?"

"Not yet."

I was just coming around after the mountain lion attack the first time I asked Sun Shu about her husband's return. Now more time had passed. I realized Sun Shu and my mom could share their burdens. I hoped fervently Sun Shu's vigil wouldn't suffer the same outcome.

She bent to untangle some wash. "When we learn of any Celestials who have come through San Francisco, Uncle Chen or Gao Chung ask them about Yang Ho. None have had any word for us. But it is just a matter of time, I'm sure."

She stepped over to stir the starch pot, and I added water from the big barrels against the wall to the wash tubs.

"Thank you," she said simply.

Sun Shu was too polite to ask why I was in town, so I offered. "I was hoping I could use Chen Yi's scales to weigh some gold."

She took up her stick to stir the clothes. "I cannot speak for him, but I am glad for your good fortune." She glanced up shyly. "Will you stay and eat with us?"

.   .   .

Supper with Sun Shu, Gao Chung, and Chen Yi was a nice change from miners' fare, and I sure appreciated the company of my good friends. The talk flowed like a friendly brook tumbling along its way. When our bowls were empty, I asked if Sun Shu could go with me to the express office and talk to the agent for me.

After closing time, Chen Yi and I made ten piles of my gold on the counter. With a certain ceremony, Chen Yi brought his scales to the counter and we began. It took some finicky doings to get each of the piles to weigh the same.

At last, we cinched up the bag between each portion with a length of twine. The Pegg family's portion was at one end, Mr. Pruitt in the middle, and Mr. Hoyt's portion was at the other end.

Chen Yi cast a skeptical eye on our handy work. "Like sausages made by drunk sausage-man."

This time, Sun Shu covered her smile.

Before we left, she said, "Perhaps if we brought a small gift to Miss Lila, she might look more kindly on our visit."

I was happy to do anything that would make for smooth sailing at the express office, especially since I had a hunch what I wanted to do was stretching the rules. Sun Shu showed me a small tin of green tea. "Good for soothing the spirit," she said as she wrapped it in a green silk cloth.

"Thank you, Ma'am. I'm sure she'll like that."

It was deep night. I worried that Lila might have finished her work and gone home. Chen Yi insisted Gao Chung go with us. Sun Shu carried the tea, and I carried the partitioned bag. Not many lingered in the street—some passed out, some scurrying to get out of the chill. At the express office, Gao Chung sat himself down on the steps, facing the street. Of course, Lila was still working.

"These are not regular business hours, young man," Lila said, holding the door open for us. "If you make a habit of it, others will feel free, and I will never get my work done. Good evening, Miss Sun."

Sun Shu didn't protest that she was married. "Good evening, Miss—?" she said as she stepped inside.

"Rose, dear," Lila smiled. "Lila Mae Rose." She closed the door firmly behind us.

I blurted, "I know we're interrupting you, Ma'am, but I have an unusual problem."

Lila arched an eyebrow at me. "I have not known you to have any other kind."

Sun Shu and I followed her to the counter. Sun Shu handed me the gift, and I offered it to Lila. "Ma'am, we brought you some tea."

"To butter me up?"

I twisted around to Sun Shu to see what I should do. She was holding her face very still. That meant she was uncertain, too.

Lila said, "I— I'm sorry. That was uncalled for. I thank you. I do. This is very nice." She rubbed her brow with stiff fingers. "It's been a *long* day!"

Sun Shu said, "Perhaps I could brew some of it while Mr. Pegg is telling you the reason for our visit."

Lila looked relieved. Her shoulders relaxed. "Yes! Oh, that would be lovely. Thank you. Please!" She handed back the gift to Sun Shu and pointed to the kettle on the stove and the teapot and cups on the shelf above it. "Just there. Thank you."

Lila turned to me. "I have not seen you since I gave you Mr. Simpson's letter. Before we discuss *your* business, there remains some of *his* we must conclude."

I was puzzled. "Yes, Ma'am."

She let out a sigh. "Once again, I am not pleased with the circumstances, but there it is." Her brows gathered together in disapproval. "Mr. Simpson should have asked you to be present at this transfer of claims, but he chose to cut and run, as did the other gentleman who left you *his* claim."

I thought back to the note R. C. had left me. He was up on the Feather River now. "Does that mean Mr. Simpson left me his claims?"

I hoped he was having better luck, on his way to another ten thousand dollars.

She let me stew for a heartbeat. "Indeed. Your presumption is correct. Would you like me to point them out to you?"

"That would be helpful, Ma'am. Sure wouldn't want to accidently intrude on someone else's claim."

Lila consulted the claims ledger and took me over to the map. She pointed to two of the small boxes with their even tinier numbers, went back to the ledger and made the required changes. I studied the bends in the river to use as landmarks.

"And now, Mr. Pegg…" She looked up, "You are still going by Pegg, I presume."

"Yes, Ma'am. I am."

"What is your business?" she said.

I explained my situation, and about Mr. Hoyt, adding, "And Sun Shu said she would speak to the situation on my behalf, if need be."

Lila spoke primly, her voice freighted with weary experience. "There are stories and schemes galore in this benighted country. I can only be interested in deposits, withdrawals, and transfers. I am responsible for the fruit of your labors, not of your skullduggery. There are fists and guns for that."

"Yes, Ma'am." I was getting worried she wouldn't agree to my scheme.

"Nonetheless," she went on, "I am obliged to ask—how may I be of help in this swamp of intrigue you're making for yourself?"

Here we go. "Well, Ma'am, I'm sorry to trouble you, but I would like to open another account."

"Not as much trouble as some," said Lila, as much to herself as to me, reaching for the ledger.

"Actually, two more accounts—under different names," I finished.

"Obviously," said Lila. She opened the ledger cover and took the pencil from behind her ear.

"Thank you. Ma'am," I said.

"Be careful. Too many thank you's will spoil me." Something besides censure sparked in her eyes. "And what is the name for the first of these new accounts?"

"Will Smith," I announced.

Lila flipped through her ledger to the "S" page. She tracked down the page with her pencil, like she always did. Her pencil paused and her eyebrows twitched in concern. This happened a couple of times. She had more "S's" on a second page, and one more pause.

"I'm afraid I already have three versions of that name. 'Will Smith,' 'William Smith,' and 'William B. Smith.' As you can see, the last individual was at pains to make his version unique. If you want to keep that name, you will have to do something of a similar nature."

My friend Will's name fit in so well, there were three of them. What could I do to Will's name to make it different from the others? *William C. Smith*? The "C" could stand for "crazy," but he wasn't actually crazy. *"R" for "rascal?"* I was getting too fancy again. It had to be something real, so I could remember it. My dad immediately appeared in my mind. *James Madison Pegg.* I all but stumbled where I stood. I went for the "James" without even trying. That would be the name for the secret account, Mr. Pruitt's account.

I lifted my chin to Lila. "Will James."

"Will James," she repeated, and searched through the "J" page. She made the entry. "And what is to be the name on the other account?"

That was the easy one. "Hoyt. Fred Hoyt."

"Ah, the mysterious Mr. Hoyt," murmured Lila, turning to the "H" page.

I kept quiet. I glanced back at Sun Shu. She waited still as a statue.

"It's none of my business," Lila offered, her pencil poised above the page. "But I would recommend you make these new accounts joint accounts, so that you might have some control over them?"

She might as well have told me to hang onto a rattlesnake. I wanted as little to do with the Hoyt account as possible—just make the deposits of his share. The whole purpose of having all these accounts was to keep him in ignorance. I didn't want my name appearing anywhere in the deposits book, to give Mr. Hoyt tracks to follow. "Excuse me, Ma'am. I don't want any control over *his*. It's his fair share to do with as he pleases."

She let her pencil settle to the page. "You're speaking as if you're certain he will come back. What if he doesn't? If your name is not on his account, you will have to leave that gold behind when you go home." She regarded me somberly. "And I am afraid that will be true of the other accounts when it comes time to close them out."

I cast a quick glance back to Sun Shu as if she had an answer for me. She looked worried, but said nothing. I turned back to Lila and clutched the counter ledge. "But if he sees my name all over the deposit book, he'll figure out what I'm doing."

Lila reared back. "Only if I show it to him. According to our regulations, only employees and the auditors have access to our books."

"Mr. Hoyt can be very unpleasant when he wants his way."

Lila worked up a frown. "He has already exhibited that with Mr. Hamblin, my associate. As for myself, I am not happy to confess I have exchanged words with the coarsest members of the population and held my own." The creases faded from her brow. "But if your Mr. Hoyt chooses not to return, I shall not be tested." She almost smiled. "Which brings us back to you." She raised her eyebrows at me. "Would you like your accounts to be joint accounts?"

I let go of the counter and eased back. "Doesn't look like I have much choice."

She waited placidly, her hands resting on the ledger, one over the other, the pencil sprouting between her fingers.

"Yes Ma'am."

She made the entries. "And do you have anything to deposit in these new accounts?"

I hefted the trouser bag onto the counter.

"What's this?" Lila exclaimed. "Badly made sausage?"

I burst out laughing and Sun Shu smiled, but quickly covered her mouth.

Lila looked confused and uncomfortable. "Have I said something out of place?"

"No, Ma'am. Not at all! It's gold." I pointed to each section of the bag. "This part goes to 'Hoyt,' this part goes to 'Will James,' and this part goes to 'Hally Forsyth.'"

Lila briskly set about her business, weighing the nuggets from each section on her scales and noting the ounces in her ledger. I saved out a few nuggets from the Hally Forsyth deposit to buy supplies. I also sent some money from that account home to my family.

.   .   .

Gao Chung was waiting outside the express office. He fell into silent step with us, a pace behind, to Sun Shu's right. Even at this late hour, the saloons and gambling halls still throbbed with life. The street was all but deserted. I didn't count the ones sleeping off their drunks. As we walked back to the laundry, Sun Shu said, "May I speak, honorable Pegg?"

"Sure," I said, dismayed at her return to caution.

"What is your goal? With this plan, I mean."

My immediate goal was to keep what gold I found out of Mr. Hoyt's clutches. I hadn't thought beyond that. And I said as much.

Sun Shu replied, "Are you going to stop when you have matched what Mr. Pruitt and the neighbors put into it?"

"Well..."

"Permit me to say, I don't think they would be happy with that. This you probably already know."

"I know. But I don't want to stay here forever. It kind of depends on how much gold I find."

"Perhaps it also depends on how long you will be able to fool Mr. Hoyt."

"That's for sure," I was getting the knot in my stomach again.

"It is no pleasure to live in fear." Sun Shu seemed to be speaking to herself, as much as me.

I refused Sun Shu's room and slept behind the counter in the front room. While I was trying to fall asleep, I worried. About Mr. Hoyt, my mother and sister, about when I would have enough gold to go back home. It seemed like everything hinged on Mr. Hoyt. As my friend Will would say, *Fun times ahead.*

.   .   .

Before I left town, I bought brass scale and counterweights, paper and pencil, a pair of trousers, another blanket, a side of bacon, and a sack of beans. I also went to see the blacksmith.

The ring of a hammer pounding on iron reached me before I got there. His shop was more like a barn than anything, a ramshackle building with a great opening at the front. In the midst of a dusty clutter of iron and tools, the smith stood at his anvil, the forge glowing next to him, while the sharp smell of hot metal filled the air.

The blacksmith was a big Negro man with a bull neck and powerful arms. Over his shirt and trousers, he wore a big leather apron, the bottom half split down the middle to facilitate the shoeing of horses. At the moment I stepped inside, he was making a horseshoe. The metal he was shaping glowed orange.

I waited by the door with Bugle until he looked up.

"Where's your horse, Sonny?" boomed the smith. "I don't shoe dogs!" He laughed a big belly laugh.

"I need a digging tool," I said, stepping farther into the building. It was as warm as an oven.

"There's picks and shovels over at Gwynn's," he chuckled. "Already made!"

When his high spirits ebbed to mere cheerfulness, I explained. "Well, no, Sir. Something more like a pry bar."

"Gwynn's got them, too!" He pronounced gleefully. Both his front teeth were gold. He shoved the half-made horseshoe back into the glowing coals and worked the bellows.

"…already made," I said in a quiet voice, right along with him. "What I need is one short enough and light enough to use with just one hand."

"Can't say as I've ever heard of such a thing." He worked the horseshoe deeper into the coals.

"I thought we could take an old horseshoe—"

"We?" he turned, still smiling, his eyebrows rising.

"Excuse me, Sir. *You*—could start with an old horseshoe you didn't need—"

"Well, why didn't you say so, Son? That'd be no trouble at all." He withdrew the shoe he was working on and tossed it in the cooling tub.

At the risk of insulting him, I added, "And a point on one end…"

"Well, o'course. I wasn't born yesterday," chortled the smith. With long iron tongs he snatched up a discarded horseshoe and worked it in among the glowing coals while pumping the bellows vigorously. The oxygen fed the coals, orange to yellow to white. As the fire got hotter, the dull black of the horseshoe soon glowed cherry-red. The smith moved the shoe around like a cook tending meat on a grill. Sparks spit up. When the metal was glowing orange, he pulled it out and laid it on his anvil.

With powerful blows, he straightened it out into a tool about nine inches long. He tapered the business end to a sturdy point. The holes were still there, but that was okay. He had pounded the other end into a sort of cap, so it wouldn't slip easily out of my hand.

He held it up in the tongs for my approval. "That what you had in mind?" The orange color cooled to red, the red grew dull.

I nodded. "Yessir. That's perfect."

Another chuckle rumbled out of him. "Well, don't hear that too often." The new tool hissed vigorously when he plunged it into the cooling tub.

When, at last, it was black again—and cool enough—he handed it to me.

"Thank you, Sir. I appreciate your help." I handed him a nugget.

"That's very generous, young fella," said the blacksmith, accepting the nugget. "A specimen half that size would be too much."

"Can I put it on credit for when I want to shoe my dog?"

The blacksmith's eyes popped wide and his mouth fell open, and I heard his booming laughter as I walked away. "Anytime, Sonny! Anytime at all!" he called, and went on laughing.

CHAPTER 27

When I reached the river, I discovered some of my neighbors had returned, and were hard at it. Osher Phelps, with the claim next to me upstream, on the other side of the Grandfather Oak. Harvey Drummond, across from me on the north bank. A few others scattered up and down the river. As the river's flow increased, so would the miners' return.

The tool worked just as I had hoped it would. I pried loose nuggets during one dive and put them in the belt bag on the next dive. It was a one-handed operation. My other hand hung on to the rope. The dives never seemed long enough.

After four bags of nuggets, *big* nuggets, I was chilled through and through: a good time to quit for the afternoon. I warmed myself by the fire, bedazzled by the bounty of the seam and glad no one around seemed to care about my time in the river. *How had such a bonanza been overlooked?* I wondered. Most likely because people couldn't swim. A lot of people were skittish about water in the first place, be it a river or a bath.

I consulted quietly with Bugle. "If this keeps up, I'm gonna have to figure out how to move along the seam."

Bugle tilted his head and worked his eyebrows, but made no other comment.

"Of course, that's if it keeps up. It could play out," I snapped my fingers, "like that!"

Bugle barked his agreement.

"So, we shouldn't get uppity, should we?" I leaned toward him and whispered, wild-eyed. "But we've already dug out more gold than most folks see in their whole lives!"

I washed the nuggets and piled them on my table. If the next couple of days were like today, I would have to head into town again and make another deposit. I hadn't yet dug that new hiding hole I was thinking about, and I was uncomfortable having this much gold sitting around in my flimsy little shelter. I fell asleep gazing at my pile of gold.

I decided to use Chen Yi's request for more laundry as my cover. As soon as he was up and moving, I approached my neighbor, Osher Phelps. "'Morning, Mr. Phelps."

He was making biscuits. He looked over his shoulder. "'Morning to you, Pegg."

I tried to sound casual. "I'm heading into town to take in some laundry and get some supplies. If you have any laundry needs doing, I could take it in for you."

"Well, that's right kind of you," he replied. "I'd be much obliged."

So I headed into town with about a third of my gold hidden in a bundle of laundry. Thanks to my new scales, it was already divided in the proper portions.

I dumped that laundry onto the counter and put aside the divided bag.

"Ah, so, Pegg-son!" exclaimed Chen Yi. "You find more bad sausage."

I grinned at him. "Yessir, I did."

Chen Yi grinned back. "Fortune not just smile you. She sing you song!" He jigged his shoulders in silent laughter.

"And it is a sweet song." I separated Mr. Phelps' laundry from mine. "This pile is for Osher Phelps." It was an odd name, so I spelled it out for Chen Yi. Then I rested my hand on my bundle of shirts. "And this pile is for me."

"Starch? No starch?" Chen Yi said, all business.

I had forgotten to ask Mr. Phelps if he wanted starch in his shirts. I took a chance. "Starch all around."

Chen Yi wrote out the two tickets and handed them to me. "No lose ticket," he said solemnly. He had just scooped away the laundry when another customer came in. I stepped back to let Chen Yi serve him. The miner spotted my bag on the counter.

"Hey, Sam," he laughed, "What's this?"

I quaked. If the man touched it, he would know.

Chen Yi slid the bag over by other piles of laundry, making a sour face. "Try sausage business, but too spicy. Stick to washee business." And reached for the miner's washing.

The man left with his ticket and Chen Yi brought my bag forward on the counter.

"Chen Yi, I would like to ask your help."

He held up a finger. "Wait, please," he said. "Bring Sun Shu."

A moment later I returned with Sun Shu.

Chen Yi said, very seriously, "This about sausage bag?"

"Yessir, it is," I said.

"Talk other room. This room many eyes, ears."

Chen Yi guided us over to the second ironing table. I had no sooner begun speaking when the bell announced another customer. Chen Yi said in a low voice, "Talk Sun Shu. I hear later," and he hurried away.

I turned to Sun Shu and patted the misshapen bag. "I have this much still back at my cabin—shelter."

Sun Shu got a concerned look. "…Shelter?"

I put my hands up in defense. "I'm okay. I'm warm, I'm dry, I'm well-fed." I rushed on. "And it looks like there may be even more where this came from. If others see me with all this gold, they'll be like moths to the flame." I paused. "Do you know that saying?"

"Yes. I do." She studied the bag for a moment. "But how can you keep all this a secret?"

"That's why I need your help."

"Yes," she said without hesitation. "How may I help?"

"Here's my idea. Instead of taking this whole bunch to the express office in one visit, we—you, me, ChenYi, maybe even Gao Chung—take in a small part of it every once in a while. Do it at all different times. Nobody sees a pattern. Would you and Chen Yi be willing to do that?"

I was too concerned with my own plight to consider what danger this might put them in.

"You would trust us with your gold?" Sun Shu arched her eyebrows in worry.

"I would trust you with my life."

She looked at me so steadily, I got nervous. "People would be suspicious of Chinese bringing in this much gold."

"Like I said, take a little bit at a time." I was desperate for her to accept my plan. "Even a few nuggets in your pocket. It doesn't matter how long it takes." Then my shoulders sagged. "Actually, it does matter how long it takes."

"Have you had word from him?"

"No. But I have to plan as if he is coming back."

"So then we must move as briskly as we can."

"Yes. Any of this—" I touched the bag again. "—that isn't hidden out of his reach, he's going to claim."

I handed Sun Shu a drawing of the bag cinched into three portions. "I made this for you." I had labeled it across the top, "Fred Hoyt, Will James, Hally Forsyth," with arrows pointing to each section. "I will have the gold all measured out before I come in. I have a set of scales now."

Sun Shu put down the drawing. She settled her hands on the table and looked down at them. She spoke quietly. "Does this mean you will be going home soon—back to Vermont?"

CHAPTER 28

After taking my leave of Sun Shu, I stopped by to see Lila on my way out of town, and told her about forthcoming visits by my Celestial friends. Her brows drew slowly together. I finished by saying, "So, if you don't mind, expect Chen Yi or Sun Shu, maybe even Gao Chung, to make deposits in one of the three accounts."

She tapped her pencil on her ledger.

"Ma'am?"

"It's none of my business, Pegg, but. . ." She closed her eyes resolutely, then opened them again. "Is it wise to put such great trust in people you've known for so short a time?"

"Miss Rose, they are good people. Look how they took care of me. If not for them, I might well have perished. I trust them as much as I trust my own family."

She hadn't expected that. She regarded me seriously. "Well," she sighed. "I'm glad they will be making only deposits, not withdrawals. Deposits I can accept. But, if there are mistakes or misunderstandings, it will be up to the parties involved to sort out. If they want to make withdrawals, on the other hand, you will have to be here *with them*."

"I understand."

She nodded, short and sharp.

"Thank you, Ma'am. I appreciate your helping out."

"I am only doing my job, Pegg. If I get so much as a whiff of unsavory shenanigans, I'll show you the door before you can catch your breath. Is that understood?" She put her pencil back behind her ear.

"Yes, Ma'am. Loud and clear, Ma'am."

"Good. Kindly inform your co-conspirators of the requirements, and my concerns."

"Yes, Ma'am." I put my hat back on.

"I trust you will do it with tact. I do not wish to be seen as ill-mannered."

"Yes, Ma'am. I'll bring everything my mother ever taught me about good manners to the situation."

A hint of a smile came to Lila's lips, then it was gone. "I expect that was not inconsiderable." She looked up as a customer came in.

Leaving the express office, I reflected that Lila had addressed me as Pegg. Not Mr. Pegg. Not Young man, not Son, or Sonny. Just Pegg. I was pleased about that.

I said a little prayer for the success of my plan.

.   .   .

As the weather warmed, more miners came back to work their claims. If anyone observed me closely enough to detect any telltale pattern to my movements, they kept it to themselves. One of my decoys was taking Bugle for a run.

I was farther along the seam, toward the center of the river, diving in eight or nine feet of water. My claim officially ended at the center line. I was sure I was getting better at holding my breath. Even so, each dive seemed to end too soon.

My makeshift pry bar had proven to be all I hoped it would be. I pried at a long and skinny specimen, about the size of a finger. The shape in itself wasn't noteworthy; nuggets came in all shapes. But this one didn't end. And it kept getting wider. Before I could see any more, I had to come up for air.

I hung onto the rope, catching my breath, looking around. Everyone was minding their own business, except for Mr. Drummond, the prospector directly across from me. His gaze was steady, as if he was waiting for acknowledgement. We nodded to each other, and he went back to inspecting his pan. I wondered if he could swim.

On the next dive, I didn't worry about filling my belt bag. I just poked along to find out more about this odd specimen. It twisted and curled, looking something like a molted snakeskin, except thicker. A trembling excitement crept over me. Not only was it getting wider; in some places it hollowed out. In those cavities, smaller, loose nuggets had collected.

It took two more dives to brush away the silt that covered the other end of the nugget. It looked to be at least twenty inches long. It was too twisty and misshapen to be fool's gold. I couldn't believe my eyes. I had exposed only the top half, but likely the bottom half was gold, too.

I stared at the gnarled mass until I was about to drown. I shot to the surface and scrambled out of the river and stood, shivering, wrapped in my blanket close to the fire. I had a powerful urge to shout to the heavens. But in the next instant, I realized it should be Dad shouting to the heavens. Sobered, questions crowded thick and fast into my mind. Was that nugget as big as I thought? How much did it weigh? How was I going to get it out of the river unseen?

I shivered, but not because I was cold. I would give anything to have my dad standing here so I could lay this mighty nugget at his feet. I sank to my knees, borne down by regret. I pictured him washing dirt at the edge of the river, working beside me, steadily, quietly, like we had done so many times on the farm, then him playing his violin after supper.

Bugle stepped close and whined a question. I stroked his head. "Somebody very important is missing right now." I put my arm around his neck and stared into the fire. I made us some dinner.

I had a tough time believing what I had dug out—well, at least revealed—in the seam. It was better than any of the wildest stories I'd heard. Since coming to Rattlesnake Bar, I'd seen and heard enough to know that many an argonaut went home empty-handed, broken, worse off than they were before—if they were lucky enough to get home at all. I was humbled at my good fortune.

The value of that one nugget would surely put me much closer to making my dad's dream a reality.

With my dinner half-eaten, I went back to the seam. During my next few dives, I concentrated on taking a truer measure of the freakish specimen. It was probably closer to two feet long, and six inches at its widest. It had a number of cavities where smaller nuggets rested.

I stopped to get warm. I stood turning, toasting myself by the fire, scheming. How to get it ashore without arousing unwelcome curiosity? Doing it at night was obvious. I devoted the remaining dives of the day to making sure the nugget was loose and could be pulled free.

It took most of the next morning's dives to drag the nugget along the bottom toward shore. By the time I had it in about five feet of water, I was in the claim downstream. Thankfully, it was the one R. C. had left me.

I covered the nugget with sand and rocks, and arranged a triangle of small stones—something I could feel with my feet—at the shoreward end of the nugget. Lastly, I placed a small, white pebble against a stump on shore to show the position of the submerged treasure.

I spent the rest of the day taking more loose nuggets out of the seam. Night could not come fast enough. I collected more firewood. Never a wasted endeavor.

After supper, I gave Bugle a good scratching. We watched the white sliver of a crescent moon come sharper in the darkening sky. The comfortable patter of the miners ebbed to quiet. Their cook fires dwindled to orange smudges in the black.

At moonset, all was still, and I stirred myself to get on with my task. Bugle woke up and raised his head, expecting a new adventure. I bent down and whispered to him, "Shhhh. No barking, okay? Wait here."

Blanket in hand, I waded into the river, located the nugget, wrapped it in the blanket underwater—just in case anybody was awake—and carried it ashore. As soon as I lifted it out of the water, I got a sense of its true weight. Six or seven pounds, maybe closer to ten!

Bugle came over to inspect the strangeness.

"You keep watch, okay, Boy?" I whispered and ducked into the shelter.

Making room on my little table, I carefully set down the bundle. I lit my lantern and unrolled the soggy blanket, settling back on my heels to stare at the nugget. It gleamed softly, its presence so powerful I expected it to rise up and speak.

Outside, Bugle whined. I opened the door and brought him in. I pointed to the specimen. "Even R. C.'s eyes would pop if he could see this monster."

Bugle licked his chops.

"If I could show it to Will, he would be speechless for a week! Well, a few minutes, anyway." I settled back and gathered Bugle in for a scratch, staring at the nugget. "It has to be two feet long, if it's an inch. What do you think?"

The nugget looked very much like a good-sized lump of taffy, pulled from both ends, fat in the middle, tapering out on each end. It was very irregular and pocked with the cavities.

I moved closer, studying every inch of its contortions, careful not to spill any of the smaller nuggets. The whole thing was *real gold!* Lifting it, I judged the weight to be much closer to ten pounds. At sixteen dollars an ounce, it would be worth more than two thousand dollars. This one specimen might put us within reach of going home.

Not if Mr. Hoyt finds out about it, Will reminded me.

I regarded the great, misshapen lump. *That's why he must never see it, never know of it.*

It was so gnarled and twisted, it could well represent somebody's torment. Or nightmare.

Now it's your nightmare, Will snickered in my mind.

So I dubbed my bounty the Nightmare Nugget.

Bugle whined in sympathy. I left off appraising the nugget and cut him a piece of bacon, and one for myself.

Dad came back into my thoughts. *He should be here, celebrating our great fortune. Was all this worth losing him?* I knew what my mother would say to that. Nothing was worth losing her husband—and she'd be right.

CHAPTER 29

Never in my wildest dreams did I ever think I would find a nugget this big. How was I going to weigh this thing? The counterweights that came with my scales added up to a pound. My nightmare nugget weighed close to ten times that much. I went outside and collected some smaller river stones, about the size of my fist. I stacked all the counterweights in the right-hand dish of the scales. That dish sank to the tabletop, lifting the empty, left dish high. I tried the stones one at a time in the empty dish. When the dishes came level, I knew I had a rock that weighed a pound.

When I had weighed nine such stones, I replaced the counterweights with the Nightmare Nugget. The right dish dropped to the table with a thump. I stacked the left dish carefully with all nine of my pound stones. The dish holding the Nightmare Nugget didn't budge.

Then, even more gingerly, I added back all the counterweights in among the pound stones. The right hand dish with the Nightmare Nugget still didn't budge.

A huge yawn caught me unawares. *Yes. Enough excitement for one day.* I turned down the wick in my lantern and was soon asleep.

I knew nothing more until the clatter of breakfast fixings roused me. The smell of coffee boiling and bacon frying followed the daylight through the gaps of my shelter. My neighbors were up and busy. The previous day came rushing back when I spied the Nightmare Nugget pinning the scale dish to my tabletop. It looked different in the flat, cool, morning light. Then I realized a thin skin of silt, invisible when it was wet, had dried in the night, hiding its luster.

I wiped it down with a wet rag, restoring its seductive gleam. The elation over the wealth it contained faded. *How am I going to get this beast into town?* Most miners dealt with a pinch or two a day, or what they could carry in a poke. My great lump seemed to gloat with the challenge it posed.

I stepped outside to survey the already busy scene. The sun would crest the eastern horizon any moment. I gave a salute to Osher Phelps, who returned it, and rekindled my fire. Bugle trotted off on his morning rounds.

He returned when I was frying our bacon. He gave out with his "A visitor's coming" bark. I looked around until I caught sight of Richard Barter splashing across the river.

"Top of the mornin' to you, Lion Man?" he said with a grin.

"How're you doing?" I pointed with my fork to a keg on the other side of the fire. "Have you had breakfast?"

Richard took the seat, folding his long legs akimbo. "Yes, Thanks. A while ago." Bugle went over for a scratch. Richard obliged.

"You must have gotten an early start." I blew on a piece of bacon to cool it for Bugle and held it out to him. Then I forked up a piece for myself. "You've been a little scarce lately."

"I had a teamster job. The bloke kept me going day and night. He arranged for changing the horses, but he didn't feel the need to extend the same courtesy to his drivers."

I got stuck on the key word. "Had? What happened?"

"He sold the business," Richard sighed. "The new owner announced his intention to keep the same regimen, to which I found I had to object." Richard gave me a rueful smile. "After something of a warm exchange, we agreed it would be better if I sought employment elsewhere."

"Ah." I chewed on another piece of bacon. I marveled that he could maintain such aplomb when his situation seemed so precarious.

He lifted his hat and tossed his dark hair as if shaking loose something irksome. "That's all right. Something else will come along." Richard looked around. "Still on your own, it appears. Whatever became of that supposed partner of yours? Hoyt, wasn't it?"

"He should be showing up soon."

Richard smiled. "Then the holiday will be over, I dare say."

My spirits dimmed. Hoyt's return was a millstone that weighed grievously. He had become more adversary than partner. "But that's not my most pressing problem."

Richard's smile faded into a questioning look.

"I want to show you something." I rose to my feet and led him into the shelter.

Richard was tall. He had to bend almost double to fit inside. "Couldn't you have built it a little smaller?" he chuckled. Then he let out a long, low whistle, and stood transfixed, staring at the Nightmare Nugget.

Richard approached it cautiously. A few bits of light fell on the lumps and swirls, making them shine. I stood aside as he crouched for a closer inspection.

He ran his hand over it lightly, up and back, letting his fingers rise and fall with the pits and knobs. Then he turned with a wide grin. "I give you joy, Pegg-o. You can go home tomorrow."

I barked out a laugh. "Ha! I wish that were true." Then my hilarity faded. "But it's not all mine. Most will go to the other partners."

Richard sagged back on his heels. "Righto. I forgot." He returned his attention to the monster nugget. After a moment, he leaned forward, lifting it.

I could tell he didn't expect it to be so heavy. Richard let out another low whistle. The dish that was under the nugget followed it up. That upset the precarious arrangement of river stones and counterweights in the other dish, all of which tumbled noisily onto the table, and then to the floor. "Oh, dear. What have I done?" Richard quickly replaced the nugget.

I stopped a weight from rolling off the table. "Don't worry. That's how I know it's more than ten pounds."

Richard's spirits rebounded, and his grin grew even wilder. "You could buy half of San Francisco with this lump."

I could no longer restrain a smile. I thought of Eli Cooder's story. "I'll leave San Francisco to Sammy Brannan. This—" I poked my finger at the Nightmare Nugget, "—is going to build the best dairy farm ever, so help me, God."

Richard stuck out his hand and we shook, grinning like fools.

I sobered up. "I need to keep this a secret. Especially from Mr. Hoyt."

Richard raised a skeptical eyebrow. "But he's your partner." He sat with his back against the bed frame.

I finished gathering up the counterweights. "I have little doubt he would gamble or drink it all away. I'm pretty sure that's what he's done with the gold I've given him so far."

"Good reason to keep this a secret, then." He regarded the Nightmare Nugget once more. "But I dare say this is much too big to be kept a secret."

"I've just got to figure out a way to get it to the express office without causing a commotion."

Richard brightened. "That's simple enough. Divide it up into smaller pieces."

"What?" I scoffed. "It's gold. It won't break like other rocks, even if I had a hammer big enough."

Richard gazed, unwavering, at the nugget. "It's quite magnificent, in a strange, savage sort of way." He reached to touch it again. "I grant you, 'twould be a pity to destroy it, but with a little work, we could tear it into pieces."

I grew impatient with his whimsy. "You can't tear a rock."

Richard smiled. "Oh! Ye of little faith." He picked up one of my weighing stones. "What do you say?"

We slid the nugget out of the scales. I put the scales and counterweights away while Richard positioned the nugget on the table. He looked along its length until he settled on a spot just short of its widest point. He raised the stone over his head.

I winced. The Nightmare Nugget was bizarre, but he was right. It was magnificent in its own, wild way. "You don't have to watch," Richard smirked. "Close your eyes and think about your new farm."

"Wait." I thrust out my hand. "We'll bash the table to pieces. Let's do it on the floor. Use one of the other stones as an anvil." I picked out one with something of a flat surface. We moved the table to have more room.

Richard glanced over his shoulder. "Let's at least start on the dirt. That will muffle the sound somewhat."

I held the nugget while Richard beat on it with the stones. After the first couple of blows, he produced a small dent, and proudly pointed out his handiwork.

"A good start." I took a fresh grip on the nugget.

Richard didn't seek my opinion after that. He just kept pounding the nugget, mashing it down in the same place, making the dent deeper. I was hard put to see it as progress. "I have a hammer. Would that work better?"

Winded from his efforts, Richard wheezed, "I think it might."

I fetched him the hammer.

Wielding the hammer with even greater vigor than he had the stone, Richard concentrated his blows on the same spot. He hammered that spot flat, but the gold refused to crack or brake or part in any way. I didn't see how he would tear it or cut it as he had proposed. He kept hammering.

I stepped outside the shelter. Thankfully, the prospectors were making enough of their own racket that our pounding was just part of the din. I went back inside.

"Can I spell you?" I asked between blows.

"Certainly." He handed me the hammer. "It's your nugget, after all. Hit it in the same place," he cautioned, pointing to the furrow he had created. "Now it's time for something firmer." He retrieved the stone I wanted to use for an anvil and placed it under the part of the nugget I was pounding.

I began pounding in earnest. Richard held the nugget steady, as I had done. But no matter how much we beat on the gold, it wouldn't break apart.

Richard instructed me to extend the furrow until it reached across the width of the nugget. We spelled each other, hammering. The place we pounded gave before our assault until it was perhaps an inch thick. The furrow looked like a little canyon running crossways through the uneven terrain of the nugget. Before long the floor of the canyon was as thin as a pancake. The free end of the Nightmare Nugget started to droop. Then I pounded it down as thin as a piece of paper. The free end sagged toward the floor. It still didn't break! Gold was behaving in a way that I'd never seen in any other rock. I kept pounding and got it *thinner* than a sheet of paper.

Without warning, the narrow, tissue-thin sheet of gold tore apart. The free part of the nugget dropped to the floor.

Richard lifted the part he was holding. "Alas," He sighed, feigning sadness, "beauty sacrificed to utility. Not for the first time, and certainly not the last."

I picked up the fallen half of the nugget and took a close look. The torn tissue of gold we had pounded hung like a limp rag.

Richard sank back on his heels. "What did I tell you?"

I grinned like a fool. Providing I had the patience, I could pound the Nightmare Nugget into as many pieces as I wanted. I could take it into town a thumbnail at a time, if I chose. Hoyt would never be the wiser. "Thanks. I am in your debt."

Richard waved his part of the nugget in the air. "You take this into town and you can order ten pounds of caviar and six geese-a-laying!"

I rested my part on the table. "If I can help it, no one will know it ever passed through town."

"That's the thinking." Richard said.

.   .   .

In the following days, I split my time between diving to the seam and pounding on the nugget. I divided the Nightmare Nugget into six pieces. It weighed a little over twelve pounds! This one nugget and its nestlings would provide three thousand dollars. I pulled the folded piece of paper—now brown, battered, and frayed—from my shirt pocket. I could barely make out the pencil marks with my mom's figures. Fifteen thousand dollars would meet all the obligations of the partnership.

After I had it all divided up into the three proper proportions and marked, I took the three deposits into the laundry in three different trips, hidden in bundles of laundry. Chen Yi and Sun Shu did their part, and for that, I was very grateful.

But the seam was still giving up its bounty. So, I started burying some of it on the hill behind my claim. This, too, I did at night.

What an odd situation to be in. Dame Fortune was showering me with riches, and instead of celebrating, I was scheming, hiding, and sneaking around.

.   .   .

I took a walk on downstream to Rattlesnake Bar, to visit Jacob at his claim. He had just come back from his brother's ranch. We had a good gab. He told me all about the ranch. It was hard, but I didn't say anything about the seam or the Nightmare Nugget.

Each time I went into Auburn, there were new faces, new stores, another saloon or two. I gave Lila a hand whenever I came to town. And, of course, I kept bringing laundry to my Celestial family.

I left Bugle at the laundry while I did my errands, the chief of which was to make a deposit at the express office. Most days, I took in Mr. Hoyt's portion, because it was the smallest of the three. I thought it would be more logical for a merchant, like Chen Yi, to make the bigger deposits.

I kept an eye out for Mr. Hoyt. The days were getting warmer and longer. If he intended to come back, it would be any day now. I tried to imagine what he would say, and what I would say back.

One day in late April, I took my family's portion to Lila's.

She had customers, so I took my place in line. It was a busy day for her; seven or eight people were ahead of me. Two more came in; one of them had letters to mail. An easy hubbub filled the room—miners chatting, catching up, swapping news. It reminded me of Saturday markets back home. Occasionally the clank of nuggets landing in Lila's scales dish broke through.

Most of what I could see were hats and backs of heads.

Then I spied a head and shoulders that were more familiar than most. My stomach dropped into my boots. Mr. Hoyt!

I'd know that wavy, oiled hair anywhere, the stiff, proud neck. Probably chafing at having to wait his turn like a mere mortal. Hoyt was fourth in line. I shifted a bit to see his boots. Yep. Same fancy boots. *It's him, all right. Same high cheek bones.*

He started to turn. I ducked back into the line. It was harder to hide; I was taller now. To my astonishment, his wary gaze passed over me with no hint of recognition. Frowning, he turned to face front again.

I stared at his back, relief washing over me.

Slip away now. Plan a better way to meet him.

Before I could make a move, he turned again, slowly this time, and fixed his gaze on me. His eyebrows shifted in consternation. As he stepped out of line, he spoke in a cautious voice. "Pegg?" His brows gathered together as if he wasn't sure. "Pegg? Is that you, boy?"

My chance to escape was gone. I stood, rooted. I couldn't bring myself to pretend joy at our reunion. Mr. Hoyt appeared to have no such reservations as he swaggered toward me. "Pegg, boy! There you are!" he cried.

I tried to keep my voice calm. "Mr. Hoyt." *Now the hard part begins.*

CHAPTER 30

I usually looked forward to going to the express office and matching wits with Lila in our cordial way. Now, as Mr. Hoyt left his place in line and approached, the room lost its warmth, its substance, its security. The whole world shrank to just him and me, tethered by a cold, stout iron rod anchored in my stomach.

The miners moved to fill his spot in the line. A few turned to watch this encounter unfold.

Mr. Hoyt was only a step away. "I didn't recognize you." He tilted his head. "You look half Injun."

He was probably right. I sported several visible scars courtesy of the mountain lion, had not cut my hair in months, and had been out in the sun without a hat almost every day.

If I couldn't pretend joy, I could manage a lie. "I didn't recognize you either—without your crutch."

He did a little jig. "Good as new." He stopped in front of me. "Look at you. You've grown like a weed." He looked closer at my forehead. "Got yourself some scars, I see. You been playin' rough while I was away?"

"I suppose you could say that. I had a run-in with a mountain lion."

Mr. Hoyt, unimpressed, reared back, beaming like a proud father. "Ain't this right nice timing, now? Here I am, making inquiries as to your whereabouts—and here you are!" He jabbed an accusing finger at me.

"Yessir. Here I am." I held very still. I had imagined a dozen versions of this moment, but each one was played opposite a testy, high-strung Hoyt. Now, standing here in the flesh, he appeared a jolly uncle, happy to see me. I knew I could not trust his hearty blandishments, but I realized his very unpredictability was his best weapon.

His eyes flicked down to the bundle in the crook of my arm, which held my family's portion of my latest deposit. A sly smile crept onto his face. His eyebrows lifted in delight. I realized in order to keep up the charade that only one account—in his name and mine—existed, this bundle would have to be sacrificed to that account. I hoped desperately Lila would play along.

Put on a cheery voice. "You couldn't have arrived at a better time." I made a smile at Hoyt, but not too much, and patted the parcel like I would Bugle. "I'm here to make a deposit into our account."

My long-lost partner fixed on the bundle like a cat spying a mouse. "Might I have a look?" he wheedled.

Reluctantly, I handed it to him.

He turned it over in his hands. The bundle was about two hand widths long, and as thick as a man's wrist. "This is yours, then? Ours, I mean." He didn't wait for my answer. He turned the lumpy parcel over, inspecting it, hefting it to get the feel for its weight. The nuggets rubbed against each other like dry knuckle bones. "This is a might more than a pinch of color in the bottom of a pan." Then he saw the writing on the sack. I froze. *Will he remember the name?*

He peered at it. "Hally Forsyth. Forsyth. . . Forsyth," like he was searching through his memory. He looked up, a challenge in his eye. "Wasn't there a Forsyth family on the trip out?"

I prayed my face wouldn't give me away. "Yes. There was."

He looked back at the writing. "Went on to Oregon, as I remember."

Fortunately, we had reached the counter, and it was our turn. "Good morning, Ma'am," I chirped.

She replied in her blandest express agent voice, like I was just another face in line. "Good morning. How may I help you today?"

"I would like to make a deposit." I turned to Mr. Hoyt, but he did not relinquish the bundle.

"Very well. What's the name?" She opened the ledger.

I gestured toward Mr. Hoyt. "Miss Rose, this is Fred Hoyt. He's the partner I've told you about. The other name I put on the account."

"I see," she said. "Good day to you, Mr. Hoyt. I… Pegg has advised me of your imminent arrival. Welcome to Auburn."

Hoyt beamed like a politician. "A pleasure, indeed, Madam." He touched his finger to his hat brim.

I gestured at the bundle Hoyt held. "As I said, I'd like to deposit this today, please." I moved to take the bundle. Hoyt moved it out of my reach. *What's he up to?*

Then he caught himself and glanced sheepishly at the half dozen miners who waited behind us. He let his arm down, and I took the bundle and handed it to Lila, mouthing a silent, "Thank you." She made a brief little frown with her lips tight together. She understood.

There was too much gold in the bag to weigh all at one time. She gently shook half the nuggets into one dish of the scale. Mr. Hoyt leaned over the counter, watching Lila put counterweights in the other dish. He leaned in more watch the marker creep closer to the center.

No sooner had the dishes come level with each other than Hoyt blurted, almost shouted, "How much? How many ounces?"

I wanted to crawl under the floorboards.

Lila ignored him. "You haven't been in for quite a while," she said to me, making a note in her ledger. Lila never made small talk while weighing ore. She emptied the first dish and filled it again with the remainder of my deposit. "You're having better luck these days, I see."

She's not only playing along, she's improving it. "Yes, Ma'am. Much better than it has been…thanks."

While Lila carefully noted in the ledger, she addressed Mr. Hoyt, "One pound, twelve ounces."

Out of habit, Lila handed me the receipt, but Mr. Hoyt intercepted it with lightning fingers, stuffing it into his vest pocket with smug satisfaction. "Now that I'm back, it's only fitting I take up my old responsibilities."

This was the Hoyt I'd grown to despise. Did he really expect to resume our old routine, gambling and drinking away the gold I brought him? How long before he got himself in the kind of trouble that would require a perilous escape from *this* town—as it had from Grizzly Bar? I slipped my hand under his elbow and led him away from the counter.

"I have a splendid idea," he exclaimed, still gloating in his fulsome mood "All the way here I promised myself that the first thing I would do is treat you to a king's feast."

I made to protest. "That's not necess—"

"Now, now." He held up his hand defensively. "I owe you a great deal, not the least of which is standing by me in the mountains. A dinner is but a trifle."

I'd never heard Hoyt express gratitude for anything. What had happened to him in Coloma over the winter? Had good fortune smiled on him at last? With his purse now bulging, could he afford to look upon the world with a kinder eye?

Nonetheless, I couldn't shake the foreboding feeling that he was already eyeing the account for his own use. How fast would he use it up? Could I keep it "stocked" with enough gold to avoid him getting suspicious? The knot in my stomach got bigger.

Mr. Hoyt broke into my thoughts. "We'll order the best the house has to offer. You can tell me what you've been doing, and I can tell you all about Coloma and Hang Town."

CHAPTER 31

The dining room of the Empire Hotel might have rough plank floors, but it had round tables with white tablecloths and chandeliers, and waiters dressed in clean livery. As befitted a quality establishment in a wildly prosperous town, the Empire served their wine in cut crystal goblets. The room was beginning to fill with the dinner trade, businessmen discussing deals, miners celebrating, travelers in dusty clothes. Hoyt and I halted by the entrance, waiting to be seated. The savory tang of hot roast beef drifted out from the kitchen. This would certainly be a welcome change to beans and bacon.

A waiter approached. "Two?"

We nodded and he conducted us to a small table tucked against the wall. The waiter pulled out a chair.

"I'm sorry," Hoyt said regretfully, "we'll need a bigger table. This is a special occasion."

I cast a wary glance at my partner. *Why do we need a bigger table? What are you planning?* I leaned close to him and whispered, "This table is fine. There's only the two of us."

"Ah," replied he grandly, "not today, my son. I said a celebration, and I don't mean it to be half-baked." His eyes brightened, and he gave me a nudge. "Oh. That was rather good, wasn't it?"

I gave him a smirk, hoping it would pass for an appreciation of his wit.

He looked around the room and pointed. "That one will do."

The waiter protested. "That table will seat six or eight, and we will surely fill it."

Hoyt turned an amiable smile on the waiter. "We will make it well worth your while, my friend. Please oblige us."

Miffed, the waiter led us to the table while Hoyt reassured him. "We intend to burden this noble table with your finest viands and most cherished vintages." I only half-listened. My friend Will would deem such talk hot air or worse.

Again, the waiter did us the courtesy of pulling out our chairs. Another waiter presented us our menus.

Hoyt studied the long, stiff card with a lively eye. For my part, I gazed upon a foreign country. I could recognize some of the words, like "beef," "mutton," "potatoes," or "pudding," but they were attached to words that rendered the familiar uncertain.

I knew the prices were steep. A plain omelet was three dollars, more than a week's wages in Vermont.

I stole a glance at the waiter, who stood to attention by Hoyt's right shoulder, waiting to take our orders. The expression on my partner's face grew more concerned the farther down the menu he progressed. He said, "It appears you offer nothing comparable to Porter's NewYork Ambassador's Dinner." He glanced up expectantly at our waiter.

The waiter blinked apologetically. "I'm sorry, Sir? Porter's—?"

Hoyt finished for him. "—New York Ambassador's Dinner. Surely you know Porter's. In Hang Town?"

The waiter replied stiffly, "I'm afraid I do not." It was a standoff. He clarified. "What we offer is itemized on the menu."

"Pity." Hoyt returned his gaze to the menu and, after more study, began to order what seemed like half the items listed.

We can't eat that much. When Hoyt paused for breath, I jumped in. "Surely that's enough. There's only two of us."

My partner blithely ignored me and charged on. The waiter scribbled furiously on a small slip of paper.

At last, Hoyt held the menu out to the waiter. Apparently, I was supposed to be satisfied with his choices. Even when I hesitated to surrender my menu, he ignored that I might have my own choices.

He smiled up at the waiter. "And we'll start with a bottle of your best claret."

"Very good." The waiter took my menu and stalked off.

I opened my mouth to protest the extravagance, but Hoyt spoke first. "You will soon learn to seize every opportunity to celebrate your triumphs, however modest; especially after such arduous travails."

I didn't know what 'travails' meant, but I knew, if Hoyt held true to form, I would end up paying for this celebration. I also knew that it was far more lavish than the occasion warranted.

It would be fine to hear about other gold rush towns, but I had a powerful urge to confront Hoyt about his treacherous neglect of my family. But I knew him well enough to know that my accusations would be lost in the thickets of his balderdash. *Maybe start with the softer edges.* That's what my dad called it. What he always did first was to get a person comfortable with something they could both agree on. "I'm sure glad to see your leg's all healed up. Like it never even happened."

Pretending to be awestruck by the finery, I gazed around the room, while letting my frustration simmer down.

Hoyt grunted contentedly. "Yes. Despite—what was his name?"

"MacIver. Gideon MacIver, the Chalmers Company scout. If anybody got us through two thousand miles of wilderness, he did."

"Yes. Despite that rascal's worst intentions, I seem to have emerged unscathed."

I had my own slant on the episode: *If MacIver hadn't set your leg, you probably wouldn't still have the leg. Worse, you would likely be frozen stiff on the side of a mountain.*

The waiter soon brought the bottle of claret and presented it to Hoyt, holding it in such a way that seemed he wanted Hoyt to approve it. Hoyt, for his part, gave the label only a brief glance.

"Ah. Chateau Mouton. That's more like it." He nodded to the waiter. "Very good, Garçon." The waiter opened the bottle and splashed a little wine into Hoyt's glass. It was little more than a mouthful. My worldly partner proceeded through a ritual of sniffing, gargling, and considering that wholly mystified me. At last, he swallowed and gestured with his glass for the waiter to pour.

The man filled both our glasses with no great care, thumped the bottle on the table, and left us, clearly displeased. This didn't seem to dampen Hoyt's spirits in the slightest. I stared at my glass. It held more wine than I had drunk in my entire life.

Hoyt took a long drink and sighed his satisfaction theatrically. For his part, he had no qualms about getting right to the heart of the matter. "If the deposit we just made is any indication, you've been doing well."

It was easy to lie when my family's future was at stake. "Oh! No, sir!" I laughed. "I wish I had. That was the best I've done in weeks. It was a small pocket and it played out by the end of the day." *Point up the negative.* "It hasn't all been like that, believe me." I managed another rueful laugh. "And that's not counting the weeks I was laid up recovering from the mountain lion attack, or more weeks I spent waiting for floodwaters to abate." Hoyt was studying me now. I shook my head slowly. "Aside from the delays, I've gone weeks without a speck of color."

Hoyt looked distressed. "Surely you've been keeping a tally while I've been gone. Do you know how much we have?"

"I don't exactly know, Sir. My luck has been so hit-and-miss. I'll bring you the receipts and you can count them up." Of course, I would bring him only the receipts for the Hoyt, Pegg account.

The first three courses arrived together: *potage du jour*, fried oysters, and a great slab of some kind of fish swimming in a thick, white sauce. Hoyt wasted no time in filling his plate.

I was struck immediately that I had become used to Chinese food, whenever I got away from bacon and beans. The dishes before me looked sumptuous, indeed. I tried an oyster. It tasted like fried leather. I took my chance. "How did you get on in Coloma? What was Mr. Brannan like?"

Hoyt took a drink of wine before answering. "Splendidly. The opportunities are boundless. The man is a whirlwind! A new idea, a new enterprise with every breath!"

I leaned forward eagerly. "You did well, then."

Another course arrived—boiled leg of mutton. The waiter carved it and served us. Hoyt attacked his portion with gusto. "Fred Hoyt does not waste time on laggards."

I sawed at my meat. "Combining what you made in Coloma with what I've made here, I'm sure we'll soon have enough to satisfy everyone in the partnership."

Hoyt took a forkful of mutton, gazing at me while he chewed, then broke into an patronizing laugh. "In these matters, the important thing is not what is in hand, but what the potential is."

"Oh."

He refilled his wine glass and set the bottle down, leaning forward earnestly. "It's not a simple matter of turning over a few shovels of dirt, Pegg, boy. In these enterprises, all the pieces have their unique challenges. But they must, in the fullness of time, join together harmoniously. Only then will the effort bear fruit."

I blinked at him as if I were a fledgling in the nest.

His patience was tested. "To realize a profit." He took a slug of wine. "They need tending, care, time—just like a corn crop. You can understand that."

Beating around the bush is getting me nowhere. "So, did you make money with Mr. Brannan, or not?"

Hoyt scowled for an eye blink, then smoothed his brow. He smiled benignly. "It would be better to say, 'I am making money.' The results will amaze you, Pegg,boy."

To please him, I took a small sip of wine. *He's still as slippery as an eel.*

Another course arrived—platters of roasted meat: beef, turkey, veal. The savor of roasted meat just about did me in, but I had to keep my wits about me. The platters were heaped, yet we'd barely made a dent in what was already on the table. I was dazzled by the sheer plentitude of victuals. We didn't even do this much at Christmas, back home. But I was too concerned about the treacherous road ahead to yield to gluttony.

Not so, my partner. Hoyt ordered another bottle of wine before the first bottle was empty. Unbidden, he transferred a slab of veal to my plate. My dog Bugle would benefit from this feast more than I.

"Drink up, Boy." He gestured with the depleted bottle before handing it to the waiter.

I took another sip.

He piled his plate with bloody red beef and pale veal. "Don't you worry, Pegg, boy. Now that I'm here, we'll get back to our old routine. I'll keep an eye on our situation. You just keep finding the loot." He stabbed his fork in the direction of several of the platters and motioned to my plate. "Eat up! Eat up! Don't be shy."

Going back to our old routine was exactly what I couldn't let happen.

Hoyt went on agreeably, "Is your claim close by?"

How can I keep him from coming out to it? "It's on the North Fork. Rattlesnake Bar." I was thinking of R. C.'s original claim. I'd have to hope he didn't learn of my other claims.

Hoyt helped himself to more beef. "I hear Rattlesnake Bar's paying good."

"That's old news. Maybe some of it still is. Not where I am."

He poured himself more wine. "Many men would give their right arm for the gold in that deposit, even once. We can only hope your luck continues, eh, Boy?"

The waiter brought the next two courses: giblet pie and kidneys in port sauce. He was hard-pressed to make room for them.

Hoyt scooped up a generous helping of kidney and two of giblet pie. He poured the last of the second bottle into his glass and held up the bottle for the waiter to see.

I had to make my situation as unattractive as possible. "I only have a little dugout. I'm sleeping on bare planks." I cut pieces off the veal, but ate none of them. "I think it'd just be simpler if I brought the take into town." Since he made no protest, I tried my next idea. "Why don't we pick a day, and each week I'll come into town on that day. We can meet at the express office and make the deposit."

Hoyt chuckled contentedly. "Now, now, Pegg, boy. Let's not get ahead of ourselves."

The waiter reappeared with three desserts: French pudding and two kinds of pie. The spicy aromas of the pies brought sweet memories of holiday and harvest dinners.

Hoyt took up a piece of mince pie and smothered it in French pudding. "I appreciate your thinking things through, but now that I'm back, you won't have to worry yourself with that. Of course, I'll give your ideas careful consideration, but all the options must be weighed before a decision can be made."

And, of course, he would make the decision.

At least he said he would consider my ideas. Before, he wouldn't even have listened to them. At last, I had a piece of apple pie—without the pudding. I watched him eat as I ate. *He eats like he doesn't know when he will eat again. Is that the manner of a successful man?* What would happen to all this uneaten food? I plotted a way to take a few slabs of meat to Bugle.

In that moment, I realized that I had gotten used to making my own decisions—except when Sun Shu had a better idea—and that was a very agreeable state of things.

With a theatrical sigh, Hoyt tossed his fork onto the empty plate and pushed it away. The table looked like a battlefield on which both sides lost. From across the ruins, he regarded me with concern. "You've only pecked at your food, Boy. I know it wasn't Porter's in Hang Town, but could you find nothing to your liking?"

"Yes. It was delicious. An extraordinary meal—reunion. Thank you, Sir."

He raised his glass. "To us." And drained it.

Our waiter approached with the bill and laid it on the table between Hoyt and me.

I almost choked. Seventy-two dollars! That equaled several month's wages and more back home. I would pay seventy-two dollars only to have much of the food thrown away. If my mother were here, she would fly into a rage at such waste. If Dad were here, this never would've happened.

I made the barest movement toward the bill. Hoyt snatched it up, just as he had done the receipt at Lila's. "A king's feast, Garçon," proclaimed he to the waiter. "A king's feast." He twisted to reach into his back pocket—and froze, surprise and consternation on his face.

I watched him. *Nothing's changed.* He patted another pocket experimentally. I shifted to retrieve my own poke.

Hoyt reached into his coat pocket, fishing, and broke into a beaming smile, withdrawing his wallet. "Never let it be said Fred Hoyt is not a man of his word." He plucked one-hundred dollars in folding money.

I stared, goggle-eyed. *He actually has money!*

He slapped the bills on the table.

He obviously had *some* success over the winter. Perhaps he had an account back in Hang Town, after all.

The money sat on top of the restaurant's bill. Hoyt pushed the whole stack toward the waiter. "Keep the difference, my good man. You've earned it."

The waiter took up the pile and blinked in disbelief.

Hoyt slouched back. "You won't soon forget Fred Hoyt's generosity, now, will you?"

I shifted my gape from the pile to my mercurial partner. While I could quibble over throwing in the extra thirty dollars above the cost of the feast, it was a clear-cut expression of Hoyt's newfound generosity.

The waiter turned and shuffled off, fingering his bounty.

Hoyt dropped his napkin on what remained of the fish. "He'll be licking my shoes next time I come in."

I had some rethinking to do. If this truly was a new Hoyt, perhaps I just had to get used to his bloated proclamations being merely a defense against unwanted inquiry.

I eased back my chair. "Let's see if they have a room here. I can't imagine it was an easy trip. I have to get back to the claim."

Hoyt likewise rose to his feet. "Splendid. I'll come along. Just have a look at your set-up."

A cold fist squeezed my heart. "Are you sure, sir? There's no place for you to sleep out there. You'll only have to come back in the dark." We threaded our way through the crowded tables. *He can't come out.*

"Do I detect a bit of prevarication, there, Pegg-son?" His voice remained jovial. "Something you want to keep to yourself?"

I quailed. *Too close.* "No, sir. Not at all. But you remember coming here? How slippery those oak leaves are, even dry? I don't imagine you want to risk another mishap."

We were abreast of the bar. I tipped my head that way. "Let's get you a room, and I'll come in bright and early tomorrow morning and we'll buy you an outfit." I gestured toward his shiny boots. "You don't want to ruin those squatting in the river."

When I inquired about a room, the barkeep announced, "Three dollars."

Hoyt reached for his wallet.

I held up my hand. "My treat. You saw to dinner. Welcome back." *Anything to keep him on the back foot.* I handed the barkeep a small nugget.

Hoyt nodded, dropping his hand. "Much obliged, Son. Much obliged."

I produced a hearty smile. "Gwynn's has a goodly selection of tools. We'll get you a pan, pick, and shovel. What do you like, a square mouth and round mouth? A long handle, or a D handle?"

The zest faded from my partner's face. "I'm impressed you can maintain such enthusiasm."

As I watched him walk away to the rooms, I had a sudden panic. What if, indeed, we got him an outfit and he came out to the river? I had no choice but to take him to R. C.'s played-out claim, downstream from my own. And I'd have to work R. C.'s claim with him as if it were the only one. And sooner or later, he'd find out that I had the others.

The only way to avoid disaster would be to move forward more quickly with my plans. The most important of which was to end my partnership with Hoyt. I certainly had cause enough, between what Gao Chung had seen back in Grizzly Bar, and what I myself had experienced.

I dashed back to the dining room and found our waiter, who regarded my approach with some suspicion, assuming Hoyt and I peddled the same manners. He mellowed a good deal when I asked him for a few slabs of the left-over roast beef for my dog.

He disappeared into the kitchen, and in short order, returned with a bundle wrapped in newspaper. "Say. . .ain't you the one wrestled with that mountain lion?"

I shrugged. "A while back." I took the parcel he offered; the juices were already soaking through the paper. "Much obliged for this. Thank you, Sir."

"It's your dinner," observed the waiter. "Bought and paid for."

.   .   .

I went to the laundry and found Bugle in his corner. I gave him his feast. While Chen Yi made supper, I went outside and helped Sun

Shu until she was finished. We were all sitting around the table when I announced, "Mr. Hoyt came back today."

Gao Chung said something short between mouthfuls. Chen Yi translated: "Bear come out cave."

We all made noises of agreement, except Sun Shu. She creased her brow with worry. "Oh, Pegg. Step carefully. Please, step carefully."

"Yes, Ma'am. I will."

Chen Yi put down his bowl and stared. "I have feeling send son to battle, no sword, no shield. . ."

We all looked at him. This was not his usual manner of speech.

"Uncle," Sun Shu said quietly, leaning toward him, "you have given him friendship. That is as stout a shield as any." She gave me a quick glance and went on. "And Pegg knows your house is a safe harbor in any storm."

"Yes, Daughter. You say true things. . ."

Gao Chung offered his own quiet comment.

I turned to Sun Shu.

She said, "It is a very old saying. Difficult to put into English words, but I will try."

At length, she spoke. "What your sword will be is unknown. But its strength will not only be in the blade. It will be in your courage."

CHAPTER 32

I made straight for the Empire Hotel just as the sun rose above the crest east of town. I wondered if I would have to rouse Hoyt from his slumber, as had happened in the past.

I looked in at the dining room, which had few customers at this early hour. There he was, seated at the very table he had refused yesterday, deep in conversation with an imposing gentleman of obvious refinement.

This new fellow was some bulkier than Hoyt—*cut-from-hard-granite*. He was clean shaven, and otherwise well-groomed, thick, wavy hair just greying at the temples. He wore a finely tailored suit of clothes. The two men were taking their ease over coffee. The scene was an unmistakable tableau. *Two of a kind, preening together.*

Interrupting Hoyt in any circumstance was courting censure, but my having to cross the room to reach their table allowed him plenty of time to compose a choice intimidation.

He called out before I gained their table—a big smile, an outstretched hand of welcome. "Ah, there you are, Pegg, my lad. Your name was just crossing our lips."

Is this more of the new Hoyt? I was reluctant to trust it. "Good morning, Sir." We shook hands.

He turned his beaming munificence on his tablemate. "Bill, allow me to introduce my long-suffering partner, Bartholomew Pegg." He turned back to me. "Pegg, this fine specimen is Mr. William S. Hutchins, Esquire. Late of Philadelphia."

I put out my hand. "Good to meet you, Sir."

Mr. Hutchins' grip was firm, his hand dry. Good signs. An easy grin displayed good, strong teeth. His voice was deep and rich. Unhurried, like Jacob Harper's. "Fred speaks highly of your skills, Pegg." He shifted to take in Hoyt. "How did you put it?"

Hoyt, making an even wider grin, leaned to give me a pat on the back. "Gold verily flies to his fingertips."

I cringed at such puffery. What other hoops has Hutchins held up for Hoyt to jump through?

Hutchins took a sip of his coffee.

Hoyt spoke up. "Pegg, why don't you get some breakfast. I'll catch up with you later. Bill and I—"

Hutchins broke in. "Please. I know you have business to conduct. I'll leave you to it. I look forward to continuing our discussion, Fred—" He rose from his chair.

Hoyt stood quickly. "Won't be a minute, Bill. Just a few details to work out, to set the boy on his way."

It took some effort to hold my tongue.

"Take your time." Hutchins nodded to me and moved off.

Is he relieved to get away?

Hoyt watched Hutchins a moment, then sat back down.

I turned to face him more directly. "I've had breakfast already. I thought if we got over to the store early. . ."

Hoyt drank his coffee. He put the cup down carefully. His speech was equally measured, filled with paternal concern. "Sit down, Pegg."

I didn't want one of his lectures. "Couldn't we—"

"Sit down."

I sat in Mr. Hutchins' chair without pulling it closer to the table.

Hoyt seemed to study the room for a moment. In the same deliberate voice he said, "Have you not eyes to see?"

Is this a trick question? Bemused, I looked around the room. Waiters moved quietly among the few occupied tables. A gentle murmur prevailed of people waking up, nursing their first cups of coffee. Mr. Hutchins appeared to be exchanging pleasantries with the maître de, who was folding napkins. Nothing seemed amiss, let alone extraordinary.

Hoyt must have read my puzzlement. He shook his head slowly, smiling down at his boots. "I keep forgetting. . . I keep forgetting." He looked up. "You've seen so little." His voice tightened. "I'm not speaking of the tablecloths, or the furniture, or the wretched waiters. I'm speaking of the pulse of ideas, Pegg, boy. The energy of stupendous opportunities."

Here we go. I took a breath. "I'm sorry to have interrupted. I can go to the store and get the tools, and you can come for the duds when you're finished with Mr. Hutchins."

Hoyt leaned a little forward as if to confide. "Let me speak plain. Hutchins, there—" he tilted his head toward the other—"has made me privy to prodigious enterprises under way." Hoyt's voice took on the hush of conspiracy. "Enterprises that must be pursued without hesitation."

I'd heard this before. I made a worried face. "But what about coming out to help on the claim?"

Hoyt held his free palm up defensively. "That's going to have to wait, I'm afraid." He cast a quick glance around the room— everybody was minding their own business. "Hutchins has only sketched the outlines, but the promise of truly legendary returns is already apparent."

I made my own plea, hoping he would not suspect how desperate I was to keep him away from the claim. "But with both of us working the claim—"

Hoyt reared back with a look of dismay. "And pass up the chance to be at the center of endeavors that will transform the face of the country? I hardly think that's a reasonable thing to ask."

"How long will it take? What's your part?"

"Our part," he declared confidently. "I would not leave you out of so auspicious an undertaking." Shifting uncomfortably, he busied himself sweeping invisible crumbs off the table. "Despite all the opportunities that await us—" He flicked away the last unseen mote. "—I must confess that I'm not entirely at liberty to do as I please." He puffed up his chest as if fortifying himself. "Brannan and I have agreements that continue to require my attention."

Which likely means you owe him money. I sat back to give Hoyt the impression that I duly exalted his every word. With a disappointed frown, I made one last stab. "So, should I buy a shovel and pan for when you do come out?"

He leaned forward earnestly, giving me an indulgent smile. "It should also be obvious that I can do us far greater good here—" the grand sweep of his arm told me he meant the whole town "—in the very cauldron of change, than hunkered down at the river."

Yes. In town is exactly where I want you to stay.

He could not have made it plainer that he wanted things to go on exactly as they had in Grizzly Bar. My toiler to his master. I pushed back my chair. The room was filling with customers and tobacco smoke.

"Well, I guess my part is to get to work." Standing, I paused. "I'll be back in a few days. Wish me luck."

"Good lad." He gave me a distracted smile, darting glances around the room. "Good lad. I'll join you as often as opportunity and commitments allow."

No matter how flimsy, you will never stop finding excuses to sidestep your obligations.

I passed Hutchins and the maître de on my way to the door. Hutchins lifted a finger to his brow. "Good to meet you, Pegg."

I doffed my hat. "Yessir." I couldn't manage more than the barest civility.

I had Hutchins to thank for filling Hoyt's head with fresh, grand schemes—plots and connivances that would require my partner to remain in town. I had a hunch that Hutchins had the same polished manner—concealing a ruthless temper—as the man Sweeney, who'd caused Hoyt and me to flee Grizzly Bar.

Outside, a bright sun presided over the dusty street, which rang with the shouts of miners, the calls of carpenters, the bray of a mule. I took a great quaff of air, relishing the probity of wood smoke, fresh- cut lumber, and manure. I knew that Hoyt would never settle for the drudgery of washing dirt. I could only hope that Mr. Hutchins and I, between us, had "convinced" Hoyt his best place was in town.

I moved up the street, immersing myself in humble, hard-working folk who were merely unloading sacks of flour, putting up a new building, or painting a sign.

The last two days had proven that, though Hoyt may have actually made some money, with or without Brannan, he had in no other way changed. As far as Fred Hoyt was concerned, he had only himself to think about. It was hard to remember that this was the same man who had so selflessly cared for Dad as the fever relentlessly took him.

I had my family to think about. It was clear what had to be done: End this partnership.

That thought stopped me in my tracks. And the sooner it ended, the better off I'd be, the better off everyone in the partnership would be.

A horse blew down my neck. I shied and turned. Past the muzzle of a big bay loomed a scowling teamster, half raised out of his seat. "If you ain't gonna keep movin', get out of the way."

"Sorry." I shuffled to the side, touching my finger to my hat. I let him pass and fell in a few paces behind his wagon.

Ending the partnership was a daunting prospect. But Hoyt's recklessness could now do great damage. The seam—and the Nightmare Nugget—had vastly improved the partnership's lot. The stakes were much higher now.

I tripped over a discarded shovel and made for a bench at the side before I did myself more harm.

"A penny for your thoughts," came a friendly hail from the teeming street.

I looked up to see Richard approaching my bench. I smiled and held out my hand.

We shook and he took a seat beside me. "You gave me a fright," he grinned. "I spied you in solemn deliberation and thought you needed rescuing."

His good cheer was always welcome. "You'll do me a great service if you'll listen to what I've been thinking about."

"I can imagine little better to do on this beautiful day." Richard leaned back against the wall and clasped his fingers around his upraised knee.

"I'm going to end the partnership with Fred Hoyt."

He lurched forward, owl-eyed, loosing his knee. His boot heel hit the ground with a thump. "Hosanna! At long last."

I told him the story Sun Shu had related to me: how Gao Chung saw Hoyt gamble away the gold I collected while working with the Frenchmen back in Grizzly Bar. "I still have the arm Sun Shu cut from a pair of long johns to hold that gold. Gao Chung retrieved it from under the gambling table."

Richard completed the narrative. "Where Hoyt had discarded it."

"Yes. Exactly."

Richard rested his hands on his knees like an old man, even though he was only a few years older than me. "A tidy story," he mused.

I gave him a nod, encouraged.

"There's only one problem with it."

"What?" Dread crept up on me.

"If Hoyt drags you into court, which he surely will if he sees his manna about to dry up, no one will give a brass farthing for a Chinaman's testimony."

I reared back, indignant. "What about my testimony?" But I sagged immediately. "My age."

Richard gave me a wry smirk. "Yes. Your age. In the court's eyes, if nobody else's, you are still a boy."

"So, I need new evidence."

He rubbed his chin thoughtfully. "Short of shooting the man, that would seem the best course."

How can I prove Hoyt has been throwing away the gold I've found? After all, prospectors did that all the time—celebrating their good fortune with champagne and oysters until they were poor again. But it was *their own* gold; they had no obligations to anybody but themselves. Hoyt was throwing away *other* people's money.

Richard spoke up. "Well, let's see what cards we have in our hand." When I looked puzzled, he tried again. "What do we have at our disposal with which to gather new evidence?"

I counted on my fingers. "He has a joint account at the express office. He knows it is the partnership account. He can withdraw from it however much he wants, whenever he wants. There will be no way of identifying the gold once he withdraws it."

Richard smiled out at the street. "Unless we paint all the nuggets in that account red."

"Even if Lila let us do it, Hoyt'd smell a rat." I slumped against the wall. "And what if he actually *has* an account back in Hang Town, and he claims he's using that? He waved a plenty healthy wallet around at dinner yesterday. Once the money's in his hand, there's no way of proving where it came from."

Richard took the lead. "You have to rig it so that you're absolutely certain he's gambling away gold you are digging up *for the partnership*."

"Supplying the gold will be easy enough. It's the spying part that has me stumped." I threw up my hands. "I can't go around tailing Mr. Hoyt while he withdraws funds, or stand next to the table while he plays." I paused, thinking Richard might have a response. He waited for me to continue. "I have to have somebody I can trust do that part of it. But everybody I know is too busy." I turned to the friend who was sitting next to me, a man I could trust. "Are you working right now?"

Richard stabbed his finger at the bench with a grin. "Right now?" He settled back, brushing a dust mote off his shirt sleeve. "As it happens, I'm free to entertain legitimate propositions."

"How would you like the job? It won't last long, and it pays well."

A smile creased his angular, sun-browned features. "You could not have proposed better terms. What did you have in mind?"

I got serious. "What do you know about spying?"

Richard laughed. "I hold the rank of Complete Ignoramus, but I'm willing to give it a go."

CHAPTER 33

I stood up from the bench. "Let's go to Lila's and get you a stake."

He looked concerned. "But isn't that partnership money?"

I told him how I had the accounts split up. "I'll use my family's portion for your stake, and the partnership account for—"

"—the bait," he finished, unfolding his lanky frame and rising to his feet.

Before we went in to see Lila, I scuttled around back of her office and dug out two containers from her trash. The one that would contain the bait needed to be immediately recognizable. I found a patch of Calico—light blue with small red roses—big enough to serve as a poke. I grabbed up a bottle for Richard's stake.

In short order, Richard and I were standing out in the sun again. Richard turned his bottle, speculating. The dust shimmered with its seductive luster. "It'll be interesting to see how far I can make this stretch. I'm not what you'd call a deft hand at cards."

"I have faith you'll do your best. When the gold runs out, you'll have earned your place as a spectator." I held up the calico that Lila had tied into a makeshift poke, the bait. "Just memorize this. You may only see it for a moment."

Richard eyed the calico. "We'll just have to hope that he keeps it in that poke until he spends it." He looked out into the street.

"Should we worry that we've just reviewed our plan in front of half the town?"

I glanced toward the north end, where the stream at our feet joined Auburn ravine on its journey westward. "You go that way." I nodded toward the south, toward Chen Yi's laundry. "I'll go the other."

"Wait. When do I start?"

"Tonight."

Richard knitted his brow. "Will that give you time to give him the bait?" He nodded at the calico poke.

"I'm going to find him right now." I stepped off. "But, likely, he won't join the game until he can pit himself against the big players."

Supposing Hoyt's roving, restless nature, I checked the gambling and drinking establishments before returning to the Empire Hotel. He was seated at the same table—I was coming to think of it as his roost—in the dining room, in the company of none other than William Hutchins. *Birds of a feather.*

As before, they were absorbed in earnest conversation. It was unusual to see Hoyt listening more than talking. I dreaded interrupting them again. But I scolded myself that Hoyt disappeared so frequently and so unpredictably that having him in my sights had to outweigh risking his ire.

The room was beginning to fill with early dinner trade. I spied our waiter from yesterday and nodded to him. He acknowledged me in return.

Hoyt's back was to me. Hutchins spotted me first coming through the tables to join them. He broke into a casual smile.

Hoyt twisted around to see what had distracted Hutchins. "Pegg, lad. Back so soon? I thought you were on your way to the claim."

"I forgot something." I had an impulse to apologize, but squelched it.

Hoyt shot a quick glance at his tablemate. He turned back to me while gesturing to him. "You remember Bill Hutchins."

"I do." I addressed Mr. Hutchins. "Mr. Hutchins." And stuck out my hand.

After Hutchins and I shook, Hoyt favored me with a chuckle. "It must be important to turn you from your path."

"You could say so." I pulled the calico poke out of my pocket. "I dug around a little before I left this morning and found this." I shrugged sheepishly, handing him the poke. "Like I said, you never know when you're going to get lucky."

Hoyt hefted the little sack appreciatively.

"It was after the other was already bundled up. In the excitement of meeting up with you, I forgot to deposit it."

"Don't you worry." Hoyt lofted the poke gently and caught it. "I'll take care of it."

Hutchins sat patiently, nursing his coffee.

"What did I tell you, Bill?"

"Gold verily flies to his fingertips." Hutchins managed a curl of his lip, then lifted his cup in salute.

Hoyt slipped the calico bag into his pocket. "Every little bit helps, doesn't it, Pegg, son?"

Was it a taunt? I wished I had a quicker wit. All I could muster was a scrap of defense. "Try to remember. That doesn't happen every day." I nodded to Hutchins, lifting my finger to my hat brim. "Mr. Hutchins. Good day to you, Sir."

"And to you, Sir."

I left them and found Richard trying on a black, notch collar frock coat in front of a three-sided tent. The sign perched above announced in florid script, "Stockwell's Clothing. Finest Men's Ware." Inside, the tent was crammed with shirts and trousers, hats and coats.

The storekeep moved continuously, wielding a small, square mirror, for his customer to assess the fit of the article.

I stepped up without Richard noticing. "Suits you fine."

He turned, still posing. "Indeed, it does, but, much as I crave it, it will have to wait for another day." He doffed the coat and handed it to the merchant. We moved off into the street.

Richard's eyes roved ceaselessly. "So how did you fare?"

"He's got the poke. I made sure he knows it's to be deposited for the partnership." Remember, faded blue calico with little red flowers."

He nodded. "It is seared into my brain."

"Seriously," I said. "If all you see is him spending gold, it'll prove nothing. You have to see him take it from the calico poke and spend it. That's the only way it'll count."

Richard drew us off to the side and we perched on two quiet barrels. "What if he doesn't gamble tonight?"

"I don't care what he does, so long as you see him pay for it out of the calico poke."

"Maybe we should give this a couple of days, just in case."

I growled in frustration. "That's probably right. I'll come back to town in a few days."

"Indeed," Richard said. "Off you go, then. Good luck."

"Good luck to *you*."

.   .   .

I worked my claims, trying not to worry about what was going on in Auburn. What if Richard failed to catch Hoyt losing the partnership gold? I needed the kind of proof Hoyt couldn't talk his way out of.

Whenever my conviction wavered, I recalled Hoyt's new suit of clothes while my mother and Amy huddled through the dark winter. I needed the calico bag for hard evidence so I could end the partnership.

I started planning the best time to hunt up Richard so I wouldn't run into Mr. Hoyt.

On the third morning, I vowed to go into town and find out what happened. I was in the river. As I swam toward shore with a bag of nuggets, I saw someone kneeling, adding wood to the fire. The man was being friendly with Bugle, who thumped his tail, soaking up the attention. Bugle saw me and barked. The man unfolded himself and stood up. It was Richard. I recognized his limber stance and dark clothes. He picked up a blanket I had ready on a rock by the shore and met me with it as I came out of the water.

"I imagine the water is cold, even on these beautiful days," he said, draping the blanket over my shoulders. We stepped close to the fire.

I realized, in my frenzy of diving, I had allowed no time to enjoy the clear blue sky or the bright sun. "Thanks. If I keep this up, I'll turn into a fish."

"Let's hope not," Richard chuckled. "We would be hard-pressed for good conversation. I'm afraid I don't speak Fish."

I rubbed the blanket around my head. "I was going to come into town today. Thanks for coming out."

Richard threw a quick glance back across the river. "I thought there would be less chance of being interrupted if I came out here."

"Yeah, I've worried about the same thing. Thanks."

I stowed the nuggets in the shelter, then we sat outside in the sun. I dried off.

"So, thanks again for doing that. I hope it went okay."

Richard made an apologetic face. "Well, it went fine—except for losing your gold at the table. I'm not much of a gambler, I'm afraid."

"It will be worth it if you learned something." I was impatient to get to the heart of it. "Did he bring out the calico bag?"

"He did," Richard grinned. "And it was a long, agonizing vigil, watching him lose every bit of it."

I sagged in relief. "Did he recognize you? Remember you from the time you took him into town when we first got here?"

"If he did, he gave no sign of it," Richard replied. "After I was out of the game, I stuck around to watch. By that time, the table had attracted something of a crowd. Mr. Hoyt is a surprisingly good player, but he's a sore loser. After he emptied the bag, I followed him to the express office where he withdrew more money to keep playing."

I wonder how Lila liked that interruption? "How do you know that?"

Richard grinned. "He came out with a fat little poke that he hugged for dear life. I watched him lose all that, too. Discreetly, mind. You are paying me handsomely to play detective. I couldn't do it by half, now could I?"

"Thanks," I said. "Thanks very much. I appreciate that."

"Hoyt was doing all right until Jim Yancey took the chair of someone who'd been cleaned out. Our dear Hoyt didn't have much of a chance after that, really," Richard mused.

I'd heard about Yancey. It seemed unlikely Mr. Hoyt had not. "Didn't he know about Yancey?" I asked. I ducked into my shelter, brought out some jerky and handed pieces to Richard and Bugle.

Between strenuous chewing, Richard replied, "If he did, he was vain enough to test his skill against a ruthless professional. He left the place very late and empty-handed. And with a fair bit of drink in him." Richard was quiet for a minute. "He's also got a terrible thirst to win." Richard studied his last bite of jerky. "I dare say, Pegg-o, there's a strong possibility the rest of your account may soon suffer the same fate."

"It's not my account. It's his account, to do with as he wishes."

Still, what Richard said got me to worrying about the safety of the other two accounts.

Richard slapped his hands on his knees. "Since I'm out here, I might as well make myself useful. Anything I can do to help?"

I threw some more sticks on my warming fire. "Can you swim?"

Richard gave a nervous laugh. "O-oohhh… I splashed about a bit when I was a tyke. But I doubt very much I could do what you're doing."

"Well. . . I'd ask you to look for some firewood. I'm a little low. But that would mean a fair hike." I gestured to all the stumps on the hillside behind us. "Around here has been pretty well picked clean."

"Never fear!" He stood up. "Eagle-eye Barter is here. If it is firewood you require, it is firewood you shall have."

"Would you mind taking Bugle with you? Give him a run?"

Bugle stood up, too, wagging his tail. He knew what was up.

After three dives, I emptied my bag of nuggets on my table and looked over my take. There was enough for another deposit trip into town. After one more bag, I could sort the batch and send part of it back with Richard. I went outside.

Mr. Hoyt was waiting for me.

I froze in my tracks, staring at him in disbelief. I grabbed a better hold of the blanket around my shoulders.

"Top o' the morning to you, Pegg, boy," he said. It was midday, at least. He was perched on the same rock Richard had so recently vacated.

Did he follow Richard? Is he spying on me? "Mr. Hoyt. What are you doing here?"

He blustered, "Well! That's a fine welcome for your partner, after I take the trouble to trek out here."

"I didn't mean it that way. It's just a surprise to see you here, is all."

"Why should it be a surprise? It's only fitting that I do my part. See if you need anything." He made a show of looking around the camp.

"Did you deposit the gold I brought you?"

He snapped his head back, not pleased with my impertinence. I didn't want him snooping around. I had a table full of nuggets in the shelter. Richard would be back any time. Mr. Hoyt would recognize Richard, and our goose would be cooked.

"Well, not to put too fine a point on it, I did make that deposit, Pegg-boy. I did, indeed." He gave me his smirk. "I must say, Boy, your manners have deserted you while I've been away. If I didn't know better, I would say my return is an inconvenience to you."

I shuffled my feet, a sure way of conveying deference. "Well, no. I just like getting old business out of the way before moving on."

He didn't like my answer, but he let it show for only an instant. Then he smoothed his face. "You forgot to tell me where the claim was. I had to ask." He was eyeing me.

"I did tell you where it was, pretty close, anyway," I said. "Fortunately for you, there aren't many boys and their dogs mining on the river."

"Speaking of children," Hoyt revealed his irritation in his voice, even if not in his face. "I saw you larking around in the river as I drew close. No wonder the account is so meager. How are we ever to get home if you spend your days frolicking when you should be looking for gold?"

I couldn't tell him the truth about what I was doing in the river, but I didn't feel like apologizing, either. "Have you come out to help with the prospecting?"

Hoyt jerked back like I had lunged at him. He recovered quickly, but scowled as if my question was the worst kind of insolence. "Not if what I just saw was what you call prospecting."

I let his gibe pass. "I was just on my way over to the other claim, where I've got a rocker. Maybe you could help me with it. It'd go a lot faster with two. Give me a minute to get some clothes on."

Hoyt blinked a couple of times, like he was trying to understand what was being asked of him. "Of course. . .of course. A rocker." He gave out his lop-sided grin. "Now you're talking."

I stepped toward the shelter. "I'll be right out. Could you collect the shovel?"

While buttoning my shirt I heard Bugle bark—close by.

CHAPTER 34

Scrambling out of the shelter, I found Richard just setting down his bundle of wood. Mr. Hoyt stared at him. Richard stepped forward with a jaunty grin, his hand out to shake. "Richard Barter. Pleased to meet you."

Hoyt let the shovel drop and shook Richard's hand as if in a daze. But he didn't offer his name. Richard charged on in a cheery voice. "I had the pleasure of your company at the gaming table the other night. You may remember."

I made a surprised voice. "You two know each other?"

"In a manner of speaking." Richard turned to me with a questioning look. "Mr…" He stopped, waiting for Mr. Hoyt to supply his name. Hoyt only darted his gaze between Richard and me.

"Hoyt," I said.

"Yes!" exclaimed Richard. "Mr. Hoyt and I were at the same table the other night in a very spirited game of monte." He looked to each of us like we were all long-lost kin, reunited.

Don't over-do it, I scolded him silently.

Richard said, "What a coincidence! You two are acquainted, then?"

I tried to keep a neutral voice. "We're partners."

Hoyt spoke at last. "You know each other?" I could hear the suspicion in his voice.

"We struck up a conversation the other day over breakfast," Richard said. "Found we had a lot in common."

"And I offered him a job," I said. "Helping to look for gold."

"Is that so?" Hoyt gave me an incriminating look. "I don't recall us discussing this."

"No disrespect, but you weren't around at the time." I was skating on thin ice. There had been no breakfast, no job offer. Where could this end but in disaster? "I was having a run of luck. I thought we could afford it. It could only help the work go faster..."

Richard spoke up. "Pardon me, but if there is a problem—"

Hoyt growled at him. "Hold your peace, young man. This is between me and the boy."

"Right you are," Richard said, and took a step back.

Hoyt glowered at me. "Now, we agreed, didn't we? Way back when your daddy died, that I was the decision-maker of this outfit." He waited. "Isn't that right, Pegg, boy?"

I swallowed hard, tamping down my anger. "Yessir."

Hoyt let out a big sigh and turned his baleful gaze on Richard. "Well, Mr. Garter, work off what's been agreed to, and I'll advise you if your services are needed in the future."

He turned back to me. "Don't let this happen again. Do you have anything for me to take into town?"

"No, Sir. Not today." *Not ever, if I can help it.*

Hoyt set off without further remark. He seemed to have forgotten his offer to help.

Richard and I watched him until Hoyt had crossed the river and started up the hill. Richard picked up the shovel, gritting his teeth. "'Garter,' indeed!" He took a new grasp, as if it were a weapon. "I came very close to crowning him."

I finished tucking in my shirt. "Do you think he believed the breakfast story?"

"It sounded pretty good to me, if I do say so."

"Yes it did," I smiled at him. "You'd make a better partner any day."

Richard did a little bow. "It would have been for nothing without your job idea following on!"

"Well, Garter-Barter," I joshed, "one thing's certain. You can't go back to town right on his heels when you're supposed to be working for me."

"Wise words." He looked doubtfully at the pile from his recent effort. "I suppose I could look for more firewood."

I brightened. "I think that's exactly what we should do." I took up the ax, Richard took up the carrying sling, and we set off. Bugle scampered ahead, always eager for another run.

When we gained some height up the slope, I stopped and turned to Richard. "Thank you again for doing that. For tailing him and seeing it through."

"How long can you keep the wool over Hoyt's eyes?"

"It all depends on what's left in the seam." One thing I needed to do without delay was write to Mr. Pruitt, to give him fair warning about Fred Hoyt.

·   ·   ·

Richard stayed three days. He worked R. C.'s claims while I kept diving in the river. He had a little luck. I made him keep all of what he found and added a handful of nuggets when he wasn't looking. I was being more than blessed with my river seam.

In the evenings, we'd go visit with Old Sven to hear stories about his voyages; whole islands covered with seals you could hear a mile out to sea, or the mighty, solitary albatross, bigger than any other bird in the world, soaring endlessly. Storms which left every inch of the ship coated in ice, and how they had to chop the ice away to keep the ship from sinking under the weight of it!

On the fourth day, Richard headed back to town, taking his gold and a load of laundry with him. Inside I'd hidden the Will James portion of my take.

I followed the next day with the other two portions: "Hoyt" and "Forsyth," as well as a letter for Mr. Pruitt. While trudging along, keeping an eye on Bugle, I wondered whether Hally would be mad at me for using her name in a deception. I promised myself I would write to her about it that very evening, even though I would have to wait until I had an address to mail it. I wondered how she was doing. Had her family found a place to settle? Did they get a house built before winter? What kind of winters did Oregon have?

I left the Forsyth portion with Chen Yi and took the Hoyt part to the express office. There I found a rarity. Lila had no other customers—for the moment.

"Good afternoon, Ma'am." I closed the door behind me.

Lila was at the map, meticulously drawing in little boxes to designate new claims. She straightened and turned. "Good afternoon, Pegg. What mischief are you at today?"

I put my letter in the mailbox at the end of the counter. "None today, Ma'am." I moved to stand opposite where she would stand. "But I can't say about tomorrow."

Lila didn't actually smile, but almost. I plunked my Hoyt portion on the counter. She came away from the map. "Don't trouble yourself," I said. "I can wait."

She kept coming. "Half the territory could walk through the door at any moment. One done is one less to do." She took up the bag and emptied it into the dish on her scales. "Hoyt. Yes?"

"Yes, Ma'am."

Lila placed counterweights in the other dish. She had the dishes level with each other in no time. She moved to the ledger. Having made her note, she closed the book and put the pencil behind her ear. "Surely you have something up your sleeve to enliven my day." Her eyes smiled even if her mouth didn't.

"Well, yes, Ma'am. I mean, no, Ma'am." I turned my hat in my hands.

Another customer entered. We both looked in his direction. I turned back to Lila, knowing I couldn't tarry much longer. "Can I ask one more question?"

Lila made her lips into a thin line and lifted her eyebrows at me. "Only one?"

I heard the miner shuffle to a stop a pace behind me. "Has the bear been at the honey?"

Lila blinked. She stitched a little frown, holding very still. I could well imagine her searching through her mental rulebook.

"A bear is very hungry when it comes out of hibernation," she said at last. "You know that."

I nodded, hardly daring to breathe, hoping she would say more.

"I believe the bear you have in mind is very hungry." She could see the alarm on my face and took pity on me. She glanced quickly past me to the waiting prospector, then said to me, "Please wait a moment and let me help this gentleman, then we can talk."

Lila beckoned the miner forward and took care of his deposit. Then, two more miners came in. I fidgeted and fretted. This might go on all day. I busied myself straightening up Lila's wrapping table.

Finally, we were alone again. I rushed back to the counter. "You were saying about the bear."

She put her pencil behind her ear and made a stern look. "Yes. The bear."

I almost crawled up on the counter. "Yes, Ma'am. How many withdrawals has he made?"

She blanched at my eagerness. "I can only tell you that because you have a joint account. Now, do you see the benefit?"

"Yes, Ma'am. That was good advice. I thank you for it."

Lila opened her ledger to the H pages and searched out his name. "One rather sizable one. Some smaller ones."

I followed a hunch. "Was the sizable one for a hundred dollars?"

"Yes." Lila looked up, a question in her eyes.

"That's how much he spent on our reunion dinner the day he came back."

She made to close the ledger. "Perhaps he felt entitled to be reimbursed."

I slapped my hat on the counter. "His sense of what he's entitled to would dwarf the Rocky Mountains."

Lila's eyes popped wide. I braced for a rebuke.

Instead, Lila glanced at her ledger again. "In fact, he made two withdrawals that day. The second late at night, when I was busy with my packages." She shook her head in a tight shiver of distaste. "A most truculent man. He would not be turned away."

"Did that happen again about five or six days ago?"

She checked her ledger once more. "Yes. April seventh."

That had to be the withdrawal Richard talked about while he was spying on Hoyt gambling with the gold in the calico bag. So, it seemed very likely Hoyt had blown through the hundred dollars, all the gold in the calico bag, and then come to Lila for more. *So much for a "new leaf!"*

Another miner came in. Lila squared her shoulders, speaking lightly, as if imparting no more than the time of day. "With regard to the bear, the honey is being taken from the hive faster than the bees are laying it up."

I had that sick feeling again. I knew I had to act before his account ran dry.

Lila handed me my receipt. "I hope the information was helpful."

I took up my hat. "Yes, Ma'am. Very helpful."

As I turned toward the door, one of the miners touched my shoulder. "Did you say you saw a bear. Where at?"

Luckily, I didn't have to make something up. Osher Phelps had told me about seeing a bear on the south rim of the canyon while he was gathering firewood. "Up on the south ridge."

"When?"

"A few days ago."

"Much obliged," said the miner, touching a finger to his hat.

.   .   .

I had supper with my Celestial family. They were all in a good mood. Talk bubbled easily around the little table. Chen Yi made sure our rice bowls stayed full. They tried to draw me in, asking me about the claims, but I was lost in worry. How could Mr. Hoyt do what he was doing? As far as he knew, his account was the only gold we had, and yet he was spending it like water. The man my father had entrusted to lead our partnership possessed not one scrap of honor. Rather than bring us home in triumph, Hoyt would drag us down to utter ruin. My father would be mortified if he knew how things had turned out.

"The more gold you find, the sadder you look," said Sun Shu. "I am confused." Her eyes bored into me. She wasn't confused at all, she was challenging. Her eyebrows drew down, the way Hally's used to do when she was cross with me.

They were all looking at me. I suddenly realized they were mixed up in this mess. What if Mr. Hoyt found out they had some of my gold? I had little doubt he would treat it as *his* gold. And he could bring them trouble in many forms.

My worry burst out, regardless of good manners. "You must tell me if taking the gold to the express office is too much trouble for you." I looked at each in turn. "If holding the gold here is uncomfortable for you." Briefly, I felt like the foreigner. "Please. You must tell me."

Chen Yi and Sun Shu swapped glances, but it was Gao Chung who spoke. Sun Shu translated for him. "Is the bear showing his teeth?"

Chen Yi spoke up. "We tell you. Not yet."

"But promise you will… and if you don't want to do it anymore."

"Perhaps, Pegg," Sun Shu held up her hand. "Chen Yi will decide."

I knew Sun Shu was cautioning me, but desperation pushed me to harsh words. "No 'perhaps'! You must tell me!"

They froze, staring at me.

I knew I had transgressed. A big hole opened in the pit of my stomach, even as a large wedge drove between us. "I'm sorry. I didn't mean it that way. Please! I'm sorry!"

Gao Chung said something and Chen Yi and Sun Shu relaxed. Sun Shu even broke a quick little smile.

Chen Yi spoke. "Gao Chung say 'Ancestors put many peppers you rice." And he refilled all our teacups.

"I guess so," I said sheepishly.

.   .   .

Every day brought me closer to the mid-point of the river. It was clear that not only did the seam continue over into Harvey Drummond's claim, but so did the bounty it held. Did he have any inkling of what might lay in his part of the seam? Did he even know the seam was there?

Would he know if I kept going? Would anyone know? I was under water; nobody could see what I was doing. To most people, this much water was terrifying. But I would know what I was doing, and so would my ancestors, if I used Sun Shu's thinking. I pushed ideas of cheating out of my head.

Every day also brought me closer to the end of the partnership. I had to keep reminding myself, *You're ending the partnership only with Hoyt.* I vowed I would not abandon my part of the seam as long as a single flake of gold remained. I would keep dividing up whatever I took out to honor all the partners' shares.

But confronting Hoyt filled me with dread. What would he do when I told him there would be no more gold coming into his account? He could keep whatever he had earned with Mr. Brannan over the winter, but we would go our separate ways. Of course, he wouldn't accept that. He'd unleash a tirade that would peel the bark off a tree. He would insist that we keep going—together; find a new claim on another river.

I'd had the courage to tell him "No," once before. Could I muster it again?

By now, I had taken up all the nuggets easily grabbed or pried loose with my pry bar, and was down to the smallest nuggets, flakes, and grains. These nestled in the deepest, narrowest parts of the gap. I was limited to pinching up what I could between my fingers. It took many dives to fill my belt pouch.

Coming up for air, I heard Bugle barking. I looked around to see if I had a visitor. Bugle was looking up the canyon slope, away from the river. Who would be approaching from that way? A couple of miners were looking around, as curious as I was about my dog's barking. I yelled to him. "Bugle! Hush, boy! Pipe down!"

At just that moment a black bear emerged from behind an outcrop fifty yards up the slope. Was it Osher's bear from before?

Bugle barked furiously, frantically, lunging against his lead. The bear approached my shelter, sniffing for something to eat! It was only a black bear, and not a grizzly, but it was still a danger to a small dog. For the moment, the bear was more interested in bacon and sugar, but that didn't guarantee Bugle's safety. With the bacon out of reach, the bear might turn his attention to the beagle.

I swam like crazy for shore. Relentlessly, the river carried me farther away. My Colt was in the shelter. Once I got close to shore, I could throw rocks. The bear was moving closer to Bugle, but cautiously, giving the fire a wide berth. Bugle was a crazy, jumping, dodging bundle of snapping teeth, growling and barking. Still, one good swipe with a bear paw would be the end of him.

Suddenly, a shot rang out. Whipping my head in that direction, I saw Osher Phelps pointing his revolver at the bear, smoke clearing the muzzle. He fired again, knocking a chip off a boulder near the bear. *How could he miss? He's thirty feet away!*

As soon as I felt rocks underfoot, I scrambled upright. I scooped up small stones and started hurling them at the beast, knowing it would do little but irritate it.

I stumbled to shallower water, yelling and shouting curses. Then another shot from downstream. It plowed earth well shy of the bear. Too close to my dog.

Bugle's leash came loose and he half-lunged, half-rolled under the bear. I cursed myself for not tying it tighter. The beast turned, wondering what had happened to its noisy snack. Bugle didn't waste any time. He charged in, snapping and biting at the bear's legs and belly. The bear grunted and snorted, trying to push its attacker out from under.

More shots rang out. Dirt kicked up; bark flew. From up and down the river, miners were converging, firing as they came.

Heedless of the gunfire, the bear had set his sights on Bugle, who seemed to be everywhere at once. A forepaw caught my dog, sweeping him into the air. He landed ten feet away from the bear; missed landing in the fire by inches. Nothing daunted, he found his footing and rushed at the bear again.

The bear left three long red streaks on Bugle's belly! Screaming at the top of my lungs, I kept moving in, hurling futile stones as fast as I could pick them up. I too, was heedless of the bullets flying.

The fusillade came from everywhere, but few shots came from skilled marksmen. White smoke and the sharp tang of burnt powder filled the air. I was terrified one of the shots would hit Bugle!

I realized that, dangerous as this was, the shooting was the only real chance of saving him. So I shut up and threw rocks.

The canvas on my shelter jerked as bullets tore through it. The beast stood up on its hind legs, not realizing it was offering a bigger target. A spurt of blood jetted from the bear's ear.

That decided it for the bear. It dropped back down to all fours and turned heavily, taking one last, half-hearted lunge at Bugle before it lumbered off up the hill. The miners kept firing until it was out of range. A handful of them gave chase. I wondered if the bear would still be alive by nightfall.

The crash of gunfire died away quickly once the bear lost himself in the brush and manzanita. The smoke, not being replenished, shredded and wandered away with the breeze. I ran to Bugle and scooped him up in my arms. "Good boy. Good boy." When I brushed his right front paw, he whimpered. It didn't look broken.

Being careful of his front paw, I looked him over. He had some scratches on his nose. They weren't a worry. But the three claw cuts on his belly were pretty deep. They would need sewing up. "We've got to get you some help. I know just the place." He licked my face over and over.

I carried him over to where my shirt and trousers lay and wrapped my shirt around his middle. In truth, he was lucky to be alive. If the bear's claws had struck true, Bugle's innards would be strewn all over the gravel. When I set him back on the ground he held his paw off the ground.

Osher Phelps came up, shaking his shaggy head. "I thought sure you were gonna catch a slug or two, yourself, you were in so close." He knelt and patted Bugle gently on his head. "Mighty scrappy mutt you got here."

Hooting and hollering, the rest of the miners returned to their claims, reviewing the action, already turning it into a story. You'd think they had just won a battle. One or two fired frivolous shots in the air, reminding me of the reckless shooting sprees on the wagon train. I shuddered. As Osher pointed out, I could have easily been hit. But my only thought was: *They saved my dog.*

I climbed up on one of the larger rocks and faced downstream, shouting at the top of my voice, "THANK YOU!" Then I turned upstream. "THANK YOU!"

CHAPTER 35

I laid my wounded dog on my bed and wrapped him in a blanket and hustled into town to Chen Yi's laundry. As soon as they saw him, Chen Yi and Sun Shu took over without a word. For that I was grateful. They unwrapped my crude bandage and brought out the same chest of medicines they had used on me. While they tended him, I told Sun Shu and Chen Yi the story of the bear.

"You life fill up bears," said Chen Yi.

"It seems so." I held Bugle still, nattering encouragement at him, while Sun Shu sewed him up.

"Bugle stay here. No bears laundry," Chen Yi said as he gently spread his ointments on Bugle's cuts.

"I can't ask you to do that again." I hoped Chen Yi would disagree.

"Bugle dog safe here," he replied. "Bugle dog welcome here."

"Thanks. I'll pay for Bugle's food and anything else he needs."

Chen Yi waved his hand at me. "Old talk. All settled."

"Yessir." I knew better than to insist. "Thank you. Thank you very much."

Sun Shu wrapped new bandages over her stitching. She glanced at me and said, "You must buy a rifle."

"Ohhh, now…" I smiled at her, patting the Colt in my belt. "I—"

Her eyes spit fire. "First floods, then mountain lions, now bears!" She made her graceful hands into fists. "What will be next?"

I held up my hands defensively. "I'll buy a rifle. I will! I will!"

Gao Chung came into the room. Sun Shu snapped at him in their language, and he smiled and ducked back out again. A moment later, he reappeared with a bowl of water for Bugle.

Bugle regarded us with sad eyes. Sun Shu moved him carefully to the edge of the bed while Gao Chung held the bowl low so he could drink.

■　　　■　　　■

I stayed at the laundry that night. In the morning, I bought a Sharps rifle and ammunition. I also bought flitches of bacon and sacks of flour to distribute among all the prospectors who'd helped drive off the bear. Sun Shu inspected the rifle approvingly, knowingly. I thought back to when I first met her, on the night of the Grizzly Bar fire. I'd given her a rifle to guard their merchandise. She must have gotten more comfortable with firearms since then.

I left Bugle with Sun Shu to complete his recovery and went back to the river. The miners who pursued the beast had come back empty-handed. The next day, out looking for firewood, I spotted a trail of drops of dried blood, more than likely the bear's. His pursuers must have missed the sign.

City boys, Will chuckled in my mind.

It seemed we had convinced the brute he was not welcome, for he had not returned. Nonetheless, I moved my living quarters into the Grandfather Oak. Among several stout branches, I built a platform large enough for my bed and my table, and rigged a simple tent over it. I didn't need much more. I would be going home before too long. I left the cook fire where it was and hoisted my food bag higher in the tree.

After another four days of diving, I reached the halfway point across the river, the limit of my claim. I could see that the gold continued in the trough of the seam. The temptation to continue into Harvey Drummond's claim lasted about a heartbeat. I came up for air and hung onto the stick, looking over to Harvey Drummond, crouched by the river, intently working his new rocker, hoping.

I gave thanks for who my folks were and what they had taught me, not the least of which was how to swim.

The day of reckoning with Mr. Hoyt was at hand. All that remained was to empty Mr. Pruitt's account and my family's portion from the express office.

I took a load of miners' laundry into town with my gold hidden inside. After dropping the laundry off at Chen Yi's, I took Hoyt's portion over to the express office. Maybe thirty paces from Lila's office, who should I see pushing his way out the door but Hoyt himself. The busy street partly obscured my view of him—as it did his view of me, should he glance my way.

I thought of calling out to him. After all, I had his portion of the gold to deposit in his account. Then I checked myself. His face seethed with anger. Why was anybody's guess. I slowed to grow the distance between us, watching people duck out of his way as he stormed up the street.

Another man was a few paces ahead of me going up the steps to Lila's office. He and I were the only customers in the room. The man conducted his business and left. I stepped up to the counter, planning a jaunty greeting. Then I stopped short and sucked in air.

A fresh bruise marred Lila's cheek. Her impassive demeanor was nowhere to be seen. In its place was a lady struggling to reclaim her bearings.

"What happened?" I asked, touching my own cheek. "Are you okay?"

Lila frowned. "You're sweet, Pegg. I tripped. It's nothing. Thank you for your concern."

An alarm went off in my head. My friend Will, fresh from his fights, often sported bruises just like that. "Did somebody hit you?" Lila was the last person in the world who would ever incite someone's wrath. Except if that someone needed little excuse to display anger.

Lila pressed her lips into a thin line. "Don't concern yourself, Pegg. Please." With a composed face, she rested her hands on her ledgers. "How may I help you today?"

"Who hit you?" I demanded. But I had a dreadful suspicion I knew: someone who had come looking for information and didn't get what he wanted.

Lila glanced quickly at the door. "Please, Pegg. You have enough to deal with. I don't want to make it worse."

"Was it Mr. Hoyt?"

Lila flinched. A tiny gesture, but unmistakable. "Please," she pleaded. "Don't trouble yourself."

"I *will* trouble myself! I'll blow his damn head off if he hit you!" The fierceness of my anger startled me.

Lila's eyes popped wide, and she went pale. She took a better grip of her ledgers. "Pegg. You mustn't be rash."

"Why did he do it?"

She wasn't steering me away from Mr. Hoyt. She began to speak, halted, began again. "He started asking questions I couldn't answer. You know how I am about business. It's my job."

"Was nobody here to stop him?"

Her voice was unsteady. "I kept hoping someone would come in, but no one did."

I was riled. I wanted to take a shovel to Fred Hoyt.

Lila was close to tears. "You must be assured I told him nothing. Not about Will James, not about Forsyth. Nothing."

She squeezed her eyes shut. Her brow creased in misery and she put out a hand. "Please, Pegg. Don't do anything foolish. You have your whole life—he's scum. He's not worth it."

I was shocked. I had never heard Lila talk like that before.

"Oh, dear," she said. "I've said too much. I shouldn't have—"

"It's all right, Ma'am. You're right. He *is* scum."

"Promise me you won't do anything you will regret. Please."

It was a promise I didn't want to make. "Yes, Ma'am. I hear you."

Even in her anguish she managed a scowl. "That's not what I want to hear." She held my gaze.

I smiled. The Lila I knew and loved was back in the saddle. "Yes, Ma'am. I promise you I will not do anything rash, anything I would regret."

.   .   .

Back at the laundry, I asked Chen Yi if Mr. Hoyt had been around asking questions.

"No. No dark cloud today," he replied.

Unsettled, I went out the side door to see what needed doing. Sun Shu was busy. I gave her a wave and hurried to top up the water barrels, not trusting myself to speak. As I worked, I tried imagining what was in Hoyt's head. He must be getting close to using up his account. What else could drive him to such behavior?

There was no telling what he'd do next. Surely, he wouldn't be rash enough to attack Lila twice! Which brought immediately to mind Chen Yi and Sun Shu. Were they next to suffer Hoyt's ire? I couldn't leave my friends in this peril. I had to warn them.

During supper, I told them Fred Hoyt was becoming more reckless, and, since they were hiding much of my gold, they had to be extraordinarily careful.

Sun Shu spoke quietly. "Do you think it was Hoyt who attacked Lila?"

I blinked at her, flummoxed. "You heard about Lila?"

Chen Yi doled out more rice. "Small town, Mouth find ear everywhere."

After supper, I helped Sun Shu get the workyard ready for tomorrow. I could sense she had more to say, but she held her peace. When we finished, it was full dark, too late to head back to the river. I curled up in my blankets behind the laundry counter, my thoughts as troubled as ever. Much as I didn't want to admit it, the only reason for Hoyt to hit Lila was if he suspected me of hiding gold from him. Why didn't he question *me*?

I was so vexed I had to get up. I went out into Sun Shu's workyard. Fortunately, a waxing moon filled the yard with a gray, powdery light. The faint ripple of piano music faded in and out.

Quite a bit of ash had collected under the wash tubs. I found a shovel and bucket. I had to go carefully, not to make too much noise.

The water barrels always needed filling. I filled the bucket from the creek below the yard. When I got back up top, Sun Shu stood among the tubs, still as a tree. She had a gray-colored blanket gathered around her, and she was barefoot.

I began to pour water carefully into one of the barrels. To my dismay, the half-empty barrel magnified the sound. This was too noisy a task for the dead of night.

"I'll finish this first thing tomorrow," I said, forgetting to whisper. I covered my mouth with my hand, smiling, the way she usually did.

"Thank you," she whispered. Her voice still had sleep in it. With one hand she picked up the shovel and leaned it against the wall. Her hair flowed like ebony water across the blanket. "You have done so much for us…"

"Let's not play that game," I said.

"I'm sorry—"

"Don't apologize," I grinned at her.

"Don't interrupt." A smile in her voice, if not her face.

Sun Shu followed me over to what was left of their cord of firewood. "Why are you out here in the middle of the night?"

I pulled wood off the stack and cradled it in my arm. "Couldn't sleep. Too much on my mind. Why are you out here?"

"I couldn't sleep, either." A pause. "Perhaps we are afflicted with the same demons."

I carried wood to the first tub and crouched to add it. She came and stood close. I looked up at her. "I'll tell you about my demons, and maybe you can tell me about yours." I glanced at her bare feet as I set down the firewood.

"If you wish," she said above me. Something tickled in my brain. The softness in her voice felt like she wanted me to take care of her… this was an entirely new feeling, and a little scary.

"Mr. Hoyt is my demon," I said. "Mostly because he is pissing away—sorry—gambling away—our gold." I stood up to go for more wood. Back in Grizzly Bar, I could look Sun Shu in the eye. Now I had to look down at her when she stood this close. I struggled to stay focused on what I was talking about. "And in trying to keep most of the gold away from him, I have put my friends in jeopardy."

She walked with me back to the woodpile while I finished my complaint. "And now he's so desperate he struck Lila, trying to get information from her."

"And the only likely person is Mr. Hoyt?"

I pulled wood off the stack. "Lila wouldn't say straight out, but when I named him, she didn't talk me out of it, or talk about anybody else. And she made me promise not to do anything rash."

I added more wood to my load. "Now I have to figure out what to do so things don't get any worse." I headed off to another tub.

Sun Shu took up a piece of wood and walked with me. "I am not surprised these thoughts have kept you awake."

Out in the street, at some distance, a drunken voice bawled out a few bars of "Roll On, Silver Moon," and, as abruptly, ended.

I knelt. "So what are your demons?"

"Uncle Chen will be very angry with me. But this is America and one speaks plainly and directly here." I looked up at Sun Shu to encourage her. "We have the same demon."

I sprang to my feet. "Why didn't you say anything?"

Her hand reached to cover my lips, but then she withdrew it. "Shhhh. There will be big trouble if we are found out here."

I whispered. "Has he—?"

Sun Shu glanced quickly at the laundry building. "We can tell from his questions that he really knows nothing. He is only interested in us because you are here so much."

"Has he threatened you?"

"He usually goes to the front of the store. Only a few times has he come back to the workyard."

"A few times?" I said too loud.

This time she did press her fingers to my lips. "Shhhhh!" She glanced over her shoulder.

I was more riled than ever. "I'm sorry. I should never have asked you to get involved."

She held my gaze. "Can we unweave the threads that brought us together?" She took a new hold of her blanket. "Uncle Chen has faced down many unpleasant people in his life."

"You must tell me if he gives you any more trouble—any more trouble at all." The thought of beating Hoyt to a pulp brought only dread.

"That is good of you, Honorable Pegg. Uncle Chen can look after his own house." She drew the blanket closer around her shoulders. "May we go in?"

"You go ahead. I want to finish up here."

She searched my face. No doubt she saw the half a dozen feelings that were too jumbled to sort out.

"As you wish." She turned away.

There was that feeling again.

After a step, she stopped and turned. "Don't worry," she said in that same soft voice. "If Mr. Hoyt touches a hair on my head, or Uncle's, Gao Chung will spread his guts from here to San Francisco."

My jaw dropped. Sun Shu padded through the ashy dust, the blanket brushing against her ankles. I stood transfixed by the way her long, silky hair swayed with each step. She stopped, holding the door frame, to brush the soles of her feet, and then stepped neatly through the door. It took a moment to collect myself and be about my business.

. . .

I realized now I couldn't wait for a reply from Mr. Pruitt, whatever his counsel might be. I had to keep my friends from further harm, harm that could strike at any moment. The most immediate solution was to take back all the gold I had left in their care. When the break with Hoyt came, there would nothing for him to demand.

I took up a fresh sheet and made a list of what I could do to achieve that end. One, close out the Will James account and send the money to Mr. Pruitt. Two, close out the Holly Forsyth account and hide that at my claim. Or send the amount from the Forsyth account to my mother as a bank draft, submitting it to the same risks as Mr. Pruitt's bank draft. Three, leave only the Hoyt/Pegg account for Hoyt to plunder.

I fell asleep reciting to myself what I would say to Mr. Hoyt: *No rulebook said how much gold one was supposed to find. Many destitute miners could attest to that. Nor was there a mandate to say when one could stop looking.*

CHAPTER 36

After a breakfast of bean cakes and tea, I helped Sun Shu change the bandages on Bugle's belly, then set off for the express office to talk to Lila about closing the accounts and sending the money back East. As I approached the office, I saw a knot of men in the shadows of the narrow space between Lila's building and Metzger's saloon. Incidents in alleys were usually best given a wide berth. My unruly imagination suggested somebody died. *Whatever has transpired will be common knowledge soon enough.*

I poked my head around the corner to see if I might get a better idea what sort of ruckus had occurred. The onlookers were already starting to wander away. The object of interest was a man sprawled flat on his back on the ground. Was he dead? Passed out? Sick? It was difficult to tell much about the fellow except he was a man of middle height with a long coat and fine boots. *Wait a minute*! I'd seen those boots before.

I came up behind the crouching figures and found myself peering down into the battered face of Fred Hoyt!

"Mr. Hoyt?" I blurted out, suddenly feeling very young and callow.

He moved his head sluggishly from side to side. At least he wasn't dead. His whole face was a pulp of cuts and bruises. This was not bumping into a door jamb, like Lila's excuse. Somebody had dealt with him savagely. Who had Hoyt insulted? Who had he cheated?

"You know this fellow?" A man opposite trying to help Hoyt sit up frowned up at me.

"Yes. Yes, I do." Only a fearsome opponent could do that much damage. There were plenty of times I thought Mr. Hoyt deserved a good whack upside the head, but he didn't—nobody—deserved such a beating.

"Well, see to him. He doesn't seem to want any help—not from us, anyways."

"I'm sorry. Thanks for your concern."

The man rose to his feet and stepped away. Others followed the speaker, recalling past fights. A few lingered uncertainly.

"Can some of you help me get him to a doctor?" I couldn't just let Hoyt lie there in the mud, waiting for him to recover.

I dropped to my knees. "Mr. Hoyt. Can you hear me? It's Pegg!"

His head lolled loose on his neck, one eye swollen shut. The other was almost as bad. His nose was a misshapen mess, his lips swollen and split in several places. Much of the blood had crusted. This must have happened hours ago, in the dead of night. Had it happened here, or had he crawled here after?

I leaned closer. "Mr. Hoyt. We've got to get you patched up. Can you stand up?"

He mumbled. I reached out to help him, but he waved me away, grumbling. I grasped his hand and arm and tugged gently to encourage him. He winced, sucked air in through his teeth, and sank back. Maybe he had a couple of ribs bruised, or worse, broken.

A drink of water, at least. I turned to one of the miners. "Can you try to find Doc Lewis?"

The miner nodded, rose to his feet, and trotted out to the street.

I went into the express office and threaded my way to the counter. "Lila—Miss Rose! May I have a cup of water?"

"Water?" she looked up from weighing a deposit.

Her customers mumbled restively.

I said, "Mr. Hoyt's hurt outside. May I have some water for him?"

"Oh! Oh dear!" She put down the counterweight. "Yes! In the office." She pointed to the wall with the map behind her. I darted around the end of the counter and ran past the wrapping table. The hubbub of the miners grew louder.

I found a tin cup sitting on a shelf above the water barrel. When I came back out, balancing the full cup, Lila said, "I'm sorry, Pegg. I cannot leave my post."

"That's okay, Ma'am. Don't worry."

A few curious miners followed me outside. I returned to Mr. Hoyt to find only two of the original crowd still there. I knelt to offer him the water, but he waved it away impatiently, wincing in pain. I became aware of a new crowd growing around us. A moment later, the miners parted to let Lila through.

She bent to have a closer look at Hoyt and flinched back, drawing a sharp breath. Perhaps she had not expected that much ruination. She straightened and turned, picking out a miner. "Cyrus? Go see if you can raise Doctor Lewis."

A man with a long, sunburnt face answered, "Yes, Ma'am!" and hustled away.

"I already sent someone."

Lila said, "With two people looking, we might actually find him."

With much grimacing, Mr. Hoyt managed to boost himself up to a sitting position. A couple of miners moved barrels to make more room around him. I offered him the cup again. "Try to drink some water."

He shook his head sluggishly. "I don't need water." Even that took an effort. He heaved for breath. "I need a gun."

It was hard to have any pity for a man with that kind of spleen. "Let's get you looked at first." I offered him the water once more. "What happened? Who did this?"

He tried to take a drink, but most of it ran down his chin, and he choked in a fit of coughing. Hoyt threw back his head, gritting his teeth. His hand went to his side, a likely sign of injured ribs.

Lila bent closer. "Mr. Hoyt, be still. The doctor is coming." He slumped back, exhausted.

She closed her hand into a fist and brought it to her chest. "Who did this awful thing?"

Hoyt didn't answer right away, as if the outside world was slow getting through to him. Finally, he muttered, "Blasted coach…driver…"

Lila recoiled. "Oh!" Her hand flew up to cover her mouth. She threw me a quick, horrified glance.

CHAPTER 37

Lila stared down at Mr. Hoyt, her face pale with alarm. The miners nearest had heard "…coach driver…" and passed it back to their fellows. This began a rumble of speculation.

Three coaches passed through Auburn each day. Wallace Evans in the morning, on his way to Sacramento City. At midday, a coach from Sacramento City to points east, and lastly, in the evening, another coach on its way west. So "coach driver" could be, at the very least, any of three men.

I was pretty darn sure it was Wallace Evans.

Lila's eyes were wide with fear. "I'm sorry, Pegg," she said, her voice tight. Had she come to the same conclusion? She rose to her feet and rushed away to reopen the express office.

I looked around at the remaining miners. "Thanks, fellas. We'll be okay 'til the doc gets here." To them, this was just another fight. Very quickly, I was alone with my battered partner. With Hoyt so grievously beaten, I had to wonder if he put up any resistance at all. That he wouldn't was hardly credible. Would Wallace Evans next appear with equally grim evidence of their altercation?

I wanted to get Mr. Hoyt to say something that would fix beyond doubt Wallace Evans as his attacker. "Do you remember anything about the man who attacked you?"

Hoyt's speech struggled past swollen, broken lips. "…completely unprovoked…" he lifted his hand as if pushing away his opponent. "…minding my…business…"

"What did he look like?"

Hoyt lifted his head as if to rise, grimaced, and fell back. "…vile accusations… unwarranted…"

I leaned closer. "Did it happen here in the alley? Which coach driver was it?"

Hoyt ground his teeth. "Big man…bully—" This brought on another spasm of coughing and wincing. His lip started to bleed again. When he regained his breath, he grunted, "Big mustaches…long coat… big hat…"

Wallace Evans, sure as the day is long. He had one look at the bruise on Lila's cheek and coaxed the truth out of her. I was attending the results.

Hoyt tried sitting up again. I set the cup down carefully to help, but he waved me away. Moments passed as he recovered his strength. I glanced over my shoulder, hoping to see the doctor approaching.

Hoyt's thoughts still came out in pieces. "…attacking innocent bystanders…" A pause for more breath. "…attacked the wrong man." He grimaced again. "Got to get…miner's court… show the b—"

I didn't want to hear any more. Dread dropped on me like a hawk on a mouse. Based on what had happened in my dispute for Mahoney's claim, putting Hoyt's fate in the hands of a miners' court scared the daylights out of me.

I had to discourage Hoyt from such a folly. *He wouldn't stand a chance.* Almost every miner had a wife, a mother, a sister, or a daughter, waiting for him back home. The miners' one unshakable goal, like mine, was to return home to them. Lila Mae was a lady, and she was held in much the same esteem. Few villainies were held in greater contempt than hitting a lady.

"Are you sure a miners' court would be a good idea?" I asked Hoyt.

He pushed himself up a little more. His mind was clearing. His speech, though hobbled by a battered nose and ruined lips, was coherent. "Of course! How else will justice be served?"

"I just don't think you—" *Have you thought through what could come of it?*

"Am I expected to turn the other cheek?" Hoyt croaked. "Meekly swallow his insults?" Hoyt looked at the ground around him. "Where's my hat?"

This man's arrogance was monumental. I could stomach no more of it. "Don't you understand what's happened here? You struck a lady. The reason doesn't matter. And now she has been avenged." I had Hoyt's scowling attention. "Every man in three hundred miles would agree that justice has indeed been served." I froze at the thought of how much I had revealed.

Hoyt recoiled with a convincingly stricken look. "Whose side are you on? What's gotten into you?" He cast about, as if seeking witnesses for his outcry. "I leave a sweet, obedient child. I break my back through a long, hard winter, eager to return to a fruitful partnership, only to find an ill-tempered, quarrelsome ingrate." He managed something of a sneer. "It appears you have still learned nothing of the world." He turned away as if I had ceased to exist, preoccupied with his pain and indignation.

I felt compelled to speak, regardless of the consequences. "I've learned how a miners' court works. This is how they will see it. You are new to town. You dress like a gambler. Your principal occupation appears to be speculation, if not outright chicanery. Wallace Evans—yes, you've all but named him—is well-known. He has a responsible position. Cripes! He's popular enough to be mayor."

I braced for Hoyt's riposte, but he only stared. I barreled on. "What do you think he will say in his defense? It'll get you a horse-whipping, or worse."

Hoyt was fast recovering his spleen. "He called me a coward! I will not let it pass!"

I sat back on my heels and played my last card. "And what if they want to hear Lila's testimony?"

He stopped plucking at his clothes and gave me a sharp look. "How do you know it was Evans?"

I threw up my hands. "Because you just described him. A big man—big mustaches, big coat, floppy hat… that's Wallace Evans."

Thankfully, long-faced Cyrus reappeared with Doctor Lewis in tow. The doctor was a small man with silver side whiskers and black clothes to go with his black bag. He knelt down and prodded and pressed, all the while asking questions.

Hoyt responded with winces and grunts, and very little co-operation. At length, Dr. Lewis settled back with a sigh. "Well, my good man, it appears you'll live. Come to my office as soon as you are able and I'll wrap up those ribs for you." He closed up his bag and rose to his feet. "At least try to avoid any more fights until you heal up from this one." His diagnosis given, he strode out of the shadowed alley.

I called after him. "Thank you, Doctor. Thanks for coming."

He raised a wave without looking back and was soon lost in the morning bustle.

Bracing against the wall of the express office, Hoyt slowly worked his way up to standing. "You and I have matters to discuss, young man."

"I have to get back to the claim," I pronounced, "so I can keep you in gold." I was filled with disgust for this lout who was supposed to be my partner.

"That can wait."

"No, it can't." I walked away, anger welling up in me like a pot about to boil over. "I'll see you in a few days."

"Pegg! Come back here!' he threatened. He was really cross now.

I kept going, into the sunlight. "Try to remember what you did with that gold back in Grizzly Bar." I didn't care if he remembered or not; I just wanted the last word.

.   .   .

The walk back gave me a chance to simmer down. Would Hoyt be reckless enough to insist on a miners' court?

On the stagecoach road I came upon Richard Barter. I called out to him. He whipped around. "Well, if it ain't the 'Lion Man'!" He waited while I caught up to him. "I give you joy, Sir," Richard beamed.

We shook hands. "And to you, Sir. Where are you headed?"

"Old Sven's given me a few days' work. Thanks to you," he replied.

We joshed and jabbered all the way to my claim. Richard was always good for lifting the spirits. He continued on downstream to Sven's diggings. I dove on the seam to make sure I hadn't left any last little flake behind.

That evening, Richard came by after his work. He found me writing a letter. "Give me a few minutes," I said. "And I'll make some coffee."

"I owe my sister a letter." Richard settled himself on a rock and gave Bugle a scratch.

"I owe my family a letter, too. But this one's for Mr. Pruitt."

"Ah." Richard broke into a grin. "Your Declaration of Independence?"

I couldn't help but smile back. "That's a pretty good name for it."

He rose from his perch. "Well, stay with it. I'll make the coffee."

"Thanks." I pointed to my tree house. The coffee's in the red tin on the shelf."

He gazed up at the Grandfather Oak. "It's been a long time since I climbed a tree."

While Richard moved around the fire brewing coffee, I finished my letter, specifying that, to my knowledge, his stepson had already spent the greatest part of his particular share.

Richard handed me a cup of the steaming brew. "I'll bet that's a load off your shoulders."

"I think I've said everything that needs saying."

My friend assumed a serious expression. "Which begs the question, if I may?"

I found it hard to match his grave manner. I grinned, "You may."

"Have you stated, in no uncertain terms, that you consider the partnership between yourself and the other parties over? Dissolved? Ended?"

I quickly reviewed my efforts. "I hope that's what this letter is doing. And the certificate to the amount of their share is on its way to him. The one before was just to tell him there were storm clouds on the horizon."

Richard smiled. "Sounds like you're learning Miss Lila's lingo." Then he got serious again. "In these matters, one can't hit the nail too squarely on the head." He raised his cup high. "To a new life out from under Hoyt's shadow."

We drank to my new life, but I couldn't help but wonder, "What will happen to him?"

Richard chided, "Mate, best think about what will happen to you."

I handed him my letter to Mr. Pruitt. "Would you please mail that for me?"

Richard grinned as he tucked it inside his shirt. "The end of your servitude is in sight. It will be a glorious freedom, my friend."

.   .   .

I tallied the receipts from everything I had deposited with Lila. The three accounts together held a little over 14,000 dollars. This did not include the bottles with my last scrapings from the seam. In addition, there remained the gold stowed under Chen Yi's floor boards at his laundry, and I had perhaps two thousand dollars' worth stashed here at the claim. Men had gone home in triumph with far less. The only thing left to do—the hardest thing—was telling Hoyt we were done.

He'll fume and he'll rant. He'll want proof. I'd tell him if he can find any more color on those claims, he'd be welcome to it. At such impudence he'd unleash a torrent of abuse the like of which would shatter stone. But once the storm was over, I'd walk away. Maybe I wouldn't even wait for the storm to be over. *Leave him to his fate. Hadn't he done that to me?*

I prepared to take the last of the seam's treasure into town. As was my custom, I asked my neighbor miners if they had any laundry I could take the next morning for them.

Coming down off the ridge south of town, the muted clatter of Auburn's varied pursuits rose up to greet me. I realized how much I looked forward to seeing my friends. Without them, searching for treasure would be a lonesome task, indeed.

Sometimes, I liked to surprise Sun Shu. I would wait out of sight until she paused in her work, and then pop out. She always made like she was startled.

That day, I crept up to the corner of the building to judge my moment. But it was Sun Shu who surprised me. She wasn't hurrying between tubs, stirring, pouring water, adding wood. She stood stock still. She had her back to me, her shoulders hunched. She seemed fixed on the door to the ironing room.

I heard voices coming from inside the laundry. Chen Yi and Gao Chung were arguing fiercely. I had never heard them raise their voices to each other in all the time I had known them. "Sun Shu. What's wrong?" I asked, moving toward her.

She spun around. Her hair fanned loose with the force of her turn. Tears streamed down her face. Her fingers were pressed to her lips. She looked like she was holding in a mountain of emotion that wanted to burst out. "It is terrible! Terrible! He will bring destruction upon us!" Her voice trembled, her eyes full of terror.

"Who?" I had a pretty good idea. *Fred Hoyt.*

"Gao Chung!" she cried. "Oh! Talk to him, Pegg! Tell him how terrible it will be!"

As soon as I came in the door, I stopped, aghast. Chen Yi and Gao Chung were on the floor, struggling desperately. Gao Chung clutched a huge kitchen knife. Chen Yi grasped the knife-wielding wrist as if restraining Gao Chung, who was spitting what were surely Chinese curses.

The room was a shambles. Chen Yi had lost his cap and one shoe. I hardly recognized Gao Chung. His plait had come undone, his face red, his eyes bulging. Veins stood out in his neck and his temples. A line of blood ran down the side of his face.

"Chen Yi—" I shouted.

"Hoyt man come back!" he shouted back, trying to get a fresh grip on Gao Chung. "Fool Gao Chung want Hoyt blood!"

CHAPTER 38

The ironing room was a wreck! Tables were broken, shelves hung askew on the walls. The shrine and banners honoring the ancestors had been torn down. Clothes were scattered everywhere. Gao Chung's ironing table was smashed to kindling and burnt. Scorch marks stained the wall behind it. It was a wonder the whole place hadn't burned down! Chen Yi and Gao Chung struggled amidst the wreckage.

Had Hoyt done all this damage? *This was my fault.*

Chen Yi and Gao Chung were matched for the moment; their arms trembled to overcome the stalemate. Despite his wound, Gao Chung had to be the stronger of the two. Gao Chung, consumed with his rage, was in danger of stabbing the older man. *But he's not just an older man. He's my friend—darn near family!*

Chen Yi's voice rasped with desperation and exertion. "Sun Shu alone front! Gao Chung hear Hoyt insult Sun Shu. Oh! Bad! Bad! Gao Chung want vengeance."

My own rage burst upon me like a thunderclap. Did Hoyt threaten Sun Shu? I'd carve out his liver. But my revenge would have to wait. Chen Yi was endangering himself by trying to stop Gao Chung.

I moved toward the two men carefully, fearing to tip the balance one way or the other.

Chen Yi was losing strength, trying to restrain Gao Chung and talk. Sun Shu stood close behind me, peering around to see. She looked as scared as the night of the Grizzly Bar fire, when I had handed her the rifle.

I never took my eyes off the fighters. "Sun Shu. You know what will happen to Gao Chung if he goes after Mr. Hoyt."

She nodded in short jerks.

Yes. She knew. A miners' court would look very harshly on a Celestial harming an American.

"Stop! Stop before somebody gets hurt." I might as well have been shouting into a storm. Wading in to grab the knife was foolhardy, at best. "Stop! Fighting never solved anything." I felt more ineffectual with each utterance.

Sun Shu said in a hushed, hurried voice, "His family is part of Uncle Chen's family, going back many generations."

I saw a thread. "Gao Chung!" I called out. "Do you have family back in China? Are they counting on you?"

Sun Shu hovered at my shoulder, translating. Gao Chung seemed to take no notice.

Chen Yi still held him off, but with difficulty. I took a step closer and said to Gao Chung, "Think of the shame and hardship you will bring on your family if you kill Mr. Hoyt."

She translated for Gao Chung. He growled something to her.

She translated for me. "Nothing compares to the shame we will bear if this goes unanswered."

"Do you want to die?"

Sun Shu translated, but tears streamed, and her voice choked with despair. Gao Chung spat out something short and sharp.

"He says, 'Dying is a small price to save the family honor.'"

I took a step closer to Gao Chung while keeping an eye on the quivering knife. Sun Shu stayed with me, but she kept hold of my sleeve. I made my voice urgent. "Do you know, Gao Chung, how much this family—" I gestured to Chen Yi and Sun Shu "—this family, right here, counts on you? Think about how hard it would be for them without you!"

Sun Shu translated, even repeating my gestures, and then said a whole bunch more in their language. Her voice was pleading. Gao Chung slowly lowered the kitchen knife. Chen Yi cautiously released his grip. Sun Shu stepped toward the two men.

What could I say that would convince Gao Chung to give up his crazy idea? *Hoyt is scum; he isn't worth dying for. You will bring your family no honor by fighting such a lowlife.*

Sun Shu was still talking to him. Gao Chung slowly crumpled to the floor. His head drooped and his shoulders slumped. His face was pinched in anguish before he covered it with his hands, crying. Chen Yi pushed the abandoned kitchen knife out of range with his foot. Sun Shu bent and snatched it up. Chen Yi embraced Gao Chung and gathered him in, speaking quietly to him.

I could tell, even without understanding the words, that Chen Yi was reminding Gao Chung of past times, shared adventures, telling him how much he meant to him. The man who a moment ago was raving mad for revenge now curled in a heap on the floor, shaking with sobs. Chen Yi held him, soothing him.

Sun Shu tugged gently at my sleeve and drew me out into the workyard. The world was very bright after the closeness and terror of the room. The muted hubbub of the town seeped around the corner. She stabbed the kitchen knife into the door jamb.

"Thank you, Honorable Pegg," she said.

"You're welcome, but you're the one who convinced him, in the end."

"Oh Pegg, Pegg, Pegg." She headed out into her workyard. "You understand so much and, yet you understand so little." She picked up an overturned tub and set it on its stone apron. "You made him think—of what might happen, of what he would be doing to other people who care about him. I only added to your argument."

"What did you say to him?" I picked up another tub.

"You gave me the words to say to him. I reminded him of his children," she said, pulling some smoldering clothing out of a fire.

"So he does have a family. . ."

"Yes. Back home in China." Sun Shu moved to a tub that hadn't been tipped over, and began stirring the boiling clothes. "He keeps almost nothing for himself. He sends money to them with every ship."

"Will you tell me what happened with Mr. Hoyt? Did he hurt you?"

She moved to right another tub. "It will only make you angry."

"I'm already angry. I have to find a way to fix things." I found a tub that needed stirring.

She stayed where she was. "Promise me you won't go after Mr. Hoyt."

That was a daunting prospect. "I can't make that promise."

While we straightened up the workyard, Sun Shu told me the story anyway. "Mr. Hoyt came back with two men. They were armed. Mr. Hoyt was not. Uncle Chen was away on errands. Gao Chung was ironing. I was in the front, attending customers. Hoyt asked me the same questions he had asked Uncle Chen before. I told him sometimes you eat with us, and sometimes you stay the night before going back to your claim. Mr. Hoyt got very angry. He said terrible things… he threatened us… me… He—" She covered her face with her hands and shook her head. "—Very bad things would happen to us—to—to me—if I didn't tell him the truth." I had never seen Sun Shu so upset. She shook her head. "Oh, Pegg. . ."

"Tell me everything!" I barked at her. I was instantly sorry.

She tried to catch her breath. "He—he called you a thief—oh, I'm sorry, Honorable Pegg. He said if we were helping you, it was the same thing as stealing from him, and—and he would bring the miners to run us out of town…or worse! I was standing right on top of where Uncle Chen keeps your gold. I was so afraid Hoyt would find it."

I ground my teeth, cursing myself roundly in my head. "What happened?"

"He told the two men to change my mind. I was very much afraid. The two men started wrecking the store. Mr. Hoyt kept saying awful things. . .about—about Chinese people. . ."

"Did they hit you or touch you?"

Sun Shu shook her head but didn't look at me. "Three miners came in for their laundry. Mr. Hoyt and the two men fled out the side door into the workyard. One of them hit Gao Chung with his gun. As you can see, they did as much damage as they could while they ran." She was easing away from her fear. "Many clothes are ruined. With the help of the three miners, we managed to put out the fire before. . ."

The whole town went up in flames. I watched her intently. Was there more?

We stood for a minute, looking around the workyard. "I know one thing I can do so Hoyt won't bother you again."

Her face filled with worry. "Remember. You have people who are counting on you, too."

"Yes, Ma'am. That never leaves my mind." I turned to go inside.

Chen Yi and Gao Chung were cleaning up the wreckage. Chen Yi followed me as I went into the front room and knelt behind the counter. "You take gold, not visit anymore?"

"Until I finish with Mr. Hoyt, not so much." I lifted the floorboards. The six bags remaining were all the larger portions: belonging to Mr. Pruitt and my family.

Sun Shu came and stood by Chen Yi. "If you take all that to the express office now, everyone will see. And Mr. Hoyt will surely hear about it." She finished with a thought I was just forming. "And it will prove his suspicions true."

I frowned down at the lumpy sacks. "As long as the gold is here, you are in real danger. This has to end." I replaced the floorboards.

Chen Yi spoke to Sun Shu. Then Sun Shu said to me, "Uncle Chen suggests you go to Lila now and tell her you will be coming late tonight with very urgent business."

"I'll help clean up, then I'll go."

Chen Yi said, "Gao Chung give hand. Too much carry, one person."

"Thank you, Uncle. I would appreciate his help very much."

Sun Shu, Gao Chung, and I set about cleaning up and repairing the ironing room while Chen Yi sorted damaged clothes from the good. He did the diplomatic work of telling some of the miners who came by their clothes had met with an accident and would be speedily replaced by the Sam Lee Laundry.

When we were finished, I went to see Lila.

Two miners were ahead of me. One, a greenhorn mailing letters; the other an old hand, all dust and patches, who deposited a small poke of dust.

When they left, I stepped briskly up to the counter before someone else came in. Lila was still finishing her entry in the ledger.

"Good day to you, Miss Rose," I said in my cheeriest voice. "Do you have any mail for me today?"

She continued to scribe the entry. "I smell trouble, Mr. Bartholomew Pegg." She straightened, closed the ledger, and carefully slid the pencil behind her ear.

I grinned. "Well, you smelled right, Miss Lila. I've come to ask a great favor."

She folded her hands on the book. "My least favorite kind." And raised an eyebrow at me.

"I need to make a large deposit. And I don't want anybody to know about it."

She spoke with resignation. "You wish to do the impossible. I should have guessed."

I gaped at her. This was the closest she'd ever come to making a joke.

Then she got serious. "I can't blame you," she said. "How do you propose to do it?"

"I would like to come here after closing time. Maybe even late enough that most people will be asleep."

"You'll wait a long time for that, I'm afraid," Lila said. "This town never sleeps." She sighed. "But come ahead. No doubt I will still be with my packages."

"And I want to close out the accounts, except for Hoyt's."

Her eyebrows stitched up in worry. "That's a lot of money, Pegg. What will you do with it?"

"I want to send another bank draft to Mr. Pruitt in Vermont, and I will take my family's portion with me back to Vermont."

"It's none of my business. . ." she hunched her shoulders, a sure sign she was breaking another of her rules. "But will you be carrying your family's portion as bullion?"

I heard the warning in her voice. "Should I do a bank draft for them, too?"

"It will draw far less attention, to say nothing of trouble, than a trunk full of bullion."

"Then that's what I'll do."

A sadness crept into Lila's voice. "Does this mean you'll be going home soon?"

Something stopped me from answering directly. "It means that the partnership with Mr. Hoyt is officially over. He and I are going our separate ways."

More miners, boisterous friends chiding each other, came into the office.

"I understand perfectly," she said in a quick, light voice. "I'm sure everyone will be pleased with your decision."

"Thank you, Ma'am," I chirped. "I appreciate your advice," speaking as if I didn't know Lila at all.

At the laundry, we did our best to make the place ready for work in the morning. After much argument, Chen Yi accepted one of my "Hally Forsyth" bags of gold hidden under the floorboards to replace the clothing that had been ruined by Hoyt's visit. I chose to broach this idea while he was making supper, so he couldn't turn his full attention to me.

We all gabbed contentedly over supper around the little table. Only the smell of burnt wood marred the setting. I was struck that these good times would not last much longer.

Just past midnight, Gao Chung and I set out for the express office with our bags of gold. We had split the load into two canvas bundles, each slightly bigger than a saddle bag. But within each bundle, the gold was divided into smaller bags to reflect the portions of the three accounts. To the casual onlooker, we could be carrying bundles of almost anything.

The street had its usual collection of late-night stragglers. Others slept where they fell.

Lila answered the door with a shotgun in her hand and locked the door behind us. The store was dark except for one lantern by the scales. Gao Chung and I settled the bags of gold on the counter.

Lila had seen a lot of treasure come through her door, but, regarding the two bundles, her eyes widened. "As large deposits go, this is noteworthy."

"These are for all three accounts: Will James, and Hally Forsyth, as well as Fred Hoyt and Pegg." I started to untie one of the smaller bags—for the Will James account.

Lila held up her hand. "In the interests of efficiency, please stack all the bags for each account together. That should make it go a little faster."

Once again Gao Chung surprised me. I never knew how much he understood. We quickly reshuffled the bags.

"Shall we begin with the Fred Hoyt account?" She opened her deposit ledger to the "H" page and moved to her scale.

After a few entries, I said, "Maybe I could make the entries in the ledger, if that could be allowed."

"No. That's entirely against regulations…" She shifted the counterweights.

"I'm sorry, Ma'am. But isn't there something we can do to help?" I cast a quick glance toward the wrapping table.

Lila saw my glance and moved her own gaze from the bags to the scales to her ledger, working her eyebrows. Then she sighed. "You can help me with the packages when we're done here, if you're willing to stay."

I gave her a big smile. "We'll stay 'til Kingdom come, if you need us to." I glanced at Gao Chung, who nodded his agreement.

"Well, we don't know how long that will be, do we?" Lila held out her hand for another bag. "In the meantime, have a bag ready and call out who it's for."

When all the gold had been recorded, we refilled the bags and bottles and stacked them against the back wall with all the bags from other miners. The whole back wall was knee-high in containers of one kind or another.

"Don't you have a safe?" I asked Lila.

"They keep promising to send one. They will, once the place is robbed. Until then. . ."

I asked Lila to make out a bank draft for the whole of the Will James account. "And make it out to Samuel Pruitt of Richford, Vermont, please." With the ore just added, it came to 32,500 dollars! That was a king's ransom, by any measure. I would give anything to be there when Mr. Pruitt opened the envelope. Some of it would be divided among the other neighbors, but Mr. Pruitt should be more than happy with his share. I asked Lila to mail it to Mr. Pruitt.

She handed me an envelope. "Please write his name and address on this, and I will see that the bank draft leaves on the morning stage." That done, she asked, "And one for your family?"

"I'll do that in the next day or two, when I figure out what I need to keep back for my own needs. Thank you anyway, Ma'am."

After that, the three of us wrapped parcels 'til the wee hours. In the middle of it, Sun Shu brought a pot of hot tea. She reported she had not been disturbed. The street was all but deserted.

. . .

Rarely had I been up that late in my whole life. As Gao Chung and I walked back to the laundry, yellow light spilled from the windows of the few places still open. Brittle piano music drifted through the doors. Far off in the dark a coyote yapped. Two miners stumbled into the street ahead. One lost his hat, and when he bent to retrieve it, he fell down. His friend reached to help him and fell on top of the first fellow. They both just lay there, laughing helplessly.

I turned to Gao Chung. "Thank you for helping me."

He gave me a short nod. "That man," he said softly.

I looked around. "What man?" Other than the laughing drunks, only one other figure was close by, sitting with his back against a building.

Gao Chung tilted his head slightly toward that man as we came abreast of him. "Watch." Gao Chung used his finger to indicate himself and me.

I looked over to the man. Perhaps my lingering gaze unsettled him. He got up and walked away.

"What was he doing? I didn't see anything odd."

Gao Chung frowned and wiped an imaginary slate clean with his hands. He pointed to where the man had been, then to his eye, then to the two of us again.

"Was he watching us?"

Gao Chung nodded.

"Was he there before? When we came?"

Gao Chung stopped and put his hand out for me to stop. Again, he pointed to himself and me. He spoke barely above a whisper. "Go apart now. Meet laundry." And in an eye blink he had slipped into the shadows between buildings. I stood where I was. If that really was someone watching us, splitting up now was of little use: he'd seen us coming out of Lila's together. And if he watched us go in. . . I walked past the laundry then circled back, using the shadows.

When I got back to the laundry, I found Gao Chung ironing a shirt. We went into the next room where Sun Shu sat writing a letter. She was making the letters on a piece of paper with a small, delicate brush.

"How did everything go?" she asked.

"Fine. Lila sends you her greetings."

Sun Shu smiled. "Thank you."

Gao Chung spoke quietly and intensely with Sun Shu for a few moments, then he went off to bed.

Sun Shu said, "Gao Chung saw someone suspicious."

I sat down opposite her at the table. "He pointed out a man when we were coming back from Lila's. I didn't see anything unusual about him, but I guess I stared too long; he got to his feet and walked away. Gao Chung thought the man was watching us."

Sun Shu laid her brush carefully aside, "He told me that the same man had been there earlier and was watching when you went into Lila's."

A chill went down my spine. "There are always people sitting back, watching the world go by."

"Yes." She paused. "But at midnight? Gao Chung said the man's concentration was pronounced."

"Hoyt's man," I worried aloud.

Sun Shu furrowed her brow. "One time might be idle curiosity; both times, perhaps not."

CHAPTER 39

I took Sun Shu's letter to the express office first thing in the next morning. Shadows cast by the buildings stretched across the street. The air was cool and fresh. The stage was outside, still being loaded. I didn't see the mailbag yet in the boot, which meant Sun Shu's letter might go out today.

Nor did I see Wallace Evans, the whip. I smiled at the thought of his hearty raillery. But then I remembered the fight. Did he still bear evidence of his dust-up with Hoyt?

Seven passengers, already waiting by the stage, meant Wallace would have to put out the center bench. If too many more people showed up for a ride, some would have to sit on top with some of the luggage. The horses would sure earn their keep today.

I hurried my pace so I might persuade Lila to include Sun Shu's letter in the morning's mail. I was glad Mr. Pruitt's certificate was going out on this stage.

The office fairly hummed with activity. Lila was writing out tickets for two more stage passengers. Her bruise had become a livid purple. She was as efficient as ever, but I could tell she was tired. I went over to the wrapping table, still piled with packages to go out that morning. She glanced over at me. I pointed to them and then to outside.

She hesitated, but then nodded short and sharp, before turning back to the next customer. I scooped up packages and hustled outside. I stowed them in the boot of the coach as I had before. It took four trips to load all the packages. She made entries in yet a different account book. For the moment, there were no other customers. The bulging mailbag sat on the floor at the end of the counter, under the letter box. I showed her Sun Shu's letter.

"Is it too late for this to go?" I asked.

"Oh, you are a rascal." She smoothed her hand across her temple. "As long as the bag is not on the stage, it's not too late."

"Is Mr. Pruitt's certificate in here?"

Lila hurriedly wrapped one last package. "No. It's in the strong box, where it should be."

I wedged Sun Shu's letter into the mail sack and cinched it up tight.

Wallace Evans' voice boomed from outside. "Alll-l aboarrrd— for Spanish Corral and points west!"

I nodded to the package Lila just then finished. "Is that ready?"

She moved out from behind the table. "You take the mailbag. I'll take this."

We met Wallace Evans as he was coming up the stairs. He looked up with a big smile and swept off his hat, his great coat flapping like a loose sail. "How be you this fine day, Miss Lila Mae?"

I hadn't seen him since his fight with Hoyt. I could see only one small bruise, fading on his left cheek. Unless he had a couple of broken ribs, which seemed unlikely, given his sprightly movements, he bore no other signs of his recent fracas.

Lila bustled past the driver, urging me along. "Hush your nonsense, Wallace Evans. I'm the same as yesterday and the same as the day before that."

He strode along with us. "And each day is a treasure if I can catch but a glimpse of you." He swept his free arm out; with the other he held his hat against his broad chest.

I couldn't help but smile at his immodest antics toward Lila. It was hard to believe the same individual was capable of the violence he had visited on Hoyt. But I couldn't begrudge him his anger. Hoyt shouldn't have hit Lila, plain and simple. I had wanted to do the same when I thought he had hit Sun Shu.

"Hush, Wallace!" Lila scowled in a fierce whisper. "You'll make yourself a laughingstock."

I hopped up onto the boot and stowed the mailbag. Lila found a spot for the last package.

Wallace beamed down at her. "A man could have worse reasons for playing the fool, Lila Mae."

Lila pushed at him, but not very hard. "Off with you. You'll be late." Her hand took just a little longer leaving his shirt than it should have. "I don't want that on my conscience, thank you."

The last passengers clambered aboard, filling the middle seat that Wallace had set up, with the tenth man indeed clambering up among the luggage on top. Wallace cinched down the big flaps covering the luggage, mailbag, and parcels. Somehow Lila managed to be in his way, and he clasped his big arm around her shoulders before he leapt up to his seat like a sailor into the rigging. He called back, "'Til the 'morrow, sweet maid! I will count the hours!"

We heard some onlooker hoot, and Lila blushed furiously. "OH!" she exclaimed, much vexed.

Wallace gathered up the reins and called to his team. Hooves thumped in the dust as the horses leaned into their harness. Wood and leather creaked and groaned as the majestic red Concord began to move. Wallace sang out encouragement to the team as he turned the big, swaying stage into the road.

Lila was not so cross that she didn't watch until the stage was out of sight. She said, "He's only doing that because you're here, you know." She turned to go back into her office. "He had an audience."

That's silly. He has the whole town for an audience, the way he bellows—every morning! But I played dumb. "Does what, Ma'am?"

She frowned. "You know perfectly well 'what.' All that nonsense about 'sweet maid' and 'counting the hours.'" But then she looked back up the street where the last of the Concord's dust drifted.

"And he never does it any other time?" I grinned at her.

"Happily, I am not obliged to answer such an impertinent question." She opened the door.

"Yes, Ma'am. Just trying to understand the whole picture, is all."

"Shame on you," she said. "What would your mother say to such cheek?"

I didn't say anything. I wished mightily my mother could be here to say whatever Lila thought needed saying. If my sister Amy were here, she'd stick out her tongue in triumph at my scolding. I sure never thought I'd miss that.

In the express office, half a dozen customers stood waiting for Lila. I took my place at the end of the line. When it came to my turn, I asked her, "Could you please tell me the amount in the Forsyth-Pegg account?"

She opened her ledger to the "F" page, and found the entry. Instead of telling me, she took a scrap of paper and wrote the amount on it. As she handed me the note, she said, "Perhaps it would be helpful to know the balance of the other account."

That caught me off guard. "Yes. I am sure it would. Thank you."

Lila flipped forward in her ledger, checked the entry, and wrote on another scrap of paper. She handed it to me. "Thank you for your business." Prim as you please.

"Yes, Ma'am." I left the counter and found a quiet corner. The larger sum, my family's share of the partnership, read 14,000 dollars. Since mid-winter, I had sent back several drafts totaling 1,000 dollars but had not heard how many of them had gotten through.

14,000 dollars would certainly buy a good farm, and more cows than we could milk, and still leave enough money for a new, bigger house for mother. I could buy Amy a hundred ribbons, each a different color. All the suffering and hard work was going to make Dad's dream come true. If only he could be here, standing with me, gazing at this fantastic number.

I did not have the luxury of wishing. I had to be practical and sort out what I would need to live on and get back home and put the rest in a bank draft to send to my mother. As with Mr. Pruitt, I worried that it would even get to her. But the danger of Hoyt somehow getting his hands on my family's share was far greater.

The sum on the second slip of paper filled me with dread. 350 dollars. Before he returned, Hoyt's share had grown to 3,000 dollars. Now, his share of the partnership's proceeds was almost depleted. Out here, a person living frugally, modestly, could make 350 dollars last some time, but that was not the way Hoyt lived. He had already resorted to violence when his resources were merely dwindling. What extremes would he go to when they were gone?

Yet more customers had crowded into Lila's office. I decided to do my calculating in the quiet of Gao Chung's ironing room and return to Lila's later.

I stepped out into the bright sunlight to find Fred Hoyt standing in the street in front of the express office, checking his pocket watch in a casual manner. I stopped short, shoving my paper scraps into my pocket. He looked up and greeted me.

"Top of the morning to you, Lad," he sang out with apparent good cheer. I couldn't swallow it quite so easily anymore. He leaned a little to one side, as if he was favoring a sore spot, like a rib. He bore the scabs and fading bruises of his recent ordeal, and a large white bandage covered most of his nose.

But none of his injuries seemed to have taken a toll on his genial spirits. As far as I knew, he had made nothing of his threats to seek justice. Had he dismissed the whole affair as a barroom scuffle? Despite his cuts he still managed his lopsided grin. "Out about your business early, I see."

I took a firm grip on my wits. "Yes, I am." I noticed that he'd treated himself to a haircut.

Hoyt also sported a new suit of clothes: tight, striped trousers, and a matching coat and vest. A shiny silk hat perched at a jaunty angle. Only his boots were the same. His spiffy new duds were in stark contrast to his battered face.

By the way he held the watch out at the end of its chain, moving it to catch the morning sun, it was obvious I was meant to praise his new bauble. Such finery would certainly have knocked a big hole in his account.

When I offered no comment, he snapped the bezel shut and, with a flourish, tucked the time piece carefully into his vest pocket. Jutting his chin in the direction of the express office, he inquired in the same amiable tone, "Making a deposit to our account?"

"No. Not this morning. Just mailing a letter." I stepped off the boardwalk and started up the dusty street toward Chen Yi's laundry.

To my dismay, Hoyt caught up and fell into step beside me. "You've been visiting the express office a fair bit for some time, from what I hear," he observed mildly. "You must be writing an awful lot of letters."

"Is there a rule about how many letters I can write?" I hoped to shake him off before I reached the laundry. No telling what Gao Chung might do.

"Now, Pegg-son," Hoyt chuckled, but there was no mirth in it. "Don't get riled. I just want to stay informed about our situation, if that's all right with you."

I kept walking, looking straight ahead. On one side, two men on ladders were putting up a new sign while the merchant, in a long, clean apron, supervised from the street. Across the way, a rival retailer was setting out his displays.

"Anything else you want to tell me?" Hoyt inquired after a pause. "About what you've been up to?"

Don't stop. Don't give in. I kept walking.

The familiar snuffling and squealing of pigs came from behind, drew closer, and then overtook us. A herd of hogs was being driven up the street. Hoyt muttered his disgust. The swine paid heed to nothing but their progress. This resulted in trampled tools and overturned buckets, which brought vigorous protests from the miners. The sheer mass of critters left a salty tang in the air.

I waited until they drew ahead with their herder. "I've done what I felt I had to do. Just like you. You decided you had to go to Coloma. You decided what to do with that gold I got at Grizzly Bar."

Keeping pace, he threw back his shoulders. "Of course, I did. That's my job."

My anger escaped me. "You said you were going to send some of it back to my family for winter. What happened to that?"

He halted as if he had been struck. "Aw, Pegg-boy! You cut me to the quick!" Then he hustled to catch up. "I did send it."

"'It?' You only sent one? We've been here eight months."

As he so often did, Hoyt sidestepped the question. "Anything could have happened to the money between here and Vermont. The stagecoach could have been robbed! The ship could have sunk in a storm! Like the *Empress*! Remember? Eighteen tons of gold—tons, you hear! Gone!" he snapped his fingers. "Like that! You can't blame me for what happens to it after it leaves my hands!"

That stopped me short. He was right. So many things could go wrong. There were plenty of stories of robberies and mysterious disappearances. But we were talking about his promises, not the vagaries of fortune.

"That's true— *if* you'd sent any back in the first place, like you said you would. Instead, you gambled it away!"

Our raised voices drew the interest of a group of men assessing the value of a worn-out mule.

Hoyt readjusted his hat. His eyebrows arched in concern. "I don't know what's got stuck in your craw, Boy, or whose lies you been swallowin.' But your behavior leaves me no alternative. I feel it only my duty to inform Mr. Pruitt of my concerns about you." Narrowly sidestepping a miner's pit, he took up the march as if he were in charge again.

I stayed put. "I've already done that." I was glad my letters to Mr. Pruitt—and the bank drafts—were on their way.

Hoyt stopped and turned back. A storm gathered in his eyes. "*What* have you already done?"

I didn't move. "I've written to Mr. Pruitt about the situation here." I felt like I'd jumped off a cliff.

The men abandoned the mule and joined the closer miners who were watching and listening to us. Others, emerging from stores with parcels, paused as well. I spotted Osher Phelps, with a new shovel, coming over. He raised his eyebrow in question, but I shook my head to warn him back.

"Well, now." Hoyt cocked his head and made his voice cheery, but tainted with scorn. "As long as we're sharing secrets, why don't you tell me what you were doing last night with your Chinese friend? Those weren't letters, too, were they?"

So, now I knew. The man Gao Chung had seen watching us *must* have been Hoyt's man. Could I deny being with Gao Chung? "They weren't letters."

Hoyt all but sneered. "And let me guess. They weren't potatoes, either."

Was that supposed to be funny? "No. They weren't."

"Well now, Boy," he brought back his lecturing voice. "There's only one thing you would take to an express office. Did you deposit what was in those sacks?"

"I did. And you got your share." *Let him do his worst. The rest was safely out of his reach.*

Hoyt jerked as if caught unawares. "What do you mean *my* share? It's all partnership gold. What'd you do with the rest of it? Have you been skimmin' off what you want for your own purposes?" He smirked. "Buying gimcracks for your hussy? Am I cursed with a wolf in sheep's clothing? Confess your scheming." He puffed himself up. "Or do I have to write to Mr. Pruitt with bad news?"

I readied myself for his fury. "I've already told him the bad news."

"What news? What news have you told him?" Suspicion twisted Hoyt's face. He was close to shouting. "What fool thing have you done now?"

By this time, quite an audience had gathered to witness our ruckus.

"No! Let's talk about what *you* haven't told *me*!" I was shouting now, not caring about the shame of a public wrangling. "What's happened to the money you made in Coloma?" I pointed back to the express office with a stiff arm. "Or the money I've been putting into your account here? Where's it all gone? Best I can see, to fancy duds and a gold watch!"

"I knew it!" Hoyt reared back, raising his fists. "You and that express woman are in cahoots against me!" He lifted his chin righteously. "Deny it at your peril, Boy! Deny it!"

We just glared at each other. Now we were encircled by onlookers, miners interrupting their work, customers and merchants alike craning for a better view.

Hoyt ranted on. "And those lyin', thievin' Celestials, too! Have they been in on it?"

That did it. "This partnership is over! I've got nothing more to say to you."

His eyes almost started from his head. "That's not for you to decide, blast it!" He roared.

"The obligations have been met—"

"How have they been met?" Hoyt lunged forward, snarling. "With that piddling account we've got in that woman's office?"

A strange calm settled over me. The need for hiding was over. "I had a separate account for Mr. Pruitt. I've sent it to him. The obligations have been met, and more. I've told Mr. Pruitt, and I'm telling you, now. The partnership is over. You go your way; I'll go mine."

Hoyt reared back again, his eyes flaring wide, bellowing for all to hear. "This is outrageous!" He stabbed a finger at his chest. "What about the obligations to me?"

"Your share is in your account. What's left of it."

"What about your share? For your pathetic, pissant little farm. Where're you hiding that?" His voice rattled with contempt.

I realized I no longer feared him. That didn't mean I could let down my guard. "Where you can't get at it. From now on you'll have to get someone else to find your gold for you."

Red faced, Fred Hoyt waved his clenched fists wide and roared, "You'll be finished when I say you're finished, you miserable whelp!"

In a flash I was on the ground. I didn't even see Hoyt step forward and strike. I didn't see anything but bright spots for a minute. But I had heard gunshots. I looked around. The ring of people surrounding us held still. Lila stood, leveling a shotgun at Mr. Hoyt. Smoke still drifted from the muzzle. Only about five or six feet separated the muzzle from his kidneys.

But there had been two shots. I looked around more. On the other side of the circle, the side closest to Chinatown, stood Sun Shu. Her rifle was pointed at the sky, but smoking, too.

A booming voice rang out. "Don't you think that's enough, Mister?" The blacksmith who had made my digging tool stood grim-faced, with his fists clenched at his sides. An unfriendly rumble chorused the burly blacksmith's challenge.

"Butt out. This ain't your concern," Hoyt shouted, his own fists still ready, not taking his eyes off me.

"We're *makin'* it our concern," replied the blacksmith. "You'd best be leavin' off."

Hoyt hesitated, then he stepped back and lowered his fists. Pointing his finger down at me, he hissed through his teeth, "You and me ain't finished, Boy." He turned and pushed his way through the crowd.

Osher Phelps stepped in and offered me a hand up. "You okay, Pegg, lad?"

"Yessir. Thank you." I gingerly felt my lip.

The spectators began to drift away. Osher said, "I'll see you at the river."

From down the street, Hoyt called out, "You're just a snot-nosed brat! You wait 'til we get back home!"

Lila looked in his direction and fired another round into the air.

I called out after him, "I'm not going home!" Then another crazy thought escaped from me. "I *am* home!"

That startled the daylights out of me. I felt like I was soaring higher than any cliff could be—above the clouds, with the sun on my back. And I knew I could land, even if I didn't know, right then, exactly where or how. The decision must have been building while I wasn't looking. What would my family say?

Sun Shu inspected my split lip. She said quietly, "Did you mean that?"

"About not going home?" I smiled, even though my lip stung. "Yeah. I think I did."

CHAPTER 40

Sun Shu and I came into the laundry through the workyard. I saw Bugle lounging against the building. As soon as he spotted us, he was on his feet, trotting over. I knelt to give him a hug and a scrub, carefully avoiding the healing of his recent wounds. "You missed the excitement, Bugle boy. You should've seen Sun Shu and Miss Lila bringing shotgun justice down on that rascal, Mr. Hoyt."

I heard Sun Shu gasp and glanced over to see her standing close. I gave her a wink. She blushed beet red.

I turned back to Bugle. "Well, maybe not. You'd've chewed his ankles off."

Chen Yi came out into the yard and spoke to Sun Shu. She gave a short response.

He marched right up to me and inspected my split lip. "Cut lip heal quick. Cuts on heart, maybe not so quick." He searched my face.

"I'm okay, Uncle," I smiled down at him. I remembered Sun Shu's line about Hoyt. "I know who he is, so his words cannot hurt me."

Chen Yi broke into a big smile. "Ah, so! All patience pay off! You call Chen Yi 'Uncle'! Special day!" He spoke again to Sun Shu.

She smiled, too. "Yes, Uncle."

"Extra ginger today! Special day." And with that, he went back into the building.

"What did he say?"

"He said he didn't know what to expect of Gold Mountain, but he didn't expect to add to his family."

.   .   .

I had a lot to think about. I had blurted out something pretty radical in my argument with Hoyt, and then I told Sun Shu I meant it. Would my mother and sister agree to such a precipitous move? For the past year and a half, I had thought about nothing else but getting enough gold to buy a new farm—*in Vermont*.

What made me say this was home? It was reckless, crazy. But something kept me from ascribing the outburst to addled wits. Did I just want to have the last word with Hoyt? I certainly didn't want to spend the rest of my days chasing gold.

Sun Shu loaded me up with shirts to take in to Gao Chung. "Do you think you'll ever go home, Sun Shu?"

"That is not for me to say, Honorable Pegg. Yang Ho will decide what we will do when he returns. My first duty is to my husband."

Yes. Yang Ho. An odd twinge unsettled me. Yang Ho had been gone for months now, when he was only supposed to be gone ten days or so. They had sent Gao Chung to look for him, they had sent letters. It was as if the earth had swallowed him up. Sun Shu had buckets more faith than I would have. "Have you heard anything? Any word at all from him?"

But they aren't in Grizzly Bar anymore. How would he find her? I decided not to ask about that.

She picked up her stirring stick. "I think you would know if I had. . ."

I wondered if Sun Shu's reunion with her husband would be anything like my folks' reunions were when they had been apart.

They ran to each other and you couldn't pry them apart for love or money, and that after eighteen years married! I said, "I'm sorry…"

She looked up with a soft smile. "Thank you. But there is no need to be sorry."

I took the shirts in to Gao Chung. When I came back outside, I checked the fires under the tubs. All the while I was trying to form how to ask my next question. Finally, I chose the straight-ahead approach. "Well, what would you do if. . . if. . ."

"If Yang Ho doesn't come back?" she said, adding water to one of the tubs. She was braver than me.

"Yes, Ma'am."

"I will…" she broke off and said in a slightly breathless voice, full of brightness. "Lila used this phrase the other day when we were talking: cross that bridge when I come to it. That is a wonderful phrase, isn't it? And that is what I will do, cross that bridge when I come to it."

She's waiting. When does she decide to stop waiting? "Yes, Ma'am." I went over to stir the starch tub. "It would be nice if you could have a store again." Then her arms wouldn't be red, and her hands wouldn't be raw from the soap. "It sure would beat doing laundry all day." I added wood to the fires that needed it. "Do you think Chen Yi will ever open another restaurant?"

"Perhaps." She said, stirring. "He has a great affection for people, despite what life has thrown him. He loves serving good food. Presiding over the whole affair like a. . .Zheng yi pin." She saw my questioning look. "A master. A mandarin of the first rank. Making sure everybody gets plenty. You should have seen his banquets. They would go on for hours. He would bring in dancers, musicians, and poets. He used any excuse to call a gathering: births, marriages, successful business transactions. . ." She moved to another tub.

That got me to thinking about Chen Yi's life here in California. How different. . . how rough. He must have been a very successful man back home in China, big house, big family. . . Sun Shu broke into my thoughts.

"But what about you, Pegg? If you do stay, what will you do? What about your family?"

I shifted my hat. "Well, I'm glad you're not holding me to what was said in such haste."

She smiled full on—without hiding it. "I think we were all flying like kites at that moment. I was so terrified that Lila would get us in trouble."

"She sure surprised me!" I thought back to prim, proper, law-abiding Lila ready to blow Hoyt in half. I grinned. "*You* surprised me."

"Hush." Sun Shu moved to another tub. "So what do you think you would do—if you were to stay?"

Leave it to Sun Shu to see to the heart of the matter. "I don't know. The only thing I really know anything about is farming."

Will winked slyly in my mind. *And making rock fences.*

Will! Another casualty of my rash declaration. Would Will want to come to California?

Once again, Sun Shu broke into my reverie. "Why don't you do that? Both Yang Ho and Uncle Chen say the soil here is the real treasure. Especially in the great valley of the Sacramento River."

"Mmmmmm." I realized that I had been so preoccupied with gravel and rocks and river bottoms that I hadn't looked around at the soil with the eyes of a farmer. As well, I'd been fixed on my dad's dream of a dairy farm. And, of course, I hadn't been out to the great valley to the west, yet. Just seen it in the distance from the tops of ridges. There certainly seemed to be plenty of it. But I wasn't sure it would be the best place for a dairy. I said so to Sun Shu.

"Does it have to be a dairy farm?" she countered.

That stopped me. "It's what my dad wanted more than anything else…"

Sun Shu paused a moment. "If I may say, Honorable Pegg. I think your father would want to see you prosperous and happy, no matter whether you are raising cows or cabbages."

It had been a long time since I spared a thought for what I wanted, other than surviving Fred Hoyt. But I wasn't the whole show. What would my mother want, or for that matter, what would be good for Amy?

Now I had even more to think about. My head was starting to hurt. "Do you think Chen Yi or Gao Chung will ever go back home?"

"Uncle keeps saying he is an old man. His children are all married. His wife is with her ancestors. His sons and nephews are running his businesses." She lifted a big wad of clothes from a washing tub into a rinsing tub. "He says no one needs him back home." Her face got serious. "He won't say it, but now I am his only burden. He won't budge until he knows I am settled and safe."

"What about Gao Chung?"

"Gao Chung will do whatever Uncle does. Gao Chung would follow Uncle Chen into the jaws of Hell." She caught herself and started again. "No. Gao Chung would walk ahead of Uncle, slaying demons and quenching flames that dare to harm Uncle Chen."

We worked in silence for a space.

When next she spoke, her voice was soft and modest as a spring rain. "Will you go into town with me this afternoon? I want to show you something."

Yang Ho would be a fool not to come back—if he's still alive. "Yes, Ma'am. I will." I replied, flustered.

Gao Chung stuck his head out the door and called us in to dinner. It took a long time to tell my Celestial family the story because Chen Yi had to keep getting up to help customers. It took longer, too, because Sun Shu was translating for Gao Chung.

"So, no more partner Mr. Hoyt?" asked ChenYi.

"That's right, Sir. No more partners with Mr. Hoyt." I sent up a prayer that if I said it enough times the words could be my shield and armor.

When dinner was over, while I cleared the table, Sun Shu spoke quietly to Chen Yi. He glanced over at me once or twice while he listened, so I reckoned I might be the subject of their talk. At length, they drew Gao Chung into it, and just about the time I started to feel left out they broke off.

Sun Shu returned. "Chen Yi has given us his blessing, and Gao Chung has agreed to tend the workyard while I am away." She finished shyly, "Please allow me a moment and then we will go."

"Is this something where Bugle can go along, or should he stay here?"

Bugle understood we were about to go out. He looked up expectantly and wagged his tail like there was no tomorrow.

Sun Shu gave my Beagle a sad look. "Perhaps it would be better if he stayed here. We won't be that long."

I escorted Bugle to his basket in the front room. "You heard the lady, Bugle. It's best you stay. Okay? We won't be long." I gave him a scratch. His scars were no longer livid. That was good.

To my surprise, Sun Shu led the way without offering any further word about our destination. She had exchanged her work clothes for a costume of the same deep, deep blue silk that she had sported back in Grizzly Bar. Its generous sleeves and trousers flowed with her movements like eddies of night. The only thing missing was the red sash that made her look like a pirate.

We joined the throng navigating what little unbroken ground was to be found in what they were pleased to call the street, picking our way between pits filled with muddy creek water or disorderly piles of tailings. At one point, we had to cross to the other side to avoid a skirmish between a merchant in dry goods, wielding a broom, and a trio of miners who were intent on digging up his front step.

We came to a halt in front of Gwynn and House's store. Gwynn had taken on a partner, a Mr. House, who already owned the Empire Hotel. The partners were in the midst of building an even grander structure—two stories of sawn lumber—next door to their current sagging canvas tent. Gwynn and House's stocked everything from mattresses to molasses, butter to blankets to Boston crackers.

The canvas diffused a special, soft light over spades and spices alike. The space occupied easily twice the floor square feet of our cabin back home. A scattering of customers, mostly impatient greenhorns throwing together their kit, kept the two or three clerks running.

Sun Shu made straight for the fresh produce displays. I had never paid much mind to this part of the store, having restricted myself to bacon, beans, coffee, and flour. I was puzzled why Sun Shu wanted to show me groceries.

I scurried after her purposeful stride. She pulled up short at a display of radishes almost as big as my fist, and carrots twice, if not three times bigger than anything we could grow in Vermont. Tables and boxes were brimming with fat melons, giant potatoes, bright, shiny strawberries. These last were far larger than any of the wild ones we harvested back home.

Across the aisle, glossy tomatoes, a pound or more each, which I had never tasted until we got to St. Louis. My uncle Rafe grew them, but most people held the fruit in suspicion.

A short man in a striped apron, with slicked-down hair and carefully trimmed mustache, came over to us. Thankfully, the canvas of the present location muffled to some degree the clatter of construction next door. "Good morning to you, Mrs. Ho. How are you today?" he beamed in an eager voice.

He had it wrong. It should have been Mrs. Yang. The Celestials did their names the other way 'round, but I kept my mouth shut.

"Good morning, Mr. Tibbets," Sun Shu replied in a reserved but pleasant manner. "I am very well, thank you. You have a lovely selection today." She picked up the topmost fruit from a neat pyramid of some two dozen of their kind. I had never seen its like before, the size of a man's fist, a plump, round, golden fruit with the blush of a girl's cheek.

"Yes, Ma'am. Things are beginning to come in," sighed Mr. Tibbets. "I'm afraid the strawberries are almost done. . ." He gestured to a tangled heap of swollen pea pods. "Mr. Nickerson brought in a fine bushel of peas this very morning. And I'm expecting lettuce and corn anytime now."

Sun Shu held the mystery fruit out to me. But she spoke to Mr. Tibbets. "Are these peaches from Mr. Mendenhall's orchard?"

I took the fruit from her hand, marveling at its weight. I had seen a peach once. It was supposed to have come from Georgia. But I never got to taste it. That long-ago peach was nowhere near as big as this one in my hand, nor as golden. This peach all but glowed. To my surprise, it was covered in a soft down that was all but invisible.

"Yes, Ma'am," answered the clerk. "They are, indeed. From his very first picking. I had to twist his arm to leave me this small offering." He gestured sadly to the pyramid. "They'll be gone by closing." The clerk sighed again. "He can make much more money shipping them to San Francisco."

Sun Shu touched another peach lightly. "Perhaps when there are more peaches, he will have more for us."

I looked at her in wonder. This was not the shy, timorous Sun Shu I had known back in Grizzly Bar. None of the hovering behind the deference of questions.

Sun Shu said, "No doubt most of his neighbors feel the same. What is the fellow's name who grows apples?"

"Mr. Neal and Mr. Morrell both grow apples." The clerk fussed over his strawberry display. "They ship everything to San Francisco, no matter how much I plead."

"I suppose Mr. Gately is doing the same with his plums," Sun Shu said.

Mr. Tibbets got flustered. "Most likely. But it'll be a few years before his trees start bearing."

If what he had on display was the first pickings of the season, Mr. Tibbets' produce offerings would be heaped to the ceiling by late August, early September.

Sun Shu went on. "Is it true that Mr. Gately is building a new house? Perhaps it's only a rumor."

Tibbet's eyes fairly danced. "Oh! Indeed he is, Ma'am! Two stories! Two fireplaces! With the money he made growing melons! Can you imagine? Melons."

"Those must be very special melons," I blurted.

The clerk shrugged nervously. "No. He just had a good crop. He's raising melons while his fruit trees are maturing."

"Why doesn't he stick with melons if he's doing so well?" I persisted.

Sun Shu moved off to inspect other produce. Mr. Tibbets burbled on. "He says plums will bring a better price, pound for pound. Especially when he can ship them to all the markets back east."

That struck me as a crazy idea. "How's he ever going to do that? They'd rot or be mashed to pieces— likely both, before they got over the Rockies."

"Mr. Gately's pinning his hopes on the railroad," replied the clerk. "He says it's only a matter of time before it gets here."

People were building railroads left, right, and center back east. *It would be no hard thing to lay track across the prairies—you'd just need a bridge or two.* "They'll have a time of it getting across the mountains." *The Rockies would be tough enough; the Sierras would be all but impossible.*

"Maybe so," replied the clerk, "but Mr. Gately says it's destiny!"

Sun Shu rejoined us. She plucked the peach gently from my hand and held it toward Mr. Tibbets. "May I have four, please?"

"Of course, Madam," the clerk smiled. "With pleasure. Four it is. Coming right up."

▪   ▪   ▪

Sun Shu and I left Mr. Tibbets beaming and waving, standing under a halo of kettles, coffee pots, and fry pans. We ourselves bore away a bounty of peaches and peas, green beans, onions and carrots. We argued over who would carry them. She let me win.

We joined people squeezing their way along between the storefronts and the clamorous diggings in the street. Individuals joined or left the throng as their errands required.

Finally, we had some breathing space. I drew abreast of Sun Shu. "Thank you for taking me shopping, Sun Shu. But to what purpose, may I ask?"

"There are many good possibilities other than a dairy farm."

I stared at her. *You can lead a horse to water, but you can't make him drink.* I was meant to drink in the bounty of produce. I reviewed what I had seen and learned: peaches, apples, plums, peas, strawberries, melons. Was there anything you couldn't grow in California?

"You're becoming more American every day," I said, grinning.

"Oh dear. Yang Ho would not be happy to hear that."

I was just getting myself in deeper trouble. It would not do to accuse a married woman of flirting. "You were being very nice to Mr. Tibbets. . . and he was being very nice back."

She gave me a stern look. "I was not flirting." She turned back to watch her step. "I am a respectably married woman."

Only the recollection that she was a married woman with a lost husband put a damper on my unruly humor.

"You are making fun of me," she protested.

"No, no, no!" I concentrated on getting my foot out of my mouth.

CHAPTER 41

Back at the laundry, Sun Shu set out four saucers and a knife on the small table where we took our meals. She washed the peaches and put one on each plate. Two of them she cut into wedges. Juice puddled under the peach. The flesh of the fruit was even more golden than the outside. She set aside the dark, gnarled pits.

"Please take this out to Uncle Chen," she said, handing me one of the saucers.

She took the second saucer to Gao Chung.

We returned to the table and our two peaches. She cut them into wedges, as she had the others, and picked up a wedge, gazing at it. "Father Cuvier sometimes spoke of the 'nectar of the gods.' In my mind, this is it." She took a bite and closed her eyes, savoring, chewing slowly.

I thought back to Sun Shu's stories about when she was growing up in China. What a stroke of good fortune for her that Father Cuvier wandered into her village and started a school. He taught her so many things besides astronomy and good English.

I bit into my first wedge. It was incredibly juicy and sweet. I had never tasted anything so sweet! I imagined eating sunshine! "Wow!" I popped the rest of the wedge into my mouth. Juice gushed out and ran down my chin.

"My mother and Amy would love this!" I took up another wedge, scowling at it. "My brother Adam probably wouldn't get excited; he's strictly a meat and potatoes man." I took a careful bite. "Mom would figure out a dozen ways to use these. In pies, for sure, just like apples. But peach pies would be ten times juicier! "

Sun Shu offered me a towel. "It will be nice to meet them some day."

.   .   .

Without fail, Sun Shu asked me to stay to supper, which, by the time all our gabbing and storytelling was done, usually meant spending the night. But I could not forget that I had a nemesis who had a habit of showing up unannounced. And if I was with my friends when he did, they would be in harm's way, too. So, reluctantly I declined.

"There are hours of light left. I can make it back to my claim with no trouble."

Sun Shu made to protest my safety but relented and folded her hands in her lap.

I couldn't help but smile. "I know. I'll have Bugle to warn me and I'll keep the rifle close at hand."

Before leaving town, I went back to Gwynn's and purchased another peach and some green beans to augment the fiddleheads and cress I gathered. Then I went to Lila's office to close out the Hally Forsyth account. The majority went to a bank draft for eleven thousand dollars to send back to my mother, leaving two thousand for me to live on, plus a thousand set by to get back to Vermont, if it came to that. But with the draft in hand, I had a moment's pause. If I sent the draft and then persuaded them to come out to California, that would put the draft at risk twice, once going east and once more coming west with my family.

If, on the other hand, they wanted me to come home, it would be easy enough to carry the certificate with me. I decided to keep it with me until I got a response from my mother.

I headed back to the river with a light heart. I was free of Fred Hoyt at last. I had turned a blind eye to his chicanery for the sake of the partnership. I had tied myself in knots making excuses for his recklessness—until the moment I'd actually uttered the words to end the partnership.

Hoyt would have to make his own way, whatever that turned out to be. Mr. Pruitt, upon receiving my letter, would be apprised of the course of events, and I felt sure he would be pleased with the reward that justified his faith in my father and me.

Best of all, I had eliminated any reason for Hoyt to persecute my friends.

Bugle still favored his leg, so we stopped and rested often, particularly if we happened upon a trickle of a stream. The sun was warm; the world was at peace. Only the scolding jays in the trees marked our passage. The turkey buzzards soared their high, lazy circles in the great blue sky. Pine pitch and tarweed flavored the air.

We were well away from heavy mining activity, and oaks were plentiful; many rivaled the old Grandfather Oak on my claim. Tall grasses, long since toasted yellow by the sun, stood between.

We came out of a grove, to the tip of a ridge before it dropped away to lower elevations. Before us spread the great central valley, running north and south. From here I knew it would be best to cut more sharply south, to meet the river close to Rattlesnake Bar, but I was halted by the prospect of the land to the west. The great central valley, dimmed blue in the late afternoon light, swept to the purple rampart of the coast range marking its western limit. Beyond it lay the vast Pacific Ocean.

I had never laid eyes on the Atlantic. On seeing the Mississippi, I thought it a mighty impressive piece of water. How wonderful it would be to see the Pacific! The Kanakas—fellow miners: big, amiable, hard-working men—were from islands in the middle of that ocean. Sun Shu, Chen Yi, and Gao Chung had sailed across its great breadth to reach this place: Gum Shan, Gold Mountain.

I glanced down at Bugle. "Room for a lot of farms out there, eh, Boy?"

Bugle turned his head and gave me his "I know you're not finished" look.

I gazed out at the vista again. "What do you think we'll need? Ten thousand acres? Twenty? Forty thousand?" I felt my mind stretching to allow such concepts. Back in Vermont we had forty acres, and not all of that was yet under the plow. I knelt down and gave Bugle a scratch. "I'm not sure I'd like living out in the flat, though. Would you? I've got to have hills around me to feel right..."

Turning my attention once more from the oaks close by, out to the broad valley and the mountains beyond, I had to admit the idea of staying in California had taken root in my mind. "So, what do you think of staying? Huh, Boy? Staying here?"

He turned his head back for more scratching. I obliged.

"Do you think Mom and Amy and Adam would like it out here?" I stopped scratching, lost in speculation. I thought back to the bounty of the fruits and vegetables Sun Shu had shown me in Gwynn's. "Do you think Dad would be disappointed if I didn't do a dairy farm? If I did something else?"

Bugle gave me his sympathy look, reminding me I'd had only two cows to look after back home.

"It seems like you can grow just about anything you want out here. Fruit trees ought to be easier to take care of than cows."

I scratched his back; places he couldn't get to. "I guess we better have a plan if we're going to convince the family to come out here."

CHAPTER 42

By the time we got back to the claim, the twilight was deep, with hills and trees alike merged into one black silhouette. Many miners were already bedded down. Campfires on both banks, slowly dying, marked out the path of the river. A short laugh from upstream floated above the gentle warble of water. Bats, like small scraps of night, flitted low overhead, hunting their suppers.

A half-moon gave us enough light to have our own supper. I finished with the peach, cutting it in thin wedges to make it last longer. I had a time wiping up the juice running down my chin. I thought of having a whole grove of peach trees; I could walk out and pluck one off a tree.

I folded up the bank draft of my family's share into an even smaller square. Then I put it into a yeast powder tin, making sure the lid was good and tight, and buried it up the hill with the rest of my stash. Lastly, I stowed my provisions in the bag hanging from the Grandfather Oak.

Scooping up Bugle under one arm, I clambered up the rope ladder into my tree shelter and drew the ladder up after me.

Rolled up in my blankets, I gathered Bugle close. "This was a day to write home about, eh, Bugle boy? That'll be our first chore tomorrow."

I woke up to Bugle barking up a storm. He was standing so close to the edge of the platform, barking earnestly, I was afraid he would slip off.

I dared not lift the canvas to see what was upsetting him for fear he'd leap head-long into a fight. It was likely an animal, a skunk or a cougar—trouble either one, but more than likely meant something bigger than Bugle. He kept up his clamor even when I dragged him away from the edge. I figured we were safe on the platform; the food was too high for even a bear to reach. *Just wait it out.*

Bugle gradually gave up his racket, and I gathered him close.

After a few tense minutes, gunshots sounded, some ways off, downstream. Shouting erupted, too. Then more gunfire. Perhaps some miners were celebrating—or arguing—or had our four-legged visitor wandered downstream?

The gunshots grew sparse and finally stopped. Still, I waited. Caution was a much stronger impulse in the dark of night. Quiet stretched on. At last, a wolf howl, at some distance, long and mournful, then an answering call, still farther off, told us the world had resettled into its rhythm.

.   .   .

That morning, Bugle and I set out, hiking downstream. Old Sven would likely know what last night's ruckus was all about. The sun had yet to breach the rim of the eastern hills, but the brightness of the morning banished any lingering dread from the night before.

In fact, for the first time in months, I felt whole; the knot in my stomach was gone. And this elation came, I knew, from having rid myself of the one person who, without ceasing, made me feel at fault.

Bugle and I came upon Sven up and laying a new fire. When we were still some paces off, Bugle bounded ahead. The old sailor was good for a scratch whenever we visited.

Sven looked up from the dog wiggling with delight under his fingers. His silvery whiskers glistened in the early light. "Guten morgen, Pegg. How do you fare?"

"Good Morning, Sir. I'm fine, thank you." I just did what my dad did. He got along with everybody. I glanced down at the chore we had interrupted. "Your fire die on you?" You could almost always coax a fire from last night's deeply buried embers.

Sven threw a glance at his kindling. "Ja. I pay for my neglect."

"You should have it back in no time." Amongst his tinder, I spied some paper, mud-spattered and shredded, he had scavenged. How many useful things had I found that way? But I couldn't help but feel a twinge of dismay. I had always been taught paper was a precious commodity.

Sven pulled out a box of matches, something new for starting fires, and touched the burning match to his tinder.

"What was all the gunfire and shouting about last night?" I asked. "Somebody celebrating a bonanza?"

"*Nei, ungdom.* It was no party. It was a bear."

A chill touched me. I gave a silent thanks for my tree house. "I think he passed through my camp. Bugle woke me up, barking at him."

Sven watched the flames lick at the wood. "You have luck with such fair warning"

"I wonder if it was the same one that went after Bugle before?" I glanced at Bugle. He was sniffing at a tent peg belonging to Sven.

"Hard to tell…" replied Sven. He arched his eyebrows into a slant. "You stay for frokost?"

I smiled. "Breakfast?"

"Ja."

I'd jump at any chance to hear more of Sven's stories. He had sailed the seven seas. He told about places I would never get to see, but I wanted to know about them, anyway. In that way Sven reminded me of Linnaeus Peabody, who'd traveled the world, and who'd traveled west with Dad and me. Linnaeus knew all about fabulous cities and ancient empires.

Sven told about wild, lost islands belching fire, others covered in jungle; waves twice as high as the ship. Score upon score of porpoises romping in the bow wave. "I be a whaler for a while," he said before taking a swig of coffee. "I always get berth because I see good far. I see a whale," he held out his cup, pointing into the distance. "I shout 'Thar she blows!' And the skipper call up to me, 'Where away?' And I shout back down, 'Abaft the beam! Two mile!'" Then the ship be bedlam. 'Boats away! Boats away!' the skipper holler." He smiled and shook his head slowly. "But the whale take their revenge."

I gave him a questioning look.

"The try pots, they boil day and night, melting blubber to oil. Everybody work. Black smoke rise to heaven. Then we cut loose what's left for sharks, the whole ship be covered black with oil soot—even the sailors. We be two days, three, washing down everything. Scrub, scrub, scrub." Coffee sloshed out of his cup as he mimicked the work. "Sails, rigging, decks—everything—down to the waterline. Everything."

It sure didn't sound like whaling could hold a candle to being a pirate, but I spared Sven my opinion.

At length, I thanked Sven for breakfast and his stories, called Bugle away from his visiting, and headed back upstream. I kept half an eye on the high ground to my right for the bear's return.

R. C.'s first claim, which he had signed over to me, lay between Sven's claim and mine. On my way back, I stopped to poke around in the pebbles. There was always the chance the river had washed a few flakes down.

Gazing out over the water, I wondered if there were more bonanzas along the bottom, just waiting for somebody else who could swim. If the prospectors had any idea what lay down there, to what lengths would they go to get at it?

I continued on, dreaming of sliced peaches over flapjacks and syrup. When I came in sight of the Grandfather Oak, I stopped. Bugle stopped. A low growl rumbled in his throat.

Fred Hoyt sat on a stump in the shade, looking right at me.

How long had he been watching me make my way through the claims? I could feel the eyes of the miners I passed on my back. I caught sight of Osher Phelps sitting by his fire, beyond Hoyt, his gaze flicking between me and Fred Hoyt.

I thought I had prepared myself for this confrontation, but now that it was here, I realized I would never be, so might as well walk right up to it.

I touched the ruff of Bugle's neck. "Stay close, hear. Stay close"

Hoyt stood up as we approached, shaking his coat loose around his shoulders, donning his crooked grin. He had changed back into his regular duds. No fancy frock coat, no gold watch, no shiny silk hat. What was this all about?

Both the Colt and my rifle were up in the tree shelter. I stopped far enough back that I could break and run if I needed to.

"Top o' the mornin' to you, Pegg, boy." He threw a quick look at Bugle. "I heard about the pooch. How's he mending?"

He doesn't give a plug nickel about Bugle. I had to make him as unwelcome as possible. "You've got no reason to be here."

Hoyt managed to look contrite for all of an eye blink. "Well, now. I've come to apologize, Son. Hard words were dealt yesterday, hard words, indeed. Should never have been let loose."

What about blows, shall we talk about hard blows? "The partnership is over."

Hoyt rolled his head in frustration, the way somebody would roll their eyes at something silly. "Now…there's no reason at all to break up a perfectly good partnership."

The noise of close activity behind me grew quiet. Osher Phelps put down his cup, his gaze steady on Hoyt's back. I spoke up, in case I needed witnesses. "That may be how you see it. The way I see it is, I've been finding the gold, and you've been spending it."

The last of Hoyt's cordiality vanished. His brows drew down in a fierce glare. "Whatever you've found belongs to the partnership," he growled.

"What about the gold you've spent on cards? On new friends and fancy clothes? Who did that belong to?"

"I can't expect you to understand what is necessary for—"

"The partnership is over."

His face grew red; his voice grated, as if holding back an explosion. "Will you never learn? That's MY decision to make!"

I stood my ground, but I was tensed to run. "There's no rule says how long a partnership has to last! Nowhere says how much gold a body is supposed to find."

He raised his fists in the air. "I say, you insolent brat!" he roared. "I say how long it lasts!"

I glimpsed Osher Phelps rise cautiously to his feet. "Mr. Pruitt has his share. You have your share. More than your share."

Osher Phelps raised a protest. "Hey! What's goin' on?"

Hoyt swung in his direction with a clenched fist in the air and roared, "Mind your own damn business if you know what's good for you!"

He turned back to me, his eyes squinted in suspicion. "What about your family's share?"

I took a step back, bracing for an attack. "It's taken care of. You don't have to worry about it. You've got to look after your own self from now on."

"You can't do this!" He stepped forward, looming taller, throwing his massive fists out with each taunt, as if already in a fight. Bugle barked. I heard mutterings as miners behind me drew closer. Others beyond Osher's claim stopped their work, wondering at the commotion.

I tried to keep my voice steady. "Maybe you've got enough left to get home. You ought to do that." I pictured the bank draft tucked in the tobacco tin. I've got my family to look after."

I threw the quickest glance up the hill. Hoyt followed my glance. His eyes widened and he broke into a run up the hill.

I ran after him. Bugle followed, barking. When I got closer I saw why Hoyt ran this way. Little bits of gold glittered among the dried leaves and pine needles. He must have seen one of those glints.

When we got to the spot, I had a sudden sick feeling! Torn up ground! The bear! The ground was plowed up with claw marks where I had buried my gold and, most recently, the tobacco tin. The bear must have sniffed out the bacon smell on the sack that held my bottles, as well as the tin with my mother's bank draft. Shreds of the sacking were scattered all around. A few bottles were broken, hence the small nuggets reflected the sun.

Hoyt fell to his knees and began sweeping through the leaf litter for nuggets. The more he scrabbled after the nuggets, the deeper they sifted into the loose mulch. The finer dust was utterly lost among the curled leaves.

I jumped on his back and tried pulling him away. He grabbed me by the throat with an iron grip and flung me aside like I was a rag doll. I narrowly missed landing on Bugle.

I waded back in, grabbing up bottles. Most of the bottles were still intact, but the tobacco tin with the bank draft was nowhere in sight. Hoyt knocked me aside and took the few bottles I collected. "Lying, thieving wretch!" he yelled.

Bugle charged him. Hoyt backhanded my dog with a vicious swipe that sent him tumbling.

"You wait! I'll ruin you *and* your family!" All the while he scrambled this way and that, stuffing the last of the bottles into his pockets.

I scrambled, too. "*You're* the liar and the thief! You're the one's been hiding and sneaking!"

Osher stepped closer, armed only with his frying pan. He didn't look ready to use it, not yet. Bugle darted in where he could, snarling, snapping.

Then I saw the tobacco tin, all but hidden under dried leaves, half ripped open by bear claws. I jumped for it. Hoyt lunged for the tin. I rolled away with it, hoping the bank draft was still wedged inside.

Hoyt came after me, striking me again, wrenching the tin from my grip. I watched in horror as he tipped it above his palm and shook it.

I ran at him, grabbing for the tin. He held me at bay, shaking the tin violently. Nothing came out. The folded-up paper must be wedged in good.

Osher looked for an opening. Hoyt didn't give him one. Drove his fist straight into the other man's chin. Osher was not a small man, but he dropped like a stone.

More miners had gathered, closer, with looks of concern. I waved them back. I didn't want them catching any of Hoyt's anger.

Bugle tugged at his pant leg, shredding it. Hoyt shook the tin twice more, then flung it away, snarling. I lunged after it, but he struck me hard again.

I rolled up against the stump of a tree and waited. I wasn't looking for any more punishment. All I cared about was the tobacco tin, and he had cast it aside.

I watched Hoyt on his hands and knees again, groping for nuggets. Bugle harried him with barking but kept out of range. Any fool could see whatever dust remained was lost in the leaf litter. At last, even Hoyt realized it. He stood up and shoved his hat on his head. "You think you will make it home without me?" he jeered. "Look at you! Without me, your bones will bleach on these wretched hills. Your precious mother will go to her grave never knowing what became of you."

I spit in his direction. "I hope I never lay eyes on you again," I yelled. This time I was careful not to look at the tobacco tin.

He snorted contempt. "You have revealed yourself to be the worst of deceivers. I will make it known." He stomped off, flinging a dismissive wave at the gathered miners, who parted to let him pass.

When he was gone, Osher Phelps and a couple of others gathered round.

"What was that all about?" he asked. "Wasn't what I'd call a fair fight."

"I called an end to our partnership. He didn't like that."

Osher looked off to where Hoyt had begun his climb out of the canyon. "Some people want to keep 'no' for themselves, and all they want from you is, 'yes.'" He turned back to me. "You sure you're okay?"

"Yessir. I am, thanks." I got to my feet to prove it.

Everybody drifted back to their work.

I went to retrieve the tobacco tin. Looking carefully inside, it looked empty, but I wasn't ready to accept that, yet. The bear had done the tin fearful damage, whether with his teeth or claws, it didn't matter. Dried blood crusted some of the torn metal. Likely the bear's. I found a small stick and probed inside the tin. I looked around the ground; hoping the bear might have dislodged the draft. All I saw was shreds of the sacking.

Then I froze. I dropped the tin and ran.

CHAPTER 43

I dreaded it as a fool's errand, even as I ran. Tinder never survives once the fire is going. And paper was the most combustible of all. But I ran on, vaulting abandoned breakfast fires, careening around startled miners. I ignored the shouts of the curious. Bugle kept right at my heels.

I skidded to a stop at Sven's claim, outside his tent. He was at the edge of the river, pouring water into his rocker. I was too desperate to explain myself. I dropped to my hands and knees beside his fire and peered into the powdery grey ash heap. I called out while concentrating on my inspection. "Where did you get that paper?"

"What you say?"

I bent my face closer. Almost no warmth came from the remains. That gave me a slim hope. "The paper you started the fire with. Where did you get it?"

Sven set down his dipper and came to stand over me. I moved around to the other side of the fire, rocking back on my heels to look up at him. "That piece of paper you used as tinder this morning. Where did it come from?"

He spread his hands and shrugged. "It be on my doorstep when I come out this morning." He gestured toward his tent.

I dared to think there could be two pieces of paper: one stuck in Sven's fire pit, one tumbling on, even now to parts unknown? "Didn't you look at it? See if it belonged to anybody?"

"I did," he protested. "But it was. . .makulert." He made a messy movement with his hands to suggest tearing something up. "And covered in mud."

I myself had not given it a second look. "Would you mind if I looked?"

"You have your try. Tell me if I can help." He stepped away to resume his work.

"Thank you," I said. "I'll rebuild it when I'm done. I promise."

I had never picked apart an old fire grain by grain. A few chunks, not completely burned, poked out of the soft powder. I knew that disturbing embers sometimes brought forth new flames. While usually welcome, I could not afford that now. I spied an unemployed wooden bucket by Sven's tent and took it over to him.

"Can I borrow this?"

He looked from the bucket to me and grinned. "You won't burn it, ja?"

I gave him a look of reproach. "No." Then I had another thought. "Do you have a spoon I could use?"

Sven's puzzlement was becoming concern. "In tent. Left side. In front."

I found the spoon, filled the bucket from the river, and got to work. On my knees, I dissected the remains of that fire crumb by crumb, sifting for scraps of unburned paper. I moved around the circle like a mule in a grist mill, working my way toward the center.

Sure enough, as I dug, a few of the re-exposed chunks of wood sprouted new flames. I doused these pieces from the bucket so they would cause no further mischief. With each circuit around the fire, my hopes shrank.

Bugle soon lost interest in such monotony and ambled off.

I uncovered a larger piece of wood that had not burned clear through. In the dirt, I made out a black line of char whose outline matched the flat bottom of the piece of wood I had just set aside.

I blew gently at the dust inside the outline. Lettering appeared. I blew some more, my heart racing.

A bit of fancy, scroll-work border, part of a date, all very official-looking. Then handwriting: P-R-U-D-E-N-C-E. My mother's Christian name. The next stroke of the pen could only be the beginning of our family name, PEGG. Chance alone had destroyed the rest.

The wood had protected an irregular scrap about three inches on a side. Two holes punctured one edge, the size and shapes of large teeth or claws.

My excitement quailed before the challenge of extracting the bit of my bank draft from the fire pit. It was more fragile than a butterfly's wing.

Sven called out. "Why so still? You give up?"

I looked over my shoulder at him. "No. I've found it."

He grumbled, "You kidding," as he rose from his crouch. He lowered himself carefully to his knees beside me, his eyebrows drawn together, and studied the scrap a moment. "Not much left of your important paper."

"What's important is there." I leaned to point. "'Prudence Pegg.' Lila will have the rest of the information."

Sven crossed his arms. "I see no 'Pegg'."

I showed him how the tails of the "P's" matched.

He sunk his chin to his chest. "A spider web be stronger than that argument."

I didn't listen to him. "How can I get it out of there?"

Sven was not encouraging. "It fall to pieces, you look at it sideway."

The old sailor gazed down at my uncle's Bowie knife. "Your toothpick, there, do the job, I think."

I pulled it out. The blade was easily two inches from spine to cutting edge. I crouched lower to insert the point under the paper. I felt a nudge.

Sven held out his hand. I surrendered the knife and moved aside.

He came at it so that more of the blade was coming under the paper. But, in fact, he was coming in a little lower, so that he included a thin layer of old ash under the scrap. He stopped when the blade was fully under the paper. He settled back. "The rest be you responsibility."

I lifted the knife oh, so carefully, and rested it on an upturned bucket.

I stared at my predicament. I couldn't hope to carry the scrap of bank draft back to town balanced on the blade of the knife. Without comment, Sven rose up and went into his tent. He returned a moment later, flipping through a book. As he came up, he stopped flipping and exclaimed, pleased. "Ah. Here we be. 'Corinthians'." He showed me a well-thumbed Bible. "Good place to carry important paper."

I was dumbfounded. "You are very generous, Sir."

"Oh," He chuckled. "I want blood oath it will come right back to me when you be done." He dropped to his knees and set the open Bible right next to the knife on the bucket. "There you go."

I brushed away as much of the silt as I could and slid the scrap into Corinthians. In a moment it was done. Sven began to close the Bible.

"Wait." I held up a staying hand. I looked around where I knelt and found a short piece of small twig. I was about to place the marker when Sven said, "Wait."

He plucked a blade of dry, yellowed grass and laid it in the gutter of the book. "No dents."

The salvation of my fortune was in hand. Impatience drove me to my feet, eager to get to town. After a quick "Thank you," to Sven, I sprang away. Sven called something after me, but I wasn't listening. I was imagining Lila handing me a crisp new certificate. I splashed across the river and raced up the northern slope, my grip tight on the Bible.

Several times I had to switch hands, and each time I feared my scrap of bank draft would slip out, unnoticed. I'd never find it again in the gathering shadows. Bugle stopped to drink when we chanced on a trickle of water, but I didn't wait for him. He caught up easily enough.

The last, ruddy light was fading out of the western sky when I reached the ridge above town. Auburn had long since sunk in shadow, and I was grateful to have the miners' fires to light my way down. Hugging the Bible tight to my chest, I made straight for the express office. Among the roistering throng, those few sitting still stuck out like stones poking out of a river.

Hoyt's man—for it was certainly he—sat. Same hat, dark clothes, city shoes. He was foolish enough to be sitting in exactly the same spot—in the *same pose*—as he had on his last spying mission, when he had watched Gao Chung and me take gold to Lila's office.

I didn't think it would be of any consequence if he recognized me from the time before, but I had to keep him from seeing me visit Lila and thus putting her in jeopardy again.

Fortunately, the revelers in the street obscured my approach. By the time he noticed me, it was too late for him to slink away. He pulled his hat lower, dipped his head, and glanced away.

I put on the biggest grin I could muster and stepped up to him. "Good evening, Brother. How do we find you this fine evening?" We were all but toe to toe.

He acknowledged me with reluctance, glancing up with a squint. "I got no money," he grumbled. "Go on. Git." He turned his gaze resolutely away.

Not a chance. A little more concern. "Is your heart troubled? Are you low in spirit?"

"Off with you." He twisted his head the other way, avoiding my zeal. "I got no use for your gibberish. Git." He waved his hand in dismissal.

I brought the Book away from my chest and placed my other hand reverently on the cover. I dared not open it. "Have you lost your way, Brother? Are you beset by temptation?" *Lean a little closer. Bible a little forward.* "Do you despair of ever finding the one true path?" *Back a little.* "If only—"

He'd had enough. He lurched to his feet and pushed past me into the crowd.

Got to make sure. I hurried after him. "Salvation is at hand, Brother. Admit Him into your heart and be saved."

He dodged and weaved, knocking people askew, but I stayed right on his heels until the crowd swallowed him up. I thought one or two more might keep him going, but I was running out of rhetoric. "The Day of Reckoning is nigh! Flock to His side. Fall down on your knees! Repent!"

A drunk, passing close, bawled, "Have a drink!"

I fell silent and let people eddy around me. When I was sure the spy was gone, I looked down at Bugle. "You won't tell mother about that little show, will you?"

He licked his chops and thumped his tail, and we headed for Lila's office.

Lila opened the door after the fourth knock. "Only you would be so persistent." Her trim silhouette was outlined by the light of the lantern on her wrapping table. Her shotgun hung in the crook of her arm.

"Good evening, Miss Lila Mae." I propped the Bible against my hip but didn't loosen my grip on it.

Lila looked out at the street, her normally smooth brow creased with concern. "Well, come in. No sense in advertising your disrespect for office hours. You'll give people license."

I followed her into the room. She brought the lamp from the wrapping table over to the counter and stowed her shotgun below.

"What shenanigans are you embroiled in now?" She fussed over her counterweights, which were already arrayed with military precision.

"Well, Ma'am, I have a small problem I'd like to talk about."

She smiled wearily. "I pray for the day when you will come in with some perfectly mundane errand."

I settled the Bible carefully on the counter with both hands.

She gazed down at the Book. "What have we here? Have you taken up a new line of work?"

I opened the Bible very carefully at the blade of grass marker. Some of the silt had broken loose and settled in the depth of the gutter. Otherwise, the piece of bank draft rested much as Sven and I had placed it. I pointed at the singed square of paper. "This is the bank draft for my family. Remember? You made it out just the other day."

Lila peered a little closer. "There certainly isn't much of it left. I would never have guessed."

I turned the Bible so she could read the writing. "It's very fragile."

"It looks burned." She peered closer yet. "What happened?"

I told her the whole, sad story. I ended with what had convinced me that it was my family's. I pointed to my mother's name. "See there. P-R-U-D—"

"'Prudence.' I can read."

I shied, contrite. "Yes, Ma'am. That's my mother's name."

She straightened up. "Perhaps you have noticed it is much favored. Three women in my own family have that name."

I pointed to the stroke that was the beginning of 'Pegg'. "What about the last name? Pegg. That should cinch it."

She regarded the mark for a moment, her brows arched in concern. "What I see, and what I'm afraid a judge would probably see, is only a stroke of the pen. It could be an I, or part of an F— even a J—as well as part of a P."

Dismay must have been writ large on my face. It certainly clawed at my insides.

Lila tucked her head in sympathy, bending a little over the scrap. "But that's not the worst of it. All the other pertinent information--the certificate's registration number, the date, my signature—the *amount*—are missing. Even with—" She stopped with her mouth drawn down in a frown. After a pause, she said, "There's just too much missing. I'm sorry."

"But you remember? You filled it out—just the other day. It was for 11,000 dollars!" Then I had an inspiration. I pointed to some printed curlicues in one corner of the scrap. "What about this fancy work? Shouldn't that identify it as yours—I mean, as coming from here?"

Lila rubbed her brow, her eyes closed. "Oh, Pegg. I'm sorry. But you will find this type of embellishment on every sort of official document. They are almost indistinguishable, one from the other." She leaned closer. "And this is such a small portion. . ." She grew quiet.

I felt battered by a world unknown to me. "Is there *any* other way of identifying it?"

Lila regarded me with what seemed like pity. That was harder to bear than anything. At last she spoke gently. "The registration number would help, but it's missing. With so much lost, I'm afraid there's no alternatives."

Desperation took charge. "Couldn't you fill out a new one and not put it in the register?"

Lila flinched back, alarmed. "Pegg. Shame on you. You know I could never do that."

Instantly I felt bad. I knew how careful she was about following the rules. I didn't want to lose her as a friend. "I'm sorry, Ma'am. I'm sorry. I shouldn't have said that. It's just this bank draft means everything to my family."

"I'm sorry, Pegg," said Lila, "I wish I could—m" She shut her eyes and, after a troubled moment, opened them again. "You have been struck the cruelest of blows, but I'm afraid there is nothing to be done." She closed the Bible carefully and slid it towards me with equal reverence. "I'm so sorry. Truly. I know what you've been up against. You, of all people, do not deserve this."

I choked back the shout that so badly wanted to escape and spoke in a voice barely under control. "But you don't understand, Ma'am! This is all that's left! I've worked really hard. My dad died! My family is counting on me." I stabbed my finger at the Bible. "Without this, we have no future!"

Lila brought her clasped hands up under her chin and squeezed her eyes shut again. "Pegg, dear. Please. Believe me." She opened them, beseeching. "If you had suffered this loss at the hands of Fred Hoyt, I would leave no stone unturned to right this calamity. But we cannot fault a bear for being a bear, any more than we can blame a storm for sinking a ship."

It was a bitter thought. My family's fate was tied to a piece of paper—so easily destroyed. When you had a lump of gold, nobody could argue with it. Gold was all but indestructible. Everybody agreed on its worth! "Yes, Ma'am." I dragged the Bible off the counter and turned toward the door. without thanking her.

"I'm sorry, Pegg," she said, sounding as desolate as I felt.

Bugle led the way outside. I drifted into the street like a ghost.

If the whole town were on fire, I would have taken no notice. It was far too late to head back to the river. I didn't want to face Chen Yi or Sun Shu. I wandered among revelers ignorant of the desperate straits I was in.

I stumbled along with no ready destination. Shrill laughter, a grating piano, leaping, shifting shadows; all seemed to throw up a leering wall of ridicule around me. I glanced down at Bugle. He kept right at my side. He was steady when all else crumbled about me. I collided with more than a few merry-makers, and I couldn't manage the meanest civility. They all had gold aplenty to squander on drinks, cards, or a new pair of boots—even a dance with a pretty girl.

I had little reason to put one foot in front of another. I looked down to talk to Bugle, but he was gone.

I froze to the spot, twisting frantically in every direction, calling over and over, "Bugle! Bugle!" I ran back the way we had come, all the way to Lila's office, now dark. I careened back up the street, calling out, veering this way and that as impulse drove me. Peering into the blackness between buildings, calling his name. Suddenly, the same horrible fear gripped me as it had back in Grizzly Bar—when the town had burned down, and I didn't know what had become of my dog.

I retraced my steps at a run, shouting his name until I was hoarse. The rollicking crowd ignored my plight. I made a circuit of the edge of town, calling into the darkness beyond. *Why doesn't he answer? Where can he be? Has someone taken him?* Pets were almost as rare as children in this wild place. I had turned down so many entreaties to buy him. Had someone lured him away with a chunk of meat? Why didn't he bark when a stranger grabbed him?

At the point of exhaustion, I found myself back among the revelers, searching faces for likely culprits. I had not been this close to tears in a long time. It seemed to me Fortune had turned her face resolutely away. What was left to take from me? There seemed no reason even to stand, and I crumpled into the dust of the street, still clutching Sven's Good Book.

The enormity of my failure bore down on me. *I have lost everything.* My dad. Our wagon and all our kit. Our team, who, once dead, doomed the wagon. More gold than I had ever dreamed of, all lost. And now I had even lost our dog.

There would be no new farm, neither here nor back home. And we might well lose the one we had in Vermont to honor our obligations. I had nothing—nothing—to show for all that we had suffered and endured. Could I even face my mother? I had failed to keep the one promise she asked of me: *Bring your father home safe to me.*

People stumbled into me, or tripped and sprawled, cursing. Slumped in the dust, I made no protest—the curses were a distant, ill-tempered buzzing in my ear.

I had no hope of finding another bonanza that would compare to the one I had just lost. What could I do? Go to work for somebody? Richard was digging canals. Did the blacksmith need an apprentice? Could Chen Yi afford to pay for help at his laundry?

I was assailed with guilt and regret. I should have hidden the gold better. I should have closed the accounts and sent the money home sooner. As long as I stayed in Auburn, Hoyt would leave me no peace. Maybe he took Bugle. And what if he made good on his threat to slander me? I knew what malicious gossip could do.

How was I going to get home? Maybe I could get work on a ship heading back east. But I would only be earning my passage: I would arrive home with empty pockets.

But none of this was worth thinking about until I found Bugle. I couldn't lose him, too.

CHAPTER 44

I awoke with my cheek pressed into the dust, curled in the same heap in the middle of the same torn-up street—deserted at this early hour. I got an elbow under me and pushed up into a sitting position. The dark crows of my misfortunes dug strong claws into my shoulders. My clothes were as rumpled and dusty as clothes can only be when slept in. I reached for my hat, punched it back into shape, and tugged it down against my ears.

When I regained my feet, I surveyed the street, wishing desperately for Bugle to come bounding from the shadows with his happy bark. A pallid blush announcing day washed up into the sky. The aroma of boiling coffee drifted by. I slapped at my clothing to get rid of most of the dust; I couldn't do much about the wrinkles.

The sprig of grass in the Bible was gone. I flipped the pages until I found the one in Corinthians with the scrap of bank draft. Lila had pronounced it useless, but I couldn't bring myself to abandon it.

I was at the bottom of the barrel. I had known that as soon as I woke up with my face in the dirt. My friend Will had a great disdain for what he called "weeping and wailing." If he found himself in low spirits, he came back fighting. If I ever wanted to look him in the eye again, I had to do the same.

It was too expensive to stay in town while I hunted for Bugle. I would have to marshal very carefully what little remained in the

Forsyth/Pegg account. My first stop would be Chen Yi's, to ask them to keep an eye out for Bugle.

I set out for the laundry with a heavy heart. They would insist on helping. As I approached, I could see Chen Yi taking down handbills and fliers from his front window. People were always asking merchants to display notices and announcements for bear fights and traveling shows. Chen Yi was one of the merchants who made an effort to take down the old ones and put up new ones.

My spirits lifted just seeing him. I walked up to the window and stood quietly, as if I were an idler reading the postings. For a heartbeat he continued his culling unperturbed. When he recognized me, his expression changed to delight, and he beckoned me inside with heart-warming enthusiasm.

I had no sooner stepped through the door when I was greeted with a sharp bark.

"Bugle!" I lunged for him at the same time he lunged for me. We tumbled to the floor with a shrill chorus of barks and cries of relief, setting up a great din of questions and barking. "What happened? Where have you been? Did somebody take you?" This amid much rubbing and scratching and thumping of his tail. I scooted up against the wall and gathered Bugle into my lap. I scrubbed his ears. "You had me worried to death. It was the last straw." I looked up at Chen Yi to see him smiling down at our antics. Gao Chung had come to peer over his shoulder.

Chen Yi put on an inquiring face. "You spend night rolling down street?"

I laughed, overlooking his boldness, glad I could laugh. "That's about it." There were more important things at hand. "How did you find Bugle?"

"He find us."

I looked from Chen Yi to Bugle and back again.

Chen Yi went on. "I prepare day. I hear scratch door. I think skunk come back. When I open door, there sit Magic Dog. Happy see him, but worry why you not standing beside."

I had another reason to smile. Bugle and I had earned our first supper with Chen Yi, back in Grizzly Bar, by chasing a skunk away from his restaurant—without ill effects. Chen Yi ever afterward called him "Magic Dog."

I turned back to Bugle. "Did you just wander off, exploring? I looked everywhere for you."

"I think rascal steal dog." Chen Yi held out a frayed length of braided rawhide rope, one end of which was fashioned into a crude noose. "But Magic Dog chew freedom."

I inspected the frayed end of the line. It had certainly been chewed. I looked down at Bugle. "Boy, I'm sure glad you didn't just give up. Dad would be proud." I bent my face closer. "I'm proud you didn't give up." *Maybe I could learn something from my dog.*

Chen Yi picked the Bible off the floor and set it on the counter. We heard the workyard door open and close, and Sun Shu appeared in the door leading into Gao Chung's ironing room. She spoke to Chen Yi as I got up from the floor. "Oh. There you are, Pegg. Lila was asking after you."

Lila stepped in beside Sun Shu. "Good morning." She cast cautious glances at everyone.

"Good day, Miss Rose." Chen Yi did a little bow. "We welcome."

I shuffled my feet. The last conversation I'd had with Lila was not a happy one. What more was there to say?

Lila took a step forward with an earnest expression and addressed me. "Gracious, Pegg. Have you been in a fight?"

"No. Ma'am. I haven't."

She relaxed. "Now, I don't want you to get your hopes up, but I've had a visit from a man with whom you've had dealings."

I lurched forward, angry. "Is he still bothering you?"

She frowned and shook her head. "No, no. Not Hoyt. A man named Swen Bund—something."

"Sven Blundhold?"

Lila waved her hand impatiently. "Yes. He said something about you not finishing with the fire—"

My mouth dropped open like a tail gate. I hadn't finish digging out the whole of Sven's fire pit. No! I'd rushed off to town with the first pitiful snip of evidence in my grasp, leaving the remainder of the fire undisturbed. My heart began to thump faster.

Lila scowled in frustration. "He said he found two more pieces of paper under other bits of wood after you left."

Which two pieces? Which two pieces? Please, Lord, make them count. "Did you bring them with you?" I grabbed the Bible and flipped the pages, looking for "my" scrap.

"Please." Lila had a pained look. "Give me a little credit. They are every bit as fragile as what you brought in the Bible." She gestured at the book in my hand. "He brought them in a copy of the Police Gazette." She drew down her brows and muttered, "Despicable rag."

Sven had made the same perilous hike to town with his scraps nestled in only a flimsy magazine.

I owed him a lot. "Let's go see." I started dancing toward the front door with the Bible in hand. Bugle crowded underfoot.

Lila moved around the counter. "Indeed." She turned to the Celestials. "If you will excuse us. I'm sorry to have interrupted you." We had to edge our way past a couple of miners bringing their laundry to Sam Lee's.

Lila set a brisk pace. I hugged the Bible to me. I had to hustle to keep up with her. "You had to close the office? Thank you for doing that. What has happened to Mr. Hamblin? I haven't seen him for a while."

Lifting her skirts out of the dust and mud, Lila navigated pits and piles with equal agility. "He became afflicted with the same fever that has afflicted every able-bodied male. He's been gone to Dutch Flat a month now."

I thought I would display a little of my sagacity. "And the head office keeps promising to send you a replacement."

Lila, without breaking stride, threw me a sharp look. "Cynicism, though burdened with it myself, is not something I would recommend cultivating."

I should have been listening more closely, but I was pasting scraps of paper together in my mind. "Yes, Ma'am. I'll do that." That got me another sharp look. "I mean, I won't. I'll be careful not to." I wanted to deflect more censure. "Why didn't Sven come to me?"

"I suspect because he didn't know where to find you. He went by your claim, then he came into town."

For a rare moment we were abreast. "Could you tell anything? Was there any writing?"

"I gave them only a quick glance. I could see they belonged with your piece."

The miners clustered at the express office door parted at Lila's approach. When they saw I was with her, they grumbled, as if I was trying to ride in on her coattails ahead of them. Lila turned and lifted her chin and her voice. "Gentlemen. Please. This young man is on another errand that will have no need of a place in line. Please, let him pass."

Once inside, with the miners spilling in around us, Lila spoke quickly to me. "Wait by the wrapping table. I'll bring the other pieces."

At the table, I put down Sven's Bible. Lila brought over two short lengths of sawn lumber, bound together with some of her wrapping twine. She set her parcel on the table and cut the twine. "What you need is between pages 12 and 13. I'll be back when there is a quiet moment." She lifted away the top piece of lumber to reveal a well-abused copy of the Police Gazette, printed on pale pink paper. "Be careful."

I was paralyzed between anticipation and dread. "I'll wait."

"Suit yourself." She hurried off to serve her customers.

I regarded the Bible and the lurid newspaper. I knew what the Bible held. Did the Gazette hold useless scraps covered in curlicues? I watched the miners shuffle forward with their tins and bottles held like offerings. Within the hour, I would be deemed wildly richer than they, or poorer by an equal measure.

Lila poured and measured and noted with the fluency of a professional gambler, a comparison best left unspoken. At length the office was empty of prospectors. She came over with a brisk step and gazed down at the table. "My Goodness. You did wait. I'm not sure I could." Taking care to keep the magazine flat, she lifted it off the bottom piece of lumber. "Take that away."

I put both pieces of lumber on the floor.

She laid the magazine down as if she were tending a new-born and opened it to page 12.

Two pieces of singed paper, one twice the size of the other, greeted my eager gaze. There were indeed curlicues, but not much. The larger piece had a signature, with some smaller printing, and the smaller piece, a printed, official-looking number. One edge of that piece seemed to describe a corner. That's where the curlicues were, looking very much like a border. Lila nudged the pieces delicately with her fingertip, then stepped away from the table. "Get out the piece from the Bible." She soon returned with a new bank draft, snowy white, without a blemish, and laid it close by the sooty scraps from the Gazette. She took the scrap from the Bible and laid it on the table next to the larger Gazette scrap.

It was obvious that those two belonged together. A glance between the whole document and the scraps confirmed that Lila had laid out the pieces to mimic their correct positions on the document. "That's my signature." She pointed to the larger Gazette scrap, then to the corresponding part of the complete draft.

I dared not breathe.

Next, she pointed to the number. "This is our best hope. It's the registration number of this certificate. It's recorded in my ledger, here, and in a tally that I send weekly to the head office."

"Is this enough? What do we do next?"

"We—I—write to the head office, explaining the situation, and enclose the evidence. Then we hope for the best." She held up her hand. "But I make no promises. And it could be weeks; it could take months."

I looked down at the scraps. "And even then, it could be 'No.'"

"Or anything in between."

.   .   .

My first duty was to return Sven's Bible.

Out of habit, I splashed across the river at my usual place and made my way downstream. Bugle took the time to greet my fellow miners while I hurried along.

But Sven was not at his claim. I asked his immediate neighbors, and those who had noticed at all reckoned he had gone after firewood. I suppose I could've left the Bible in his tent, but I wanted to thank him. I took a seat on one of the kegs that served as furniture.

For the first time in a long time, I wasn't hustling or worrying. Waiting on Lila and the San Francisco people meant I could stop and take a breath and let it out slow. All I really had to do was steer clear of Fred Hoyt.

Two buzzards wheeled in the clear blue sky. The sun warmed my shoulders. People who'd been here since '48 said the summers were hot. I looked forward to that. It came to me that I was content in this place. The good-natured banter of the miners, the clamorous din of their industry, had come to be a genial world.

"Ahoy, Pegg!" broke my reverie. I turned to see Sven coming down the last slope onto the river bottom. He was bent under a great bundle of sticks and branches. The tumpline across his forehead was dark with sweat. His axe swung in his right hand. "Everything shipshape?"

I stood to greet him. *No weeping and wailing.* "Thanks to you, its at least got a chance of being shipshape."

Sven slid the tumpline from his forehead, leaning to his right, and the load of wood tumbled, clattering, to the ground. "What'd I do?"

"You found those other two scraps after I rushed off without finishing the job."

He joined me at the kegs. "Can't really blame you for bein' in hurry."

I sat back down. Bugle came and slumped at my feet. "Lila says the registration number is our best hope. It was on one of the pieces you found, so I thank you as much as it's possible to thank a body."

"You're welcome, then. What happens now?"

"We wait to hear back from San Francisco." I handed him his Bible. "I wanted to thank you for the use of your Good Book, too. I hope you'll find it restored as you offered it."

He spat a jet of tobacco juice into the fireplace. "I'm not worried."

I looked down at my dog. "C'mon, Bugle." We made our farewells and set off upstream.

As we drew near my claim, I saw a gaggle of miners surrounding Osher Phelps on his claim. More miners were converging, bearing letters. These they handed to Osher, who put them in a battered leather satchel hanging on his shoulder. Along with their letters, they gave him nuggets or coins to buy postage.

In the hubbub I overheard he was going to San Francisco. I almost asked him to take Lila's letter, but she'd likely insist it go by official means, to keep the main office happy. *Should I ask him to look for Yang Ho, Sun Shu's husband*? I scrambled up to my tree shelter and brought down a letter to my mother, as well as one to my aunt Joanna, telling her about R. C. Simpson. I still had no address for Hally Forsyth, the girl I'd met on the wagon train, so I couldn't mail those yet. I handed Osher my missives and a nugget.

The miners asked Osher to collect any mail waiting for them, and he wrote their names on a piece of paper. My Mom knew where I was, but I asked anyway, and Osher added my name to his list.

When everyone was drifting away, I said, "I'll keep an eye on things while you're away. How long you figure?"

He nestled the letters in the satchel. "A week, maybe a bit more."

That seemed awfully quick. I raised questioning eyebrows at him.

"The stage to Sacramento City, and a river boat to San Francisco. Same comin' back."

CHAPTER 45

The day after Osher Phelps left on his mail errand, I went hunting and brought in two good-sized jackrabbits. I was skinning them out in the shade of the Grandfather Oak, my back to the river, when I heard someone clear their throat behind me.

A short, slender, nervous-looking man stood at a respectful distance. He looked familiar. Very familiar.

He was Harvey Drummond, my prospecting neighbor from right across the river. I rarely saw him this close, and rarely in any other pose but crouched over his pan. At least once a day, for most of the last eight months or more, I had looked across the river at Harvey Drummond working his claim. Sometimes he'd be looking at me. Barely more than a dozen words had passed between us during that time. He stood now, holding his hat flat against his belly, looking worried.

"Good morning, Mr. Drummond." I laid down my knife and offered my hand. "Bartholomew Pegg, if you didn't know that already." We shook. "Good to meet you—at last."

Drummond stammered. "They… They s—said it's okay to call you Pegg. Is that all right?"

"Everybody does."

He gulped and turned his hat in his hands. "You're the kid who's b—been working in the river."

I tensed. Most people thought I was playing when I was in the river. Apparently, I had not fooled Mr. Drummond. "Everybody works in the river." How many others had the same suspicions but held their peace?

"I mean right opposite me. You been divin' in a line comin' right across."

How much does he know about the seam? "You've got a good eye." I waited.

Drummond took a fresh grip on his hat. "I waded out as far as I dared, to see if I could see what you were followin'. That ridge looked to be a possibility, and it lines up with where you been workin'."

Ridge? What with the distortion of the water, he might not have picked out the cleft in the seam that held all the gold.

He tucked in his chin. "Best I could tell, it comes on into my claim."

"I saw that from my side." *Saw it a little better when I was two feet off the bottom.*

"I appreciate you respectin' the limit."

I felt oddly affronted that he thought I wouldn't. "That's where the claims end. . .the middle of the river."

Harvey Drummond stopped fidgeting with his hat. "I… I got a proposition for you."

I had a good hunch what it was. "What's that?"

"You can have half of whatever you pull out of that ridge on my side."

Now it was time to pay attention. "You can't swim?"

"Like most," he shrugged.

I sure wasn't in any great hurry to take up with another partner. Besides, if there was justice in the world, I would be getting a bank draft from Lila soon. That represented more gold than I ever dreamed of. As long as I kept washing dirt, I'd have Hoyt breathing down my neck. And he wasn't getting any nicer about it. "Half's right generous."

Harvey shrugged. "I figure half is more than I'd have if I just left it."

I guess I took a might too long in answering because Mr. Drummond spoke on. "The truth is, whatever might be in that ridge is my last hope."

It was none of my business, but I opened my mouth anyway. "Your claim didn't pay that well?"

"Oh, I was doin' all right, but my claim is near played out." Drummond squirmed. "I got a wife and little ones waitin' on me at home. Had my sights set on openin' my own shop. Then I heard about a way I could go home flush. Fella sellin' shares in a freight line between Sacramento City and San Francisco. He said they were about to launch their first boat. Sounded like a sure thing. By the time I came to my senses, he'd talked me out of almost half my stake."

"The fella sellin' this scheme. What'd he look like?" *Could it have been Hoyt?*

Drummond wrinkled his brow, recalling. "Big fella. . .heavy set. Natty dresser. Good teeth."

Sounded more like Hutchins, the man at the Empire Hotel whose boots Hoyt was licking. "Smooth voice? Silk waistcoat? Silver stick pin?"

"That's him. You know him?"

"You could say." Suddenly, I had a worthy chore to occupy my time while waiting for my bank draft. I only hoped Harvey had learned his lesson with regard to hustlers like Hutchins. I gave him a stern look. "You keep track of my half. I'll collect when we're done."

"You'll do it?" He gulped, wide-eyed. "The missus will send prayers to heaven for you."

We shook on it. For the first time, Drummond flat-out smiled. "When can you start?"

"Tomorrow."

.   .   .

Harvey Drummond proved a very trustworthy fellow. We only washed dirt when I was out of the water. He kept a roaring fire going for me to warm up by. In the evening, over supper, we swapped stories of the trail and where we were from. One evening, with supper in our bellies, and a full moon rising plump and pale as butter over the eastern hills, I asked him how he'd decided I wasn't just larking around in the river.

Harvey filled two tin cups with coffee, gave me one, and found a seat on a small keg. "I thought that, too, at first. But the giveaway was how, when you came up, you could stay in that spot—without the river carryin' you on downstream—before you dove again."

I smiled into my cup. "That must've looked right odd."

"I looked hard when you were down, and I caught sight of the stick floatin'—and the rope that held it there." Harvey twisted his brows into a fret. "I figured there must be somethin' down there worth all that effort."

"Why didn't you come talk to me before?"

"I feared for my half. You know what happens when people get wind of a strike."

"So what decided you on talking to me now?"

"You hit the center of the river and stopped. The rest o' your claim sure looked played out. I reckoned I'd better talk to you 'fore you lit out for some other place."

Eight days into working Harvey Drummond's half of the seam, our mailman, Osher Phelps, showed up on the north bank with his satchel bulging. As he crossed, word spread like a summer grass fire, and miners came running. The only thing more precious than gold was a letter from home. I didn't expect anything, so I made one more dive before climbing out. I got dressed and joined Osher on his claim as the last few stragglers came up to see if he had anything for them. A burly man with florid whiskers said, "Fornell. Jake Fornell."

Osher consulted his list and handed Fornell three letters. The man stumbled away, gazing at his bounty as if they were the crown jewels.

I stepped closer. "If you've got anything for me, I'll buy you a steak dinner."

Osher looked up at me. "Ah. There you are, Pegg." He reached into his bag and came out with *four* letters. "You owe me a steak dinner," he grinned.

My jaw dropped. "I owe you four steak dinners." Dumbfounded, I took the letters from him.

All of them were addressed to "J. M. Pegg, General Delivery, San Francisco." A sudden dismay swept over me. These had all been written assuming Dad had made it to California and would make a trip to San Francisco to collect his mail. And if the folks in Vermont had received no word since Fort Kearny, these letters were one more confirmation that Hoyt had written no one about Dad's passing.

Three were from my mom; one was from Mr. Pruitt. That one could be trouble. I untied Bugle and went up the hill a ways to some shade, and settled down to read. "Can you believe this, Boy? How long have these been sitting in San Francisco?"

When I opened the first of my mother's letters, my heart seized at the salutation.

Dearest, beloved husband,

We have had no word since Fort Laramie, so I am addressing this to you in San Francisco, as we are told that is where everyone goes to collect their mail. We all work ceaselessly to fill the void the two of you have left. Nightly we send prayers heavenward for yours and Barti's safety.

I stopped reading. I felt like I was intruding, like when I would come around a corner in the barn and find them with their arms around each other. But there might be something I should know. I read on.

I cannot find words strong enough to say how much I miss you. Every hour, when the chores are done, is longer without you. Amy continues to grow and thrive. She has taken over many of the chores with good cheer. Boys are beginning to tease her. I am reminded of how you used to tease me, way back when. Our Adam has announced his imminent departure. He has the opportunity to buy the Ackerson place at a good price. With this development in view, Adriana's father has given his consent for Adam and Adriana to marry. He has also offered to assist in the purchase. Once Adam is gone, we will have to rely on itinerant labor, or the generosity of neighbors. Mr. Pruitt has his own concerns. Many in his employ have deserted him for California. He is finding it difficult to replace them.

I pray fervently for your speedy return. I can bear any burden if you are by my side. Know that our love surrounds you.

Please do not let up on Barti's lessons. Please write whenever you have a spare moment. We crave any word.

Until the happy moment I can be in your arms again, I remain,
Your loving wife,
Perky

I blushed. I had never heard this nickname for my mother. This was my first inkling that my parents might have a whole other life that nobody—not even my sister and I—ever knew about. I folded up the letter as if I could restore their privacy.

Her other two letters each began with news of the farm and the season, but expressed her growing desperation at the lack of word from us. Though she tried to make light of them, her pleas were heart-rending. By the end I was weeping tears of frustration and rage. All three must have been written before she got my letter from Grizzly Bar. In that letter, I'd assumed she already knew of Dad's death. Hoyt had assured me he had written to her about it.

As it was, she had to tease it out of my sidelong references. I kicked myself for taking so long to write once Hoyt and I had arrived. I sat staring for a long time, trying to right the wrongs.

At length, I took up Mr. Pruitt's letter. I opened it with a feeling of dread.

My Dear James,

We have been neighbors for a long time. You know I hold you in the highest esteem.

I take pen in hand to inquire about your situation. With no word since Fort Laramie, we are understandably concerned.

Perhaps I worry too soon. The far west, we are told, will test a man to his limits.

I fear I have given you more work than you bargained for, in having my stepson, Fred, in your party. But I have further information of which you will have need. I have discovered that Fred has been rash enough to incur considerable debts, in the vicinity, without my knowledge. What is worse, he has contrived to make me responsible for his obligations. This has been revealed to me only recently, through a series of unpleasant correspondence with his creditors. It will be no small thing to honor these commitments, if only to preserve my own good name, but it has exposed my stepson to be far more desperate a character than I have been, until now, willing to admit.

I feel it imperative to advise you, even at this late date, to exercise the greatest caution in your association with Fred Hoyt and arrange your finances so that they are beyond his grasp.

I lowered the letter and turned to Bugle, who drowsed in a patch of warm sun. "Boy. I could have used this letter a few months back." Preparing for worse, I resumed reading.

I offer my deepest, deepest apologies. I had no inkling that I was imposing upon you such an unnecessary burden. I extend my most ardent hopes that your hard work will be generously rewarded. Please be assured that our faith in you remains undiminished.

As I promised, I have, on occasion, inquired after your family, and they ask me to send you their fondest sentiments.

Please put pen to paper at your earliest opportunity that we may continue to anticipate your return with glad hearts.

Yours in peace and brotherhood,

Samuel Pruitt

Richford, Vermont

I settled Mr. Pruitt's letter in my lap, staring out at nothing. This letter, too, had been written without knowledge of Dad's death. When did Mr. Pruitt learn of it? I pictured him reading my latest letter, with its drastic declarations, and shuddered.

. . .

It took ten days for Harvey Drummond's half of the seam to give up 11,500 dollars. There were no Nightmare nuggets, but there were a number of specimens that made Harvey's eyes pop. The bonanza petered out as we got close to shore, as I thought it might.

One bright, sunny morning, with the canyon echoing the clamor of hundreds of miners beavering away, Harvey used his scale to divide the take, and we shook hands on a job well done. I feigned a stern look. "Now don't go listenin' to any more of Hutchins' malarkey."

"Don't you worry." exclaimed Harvey. "I'll be on the next boat out of here." He went from eager to worried in an eye-blink. "How about you?"

"I've got some unfinished business to see to." *Like a letter to my mother.* "It'll depend on that."

Harvey hefted his own sack. "I thank you and the missus thanks you."

Our bonhomie was interrupted. "Now ain't this a dandy sight!" called out Fred Hoyt as he approached Harvey's claim.

CHAPTER 46

As Hoyt stepped closer, Bugle rose up, growling. I snatched up my bag and sprang to my feet, cursing myself that I had not kept a sharper eye out for Hoyt or his people. "You've got no business here!" I shouted at him.

Harvey got to his feet more cautiously, staring between Hoyt and me.

Hoyt came on, like a boulder rolling down a hill, grinning his cynical smirk. "Now, Pegg, boy. Be reasonable. If you've got gold, which it sure looks like you do, then we certainly do have business." He had the look of a hungry wolf about him.

"We're not partners anymore!" I shouted, taking a step back. Bugle barked. I reached down to keep him by me. I could smell liquor coming off Hoyt in a stale cloud.

He lost his smile and his voice grew hard. "That ain't for you to say, Boy. There's more at stake here than you realize."

"It's as much for me to say as anybody!" I backed into the shallow water.

He kept advancing, his right hand closing into a fist. "As long as I'm in charge, you'll keep your place."

I kept backing up. A few miners close by looked up, curious. Mr. Drummond took a tentative step forward. "Now, listen here, Hoyt—"

Hoyt swung around, weaving, and raised his hand to strike. "You'll keep out of this if you know what's good for you!"

The only thing that spared Harvey Drummond a blow was his distance from the menace.

More miners looked up, alerted to the angry tone, if not the words themselves. I backed farther into the water. "What I've found is mine to keep. You find your own gold!"

Hoyt swung back to me and almost lost his footing on the slippery rocks.

I saw Harvey edging closer. "It's okay, Mr. Drummond," I called out. "I'll take care of this." In water up to my knees, I twisted and flung the bag over my shoulder into the center of the river. The bag went in not far from the claim line. The spout shot high, attesting to its weight.

Hoyt howled "Nooooo!" and lunged past me, knocking me aside. Down I went! But I had the advantage. Hoyt didn't know how to stand against the press of the water, nor was he moving carefully, and the current swept him off his feet. He went under and came up at once, sputtering and gasping, flailing his arms desperately, even as the river bore him persistently away. He went down again.

When he came up, farther downstream, he shouted "Pegg!"

The current was drawing him into ever deeper water. I could picture his legs thrashing, desperate for a firm footing. I knew that feeling of panic. He went under again. Not only did he not seem to know how to swim, he had no idea how to even stay afloat.

He came up even farther downstream, slapping at the water, screaming, "Pegg! Please! For pity's sake!"

Miners looked up from their work, but even as they moved to help, Hoyt was already floundering beyond their reach.

Again, he went under; his arms rose up stiff, then his head. "Pegg! P—!" He took in a mouthful of water as he went under once more.

My conscience got the better of me, and I dove after him. The combination of my swimming and the current brought me to him quickly. And just as Mr. Mahoney had done, Hoyt grabbed onto me for dear life.

But I was wrong.

He wrapped his arms around me in an iron grip and growled in my ear, "If I can't have it, you won't, either."

We went under. His grip was too strong. I could not free my arms. I kicked furiously, but to no effect. We sank deeper and deeper until Hoyt had to decide whether to go up for air or keep hold of me. I heard muffled yelling.

All my diving in the river had increased the length of time I could hold my breath under water. I followed my own rule about holding it longer: I stopped fighting and went quiet, not knowing how long I could last. Would the river get shallow enough to stand again before I ran out of air? I thought my lungs would burst. I pictured my mom and Amy, Will, and Hally. Then R. C., Linnaeus, and Richard. I might never see them again. The urge to draw breath was overwhelming.

At last, Fred Hoyt ran out of breath, and I felt his grip relax. I thrashed mightily to get free. He didn't hold me back and I shot for the surface.

I gulped precious air again and again, wiping water out of my eyes. Ragged cheers went up from both banks. I twisted to see where Hoyt was. Was he closing in for another attack? I spotted him a few yards downstream with his hair and shirt plastered against his body. I did no more than tread water. The river carried us along equally. Some miners were concerned enough to track Hoyt's progress, but none were interested in braving the deeper waters. One man, in up to his knees, held out a branch to me, but by the time I saw him I was already floating past him. Hoyt didn't change his posture as he bobbed and swung in the current. *He can't still be holding his breath.*

I bumped into a rock in midstream and clung to it, resting, still marveling that I was alive. It was a good bet my adversary had drowned. I watched until the river carried him around a bend. It could take him all the way to San Francisco, for all I cared.

Harvey Drummond had chased after us. He now stood among other miners on the north bank and called out, "Pegg! Are you all right?"

The reprieve I had been granted was still too fresh to trust speech. I waved and began swimming for the north shore. Farther downstream, I clambered out on the rocks.

Harvey met me there with a blanket. "You had me worried sure, you were under so long." He glanced off down the river. "Is he dead?"

I wrapped the blanket around my shoulders. "Likely, but I'm not certain." I thought of my attempt to save Mr. Mahoney from the flash food at Grizzly Bar, and how I'd wanted to make certain of *his* fate. "I'm going to hike down a ways and ask if anybody's seen him come out, or the body gets snagged."

Harvey gave me a wary look. "You were partners?"

"Too long. I'll see you back at your camp."

Harvey said after me, "You take it slow. He's a sidewinder, that one."

I walked downstream, giving thanks for every breath. I asked miners along the way if they'd seen a body float by, black hair, blue shirt. Some had. I persisted. "Was he swimming, or just drifting? Did you see if he got out and walked away?"

"I seen drowned buffalo floatin' down the Missouri," one old-timer said. "He was floatin' like that."

What with the asking, it took most of an hour to arrive two miles downstream. There I came upon some miners standing around a body lying on the cobbles of the south shore. I stepped up to have a closer look. Fred Hoyt looked as wet and glossy as a fresh-caught fish. His mouth was open like one, too. His skin had the yellowish pallor of the deceased.

Since I was still sopping wet, the miners figured there must be a connection.

One with very few teeth asked me, "You know this fella?"

"Yes. Thanks for fishing him out of the river."

"We didn't," replied the miner. "He got caught at the head of our flume." He pointed at the structure, which was, indeed, hard by. "Cut off the water to nothin' but a trickle. We came up to see what was what. Found your friend, here, pluggin' up the intake and drug him out of the way."

"Sorry for your trouble." I stared down at the remains of my former partner. Hoyt was troublesome even in death. The river tugged gently at his cuffs, as if to urge him onward. I would never have to worry about Fred Hoyt coming after me again. I should've been relieved, but another feeling, one of pity, crept into my thoughts. He'd chased after chimeras, and when they vanished, blamed everyone else for his misfortune. "I'll get a wagon to fetch him. Can I ask you fellas to keep the coyotes off him 'til I can get back?"

"We'd want the same, it was one of us," the spokesman said. A couple of the other miners nodded solemnly.

"Mystery's solved." The miner glanced at the body. "Sorry it had to be this."

"Thanks. I'll be quick as I can."

I took Harvey's blanket from my shoulders and spread it over Fred Hoyt and made my way back to Mr. Drummond, who poured me a cup of hot coffee. "Drowned?" he asked.

"Yes."

"What about your gold? I saw where it landed," he offered.

"So did I." I went into the river and retrieved it, already thinking about how to break the news of his stepson's demise to Mr. Pruitt.

I went into town and found Richard at the livery stable. I asked him for his help, hired a buckboard and we drove out the wagon road. We tied up Fred Hoyt in the blanket, hauled him out of the canyon and brought him back to town. I paid for the wagon and the burial out of my "Drummond take." I gave Richard three good-sized nuggets, too. Then I invited him to supper at the Empire.

"But you've already paid me." He held out his three nuggets.

"That was for your labor. This is to celebrate."

Richard wrinkled his brow. "Celebrate?"

I ducked my head. I felt like a heel. "Well, maybe not celebrate. Certainly not the death of my partner—ex-partner. But being alive." Then I confessed how Hoyt had tried to kill me. "I was thinking I have a new life, free of that dark cloud of worry and deception."

The Empire was already crowded with the supper trade, but we got the little table off to the side I had come to think of as Hoyt's roost.

"What'll you do now?" Richard asked, slicing enthusiastically into smoked tongue.

"I'm not sure, but I've been thinking about some things. I know one thing I'm not going to do, though."

"What's that?"

"I'm never going to live in fear of anybody again."

"Now, *that's* worth honoring, Mate." He nodded, topping up our glasses with wine.

When Richard and I parted company outside the Empire, I lingered a while. It was that time of day when the bustle of industry gave way to the shout of revelry. I stood savoring the sights and sounds as if they were vivid new treasures, to be all the more cherished for being so nearly lost. I had people to notify, to let them know they had nothing more to fear from Fred Hoyt.

Chen Yi's laundry, and the Celestials within, was one of those treasures never to be taken for granted again. They were done with supper, but Chen Yi insisted on preparing some dumplings for me. I was replete from my supper with Richard, but I was not about to decline Chen Yi's hospitality.

As was our custom, we clustered around the little table. They drank tea while I ate. Now I knew the meaning of Sun Shu's saying

". . .when we have eaten so much rice together." A friendship that only deepened with the sharing of many adventures.

They had heard only scraps of rumor. I gave them a complete account. Sun Shu started translating for Gao Chung, but he waved his hand "no" to her and then nodded for me to go on.

When I finished, Gao Chung muttered something, and they murmured agreement.

Chen Yi turned to me. "Gao Chung say, 'No bear, give new life.'"

After they retired, I wrote letters by lantern light.

.   .   .

I took letters for Mr. Pruitt and my family to the express office. Lila was busy. I stood back by the door, listening to the hubbub of camaraderie, waiting for the crowd to ebb. I had new ears for the clank of nuggets in the dish, the velvet timbre of Lila's voice, the respect for her I could hear in the miners' speech. *Sure would've missed this, if I hadn't survived yesterday.* And, most particularly, this lady, who I'd come to consider as light and warmth despite her stern demeanor. Lila was as much a bulwark for my well-being as my Celestial family.

When at last I reached the counter, I dropped my letters in the letterbox and beamed at her. "Good morning, Miss Rose."

Lila knitted her brow. "Oh, Pegg. We heard. Are you all right?"

"Yes, Ma'am. Thank you. Just a little waterlogged, is all."

"Well," she pursed her lips in disapproval. "I'm relieved that you're here to make light of the matter."

I blanched, foot-in-mouth again. "I meant no disrespect, Ma'am. To you, or to him—or the matter."

"I'll do my best to believe you. At least life should be a little simpler for you now."

I sure hope so. "Do I have any mail today?"

"As a matter of fact, you do." Lila handed me an envelope.

A letter from Vermont, showing the scuffs and blemishes of its long journey. It was from my sister, of all people. That was a surprise.

"Thank you very much, Miss Rose. I'll check back later."

"You are always welcome, Pegg."

I scurried out the door and plopped down at the first vacant bench I came to. The imp, the scamp, actually wrote me a letter.

Dear Brother;

This is your sister, Amy. I am old enough now to write my own letter. I have had to grow up faster than I would have liked this past winter. I would like to tell you many things. But I must apply this precious space to the most important. News of Father's death left us all in the greatest shock. I cannot imagine how you were able to continue on without him. It was an anxious time when we went so long without any word after Fort Laramie. Mr. Pruitt said he had heard nothing from his stepson, Mr. Hoyt, and said Father's passing in the middle of all that desolation was the cruelest of blows.

I must come to the heart of things. Mother is in a very bad way. She goes about in a daze. I sometimes come upon her with her face pressed into one of Father's shirts. She will allow none of his clothes to go to others' use, though it would be the charitable thing to do. I find her in the work shed running her hands over Father's tools. Other times she forgets and sets his place at the table. Reading your letters from Auburn, except that first one, are the only times Mother smiles, but even that is on the brink of tears.

We cannot go on this way. We barely got the planting in. Thankfully, the neighbors lent generous hands. More than one said they owed Father that small favor. I hope you can come home soon. But, much as we would rejoice in that happy occasion, in truth, I am not sure that it would be enough. Our farm has Father's presence in every board and beam. At every step, at every turn, there is a fresh point of grief. Adam will be away soon. Think of it—our big brother— a married man. I do not know what you can do, being so far away. In spite of all the newspapers say, California still feels like it's on the other side of the world! Please come home soon so we can figure out what to do.

Our prayers are with you,
Believe it or not, I miss you terribly.
Your loving sister,
Amy

I sat on that bench and let the day flow around me. I thought about this new person, my sister, how remarkably level-headed she was for an eight-year-old— and what she was dealing with. Her letter made clear what needed to be done.

I went back into the express office, marched up to the counter and began without preamble. "I'd like to take out another bank draft, Ma'am."

Lila looked up from writing in her ledger. "And good day to you, too," she replied tartly. I was too lathered up to realize she expected an apology. When I didn't offer one, she forged on. "Very well. For how much?" She opened the accounts ledger to the "F" page.

"Two thousand dollars." Even though her head was bowed, I could see Lila purse her lips. I spoke up. "I know. It puts a big hole in what I have on account here, but this is important. And I have what I made with Mr. Drummond to tide me over until the bank draft comes back from San Francisco."

"Pegg. . ." She squared her shoulders. "It would not be wise to put too much store in the bank draft. We have no idea what San Francisco will decide."

"Yes, Ma'am. I understand that. Could you please send it to this address." I wrote on a piece of paper and slid it across the counter to her.

She read aloud. "Mrs. Prudence Pegg, general delivery, Richford, Vermont, United States. Is that right?"

"Yes, Ma'am."

"You don't have to write 'United States' anymore," Lila smiled. "California is a state of the union now."

"Oh! Right! I forgot. And could you put a note on the draft, saying 'Please use this to come to California.'?"

Lila stared at me. "You meant it, then."

"Ma'am?"

"That you consider this home, now. You're bringing your family out."

"Yes, Ma'am." I produced a stern look, to show that I understood the portent. "If they'll come. That's not certain, yet."

She tipped her head, sounding almost wistful. "Well, we'll have to keep our fingers crossed, won't we?" She straightened up, becoming official again. "It would be better if the instruction was in your own handwriting." She produced a crisp new bank draft and laid it on the counter, running her finger along the very bottom. "Write it right along there. Don't go too far up and run into the signature block." She put a pen and ink bottle in front of me. "Then I'll fill out the rest and send it off."

"Thank you, Ma'am."

"And do me a favor?" she said.

"Yes, Ma'am!"

"Call me 'Lila' once in a while."

CHAPTER 47

Richard and I were taking our ease in the afternoon sun outside Gwynn and House's Mercantile and I was fretting out loud. Lila had warned me three different times about putting too much store in the restoration of my bank draft, and it had finally sunk in. I was worried.

After a pause, Richard spoke. "Have you thought about your claims?"

"What about them? I've scraped every last flake out of each one of 'em."

"Greenhorns don't seem to take that much into account." Richard looked off down the street. "Heard about a fellow who sold his claim to a yokel just off the boat for a thousand dollars." Another pause. "Over on the Feather River."

"Did the fella who sold it know it was played out?"

"I guess he thought so. I wasn't there at the time."

Up the street, a four-mule team set up a terrific braying, augmented by their teamster's curses.

Richard finished his line of thinking. "You could have three thousand dollars quick as spit."

"That sounds like something Hoyt would do." I scowled righteously.

"Seems it's common practice," came the bland reply.

"I wouldn't feel right."

"So, ask five hundred, if it'll soothe your troubled soul."

Regardless of my perilous circumstances, I proclaimed, "two hundred, tops. And they're not even worth that."

Richard pulled himself out of his slouch. "People will think you daft."

"When my bank draft comes through, I'll have the last laugh." A twinge of doubt poked me. "Will you put the word out?" I looked at him.

He got to his feet. "Wait here. I won't be a minute."

I called after him. "Make sure they know the claims've been worked."

Within fifteen minutes, Richard returned, leading a group of perhaps thirty men. Some "squeaked," they were so new. By their attire, these greenhorns belied a variety of means. I spied a few shabby sandhogs, probably looking for a new start, but I stuck to my guns, and in short order I had six hundred dollars in hand. That would get me back to Vermont, if need be.

The proud new owners of my claims were three fellows to instantly inspire pity. Two had come by way of Panama and had the sallow, feverish look to show for it; the other had come 'round the horn, and had spent most of the journey sea-sick. Yet they beamed as if they had been given the keys to King Solomon's mines.

Lambs to the slaughter. I tried to be civil. "You fellas have any idea what you're about?"

They exchanged glances.

I pointed over my shoulder to the store. "Step inside there and get yourselves a pan, a pick, and a shovel—each. Meet me right here tomorrow morning, and I'll take you to the river. Show you your claims."

Richard, standing back, shook his head, smiling. As soon as the greenhorns had hustled inside, he returned to sit at the bench. "People will pronounce you daft."

"Can't help that." I'd had so many people help me, this repayment, if that's what it was, was a pittance.

.   .   .

I led the greenhorns to R. C.'s first claim, down on Rattlesnake Bar. The whole exercise turned into something of a circus. The greenhorn who came the long way, a big fellow with a derby hat, struggled with how much to tip the pan. The one who had come way of Panama complained about ruining his boots, while his companion managed to wash out one tiny glittering flake, which surprised us both. However, I did not join him in dancing around like a mad man.

I watched my charges crouched on the river stones at the water's edge, using too much water, tipping the pan too steeply, or not steeply enough.

Richard Barter came splashing across the river to the south bank. He stood back until he saw a pause in my teaching, then beckoned me over. "Miss Rose said you might be interested in dropping by the express office—" He looked over at my students. "—at your convenience."

I brushed by him and sprinted up the slope.

He called after me. "I'll look after your—pupils."

Bugle caught up and raced ahead. I was running flat out with the thought, *She wouldn't be calling unless it was the about bank draft.* And a heartbeat later, *The answer could still be No.*

Lila's office was jammed, no doubt Providence chastising me for wanting to barrel through the crowd and climb up on the counter. I waited by the wrapping table, wrestling down my impatience. *It's got to be Yes. It's got to be!* I watched Lila, but could read nothing on her face.

After a minor eternity, the room was empty. I stood, rooted. In a moment, I was going to be very happy or very sad. Lila reached below the counter and came forward with a piece of paper. She handed me the snowy white sheet.

I gazed at every square inch of it. It was all there: 11,000 dollars, to Prudence Pegg, the curlicue borders, Lila's officiating signature; the date, May 27, 1851. While I was savoring every detail, she said, "Try not to let the bears get at this one."

I looked up and let out a whoop and gave Lila an impetuous hug. She let out a squeak.

"I'm sorry, Ma'am. I'm sorry. That was uncalled for."

Flustered, she smoothed her dress. "Nonsense. It was completely called for. Congratulations." Primping her hair but smiling without reserve.

I couldn't stop grinning. "Thank you, Ma'am. Thank you, thank you." Then I took up dancing around the room like a mad man.

I asked Lila for some paper, and if I might use her pen and ink, and sat at the wrapping table to write a letter.

Dearest Mother and Amy,

I do not know which has gotten to you first, this letter or the bank draft. If it was the bank draft, I am sorry to have left you in a mystery about it. If you have received this letter first, then the arrival of the bank draft will provide the means to carry out what I suggest below.

I cannot tell you how much I miss you both. I have discovered many wonderful things besides gold in this place called California. While the hills are swarming with people hunting the elusive ore, the great central valley is blooming with vast farms (called ranches here). Many are of the opinion that the real gold of California is its soil and mild climate. The harshest winter in these foothills is like autumn in Vermont. There are bustling cities that swarm with enterprising, ambitious people. But there are also vast tracts of countryside that hear only the call of the coyote.

Many people have given up the gold fields for a better life. A man named Mendenhall supplies both local stores and bustling cities with fruit from his ranch. I have seen watermelons almost as big as barrels. Indeed, a Mr. Gately is building a new house from the money he made selling melons. People are growing wheat, grapes for wine, and every kind of fruit and vegetable.

I propose we make a new life here. I propose this for all the reasons I have stated above. It may not be a dairy farm, but I think Father would be happy to see us together with a successful farm, no matter whether we are growing cabbages or cows. I would like to grow peaches. Out here they are as big as a man's fist! If, however, it is your wish, I will come home. I can bring home enough money to buy a better place back there.

But this place has won me. And I hope you will be willing to give it a chance to win you, too. The bank draft is for two tickets around the Horn to San Francisco. No matter what you are told, do NOT go by way of Panama. It is universally known to be nothing but disease-infested misery and danger. Worse, uncertainty about further progress awaits you on the Pacific side. Please let me know as soon as you can what you would like to do.

Until then, I remain,
Your dutiful and loving son and brother,
Bartholomew

I mailed that letter and prayed Mother would see it in a good light. Over the next few weeks, I sent two copies of that letter spaced in separate mails. One of them was bound to get through.

A couple months later, when I paid one of my frequent visits to Lila's express office, I received an answer.

Dearest Barti,
This is the third copy of this letter, in imitation of your scheme. to outwit the unreliable postal service. If you are reading this copy, you may disregard the next two. We received the second copy of your letter making your proposal.

Your idea has created a level of excitement seldom seen in this household. The desire to be together as a family far outshines all else.

Your beloved sister is beside herself. She has already packed and repacked half a dozen times, fretting over what she wants and what she might need, She would be off down the road this very moment were not certain practicalities impeding her.

Starting a new life in a place so far and so different from all we know and cherish is daunting, indeed, but we are committed. I have faith that you have inherited your father's soberness of mind, and the superlatives you apply to that place are close enough to the facts to bear our trust.

Your friend Will caught wind of our plans and came by to offer his assistance, helping Mr. Milbray load furniture, organizing an auction for our tools, and a bevy of other chores. I suspect, at bottom, it was his way of hanging on to you a bit longer. He would never admit it baldly, but he misses you greatly. He declared he might entertain a visit to ensure your activities are on the up and up.

Mr. Pruitt wishes me to assure you he received the bank draft, and to impart his utmost gratitude for honoring the commitment you and your father made to him and the other partners. I can say from what others have said to me, everyone is pleased with their return.

Our preparations are well underway. Mr. Pruitt earned an everlasting place in our affections by offering the best possible price for the farm. As I alluded earlier, the Milbrays bought all of our household goods with a portion of their share of the partnership. I have booked passage on the Sarasota. We will embark at Baltimore on April twenty-third.

Oh my goodness. Not only had she agreed. She was already on her way with Amy. I returned to see what else was in the letter.

The Sarasota is a newly refitted whaler, commissioned expressly for the purpose of conveying gold-seekers to that wild coast. The shipping agent assured me that the Sarasota has been provided with all the best accommodations. If Providence watches over us, we will arrive at San Francisco in early-October.

My dearest Barti, I count the days until our family will be reunited. We must be brave and carry on without your father, who was our strength, our light, the very breath of our soul. I feel if we create this new life, it will be the best way to honor his memory.

I count the minutes until we embrace in San Francisco.

To my last breath, I remain,

Your devoted mother

I heaved a huge sigh of relief. She had agreed. She and Amy were coming out to California. Our family would be together again, even if diminished. The letter I held in my hand proved my scheme was worth the effort: six copies of each of these crucial letters, mailed two weeks apart, so that at least one had a chance of getting through.

I hunkered down outside the express office, holding the letter in both hands as if it were sacred. The street bustled around me, but my mind was thousands of miles away in Vermont, basking in the great joy of our reunion. I gained a new appreciation for my mother's brisk movements, her sensible turn of mind, her wonderful cooking. I could resume honing my wit on my sister's chiding.

I got up and paced, glancing now and again at the pages to reassure myself I had read them right. Again and again, the thought of our being together again lit me up like the morning sun breaking the horizon. I repeated the ship's name, *Sarasota*, to fix it in my mind.

.   .   .

Making my way to the river late in the day, I kept to high ridges before cutting down into the canyon. Bugle was in hog-heaven, our traverse being new territory for him to explore and claim. The sun sat low to the horizon, a plump, simmering ball. Shadows stretched long behind us. I emerged from a scattering of oaks to a scene bathed in light that seemed the color of peaches. I stopped to take in the tranquil prospect. Bugle rejoined me and sat on his haunches, panting contentedly. The land stepped in ridges down to the vast plain of the central valley. The low mountains marking its western limit made a bumpy rampart running north and south. The limitless sky soared above, not a wisp of cloud in the whole of it. My chest filled with elation that I could be in this grand place.

Recalling the challenge I had made at the beginning of this journey, I looked again at the setting sun. *"I have caught you at last."*

THE END

ABOUT THE AUTHOR

Frank Nissen grew up in the gold country he loves to write about. *Fortune's Call*, published in 2022, is the first volume of his Gold Rush Odyssey saga. When not giving presentations based on his research, Frank is busily at work on book three.

After a career as an animator, story board artist and story developer he enjoys hobnobbing with fellow writers and old school chums. Frank finds inspiration in people's stories, as well as horizons filled with trees rather than buildings.

He invites readers to follow his escapades, read his musings, and see his latest doodles on Facebook at Frank Nissen Author.

OTHER TITLES BY FRANK NISSEN

NOTE FROM FRANK NISSEN

Word-of-mouth is crucial for any author to succeed. If you enjoyed *Fortune's Price*, please leave a review online—anywhere you are able. Even if it's just a sentence or two. It would make all the difference and would be very much appreciated.

Thanks!
Frank Nissen

We hope you enjoyed reading this title from:

www.blackrosewriting.com

Subscribe to our mailing list – *The Rosevine* – and receive **FREE** books, daily
deals, and stay current with news about upcoming
releases and our hottest authors.
Scan the QR code below to sign up.

Already a subscriber? Please accept a sincere thank you for being a fan of
Black Rose Writing authors.

View other Black Rose Writing titles at
www.blackrosewriting.com/books and use promo code
PRINT to receive a **20% discount** when purchasing.